Published by SLG Publishing

P.O. Box 26427
San Jose, California 95159
www.slgcomic.com

President and Publisher: Dan Vado
Editor-in-Chief: Jennifer de Guzman

First Printing: January 2010
ISBN-13: 978-1-59362-183-4

Book design by Jennifer de Guzman

This volume collects *Gordon Yamamoto and the King of the Geeks* and *Loyola Chin and the San Peligran Order*, both previously published by SLG Publishing.

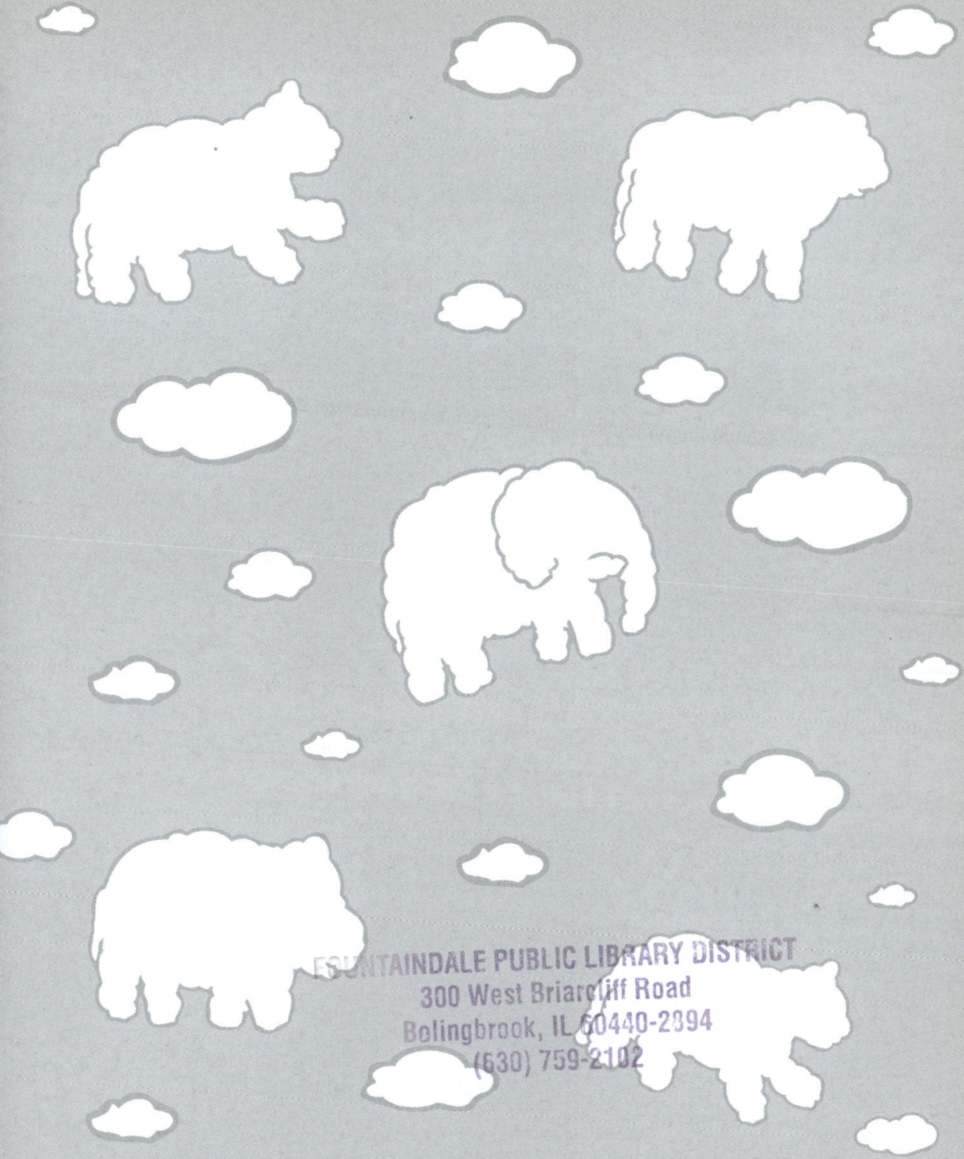

ANIMAL CRACKERS

by Gene Luen Yang

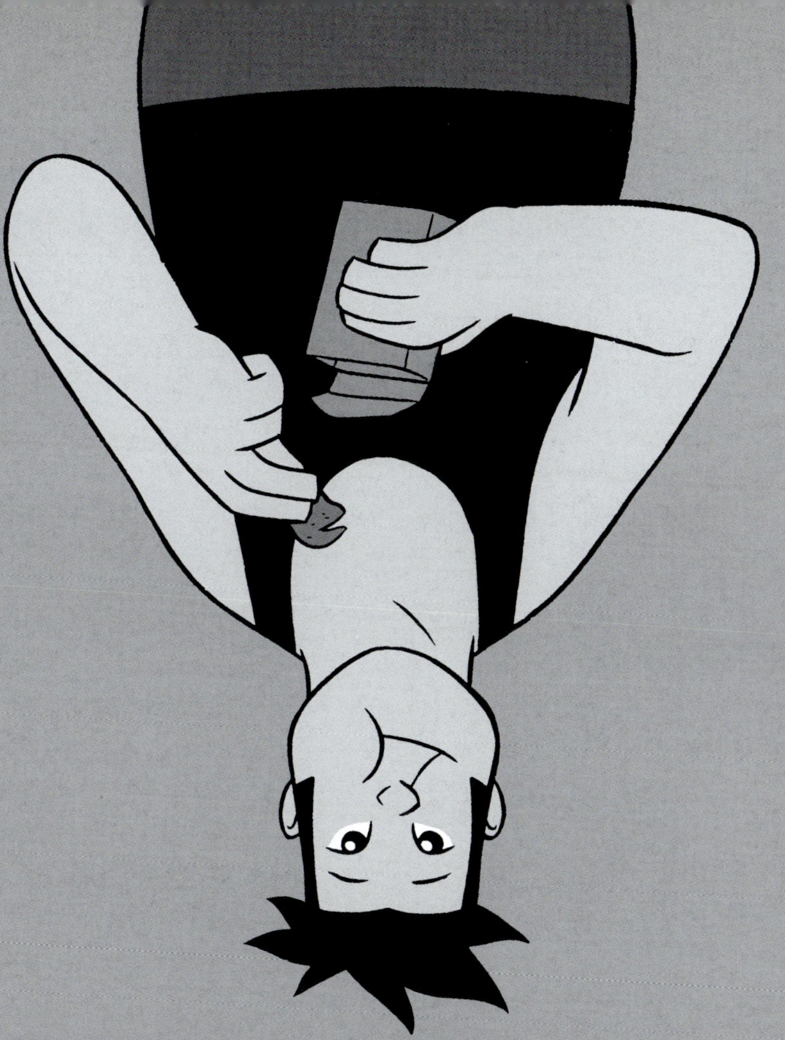

GORDON YAMAMOTO
and THE KING of THE GEEKS

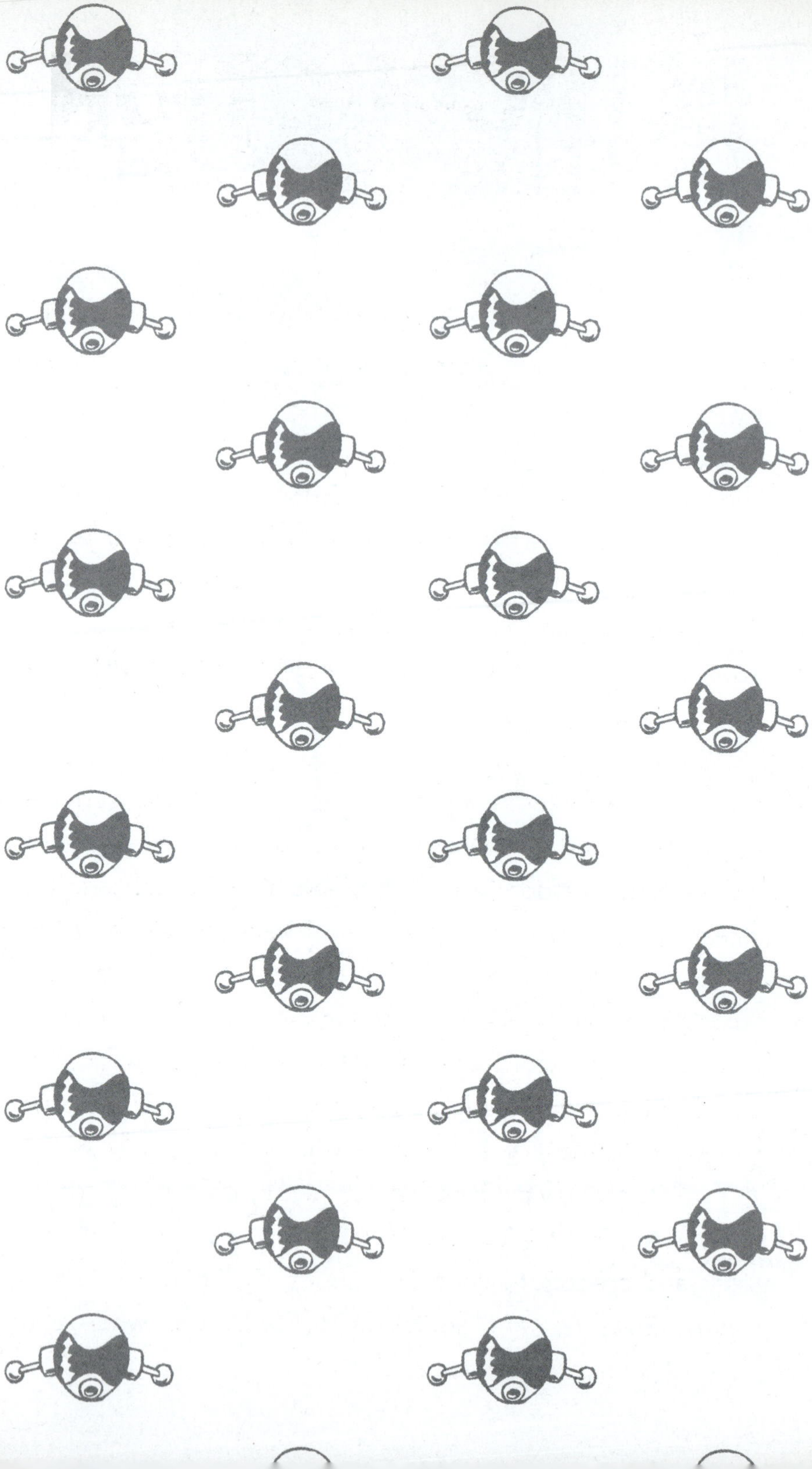

INTRODUCTION
BY DEREK KIRK KIM

Magical.

There are very few works of fiction upon which I could affix that adjective without half a sardonic smirk on my face. *The Little Prince, My Neighbor Totoro, A Wrinkle in Time* are a few that come to mind. Funny how none of these are comics. How sad, actually. You would think a medium seeping with yarns of flying men, talking animals, rocket ships, vampires, witches, and princesses would be filled with nothing but magical stories. But we all know a story isn't made "magical" simply by stuffing it with fairies and magical potions.

Gordon Yamamoto and the King of the Geeks is that rarest of all breeds—a story that embodies the genuine enthusiasm and boundless imagination of a ten-year-old kid with the wisdom and craftsmanship of a contemplative adult. In an industry where childhood fancies have been manufactured through cold, careful dissection and "market research," Gene Yang doesn't even have to try. It simply flows out of him like battles you waged with your Transformers on a shag carpet back when rushing home to watch cartoons was the highlight of your day.

Although David Copperfield might disagree, Gene is a magician. He tricks you. He messes with your predictions and preconceptions. He clouds your mind with stories insanely fun and addicting to read. Then when you least expect it, he clears away the smoke and lets the themes bubbling under the surface blow up in your face. But it's never painful or didactic, and that's the greatest trick of all. He gently and humble engages you with everyday issues and struggles that concern all of us: forgiveness, conformity social hierarchy, and tolerance. All that bookeneded with a boy shoving a TV cable up his nose and animal crackers come to manic life.

That's *Gordon Yamamoto and the King of the Geeks.*

That's magical.

Derek Kirk Kim, April 2004
Same Difference and Other Stories
The Eternal Smile

CHAPTER ONE

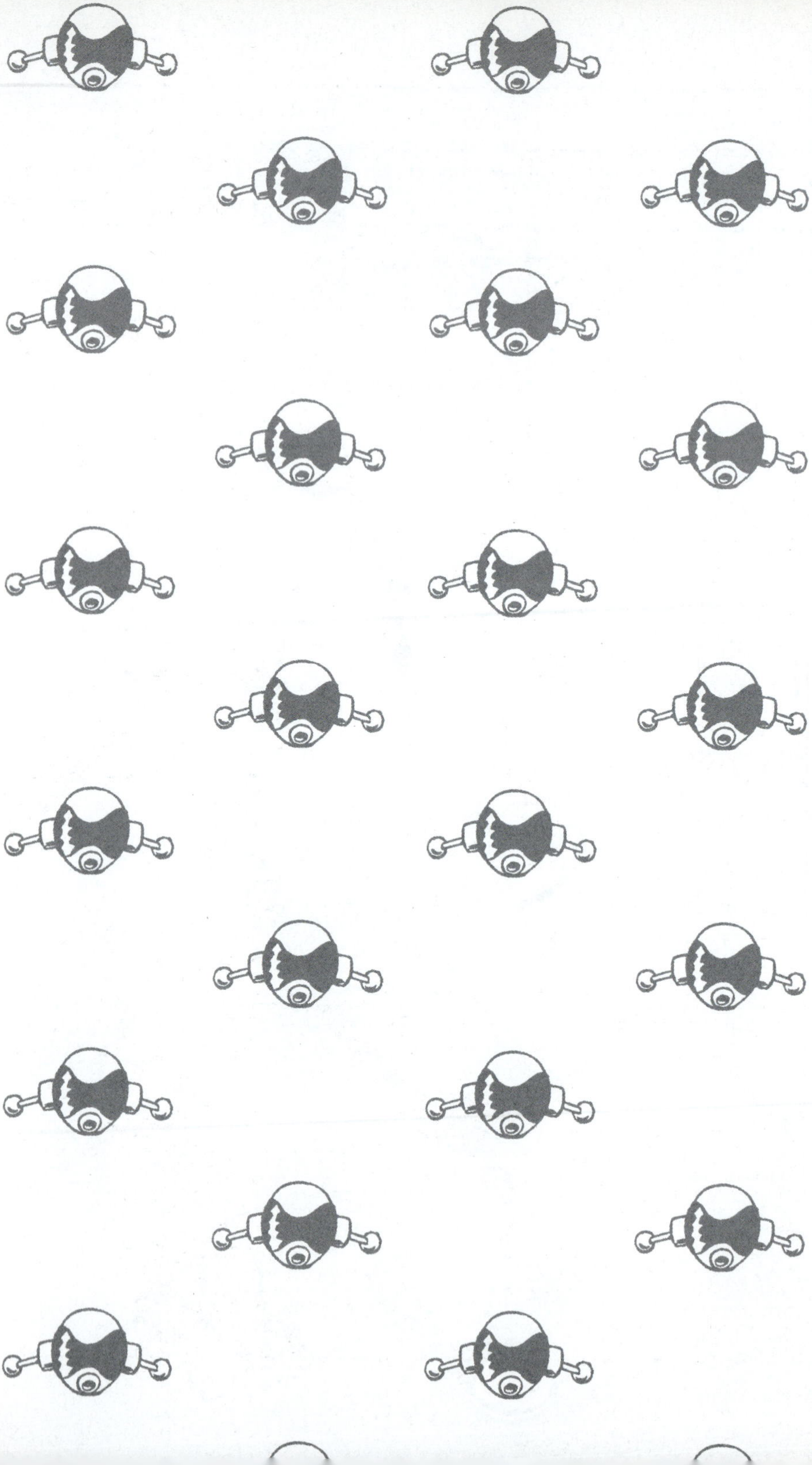

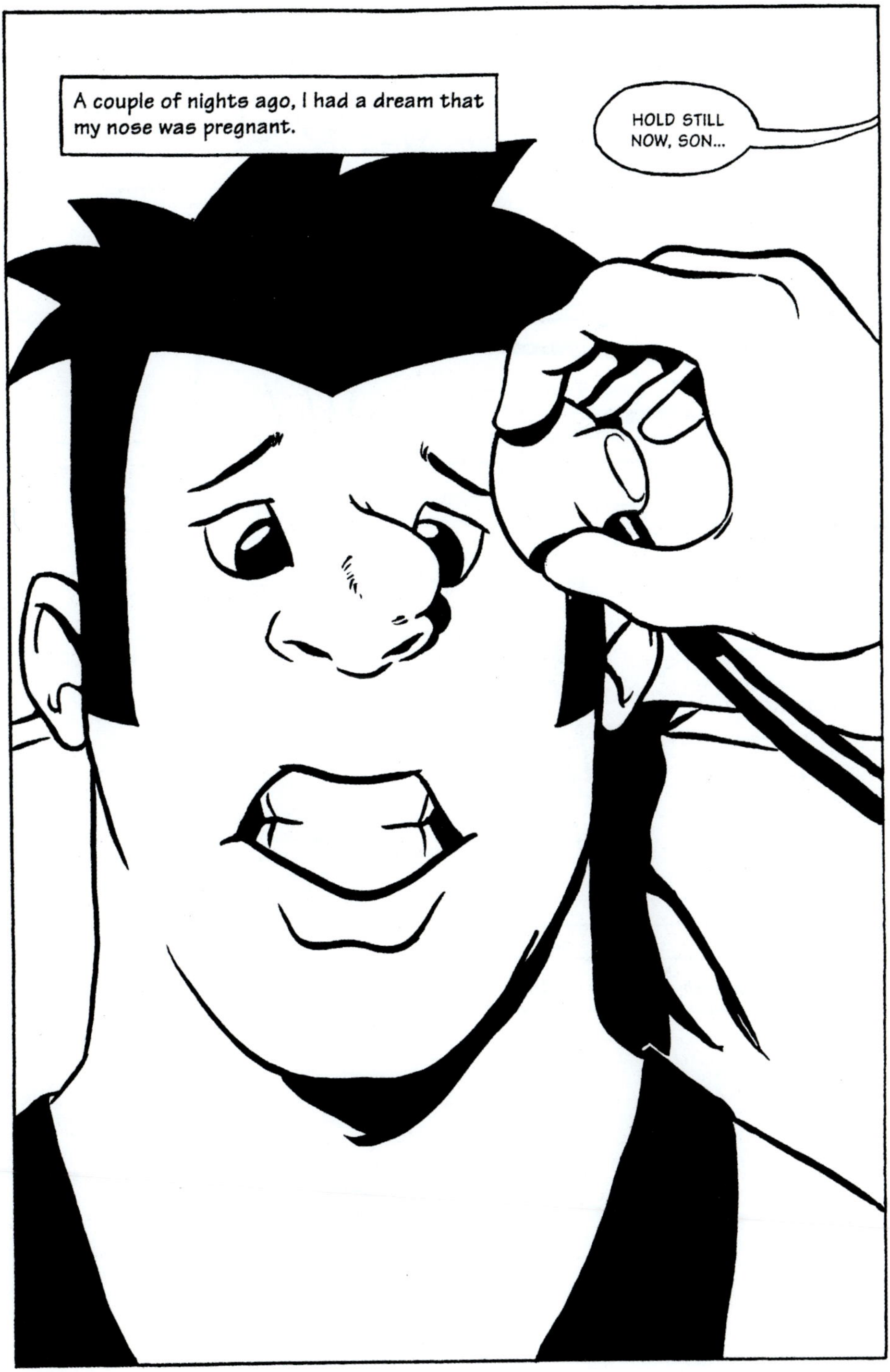
A couple of nights ago, I had a dream that my nose was pregnant.
HOLD STILL NOW, SON...

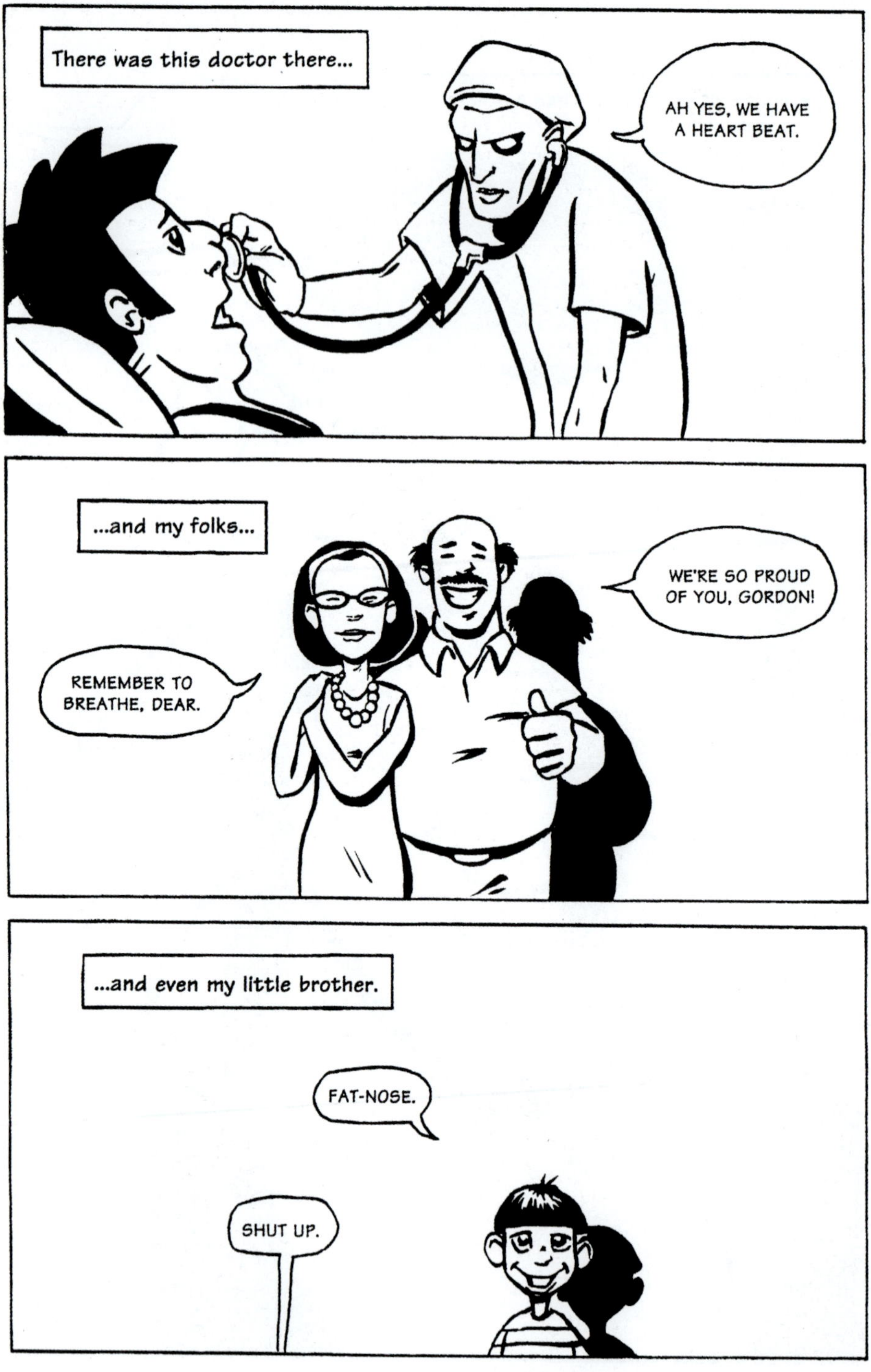
There was this doctor there...
AH YES, WE HAVE A HEART BEAT.
...and my folks...
WE'RE SO PROUD OF YOU, GORDON!
REMEMBER TO BREATHE, DEAR.
...and even my little brother.
FAT-NOSE.
SHUT UP.

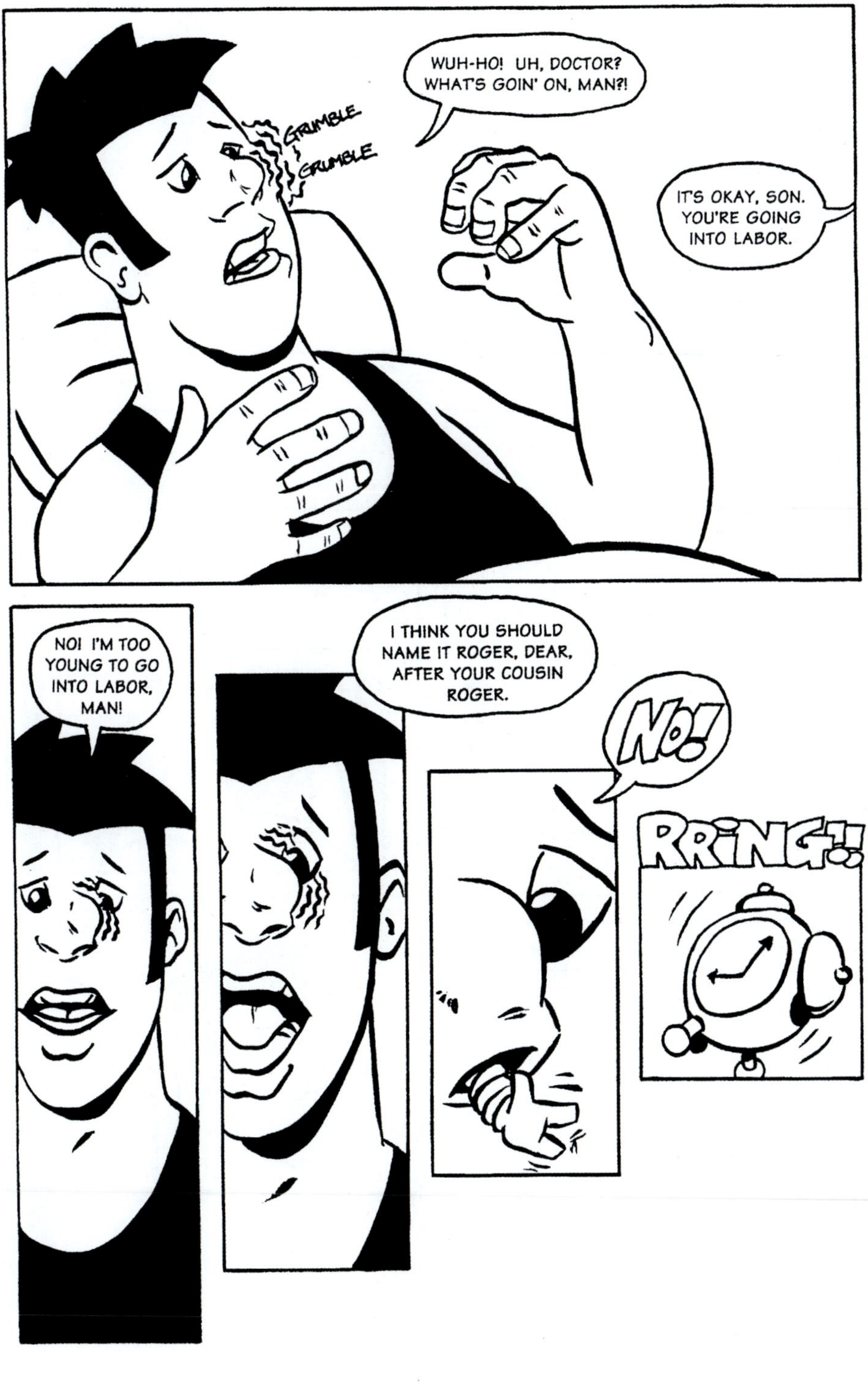
WUH-HO! UH, DOCTOR? WHAT'S GOIN' ON, MAN?!
GRUMBLE GRUMBLE
IT'S OKAY, SON. YOU'RE GOING INTO LABOR.
NO! I'M TOO YOUNG TO GO INTO LABOR, MAN!
I THINK YOU SHOULD NAME IT ROGER, DEAR, AFTER YOUR COUSIN ROGER.
NO!
RRING!!

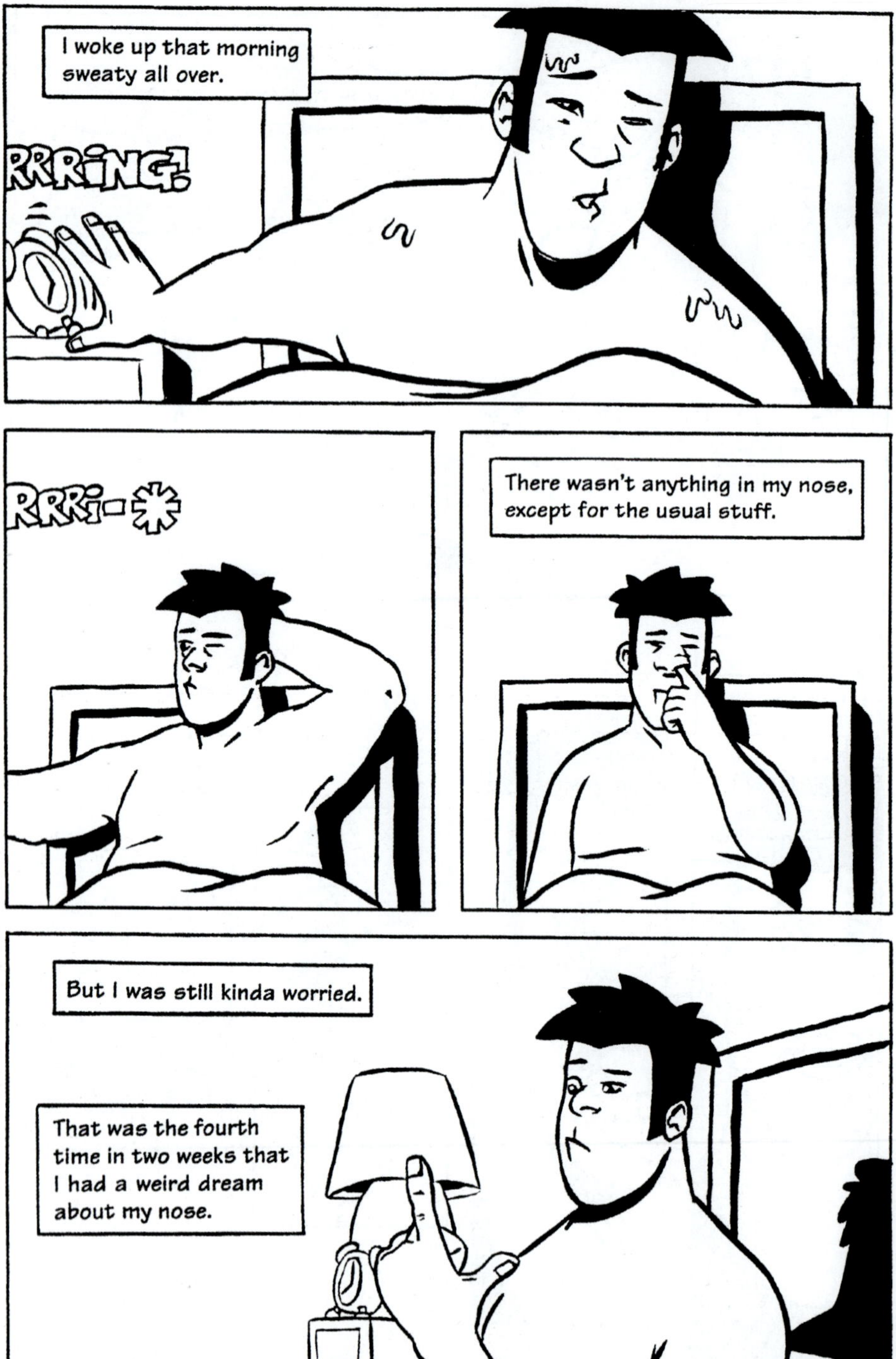
I woke up that morning sweaty all over.
RRRING!
RRRi-
There wasn't anything in my nose, except for the usual stuff.
But I was still kinda worried.
That was the fourth time in two weeks that I had a weird dream about my nose.

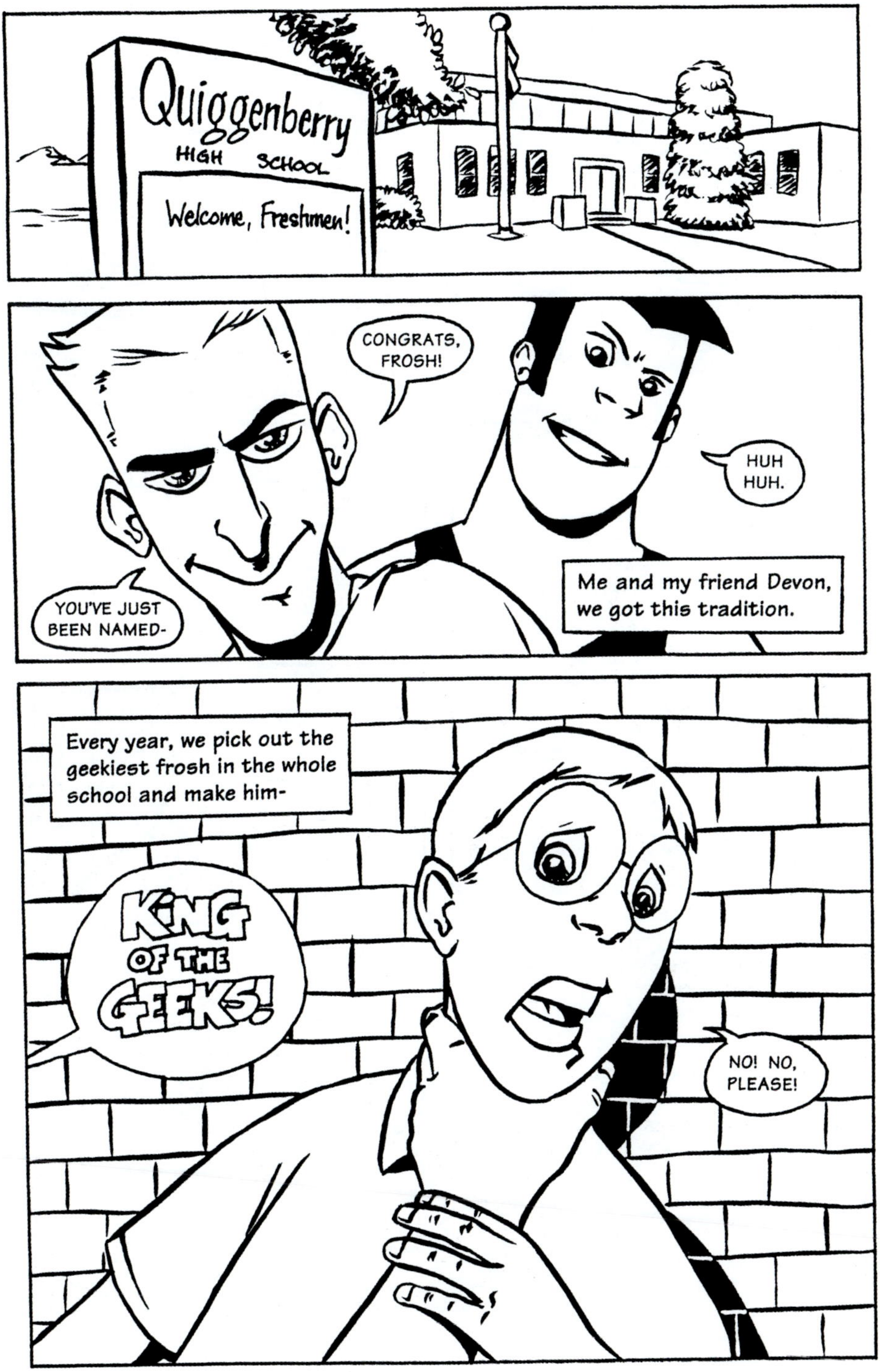
Quiggenberry
HIGH SCHOOL
Welcome, Freshmen!
CONGRATS, FROSH!
HUH HUH.
YOU'VE JUST BEEN NAMED-
Me and my friend Devon, we got this tradition.
Every year, we pick out the geekiest frosh in the whole school and make him-
KING OF THE GEEKS!
NO! NO, PLEASE!

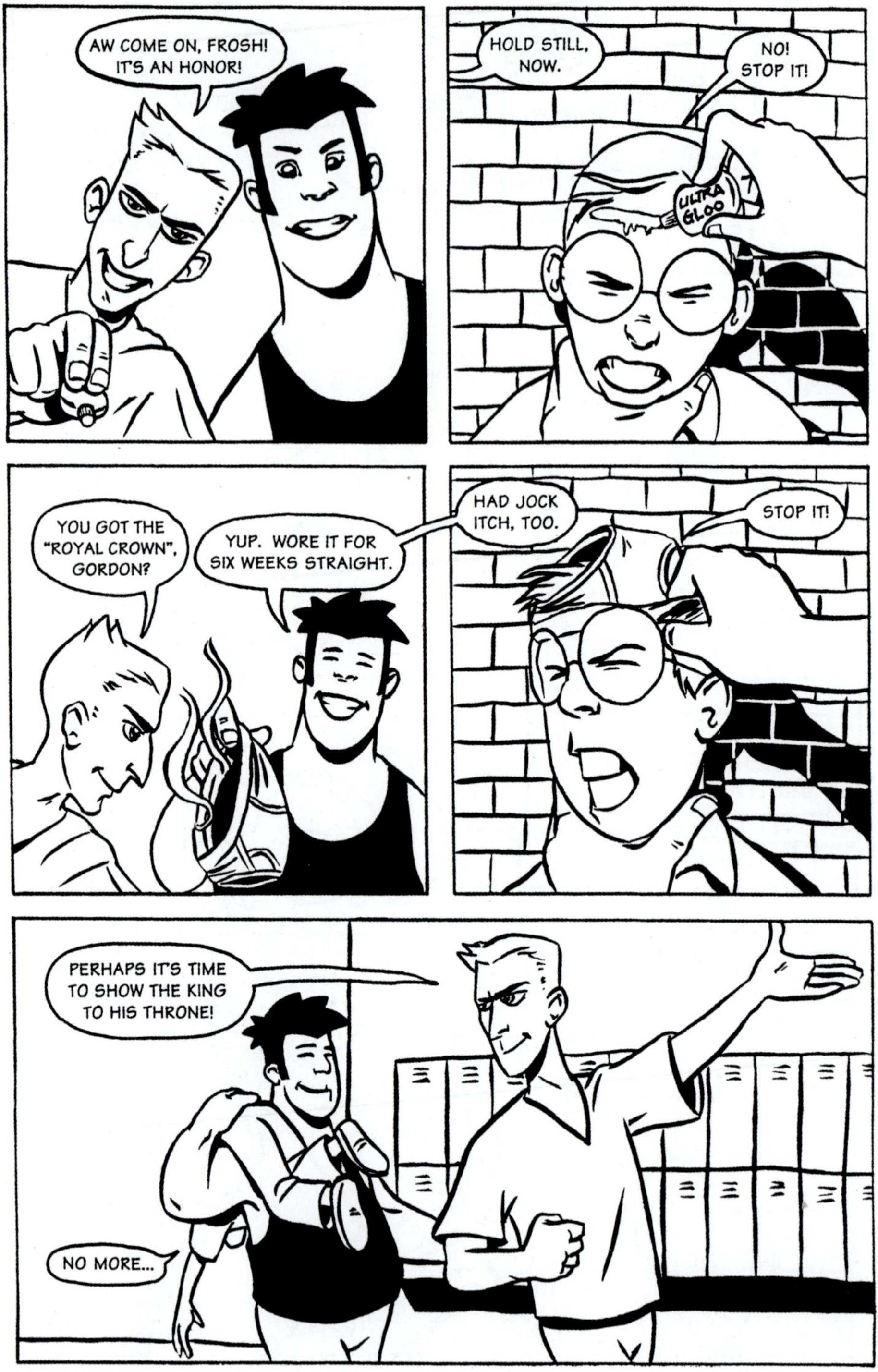
AW COME ON, FROSH! IT'S AN HONOR!
HOLD STILL, NOW.
NO! STOP IT!
ULTRA GLOO
YOU GOT THE "ROYAL CROWN", GORDON?
YUP. WORE IT FOR SIX WEEKS STRAIGHT.
HAD JOCK ITCH, TOO.
STOP IT!
PERHAPS IT'S TIME TO SHOW THE KING TO HIS THRONE!
NO MORE...

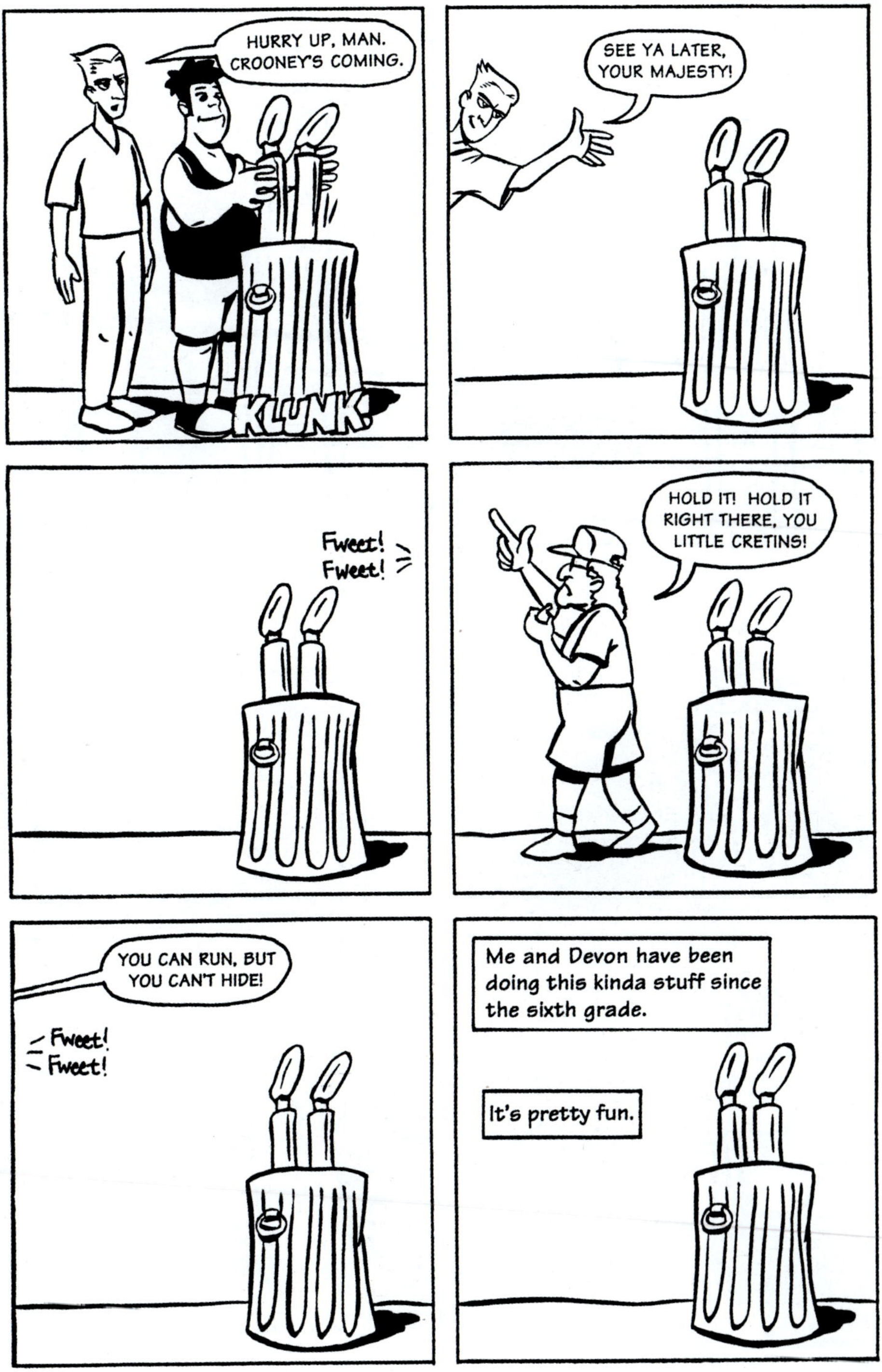
HURRY UP, MAN. CROONEY'S COMING.
KLUNK!
SEE YA LATER, YOUR MAJESTY!
Fweet!
Fweet!
HOLD IT! HOLD IT RIGHT THERE, YOU LITTLE CRETINS!
YOU CAN RUN, BUT YOU CAN'T HIDE!
Fweet!
Fweet!
Me and Devon have been doing this kinda stuff since the sixth grade.
It's pretty fun.

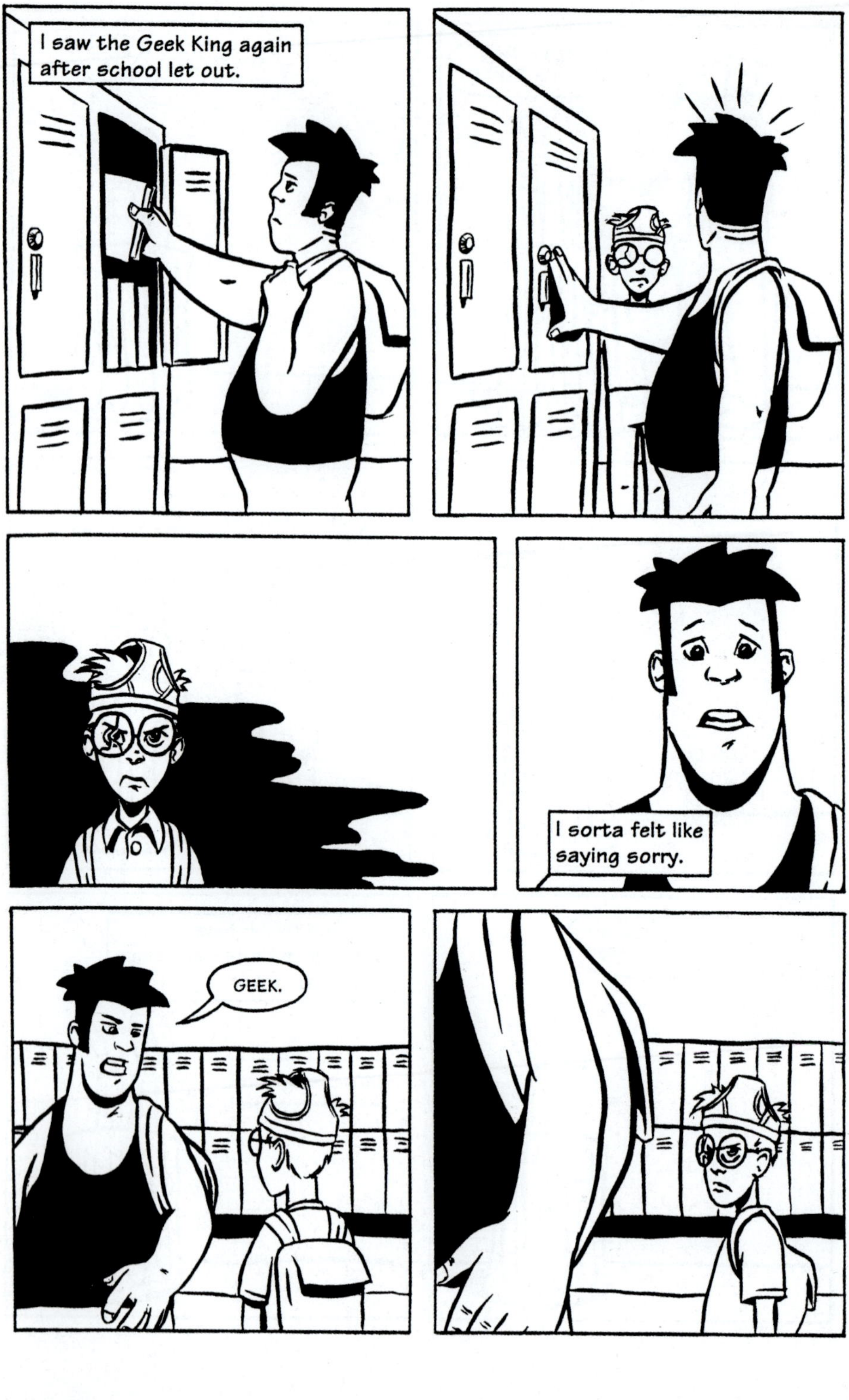
I saw the Geek King again after school let out.
I sorta felt like saying sorry.
GEEK.

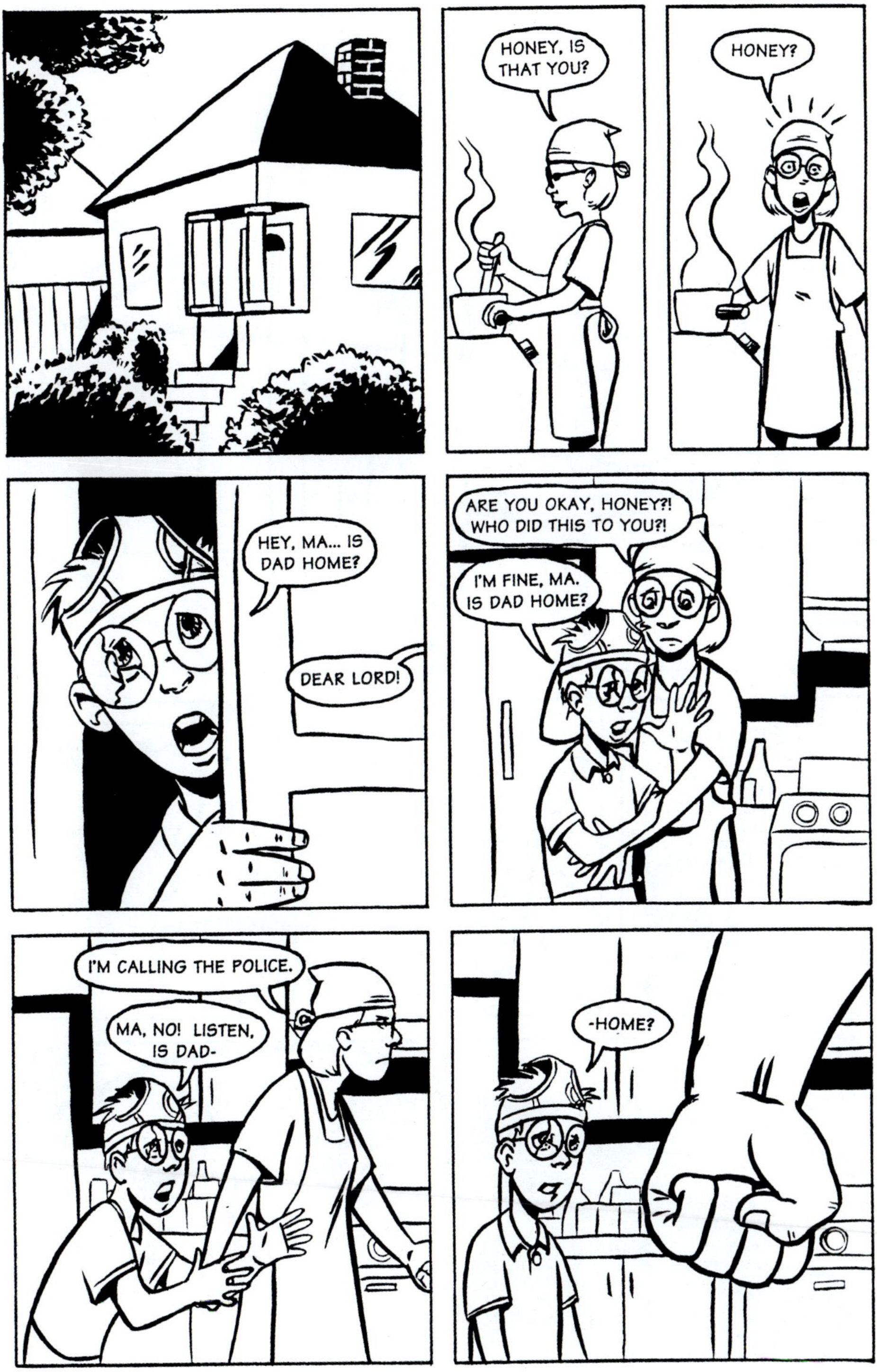
HONEY, IS THAT YOU?
HONEY?
HEY, MA... IS DAD HOME?
DEAR LORD!
ARE YOU OKAY, HONEY?! WHO DID THIS TO YOU?!
I'M FINE, MA. IS DAD HOME?
I'M CALLING THE POLICE.
MA, NO! LISTEN, IS DAD-
-HOME?

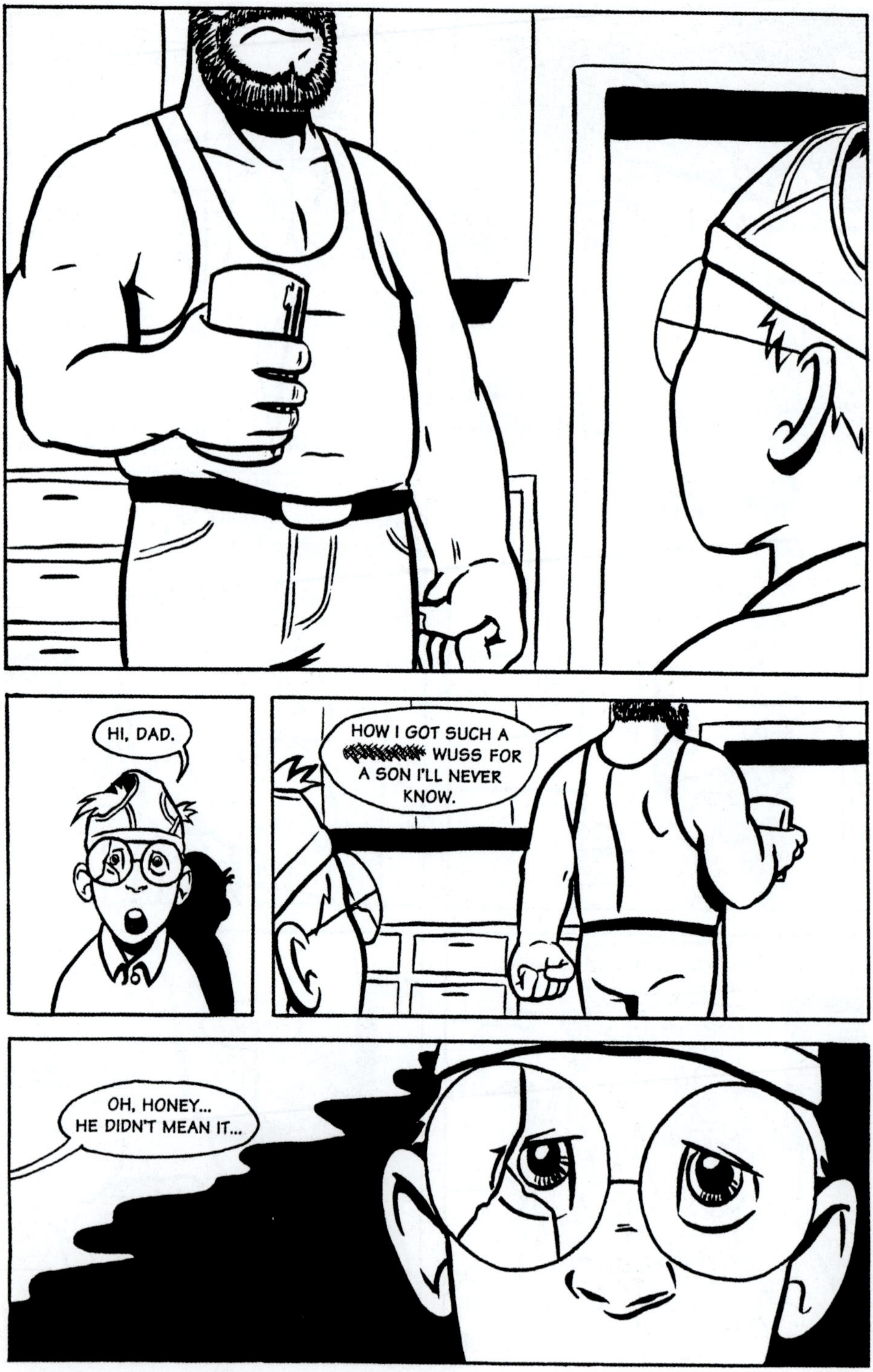
HI, DAD.
HOW I GOT SUCH A [redacted] WUSS FOR A SON I'LL NEVER KNOW.
OH, HONEY... HE DIDN'T MEAN IT...

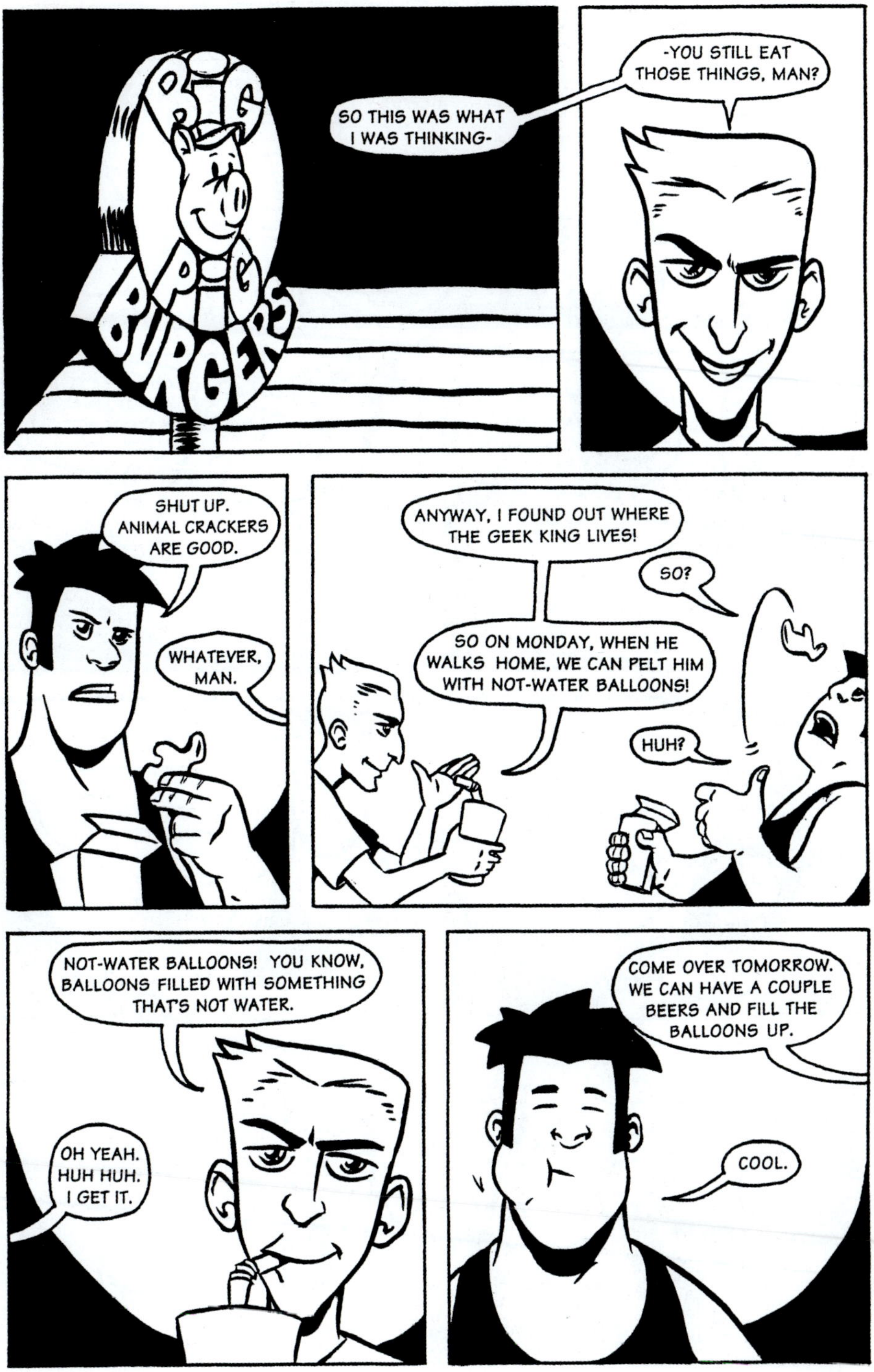
BIG
PIG
BURGERS
SO THIS WAS WHAT I WAS THINKING-
-YOU STILL EAT THOSE THINGS, MAN?
SHUT UP. ANIMAL CRACKERS ARE GOOD.
WHATEVER, MAN.
ANYWAY, I FOUND OUT WHERE THE GEEK KING LIVES!
SO?
SO ON MONDAY, WHEN HE WALKS HOME, WE CAN PELT HIM WITH NOT-WATER BALLOONS!
HUH?
NOT-WATER BALLOONS! YOU KNOW, BALLOONS FILLED WITH SOMETHING THAT'S NOT WATER.
OH YEAH. HUH HUH. I GET IT.
COME OVER TOMORROW. WE CAN HAVE A COUPLE BEERS AND FILL THE BALLOONS UP.
COOL.

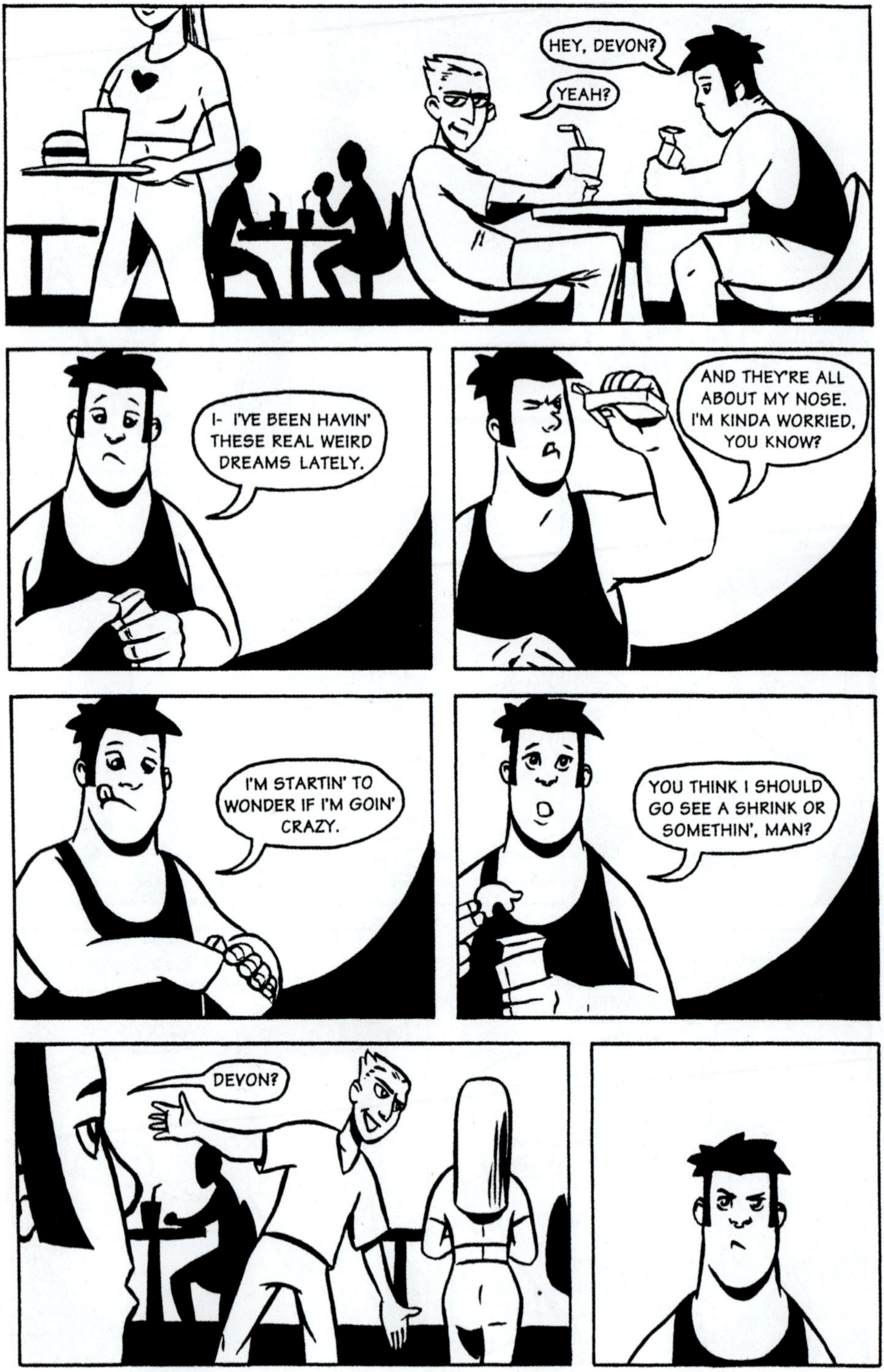
HEY, DEVON?
YEAH?
I- I'VE BEEN HAVIN' THESE REAL WEIRD DREAMS LATELY.
AND THEY'RE ALL ABOUT MY NOSE. I'M KINDA WORRIED, YOU KNOW?
I'M STARTIN' TO WONDER IF I'M GOIN' CRAZY.
YOU THINK I SHOULD GO SEE A SHRINK OR SOMETHIN', MAN?
DEVON?

HONEY...
HONEY...
DINNER'S READY!
BE RIGHT THERE, MA.
HOW TO MAKE BOMBS

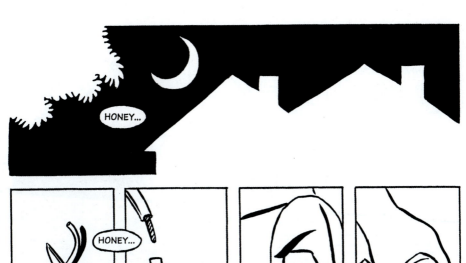

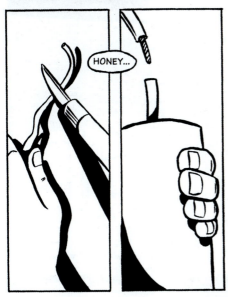

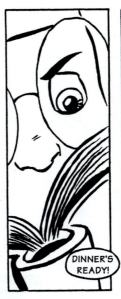

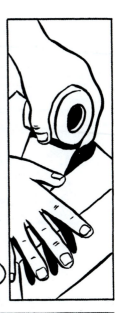

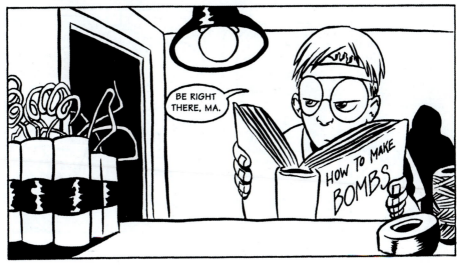

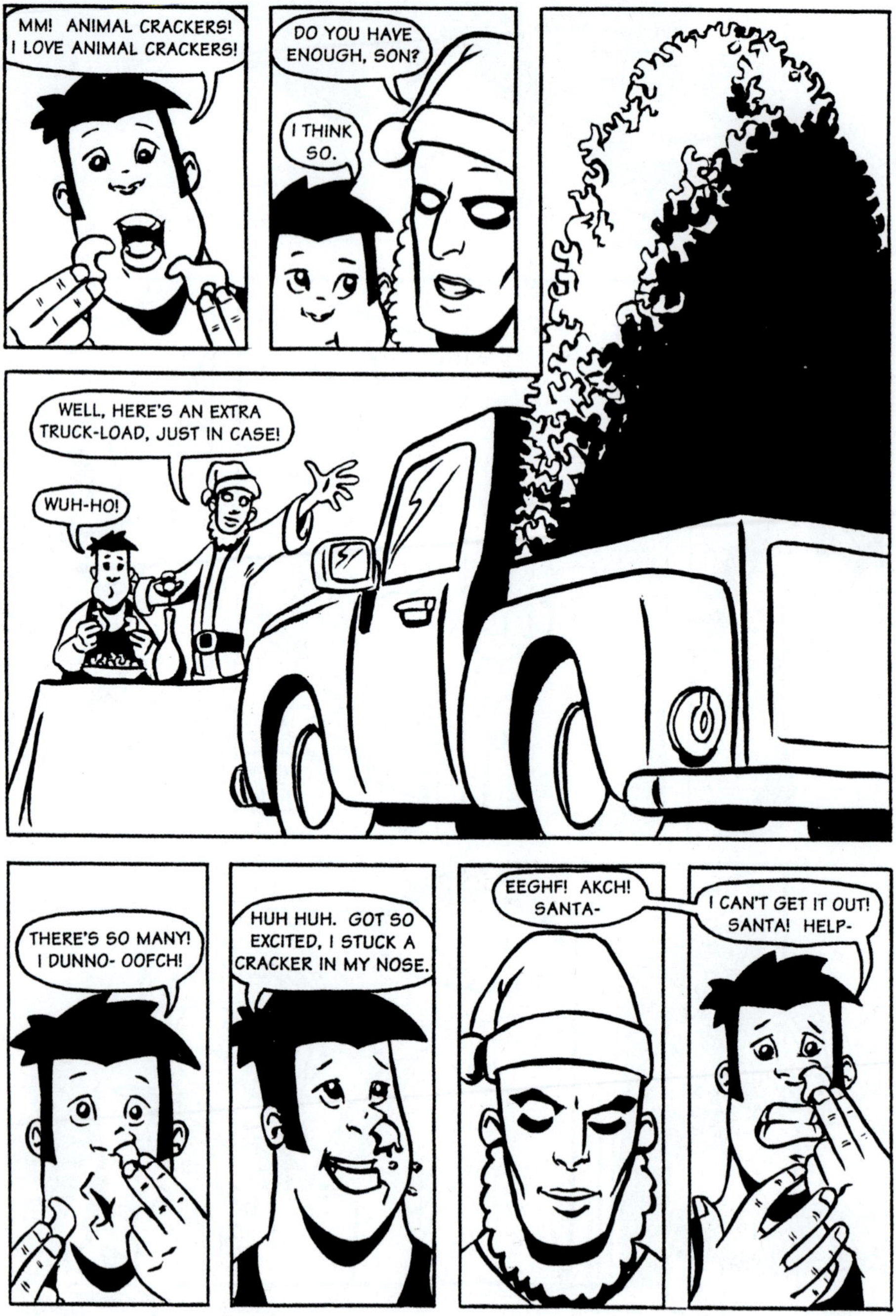
MM! ANIMAL CRACKERS! I LOVE ANIMAL CRACKERS!
DO YOU HAVE ENOUGH, SON?
I THINK SO.
WELL, HERE'S AN EXTRA TRUCK-LOAD, JUST IN CASE!
WUH-HO!
THERE'S SO MANY! I DUNNO- OOFCH!
HUH HUH. GOT SO EXCITED, I STUCK A CRACKER IN MY NOSE.
EEGHF! AKCH! SANTA-
I CAN'T GET IT OUT! SANTA! HELP-

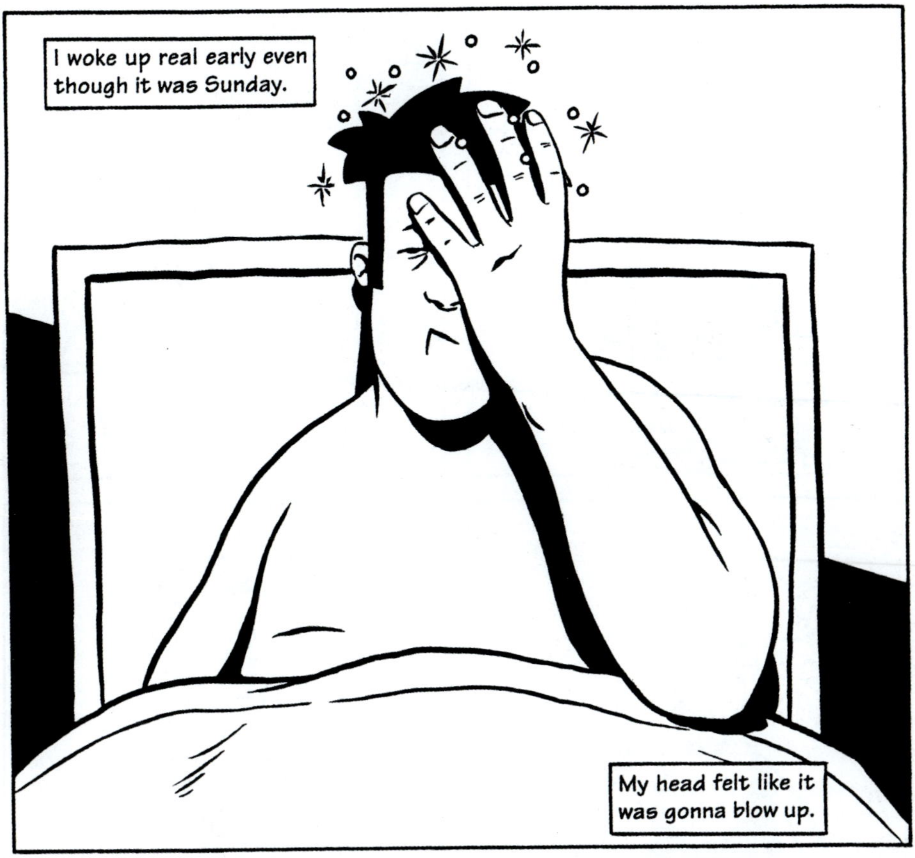
I woke up real early even though it was Sunday.
My head felt like it was gonna blow up.

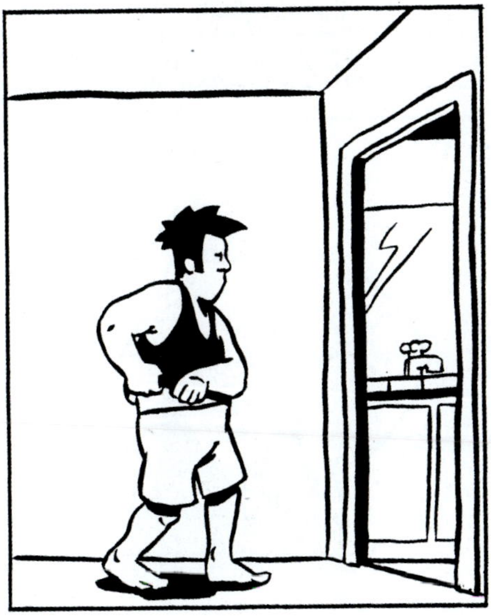

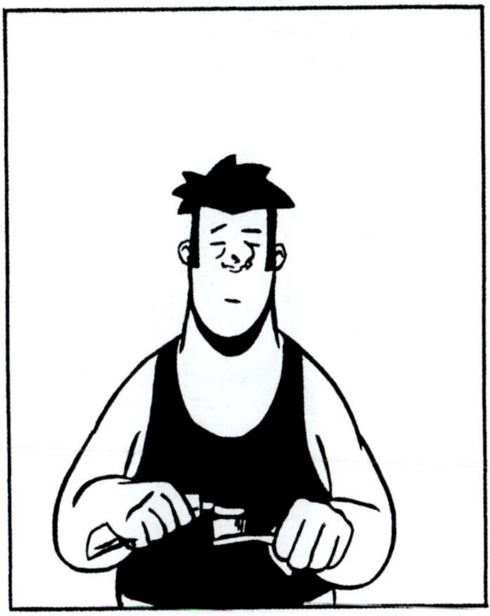

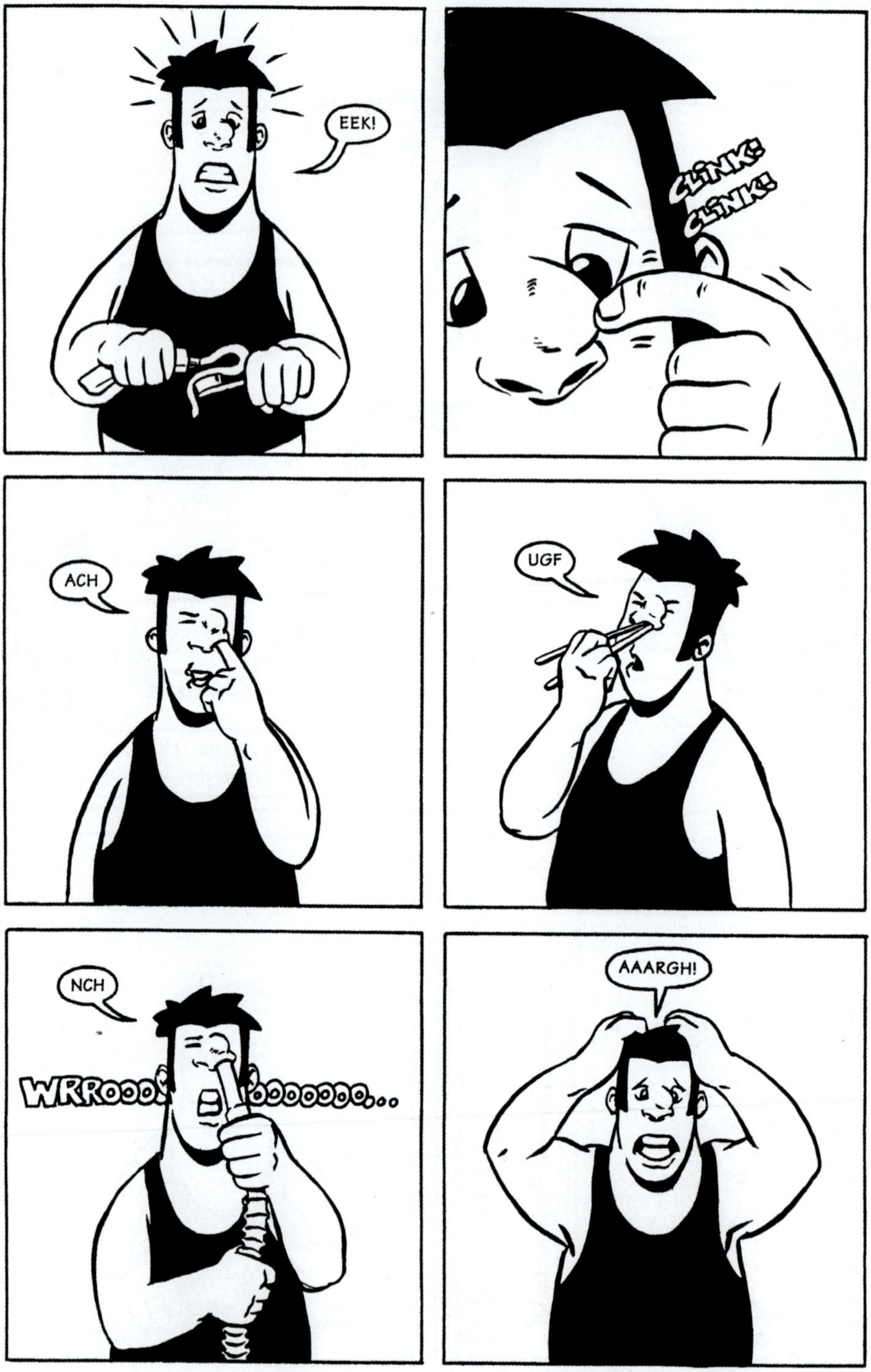
EEK!
CLINK!
CLINK!
ACH
UGF
NCH
WRROOO OOOOOOOO...
AAARGH!

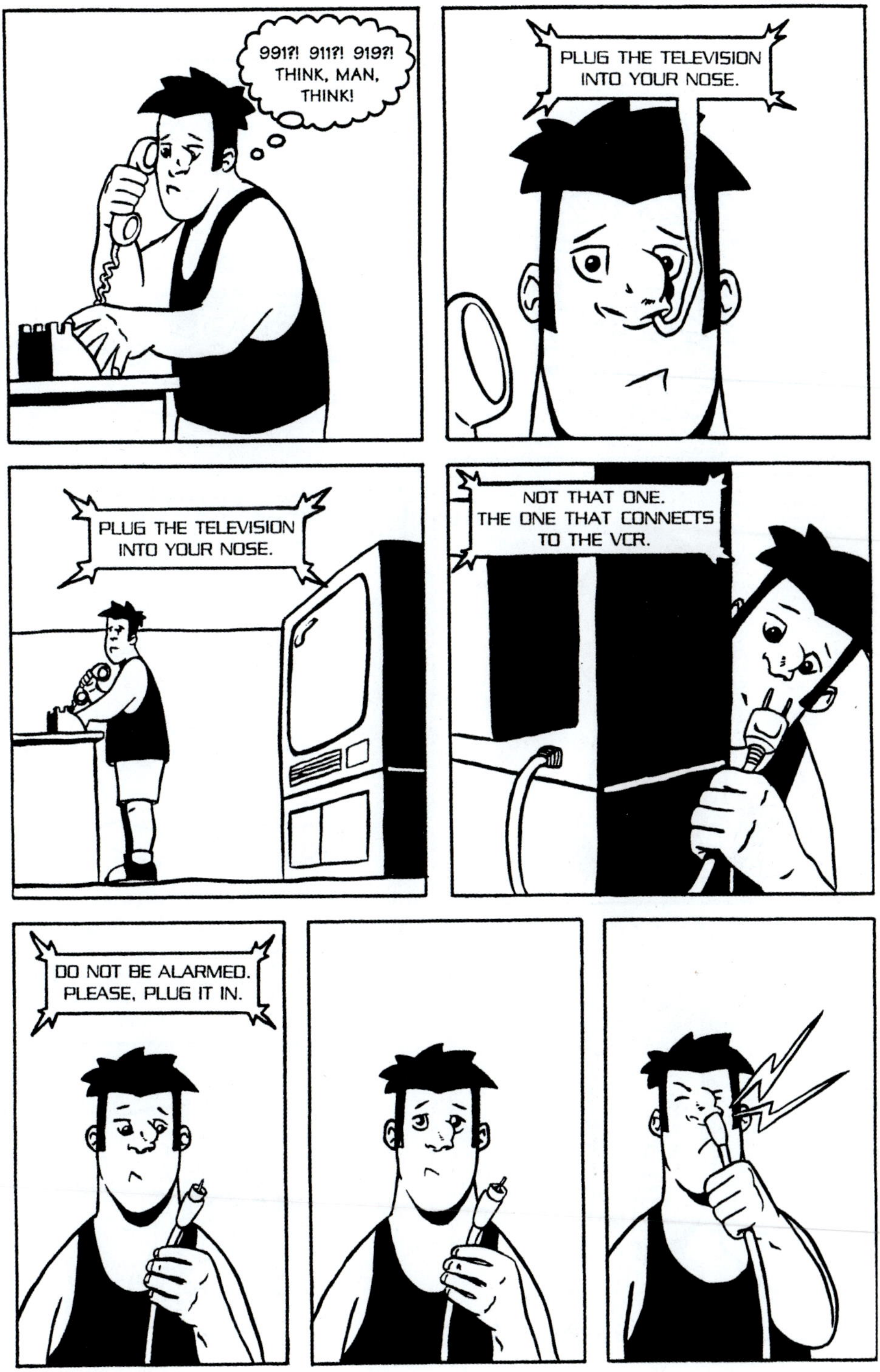
991?! 911?! 919?!
THINK, MAN,
THINK!
PLUG THE TELEVISION
INTO YOUR NOSE.
PLUG THE TELEVISION
INTO YOUR NOSE.
NOT THAT ONE.
THE ONE THAT CONNECTS
TO THE VCR.
DO NOT BE ALARMED.
PLEASE, PLUG IT IN.

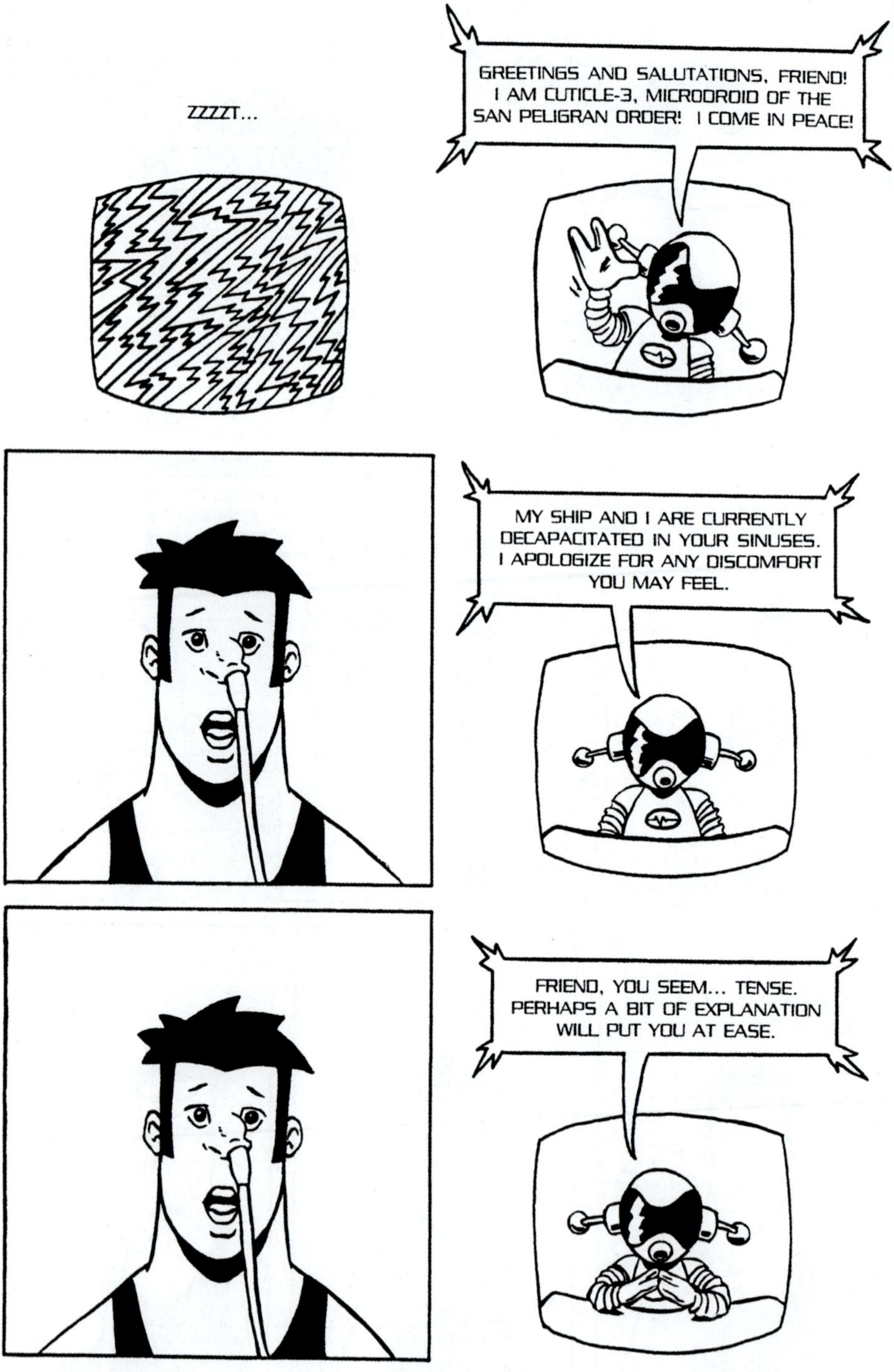
ZZZZT...
GREETINGS AND SALUTATIONS, FRIEND! I AM CUTICLE-3, MICRODROID OF THE SAN PELIGRAN ORDER! I COME IN PEACE!
MY SHIP AND I ARE CURRENTLY DECAPACITATED IN YOUR SINUSES. I APOLOGIZE FOR ANY DISCOMFORT YOU MAY FEEL.
FRIEND, YOU SEEM... TENSE. PERHAPS A BIT OF EXPLANATION WILL PUT YOU AT EASE.

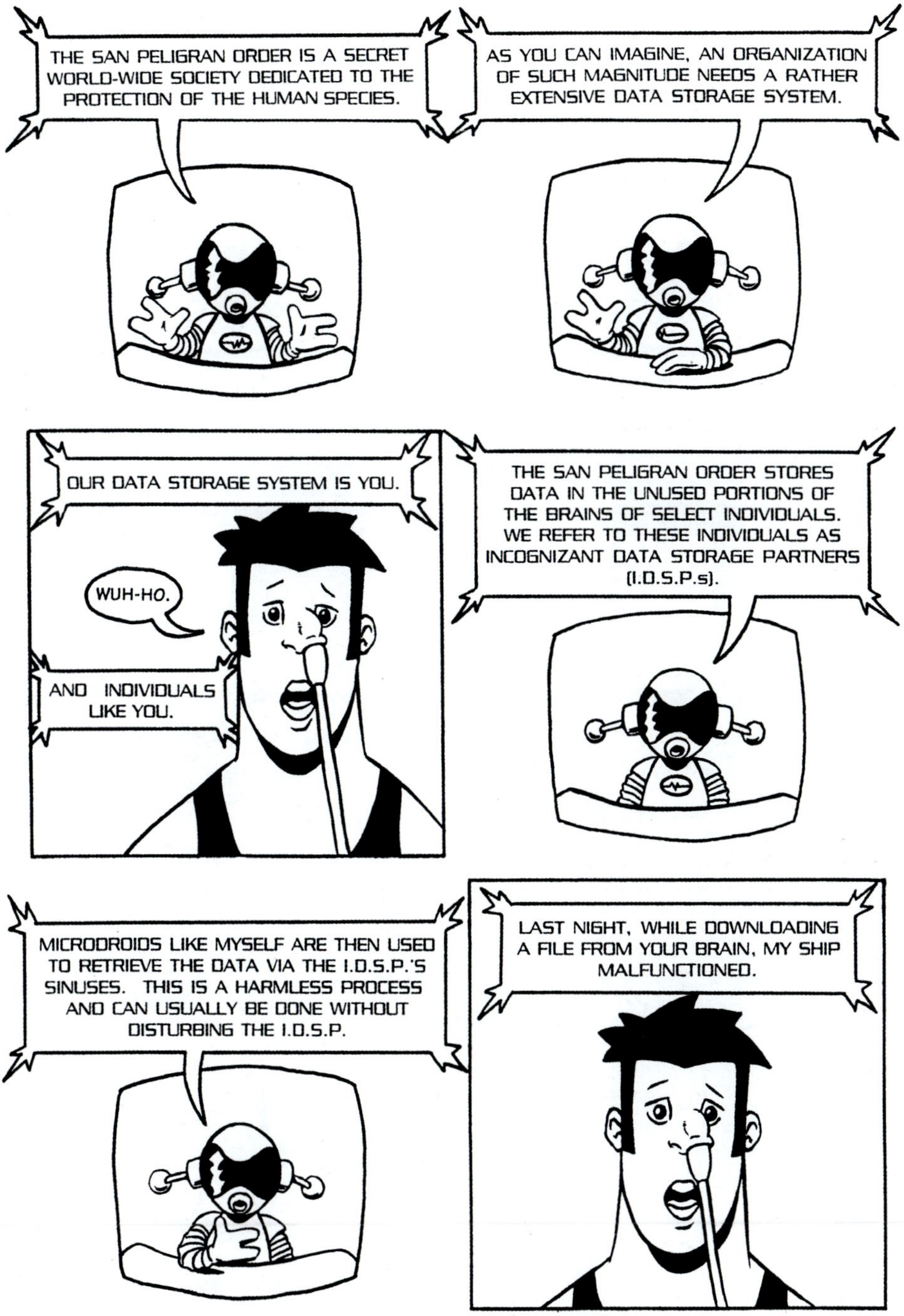
THE SAN PELIGRAN ORDER IS A SECRET WORLD-WIDE SOCIETY DEDICATED TO THE PROTECTION OF THE HUMAN SPECIES.
AS YOU CAN IMAGINE, AN ORGANIZATION OF SUCH MAGNITUDE NEEDS A RATHER EXTENSIVE DATA STORAGE SYSTEM.
OUR DATA STORAGE SYSTEM IS YOU.
WUH-HO.
AND INDIVIDUALS LIKE YOU.
THE SAN PELIGRAN ORDER STORES DATA IN THE UNUSED PORTIONS OF THE BRAINS OF SELECT INDIVIDUALS. WE REFER TO THESE INDIVIDUALS AS INCOGNIZANT DATA STORAGE PARTNERS (I.D.S.P.s).
MICRODROIDS LIKE MYSELF ARE THEN USED TO RETRIEVE THE DATA VIA THE I.D.S.P.'S SINUSES. THIS IS A HARMLESS PROCESS AND CAN USUALLY BE DONE WITHOUT DISTURBING THE I.D.S.P.
LAST NIGHT, WHILE DOWNLOADING A FILE FROM YOUR BRAIN, MY SHIP MALFUNCTIONED.

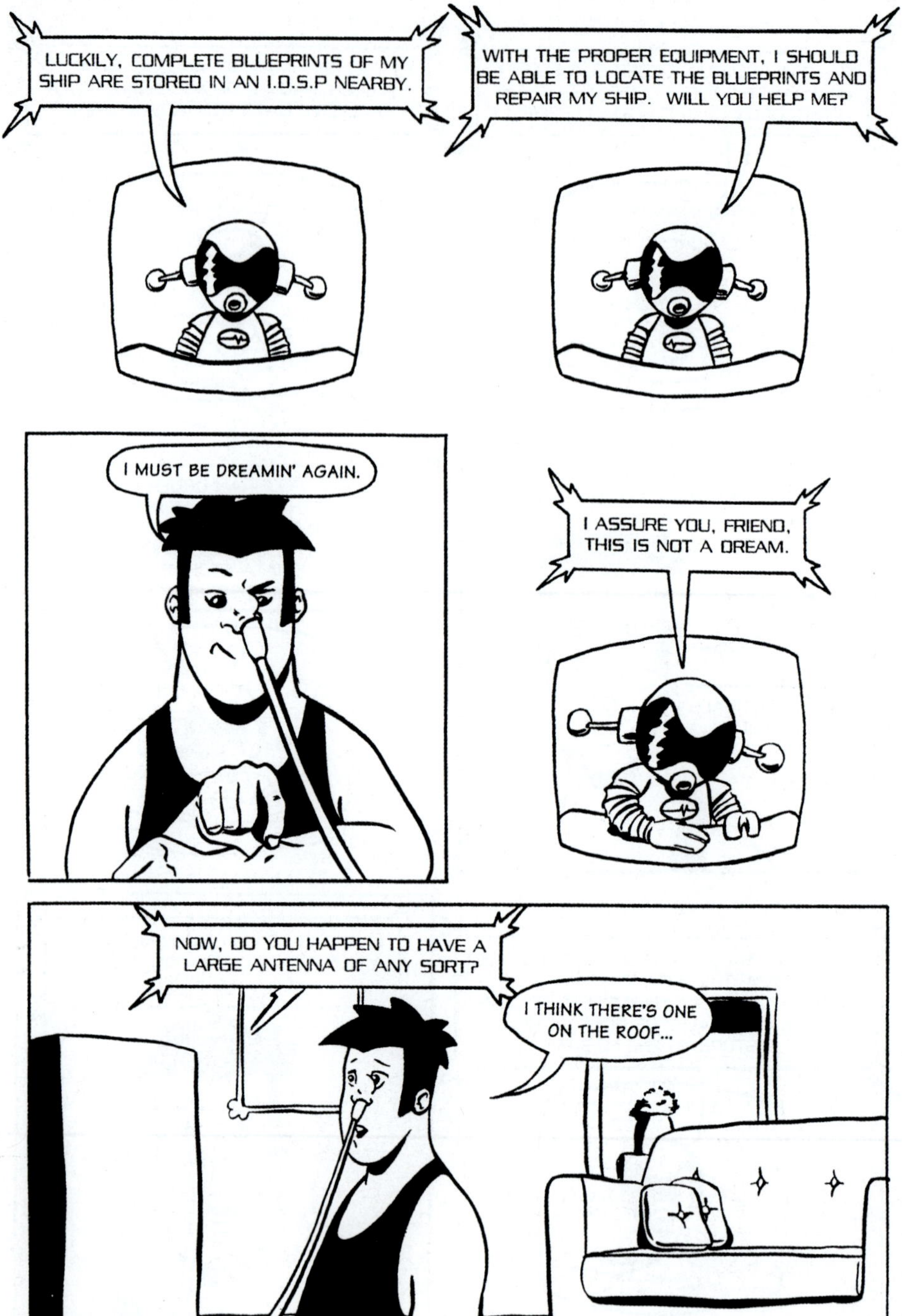
LUCKILY, COMPLETE BLUEPRINTS OF MY SHIP ARE STORED IN AN I.D.S.P NEARBY.
WITH THE PROPER EQUIPMENT, I SHOULD BE ABLE TO LOCATE THE BLUEPRINTS AND REPAIR MY SHIP. WILL YOU HELP ME?
I MUST BE DREAMIN' AGAIN.
I ASSURE YOU, FRIEND, THIS IS NOT A DREAM.
NOW, DO YOU HAPPEN TO HAVE A LARGE ANTENNA OF ANY SORT?
I THINK THERE'S ONE ON THE ROOF...

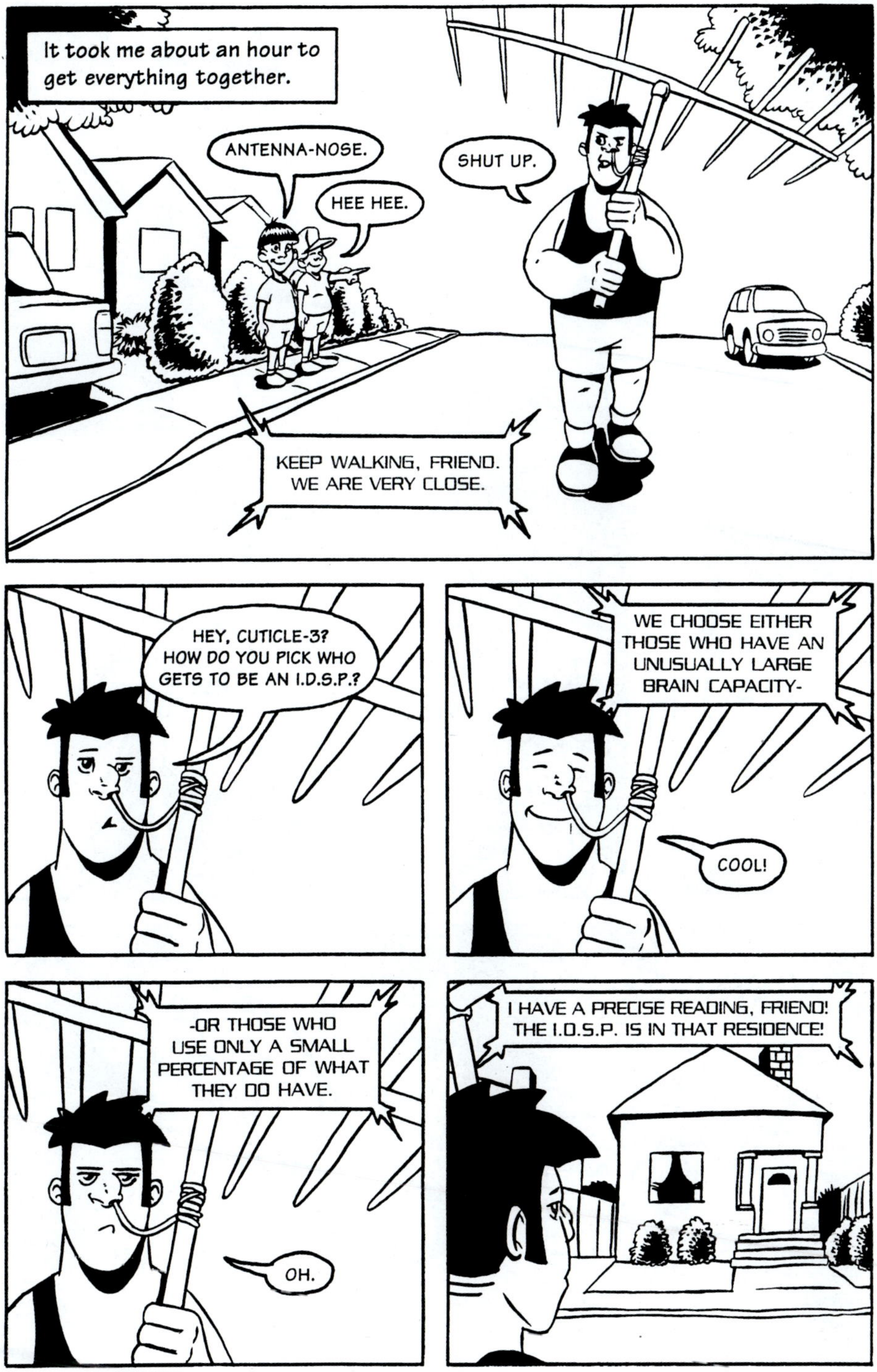
It took me about an hour to get everything together.
ANTENNA-NOSE.
HEE HEE.
SHUT UP.
KEEP WALKING, FRIEND. WE ARE VERY CLOSE.
HEY, CUTICLE-3? HOW DO YOU PICK WHO GETS TO BE AN I.D.S.P.?
WE CHOOSE EITHER THOSE WHO HAVE AN UNUSUALLY LARGE BRAIN CAPACITY-
COOL!
-OR THOSE WHO USE ONLY A SMALL PERCENTAGE OF WHAT THEY DO HAVE.
OH.
I HAVE A PRECISE READING, FRIEND! THE I.D.S.P. IS IN THAT RESIDENCE!

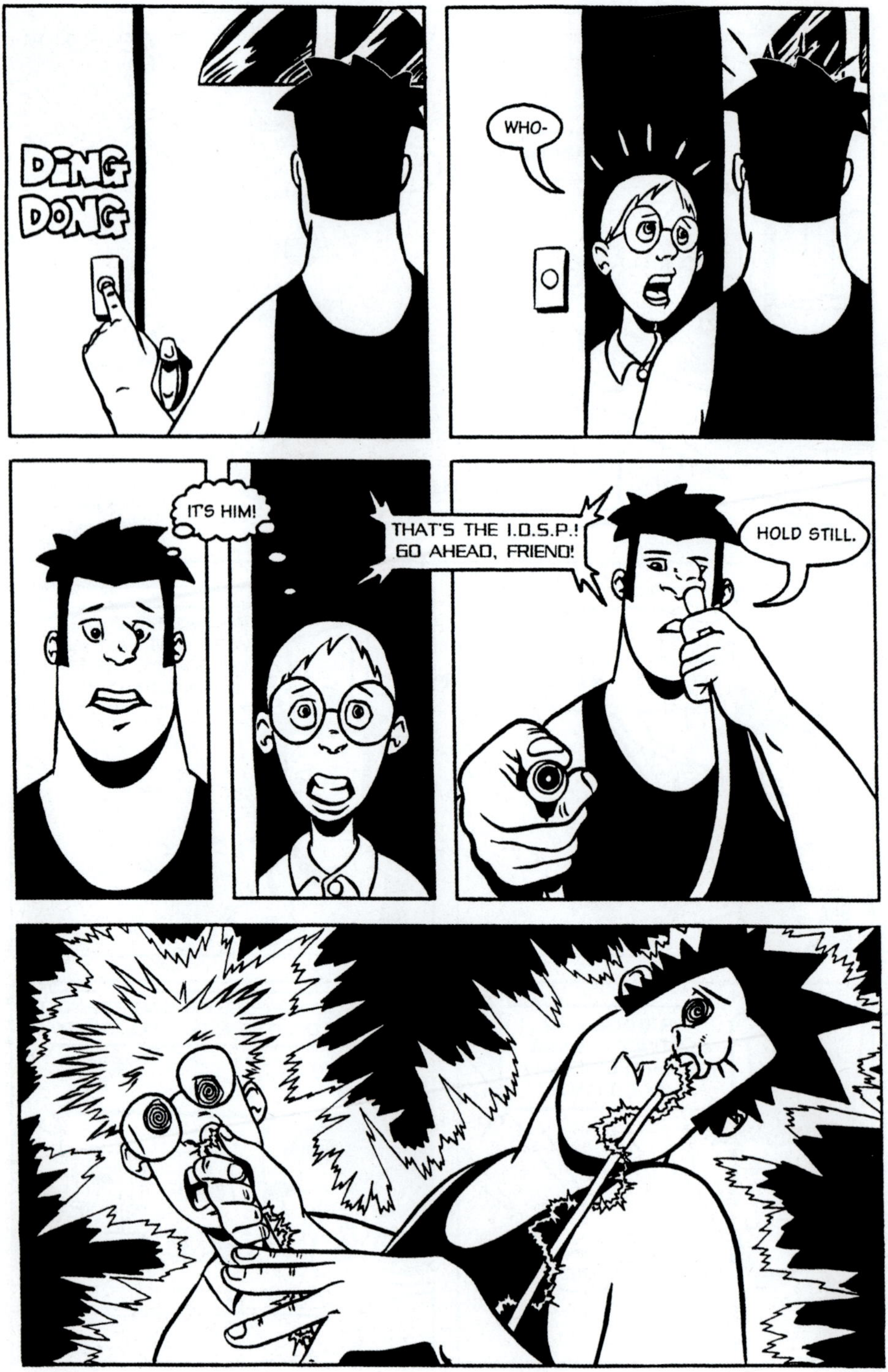
DING DONG
WHO-
IT'S HIM!
THAT'S THE I.D.S.P.! GO AHEAD, FRIEND!
HOLD STILL.

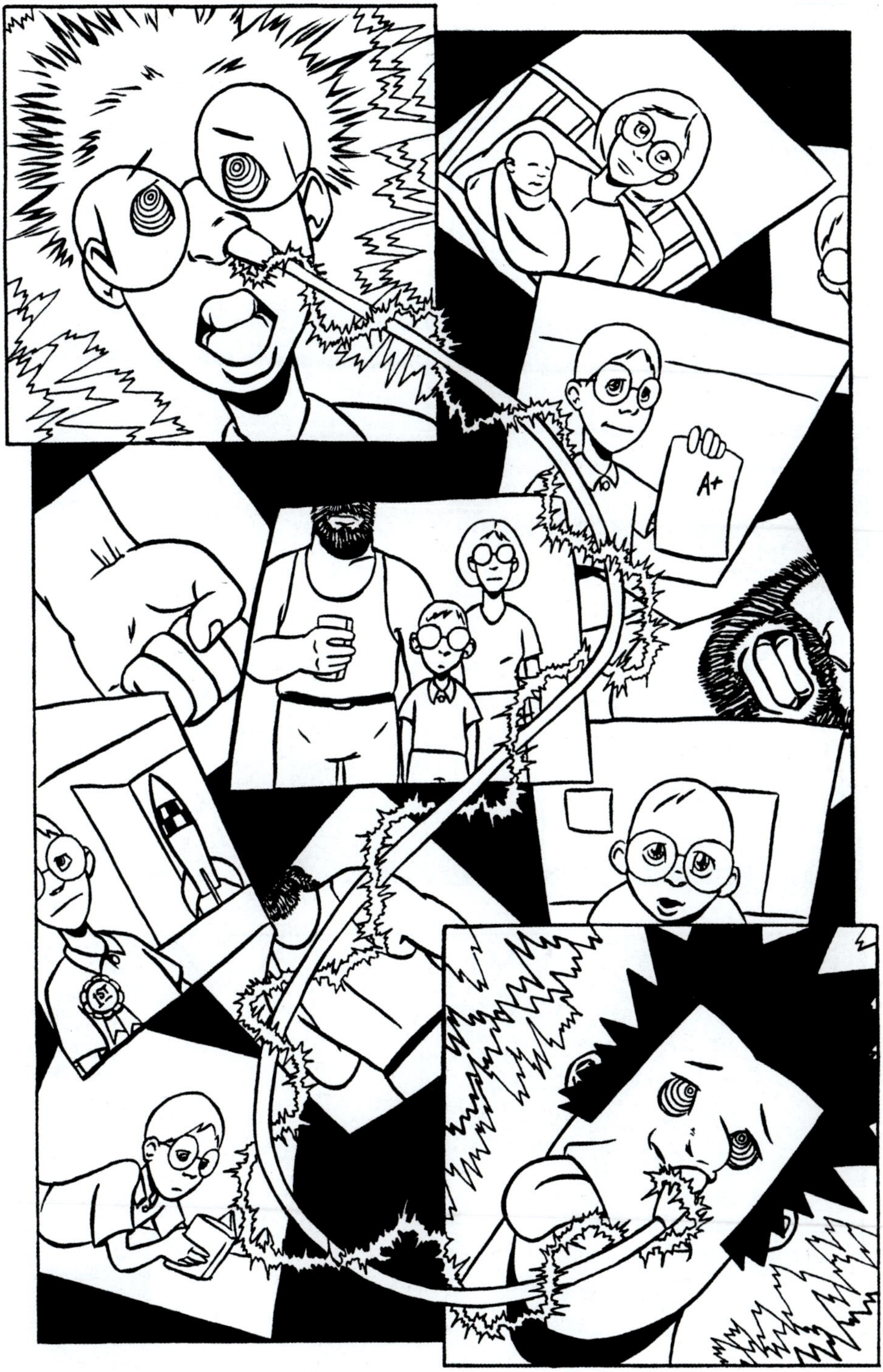
A+

OH DEAR. I MISTAKENLY DOWNLOADED THE I.D.S.P.'S MEMORIES INTO YOUR BRAIN, FRIEND. I APOLOGIZE PROFUSELY!
THERE! THAT SHOULD BE THE BLUEPRINTS.
SLAM

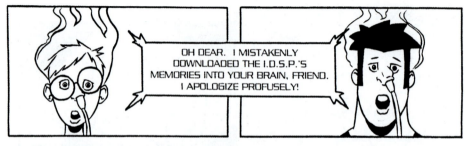

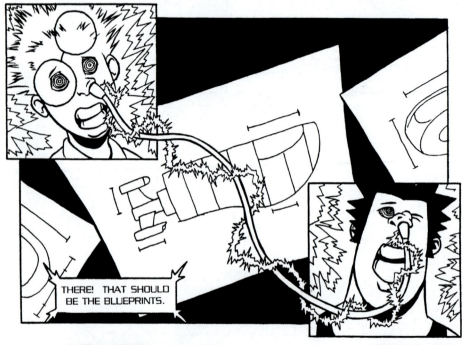

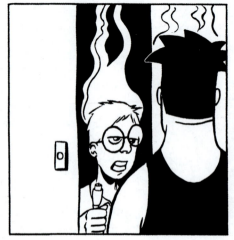

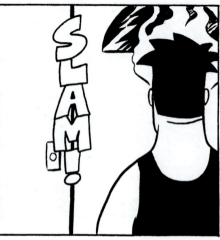

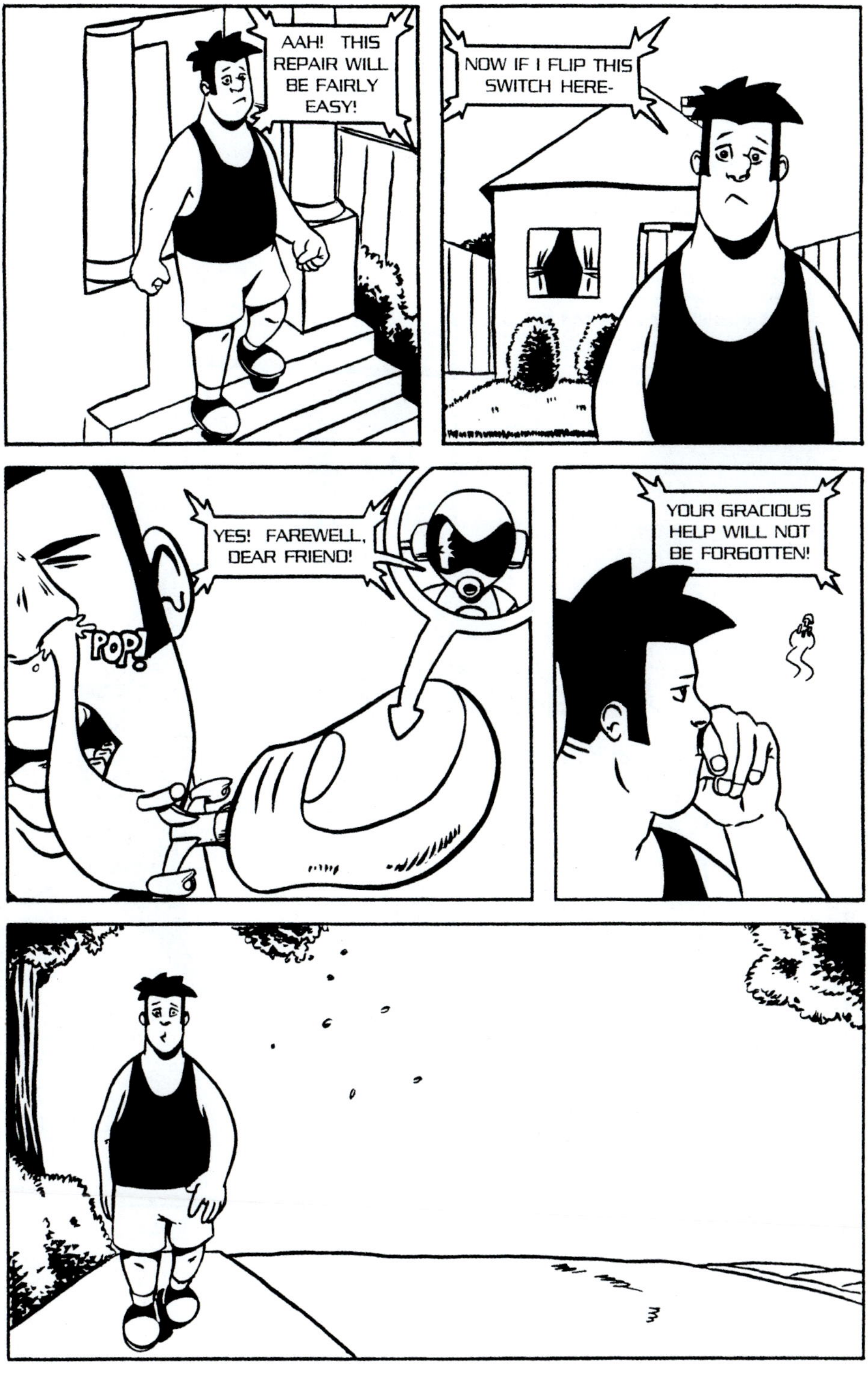
AAH! THIS REPAIR WILL BE FAIRLY EASY!
NOW IF I FLIP THIS SWITCH HERE-
YES! FAREWELL, DEAR FRIEND!
POP!
YOUR GRACIOUS HELP WILL NOT BE FORGOTTEN!

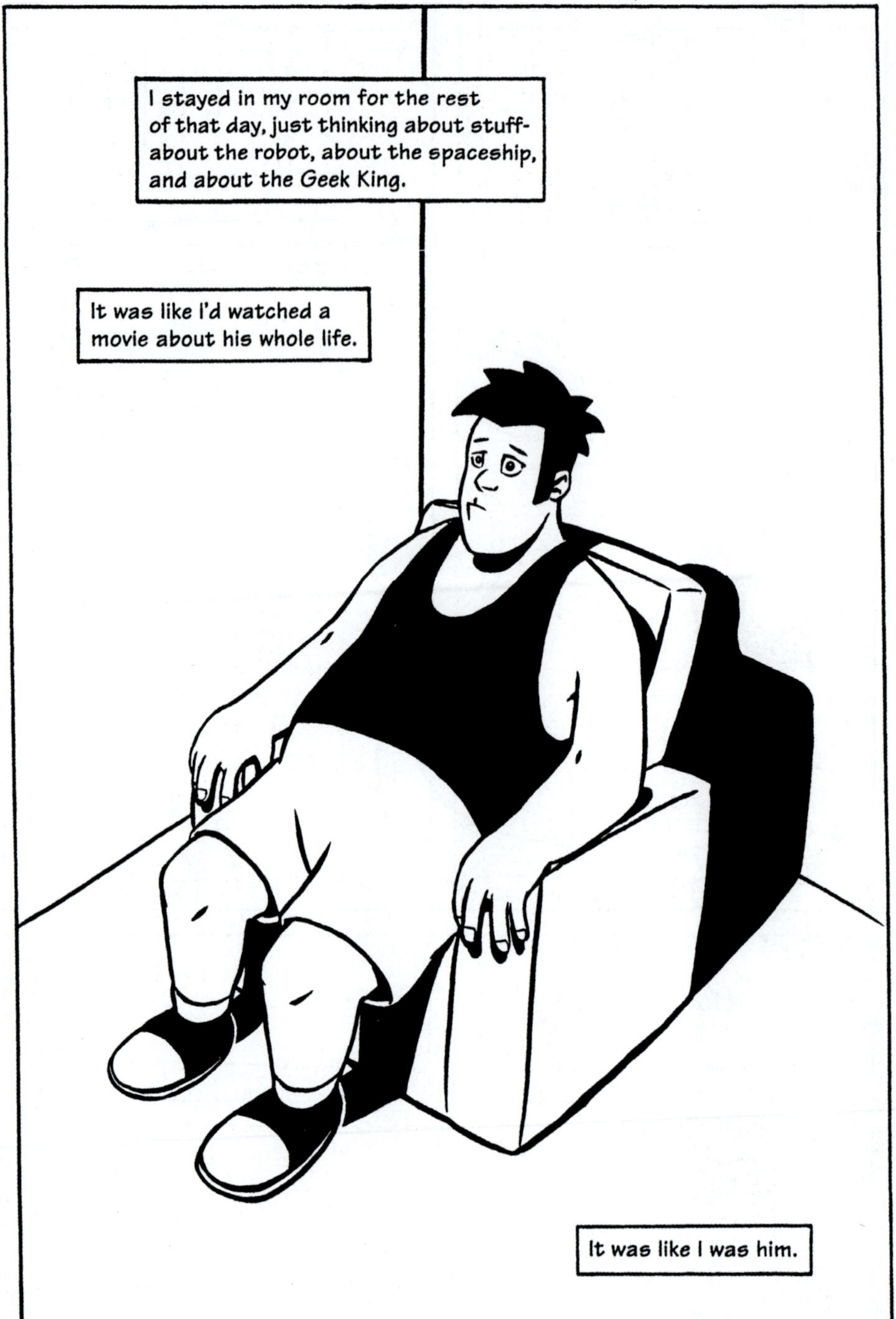
I stayed in my room for the rest of that day, just thinking about stuff- about the robot, about the spaceship, and about the Geek King.
It was like I'd watched a movie about his whole life.
It was like I was him.

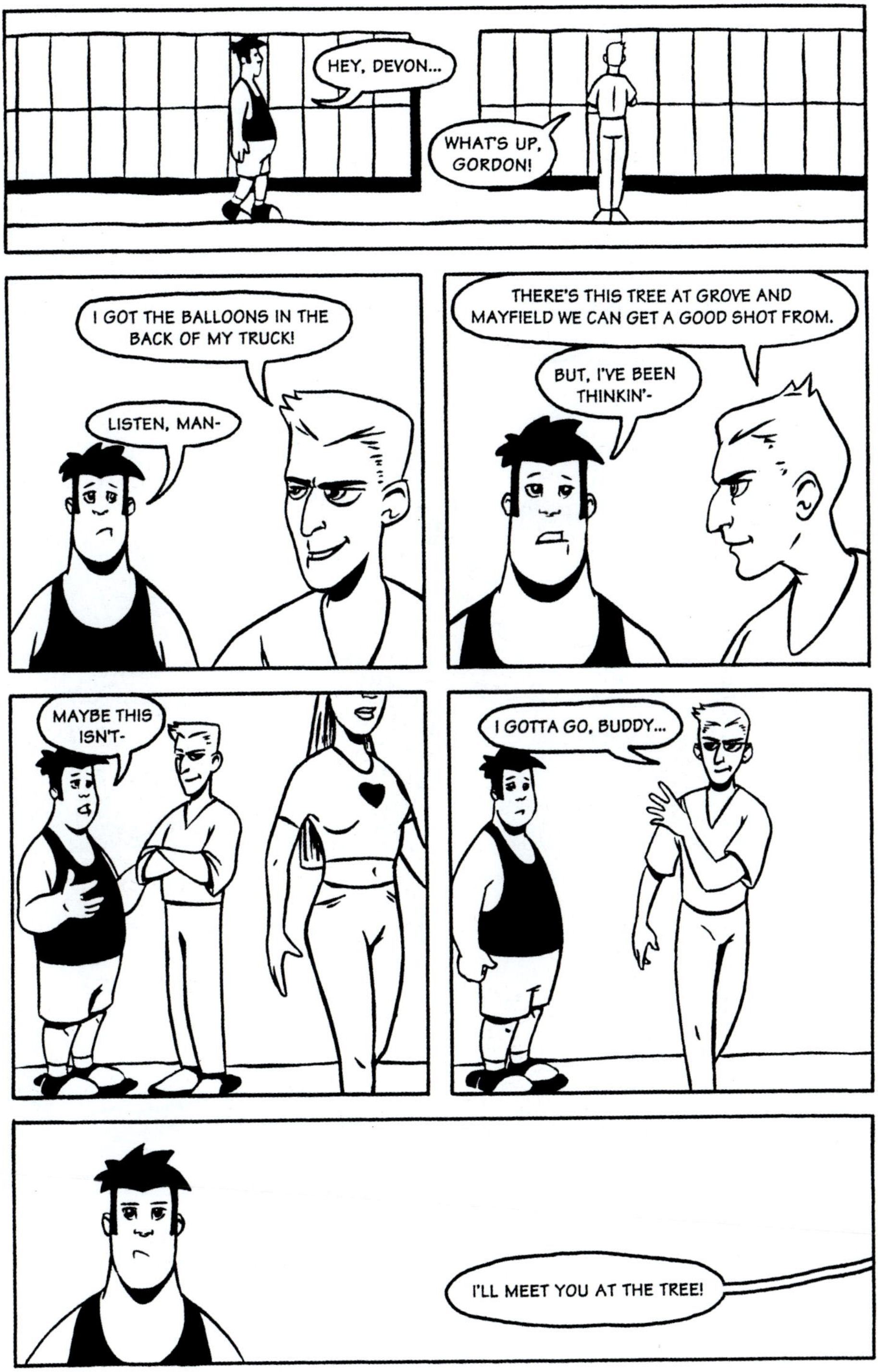
HEY, DEVON...
WHAT'S UP, GORDON!
I GOT THE BALLOONS IN THE BACK OF MY TRUCK!
LISTEN, MAN-
THERE'S THIS TREE AT GROVE AND MAYFIELD WE CAN GET A GOOD SHOT FROM.
BUT, I'VE BEEN THINKIN'-
MAYBE THIS ISN'T-
I GOTTA GO, BUDDY...
I'LL MEET YOU AT THE TREE!

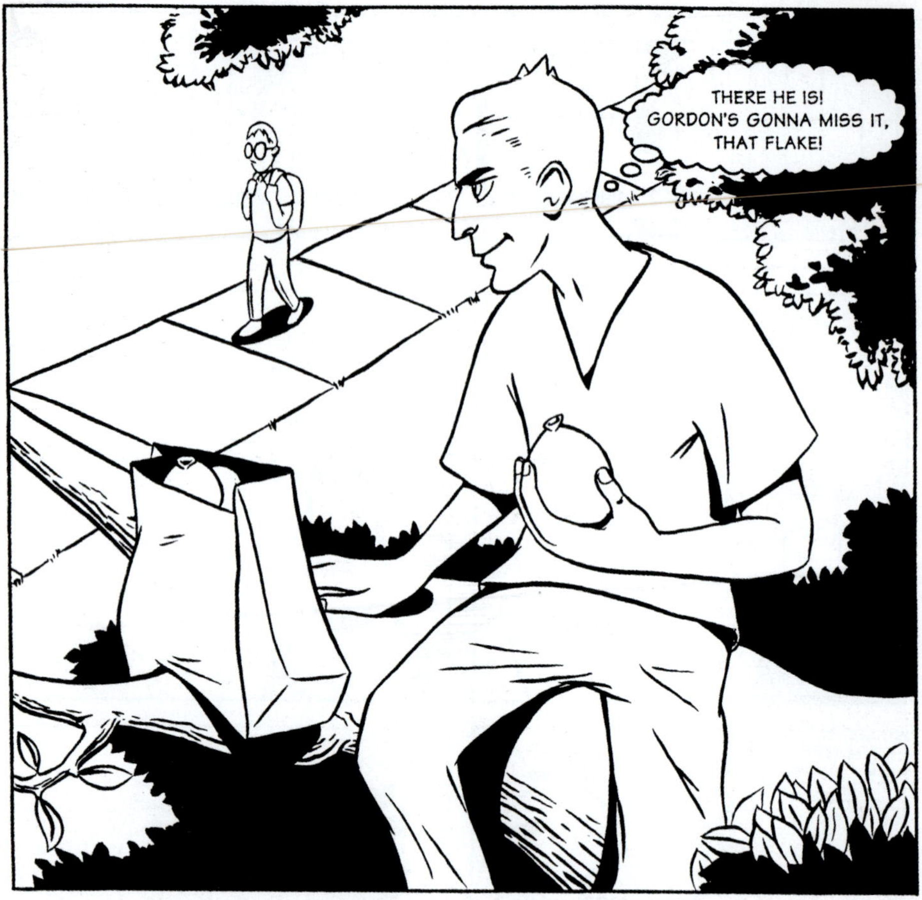
THERE HE IS! GORDON'S GONNA MISS IT, THAT FLAKE!

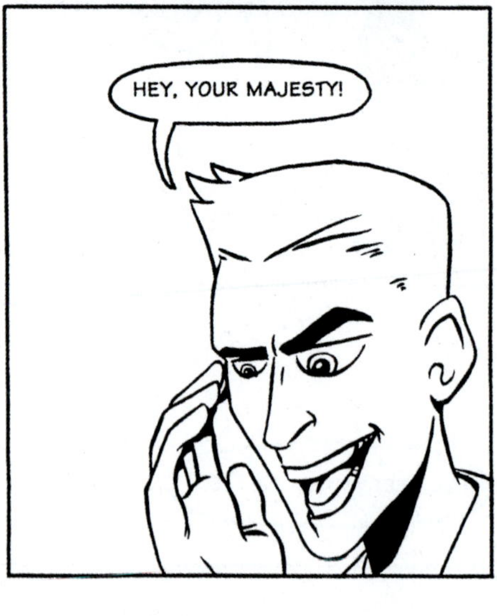
HEY, YOUR MAJESTY!

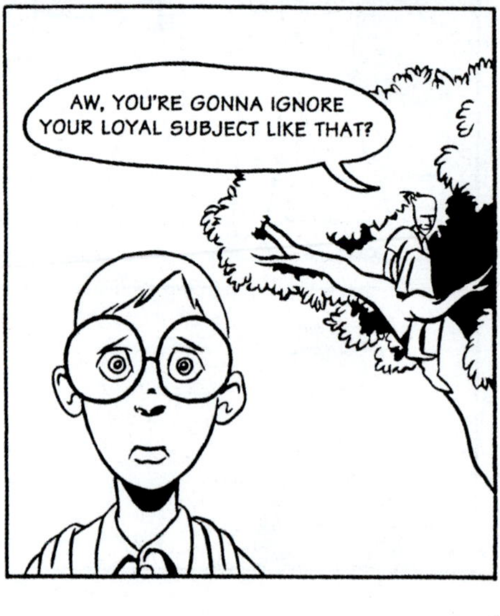
AW, YOU'RE GONNA IGNORE YOUR LOYAL SUBJECT LIKE THAT?

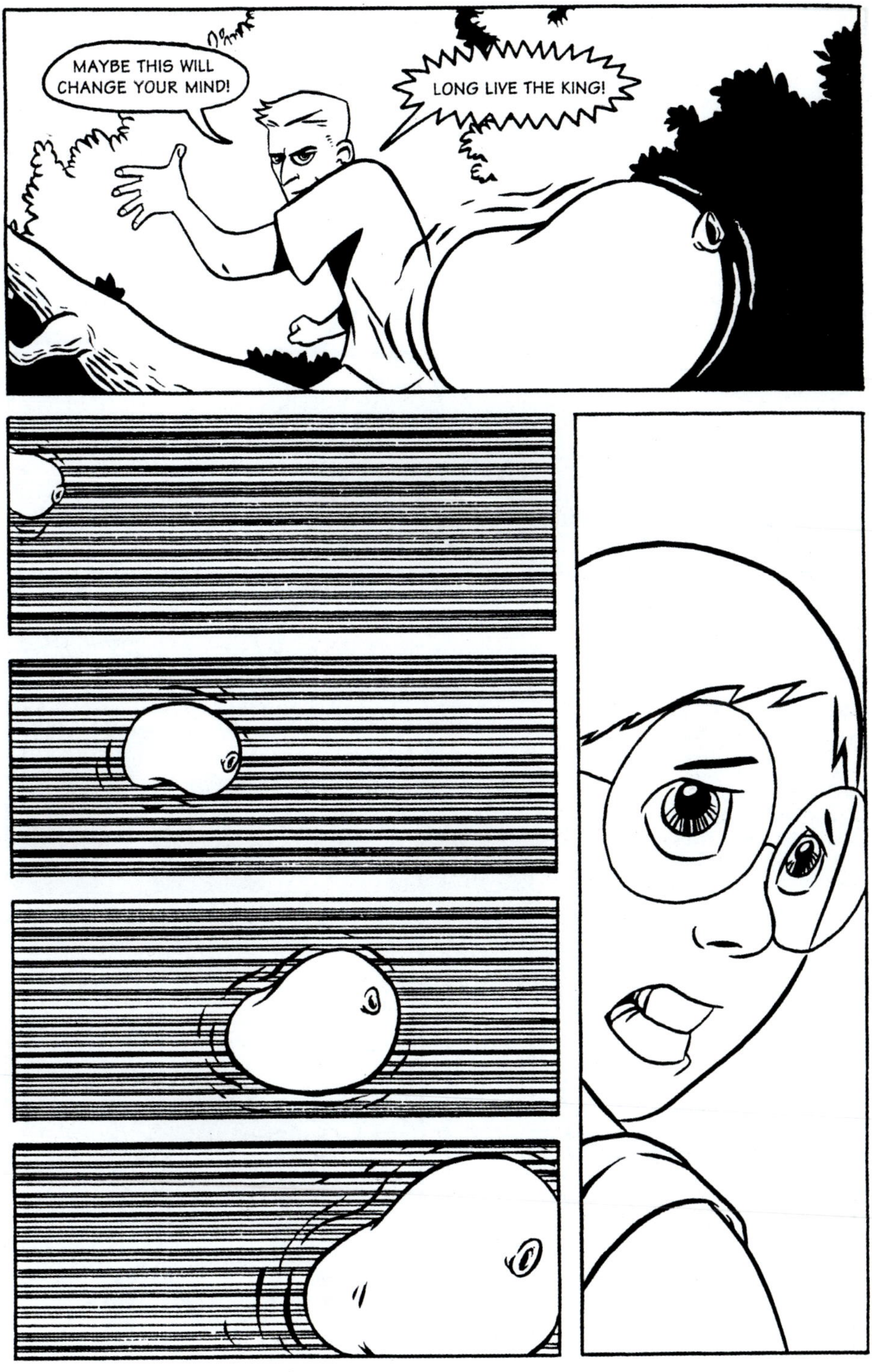
MAYBE THIS WILL CHANGE YOUR MIND!
LONG LIVE THE KING!

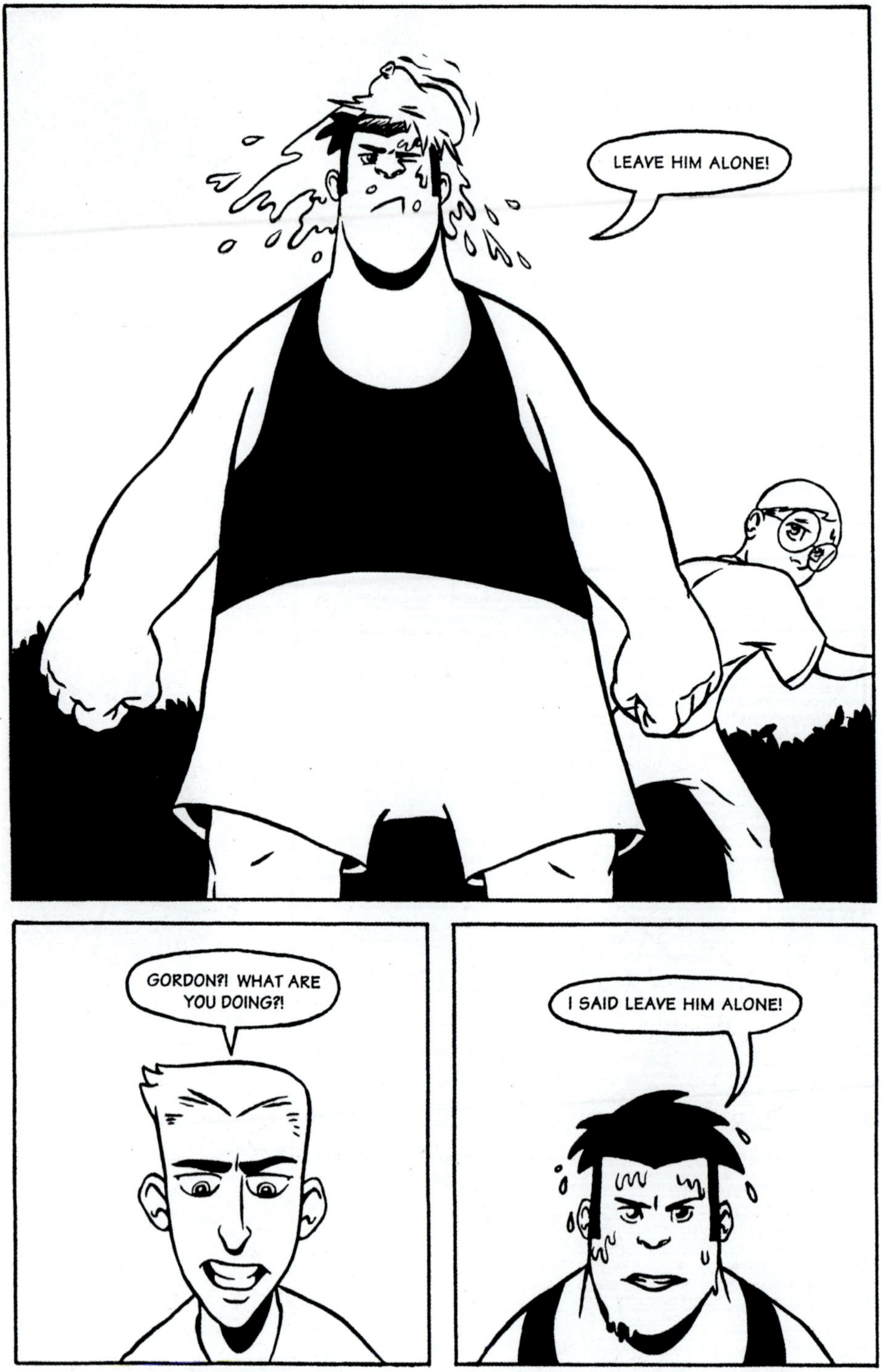
LEAVE HIM ALONE!
GORDON?! WHAT ARE YOU DOING?!
I SAID LEAVE HIM ALONE!

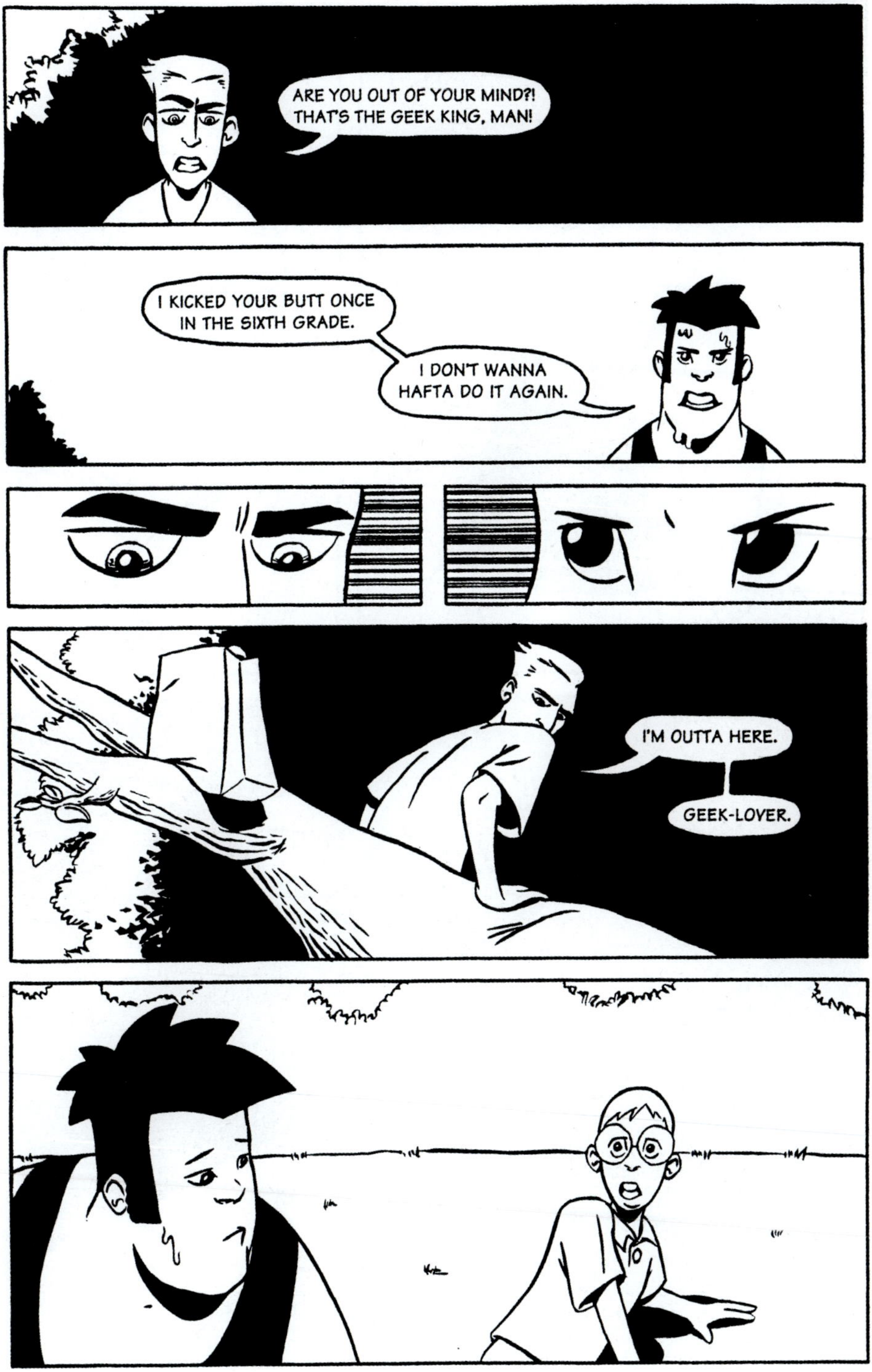
ARE YOU OUT OF YOUR MIND?! THAT'S THE GEEK KING, MAN!
I KICKED YOUR BUTT ONCE IN THE SIXTH GRADE.
I DON'T WANNA HAFTA DO IT AGAIN.
I'M OUTTA HERE.
GEEK-LOVER.

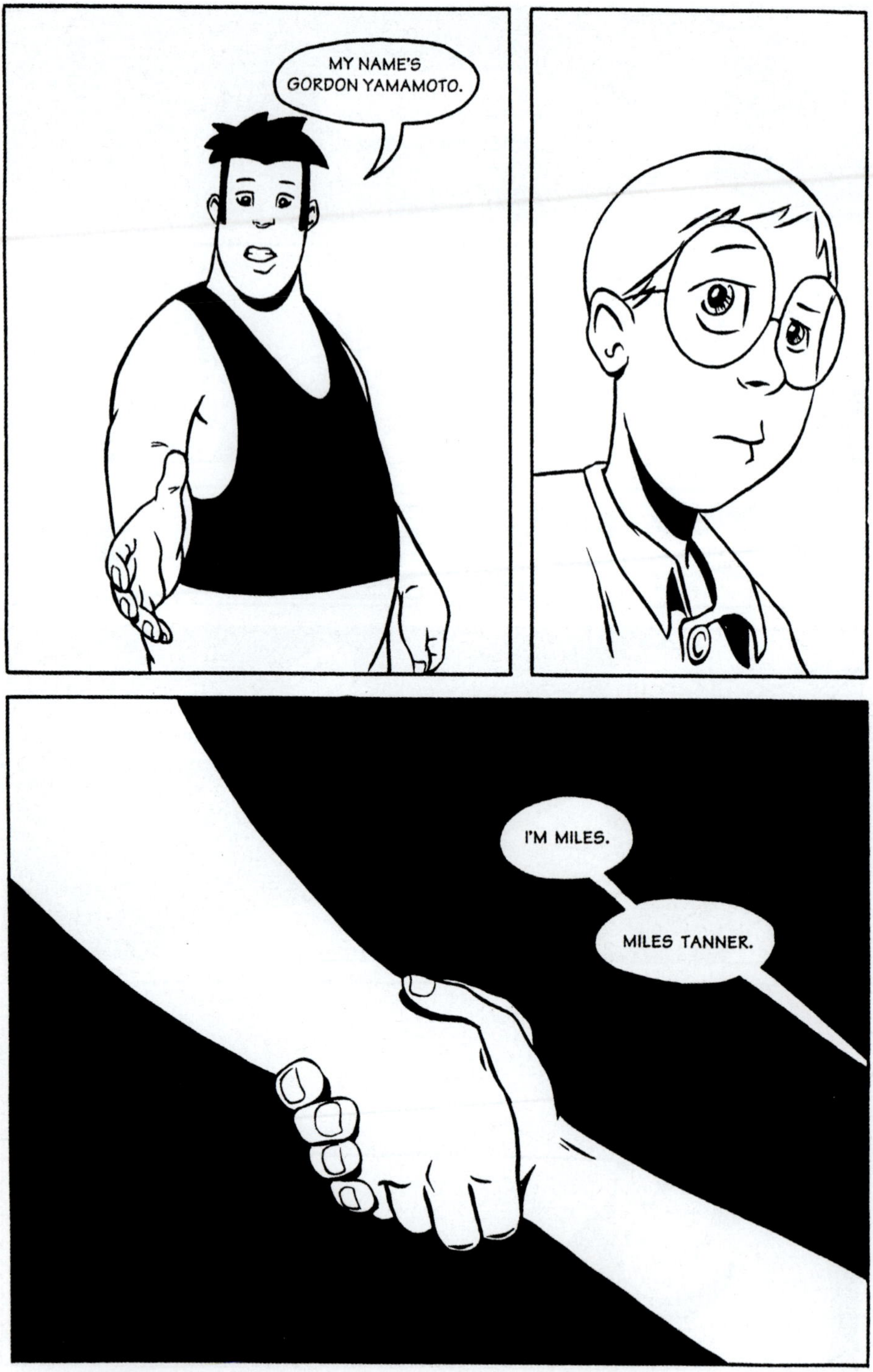
MY NAME'S GORDON YAMAMOTO.
I'M MILES.
MILES TANNER.

CHAPTER
TWO

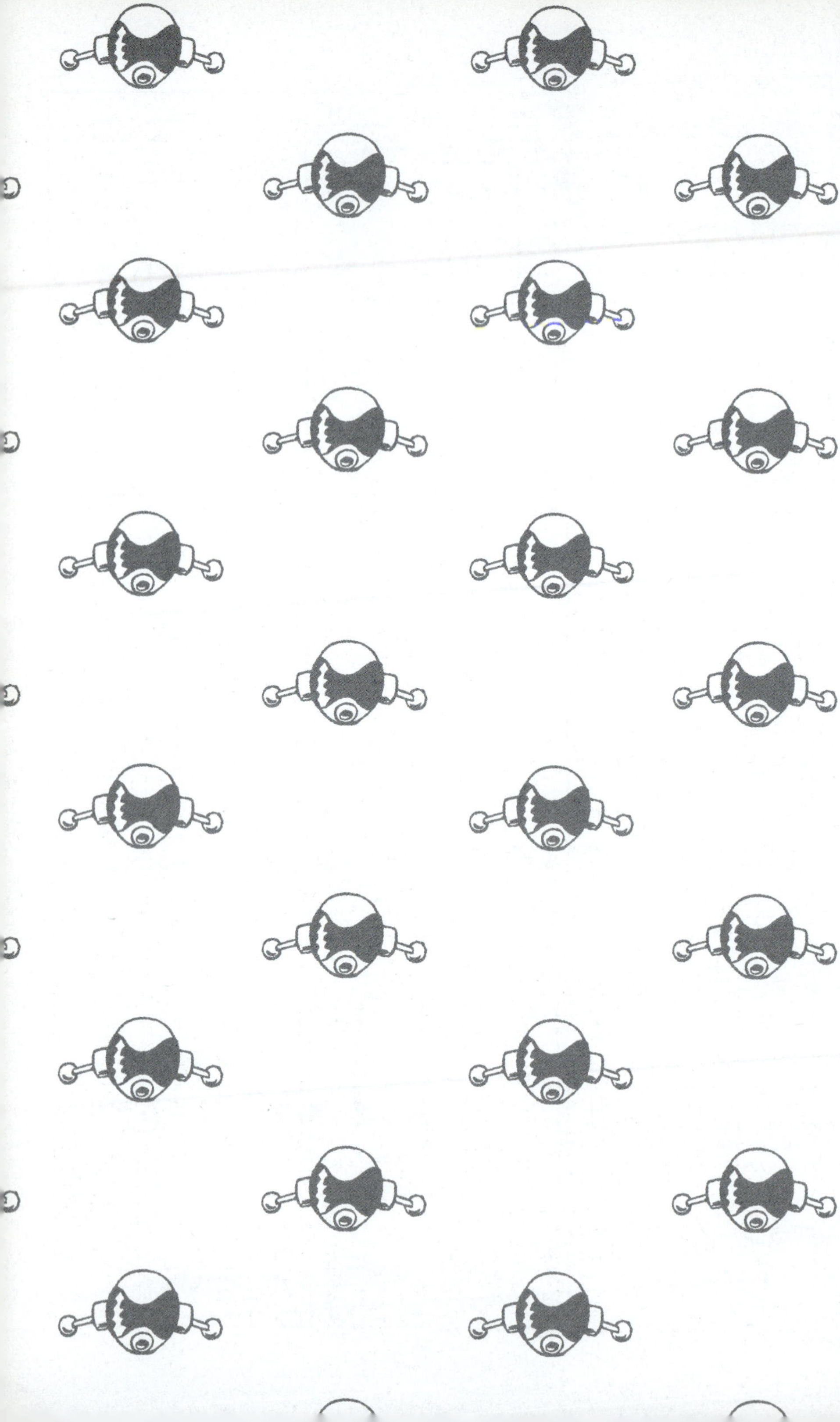

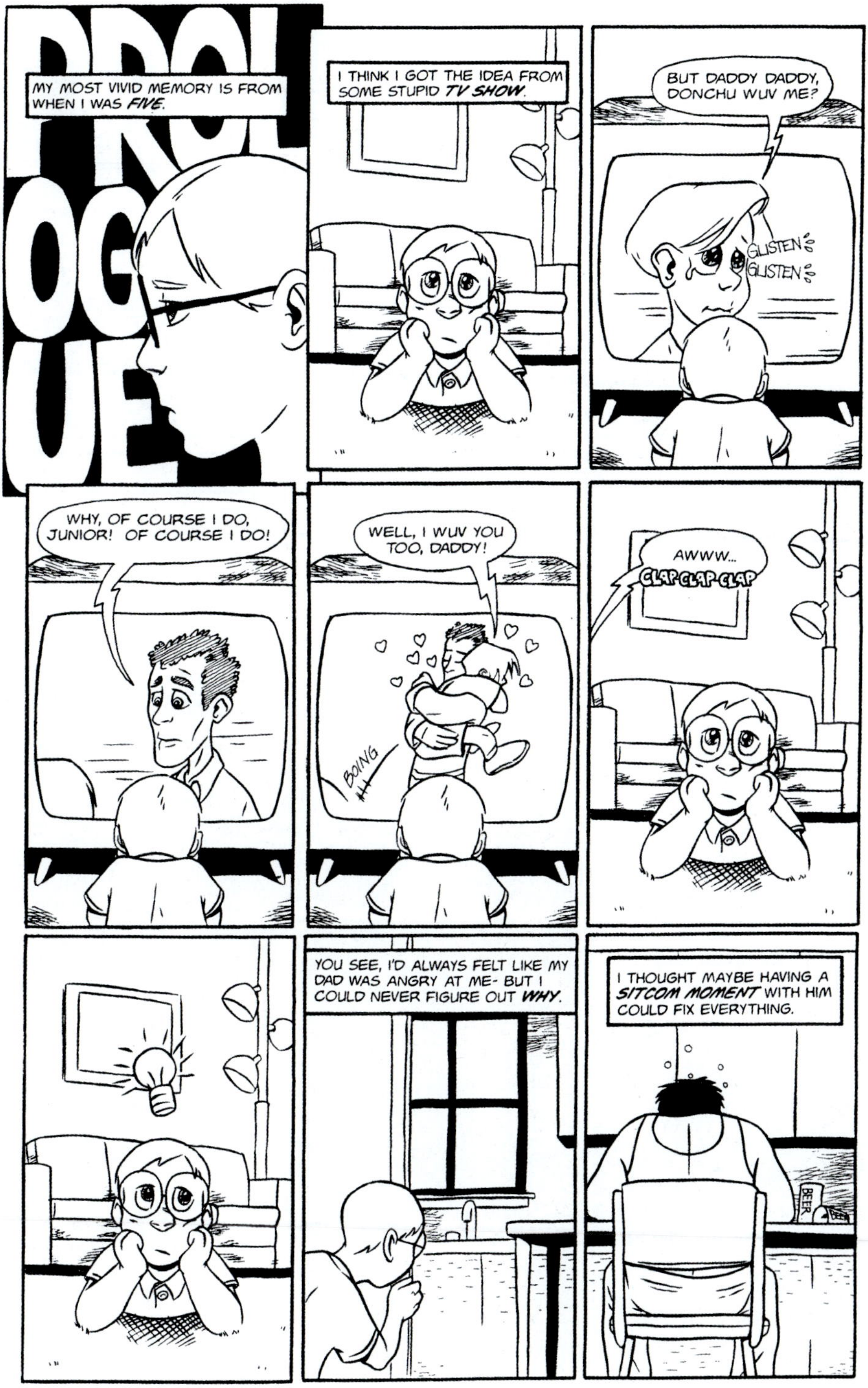
PROLOGUE
MY MOST VIVID MEMORY IS FROM WHEN I WAS *FIVE*.
I THINK I GOT THE IDEA FROM SOME STUPID *TV SHOW*.
BUT DADDY DADDY, DONCHU WUV ME?
GLISTEN
GLISTEN
WHY, OF COURSE I DO, JUNIOR! OF COURSE I DO!
WELL, I WUV YOU TOO, DADDY!
BOING
AWWW...
CLAP CLAP CLAP
YOU SEE, I'D ALWAYS FELT LIKE MY DAD WAS ANGRY AT ME- BUT I COULD NEVER FIGURE OUT *WHY*.
I THOUGHT MAYBE HAVING A *SITCOM MOMENT* WITH HIM COULD FIX EVERYTHING.
BEER

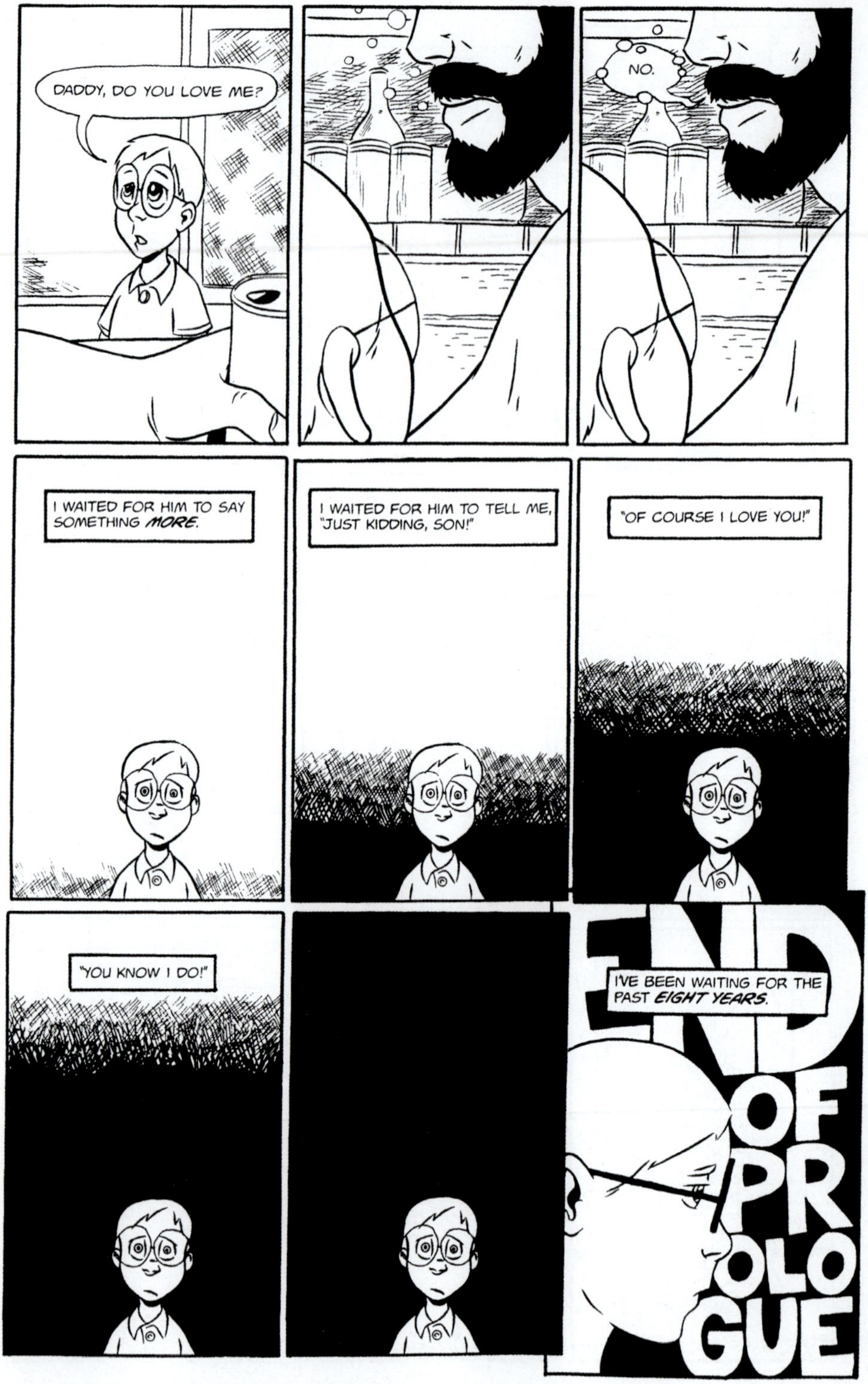
DADDY, DO YOU LOVE ME?
NO.
I WAITED FOR HIM TO SAY SOMETHING MORE.
I WAITED FOR HIM TO TELL ME, "JUST KIDDING, SON!"
"OF COURSE I LOVE YOU!"
"YOU KNOW I DO!"
END OF PROLOGUE
I'VE BEEN WAITING FOR THE PAST EIGHT YEARS.

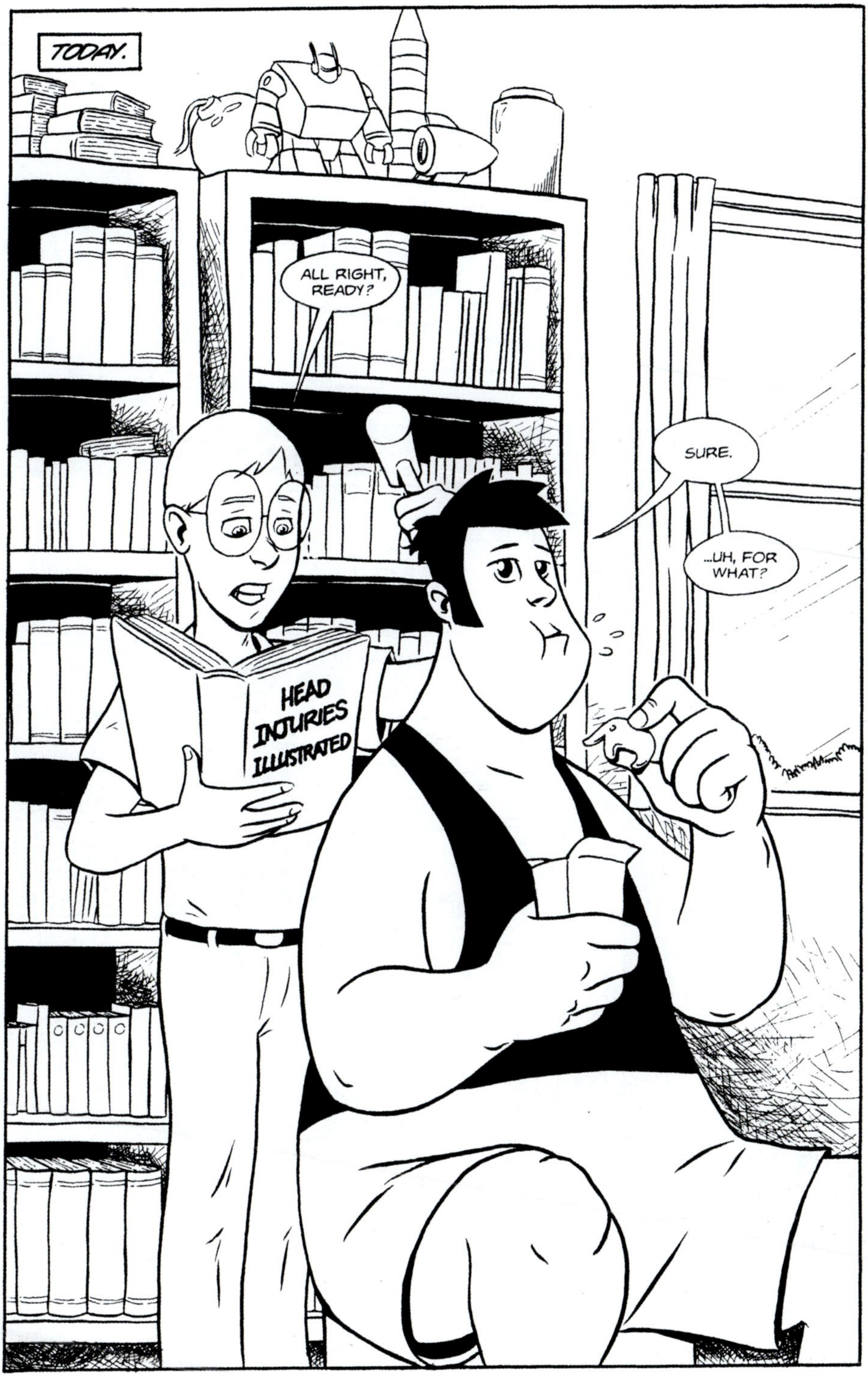
TODAY.
ALL RIGHT, READY?
SURE.
...UH, FOR WHAT?
HEAD INJURIES ILLUSTRATED

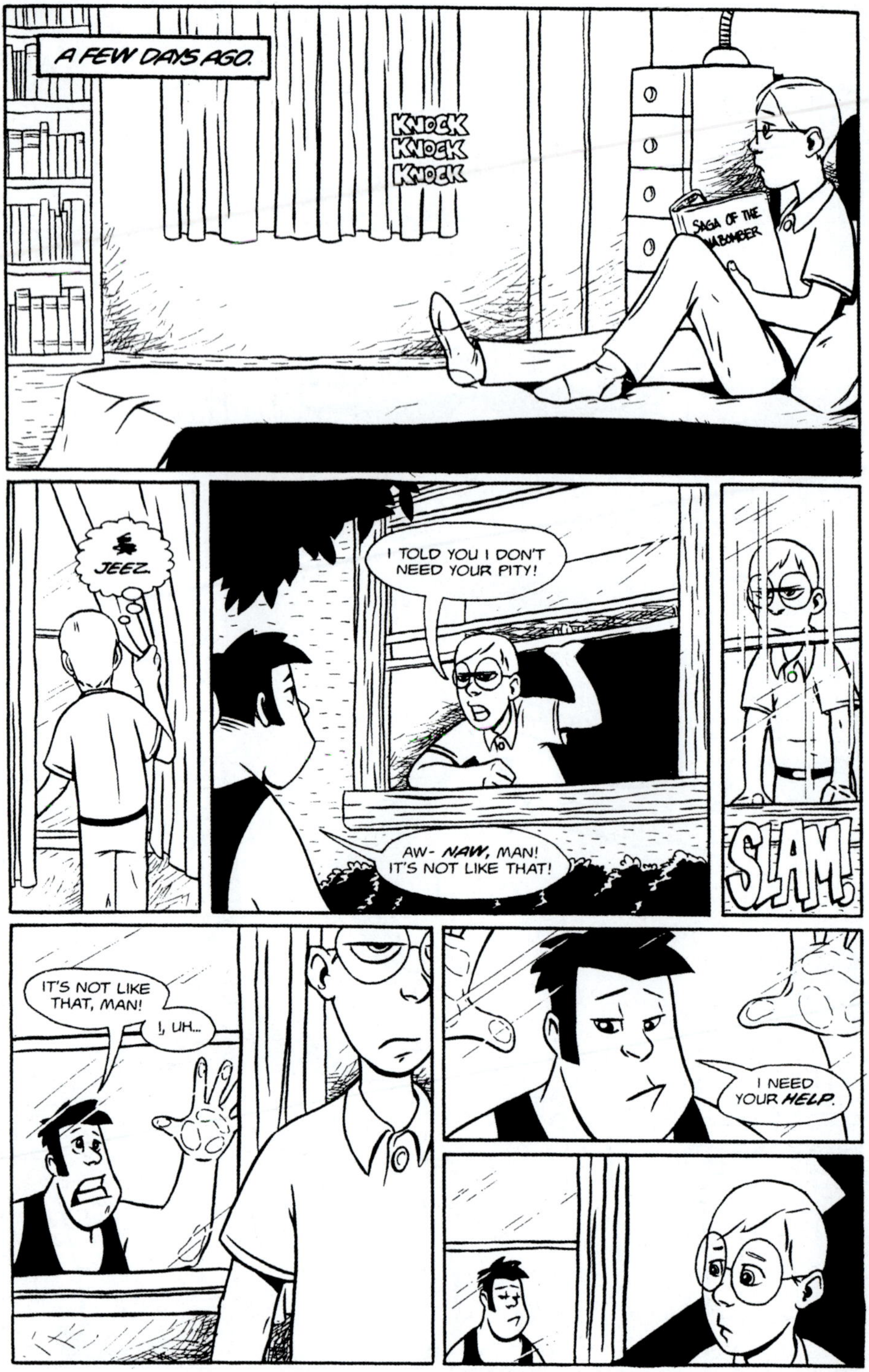
A FEW DAYS AGO.
KNOCK KNOCK KNOCK
SAGA OF THE UNABOMBER
JEEZ.
I TOLD YOU I DON'T NEED YOUR PITY!
AW- NAW, MAN! IT'S NOT LIKE THAT!
SLAM!
IT'S NOT LIKE THAT, MAN!
I, UH...
I NEED YOUR HELP.

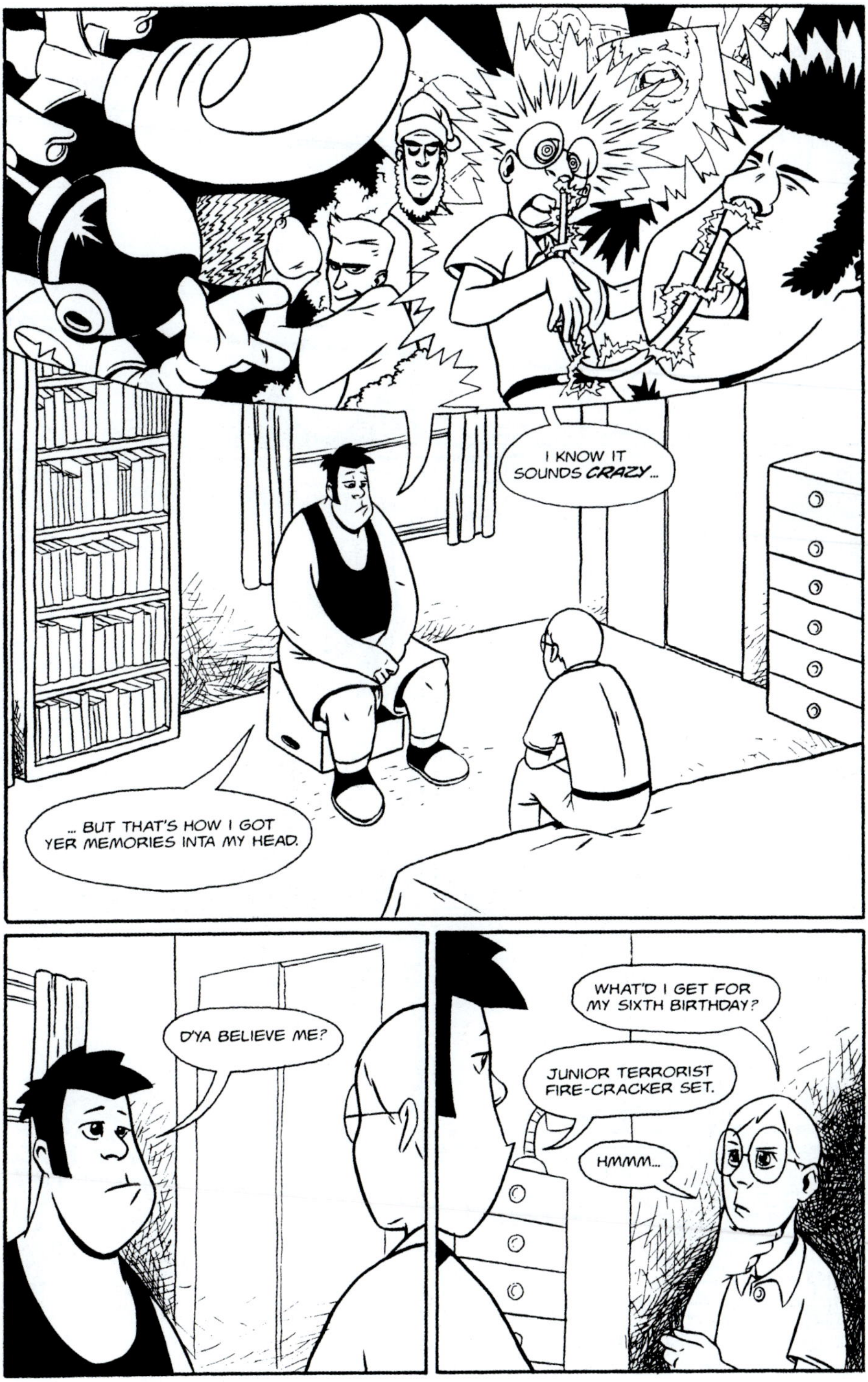
I KNOW IT SOUNDS CRAZY...
... BUT THAT'S HOW I GOT YER MEMORIES INTA MY HEAD.
D'YA BELIEVE ME?
WHAT'D I GET FOR MY SIXTH BIRTHDAY?
JUNIOR TERRORIST FIRE-CRACKER SET.
HMMM...

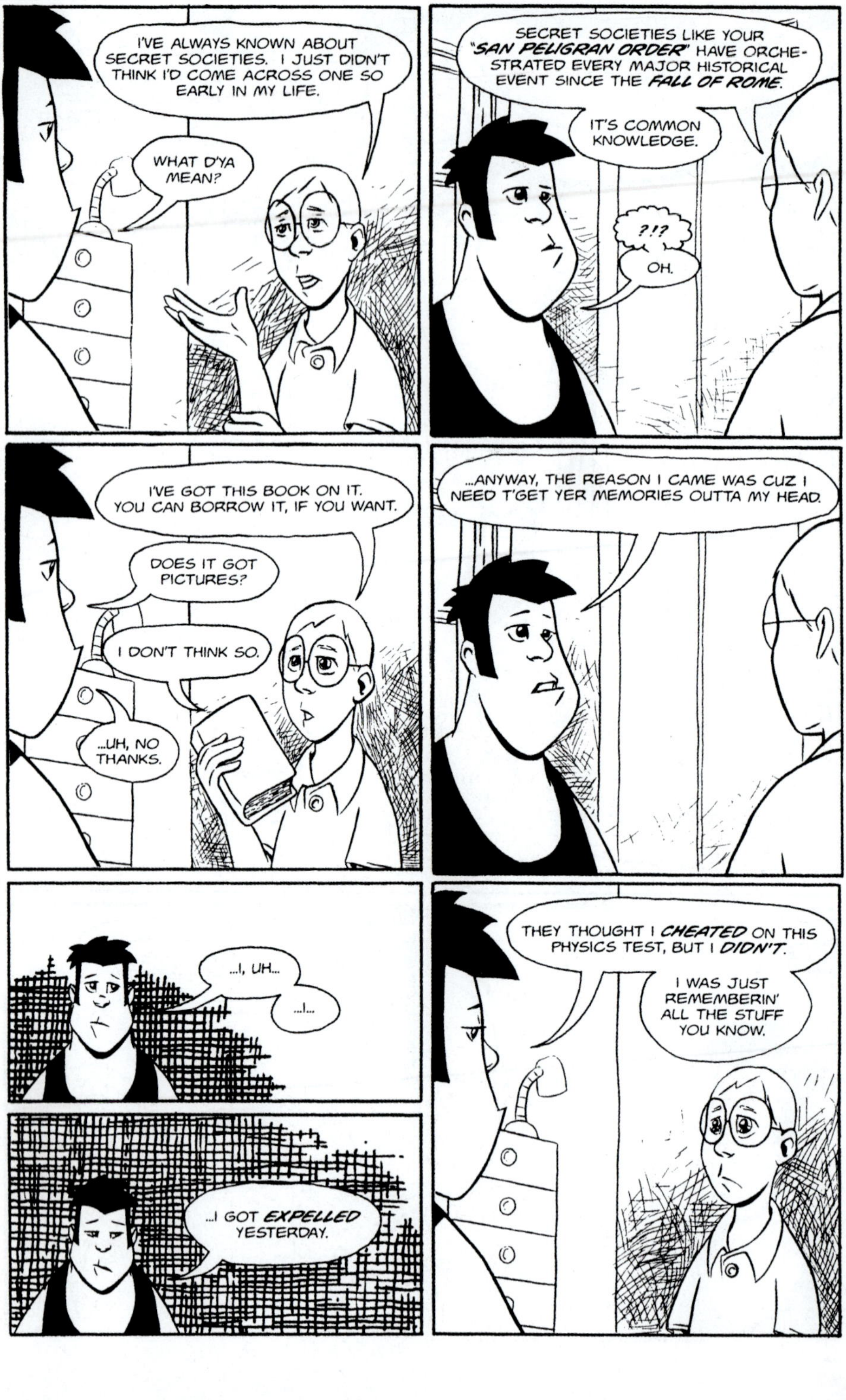
I'VE ALWAYS KNOWN ABOUT SECRET SOCIETIES. I JUST DIDN'T THINK I'D COME ACROSS ONE SO EARLY IN MY LIFE.
WHAT D'YA MEAN?
SECRET SOCIETIES LIKE YOUR "SAN PELIGRAN ORDER" HAVE ORCHESTRATED EVERY MAJOR HISTORICAL EVENT SINCE THE FALL OF ROME.
IT'S COMMON KNOWLEDGE.
?!?
OH.
I'VE GOT THIS BOOK ON IT. YOU CAN BORROW IT, IF YOU WANT.
DOES IT GOT PICTURES?
I DON'T THINK SO.
...UH, NO THANKS.
...ANYWAY, THE REASON I CAME WAS CUZ I NEED T'GET YER MEMORIES OUTTA MY HEAD.
...I, UH...
...I...
...I GOT EXPELLED YESTERDAY.
THEY THOUGHT I CHEATED ON THIS PHYSICS TEST, BUT I DIDN'T.
I WAS JUST REMEMBERIN' ALL THE STUFF YOU KNOW.

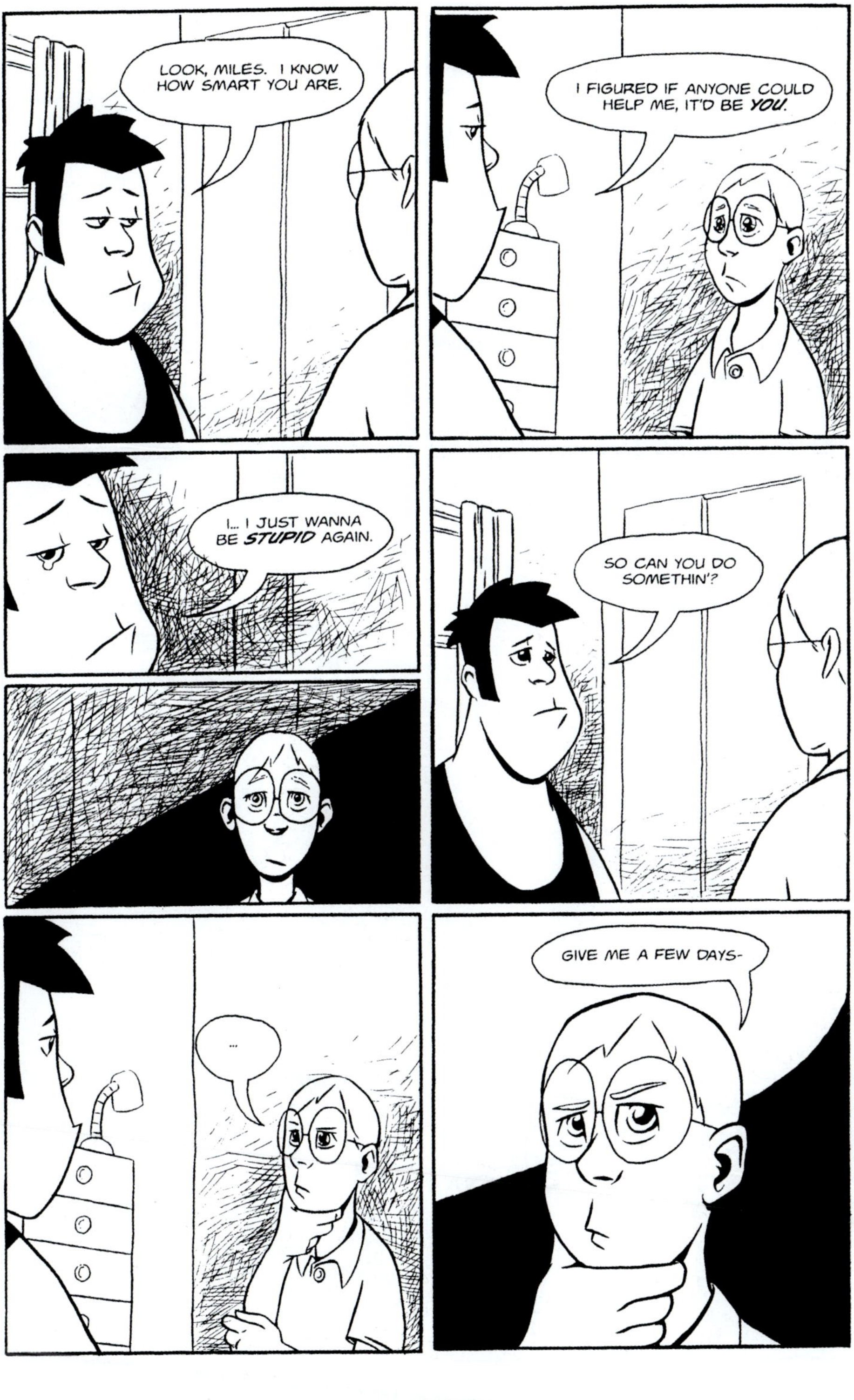
LOOK, MILES. I KNOW HOW SMART YOU ARE.
I FIGURED IF ANYONE COULD HELP ME, IT'D BE *YOU*.
I... I JUST WANNA BE ***STUPID*** AGAIN.
SO CAN YOU DO SOMETHIN'?
...
GIVE ME A FEW DAYS-

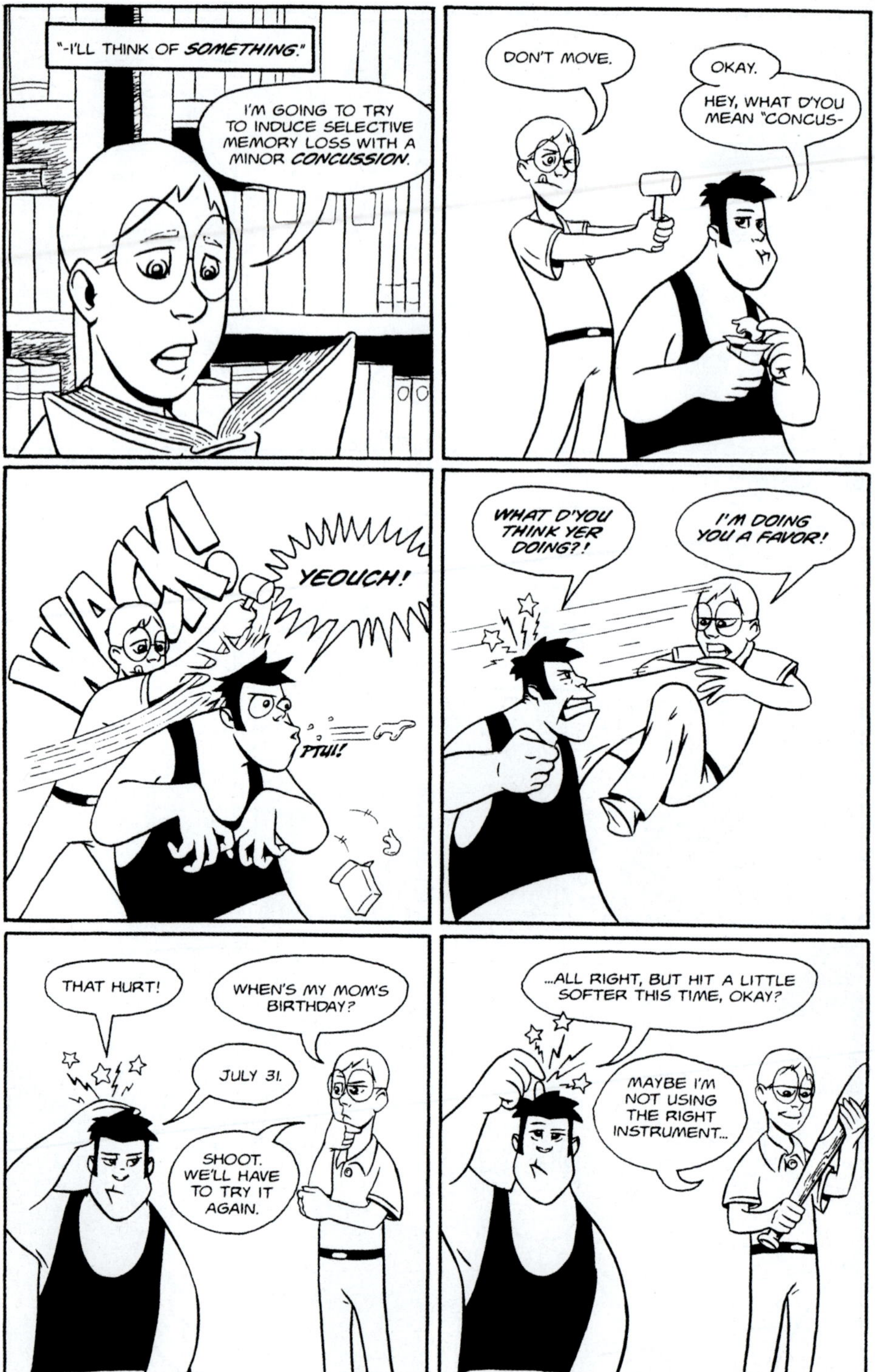
"-I'LL THINK OF *SOMETHING*."
I'M GOING TO TRY TO INDUCE SELECTIVE MEMORY LOSS WITH A MINOR *CONCUSSION*.
DON'T MOVE.
OKAY.
HEY, WHAT D'YOU MEAN "CONCUS-
WACK!
YEOUCH!
PTUI!
WHAT D'YOU THINK YER DOING?!
I'M DOING YOU A FAVOR!
THAT HURT!
WHEN'S MY MOM'S BIRTHDAY?
JULY 31.
SHOOT. WE'LL HAVE TO TRY IT AGAIN.
...ALL RIGHT, BUT HIT A LITTLE SOFTER THIS TIME, OKAY?
MAYBE I'M NOT USING THE RIGHT INSTRUMENT...

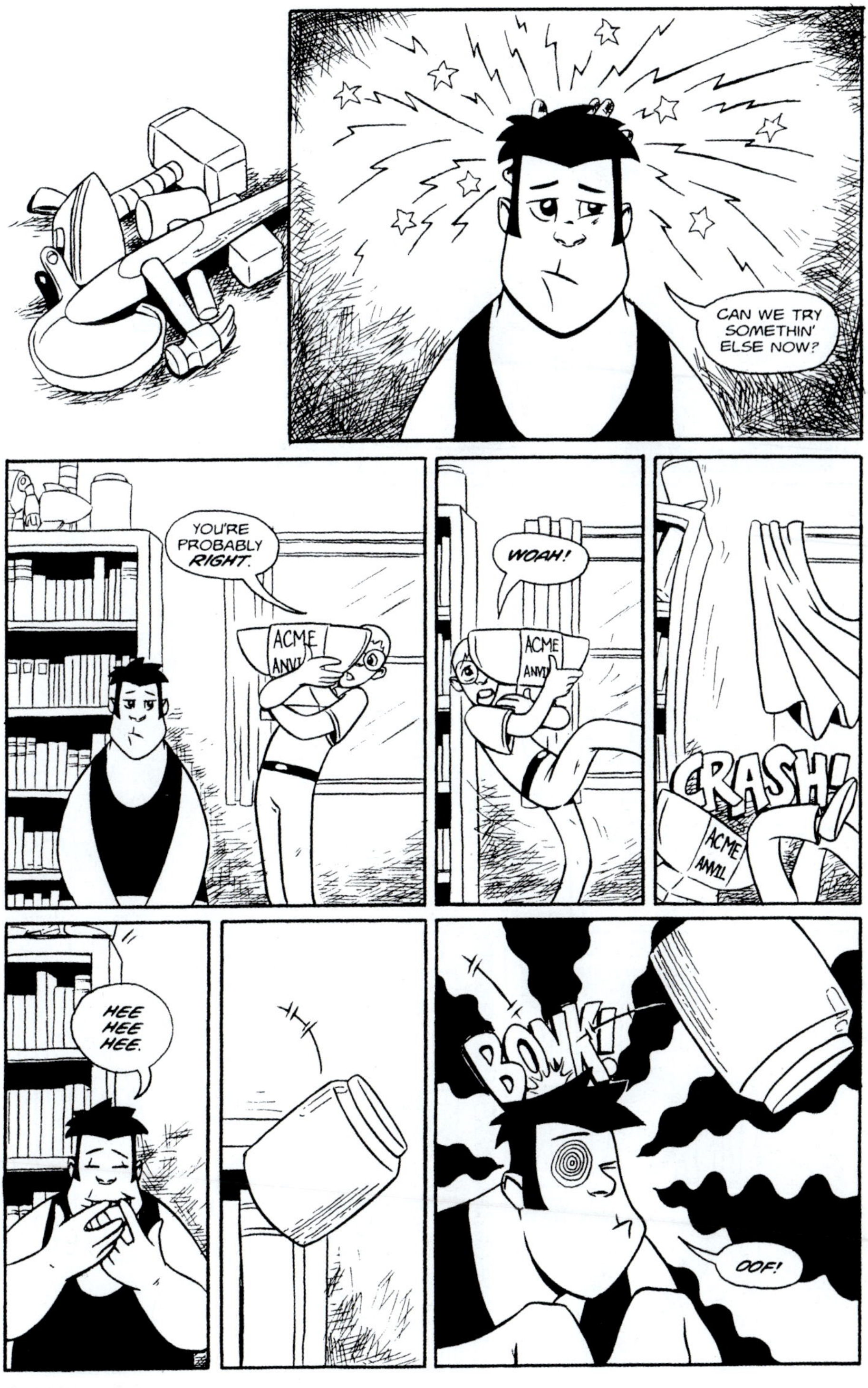
CAN WE TRY SOMETHIN' ELSE NOW?
YOU'RE PROBABLY *RIGHT*.
ACME ANVIL
WOAH!
ACME ANVIL
CRASH!
ACME ANVIL
HEE HEE HEE.
BONK!
OOF!

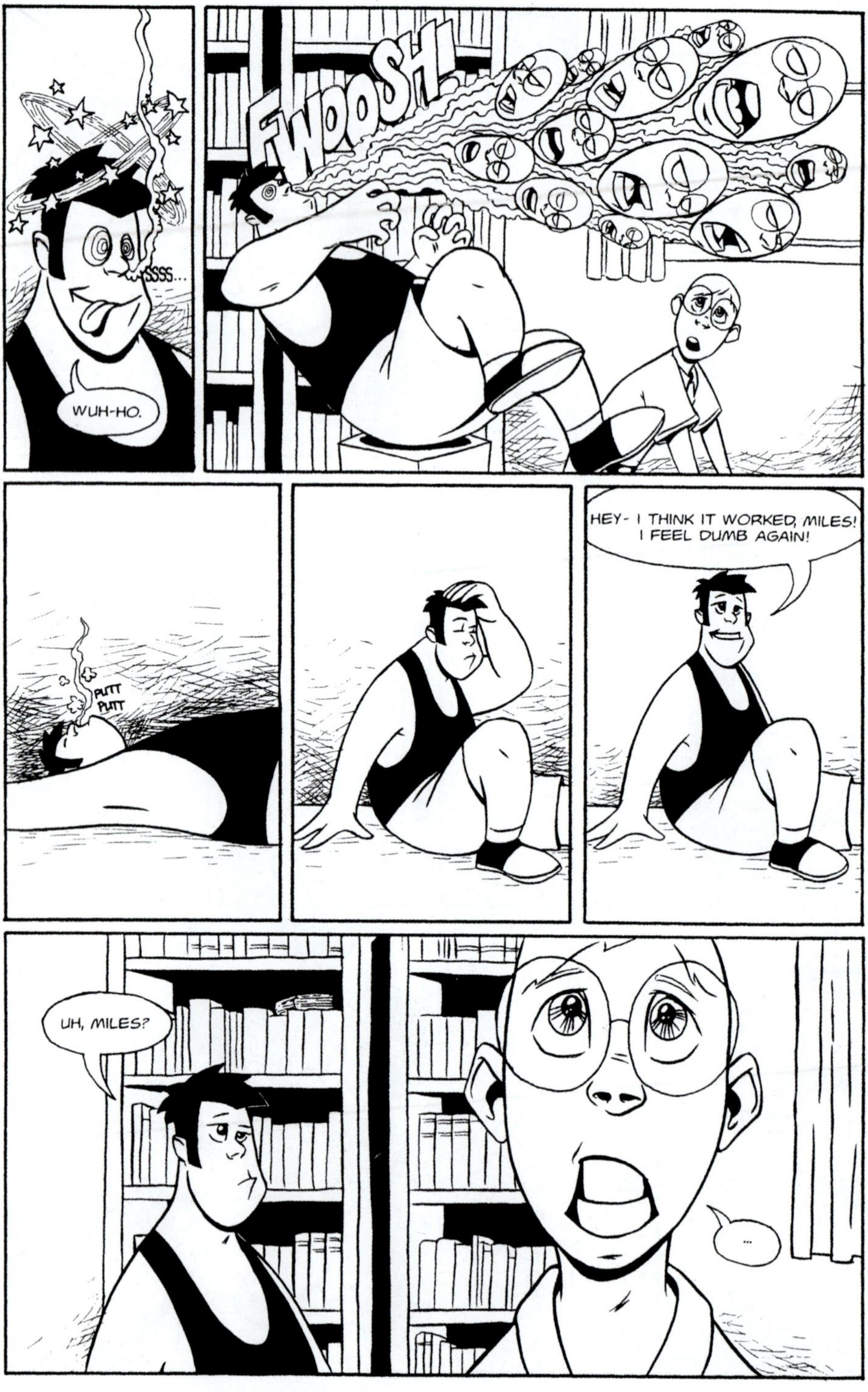
SSSS...
WUH-HO.
FWOOSH!
PUTT PUTT
HEY- I THINK IT WORKED, MILES! I FEEL DUMB AGAIN!
UH, MILES?
...

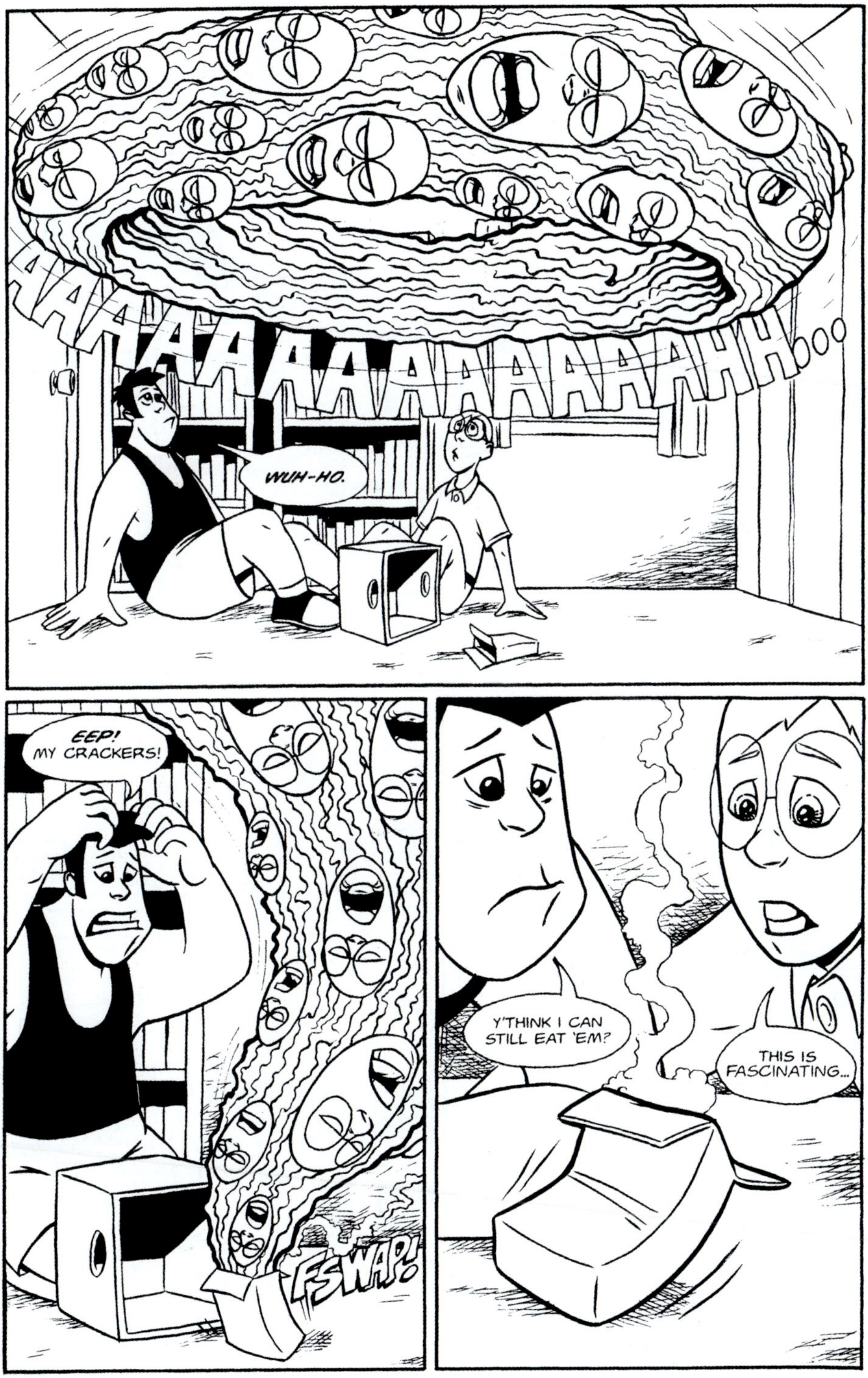
AAAAAAAAAAAAAAAAAHH...
WUH-HO.
EEP!
MY CRACKERS!
FSWAP!
Y'THINK I CAN
STILL EAT 'EM?
THIS IS
FASCINATING...

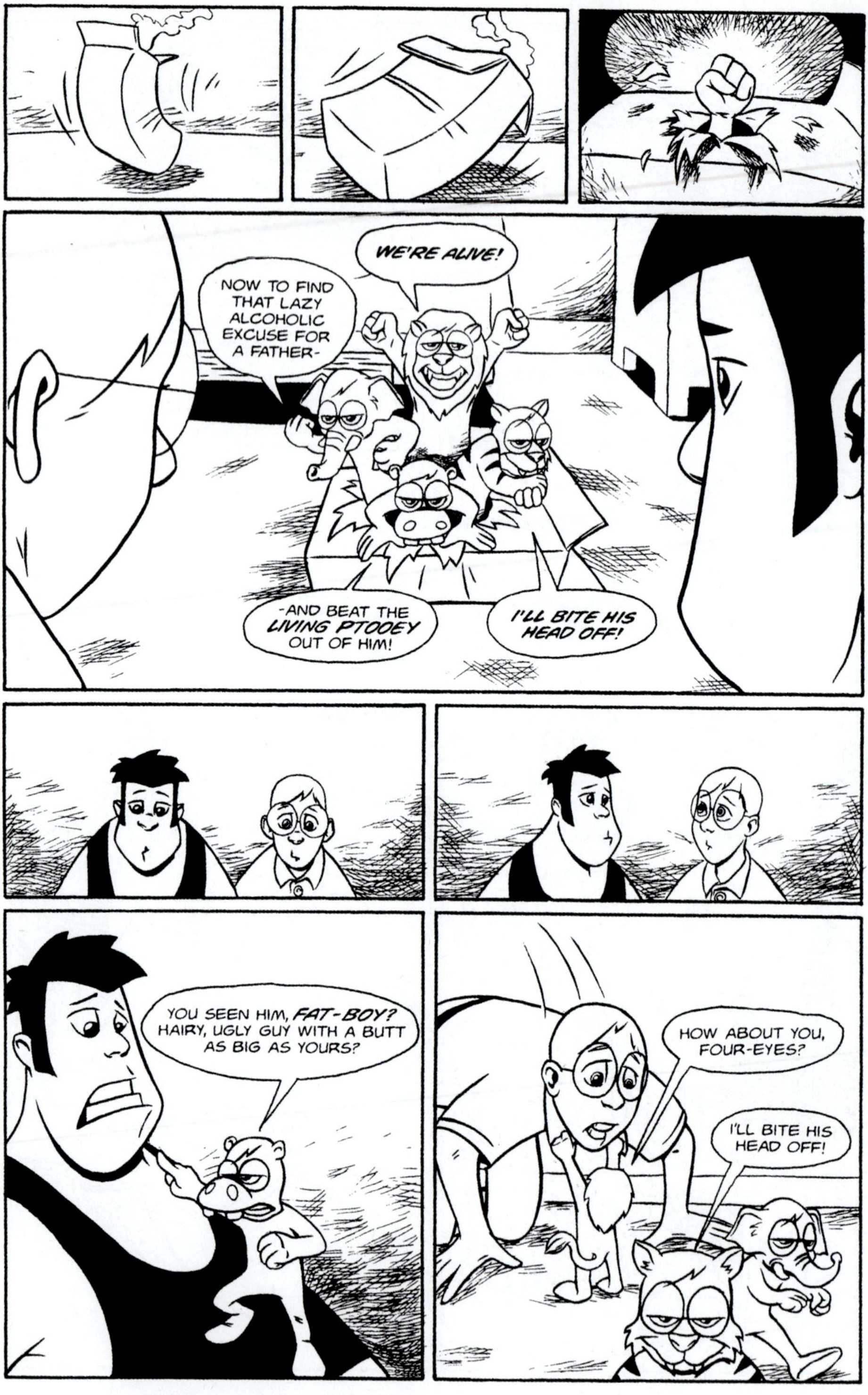
NOW TO FIND THAT LAZY ALCOHOLIC EXCUSE FOR A FATHER-
WE'RE ALIVE!
-AND BEAT THE LIVING PTOOEY OUT OF HIM!
I'LL BITE HIS HEAD OFF!
YOU SEEN HIM, FAT-BOY? HAIRY, UGLY GUY WITH A BUTT AS BIG AS YOURS?
HOW ABOUT YOU, FOUR-EYES?
I'LL BITE HIS HEAD OFF!

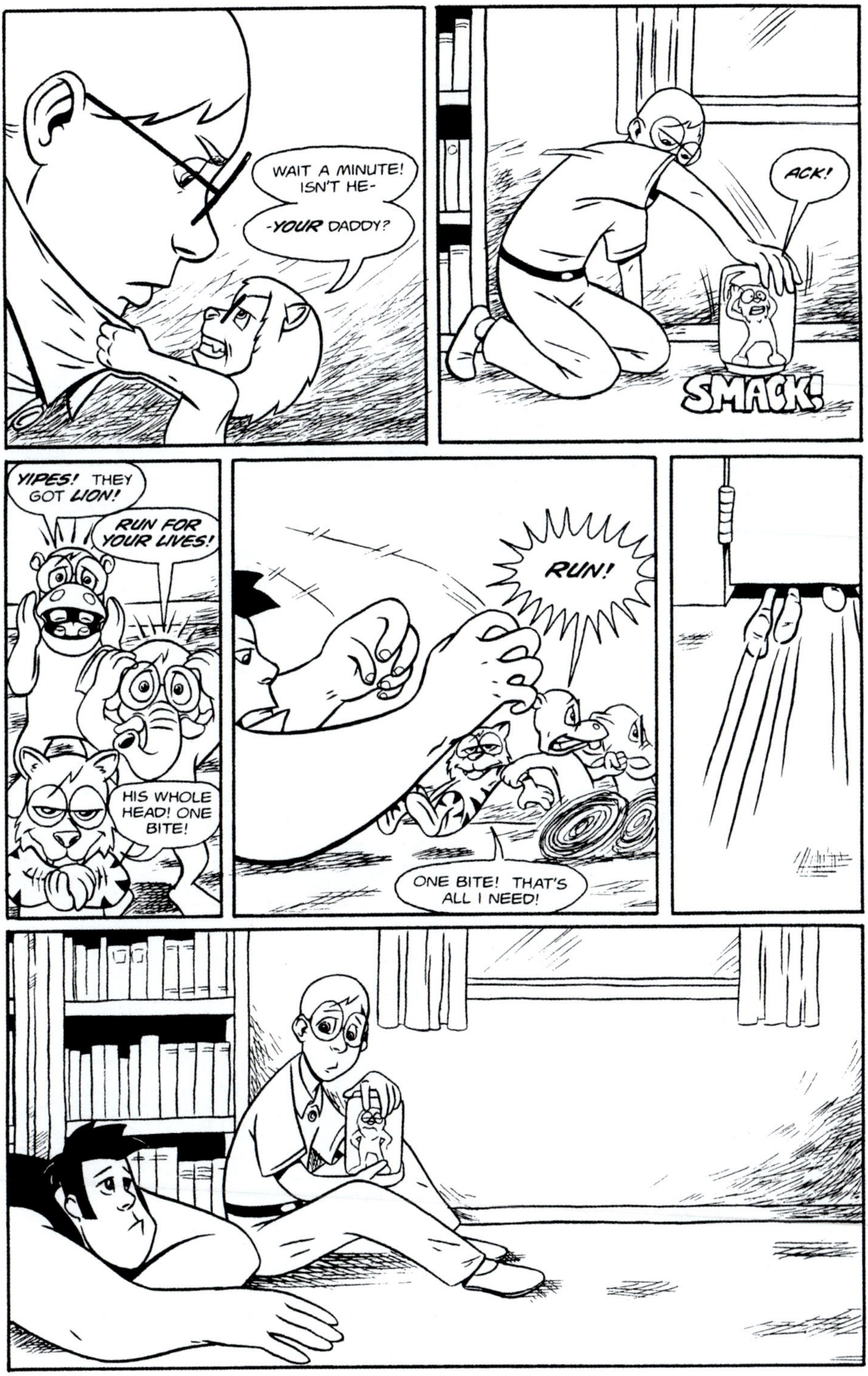
WAIT A MINUTE! ISN'T HE-
-YOUR DADDY?
ACK!
SMACK!
YIPES! THEY GOT LION!
RUN FOR YOUR LIVES!
HIS WHOLE HEAD! ONE BITE!
RUN!
ONE BITE! THAT'S ALL I NEED!

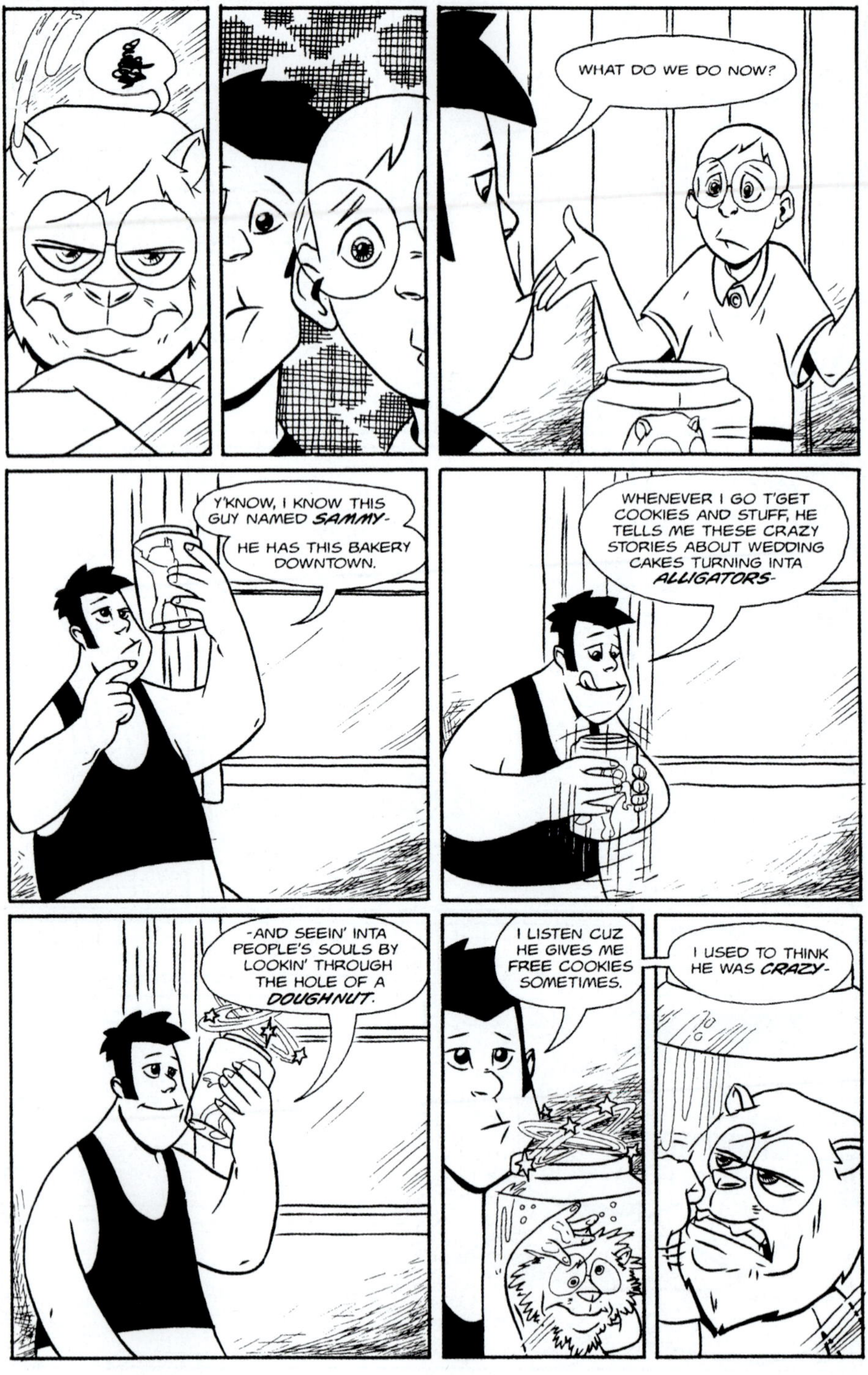
WHAT DO WE DO NOW?
Y'KNOW, I KNOW THIS GUY NAMED SAMMY-
HE HAS THIS BAKERY DOWNTOWN.
WHENEVER I GO T'GET COOKIES AND STUFF, HE TELLS ME THESE CRAZY STORIES ABOUT WEDDING CAKES TURNING INTA ALLIGATORS-
-AND SEEIN' INTA PEOPLE'S SOULS BY LOOKIN' THROUGH THE HOLE OF A DOUGHNUT.
I LISTEN CUZ HE GIVES ME FREE COOKIES SOMETIMES.
I USED TO THINK HE WAS CRAZY-

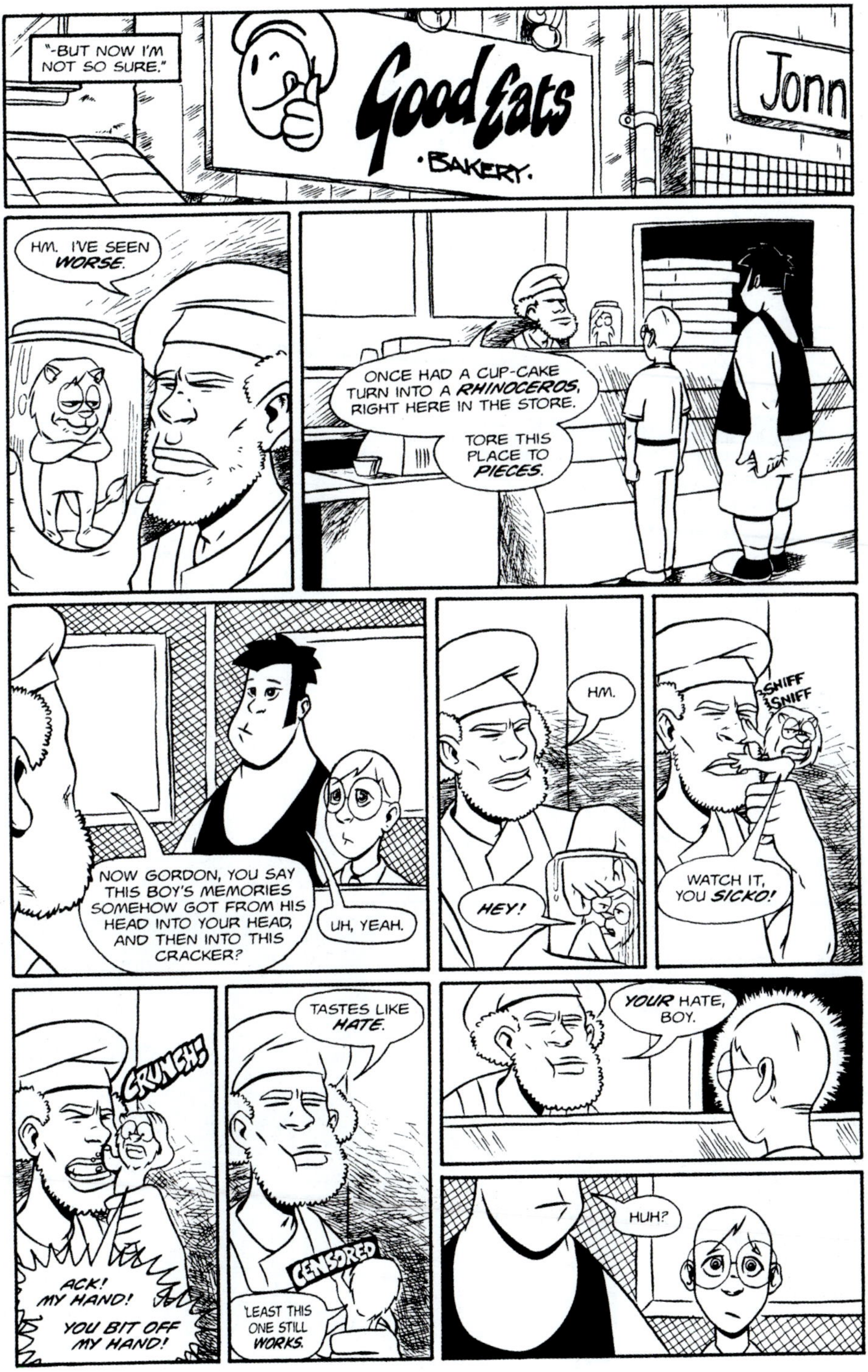
"-BUT NOW I'M NOT SO SURE."
Good Eats
·BAKERY·
Jonn
HM. I'VE SEEN WORSE.
ONCE HAD A CUP-CAKE TURN INTO A RHINOCEROS, RIGHT HERE IN THE STORE.
TORE THIS PLACE TO PIECES.
NOW GORDON, YOU SAY THIS BOY'S MEMORIES SOMEHOW GOT FROM HIS HEAD INTO YOUR HEAD, AND THEN INTO THIS CRACKER?
UH, YEAH.
HM.
HEY!
SNIFF SNIFF
WATCH IT, YOU SICKO!
CRUNCH!
ACK! MY HAND!
YOU BIT OFF MY HAND!
TASTES LIKE HATE.
CENSORED
'LEAST THIS ONE STILL WORKS.
YOUR HATE, BOY.
HUH?

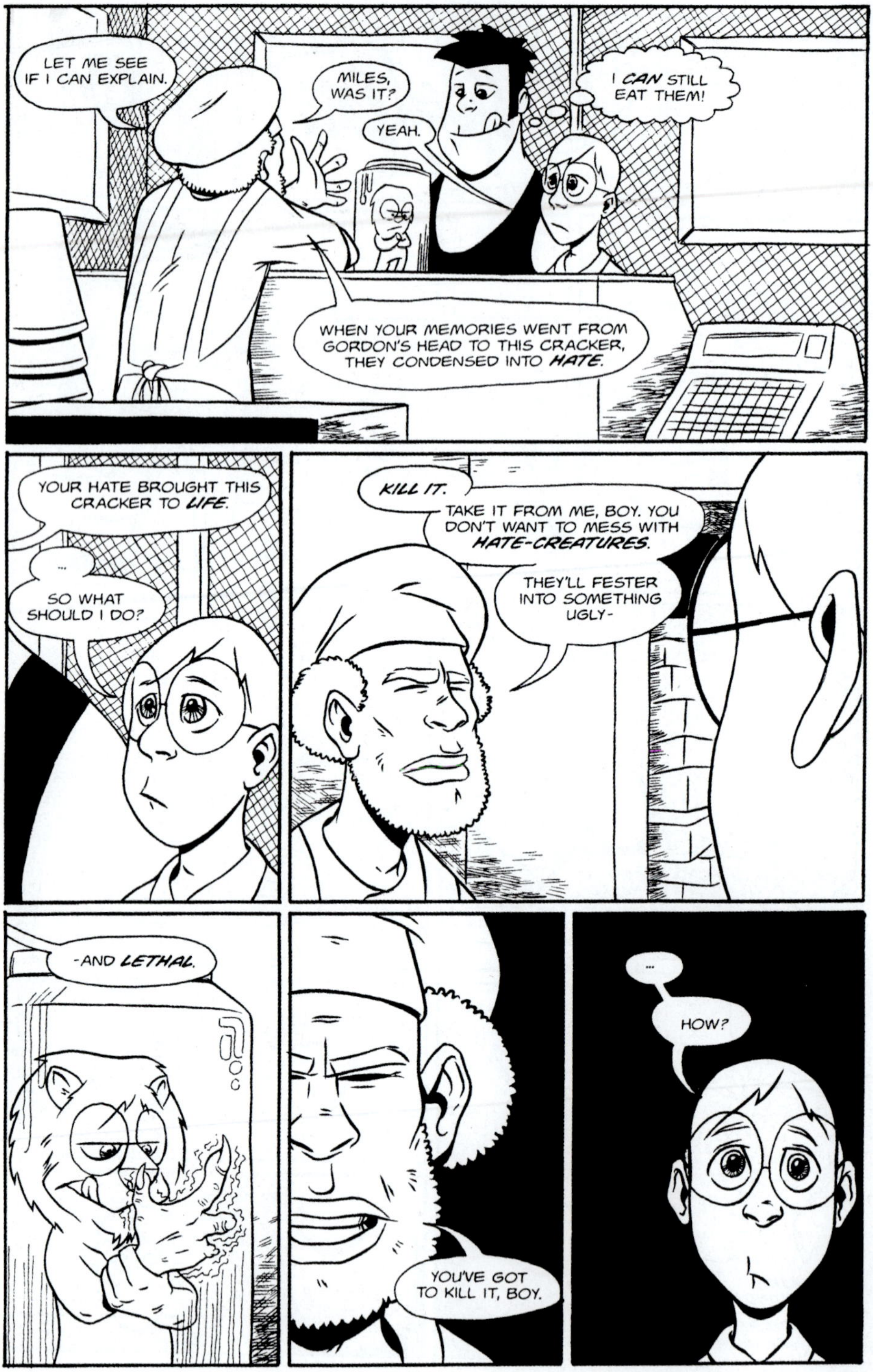
LET ME SEE IF I CAN EXPLAIN.
MILES, WAS IT?
YEAH.
I CAN STILL EAT THEM!
WHEN YOUR MEMORIES WENT FROM GORDON'S HEAD TO THIS CRACKER, THEY CONDENSED INTO HATE.
YOUR HATE BROUGHT THIS CRACKER TO LIFE.
...
SO WHAT SHOULD I DO?
KILL IT.
TAKE IT FROM ME, BOY. YOU DON'T WANT TO MESS WITH HATE-CREATURES.
THEY'LL FESTER INTO SOMETHING UGLY-
-AND LETHAL.
YOU'VE GOT TO KILL IT, BOY.
...
HOW?

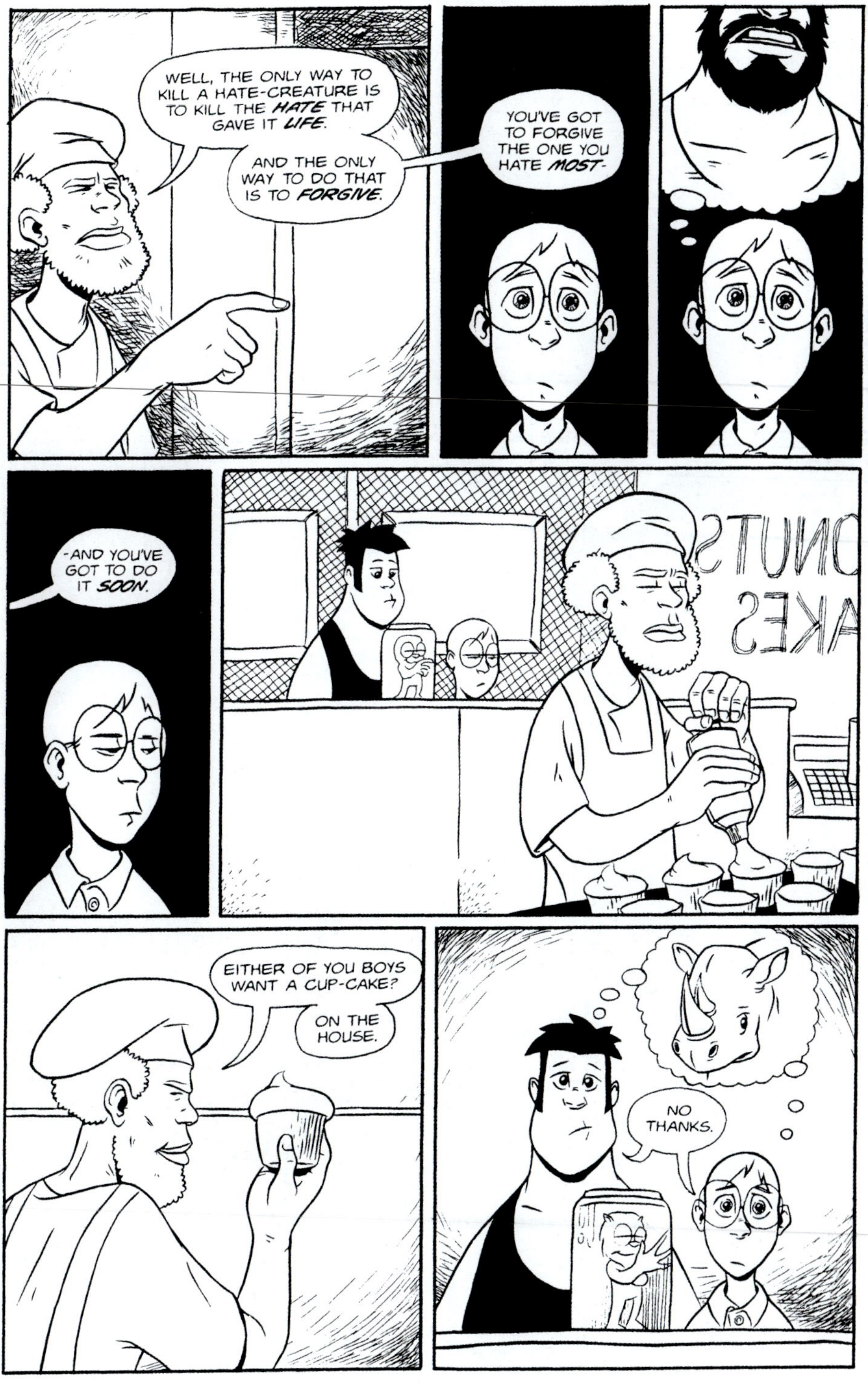
WELL, THE ONLY WAY TO KILL A HATE-CREATURE IS TO KILL THE *HATE* THAT GAVE IT *LIFE*.
AND THE ONLY WAY TO DO THAT IS TO *FORGIVE*.
YOU'VE GOT TO FORGIVE THE ONE YOU HATE *MOST*-
-AND YOU'VE GOT TO DO IT *SOON*.
ONUTS
AKES
EITHER OF YOU BOYS WANT A CUP-CAKE?
ON THE HOUSE.
NO THANKS.

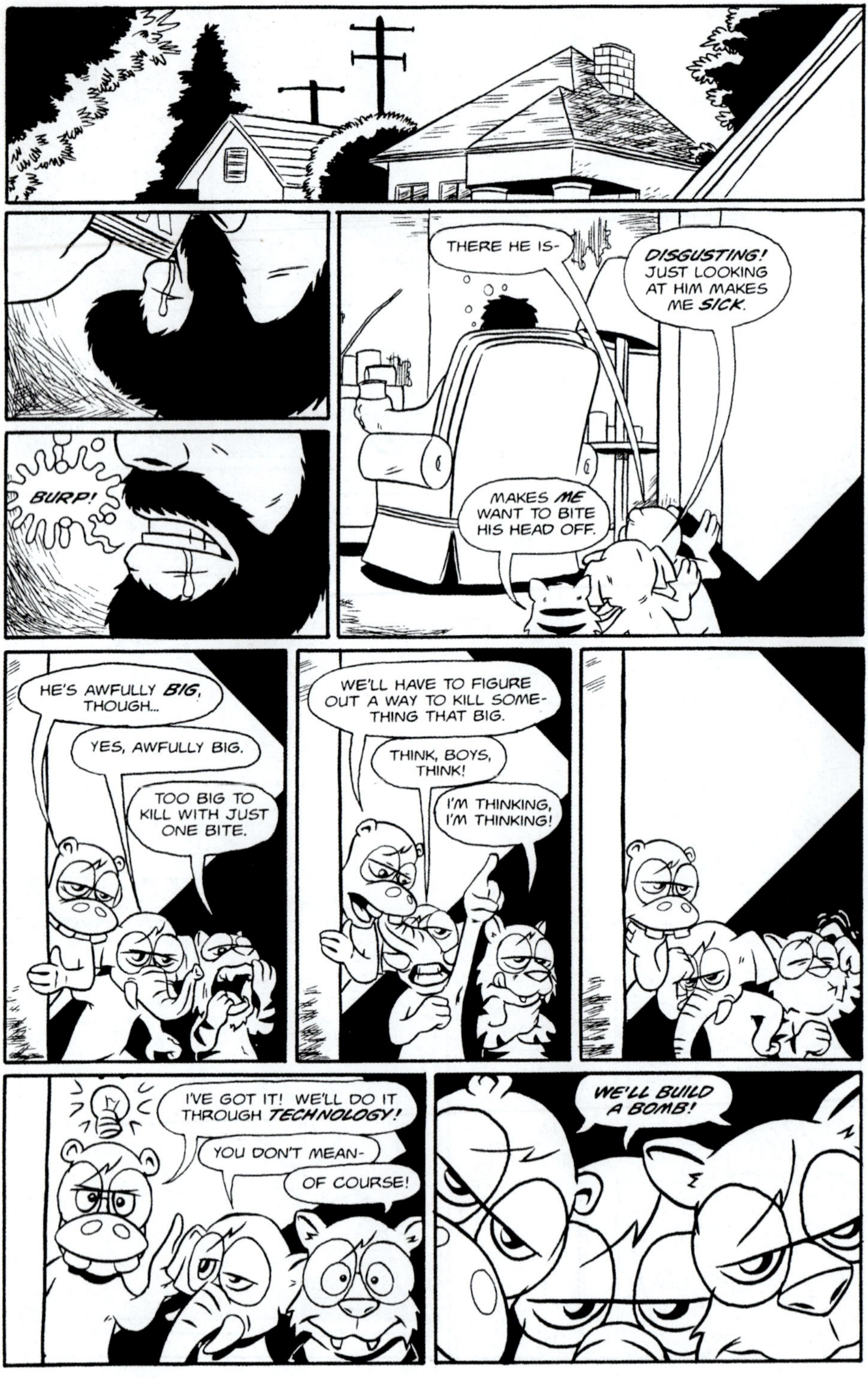
THERE HE IS-
DISGUSTING! JUST LOOKING AT HIM MAKES ME SICK.
BURP!
MAKES ME WANT TO BITE HIS HEAD OFF.
HE'S AWFULLY BIG, THOUGH...
YES, AWFULLY BIG.
TOO BIG TO KILL WITH JUST ONE BITE.
WE'LL HAVE TO FIGURE OUT A WAY TO KILL SOMETHING THAT BIG.
THINK, BOYS, THINK!
I'M THINKING, I'M THINKING!
I'VE GOT IT! WE'LL DO IT THROUGH TECHNOLOGY!
YOU DON'T MEAN-
OF COURSE!
WE'LL BUILD A BOMB!

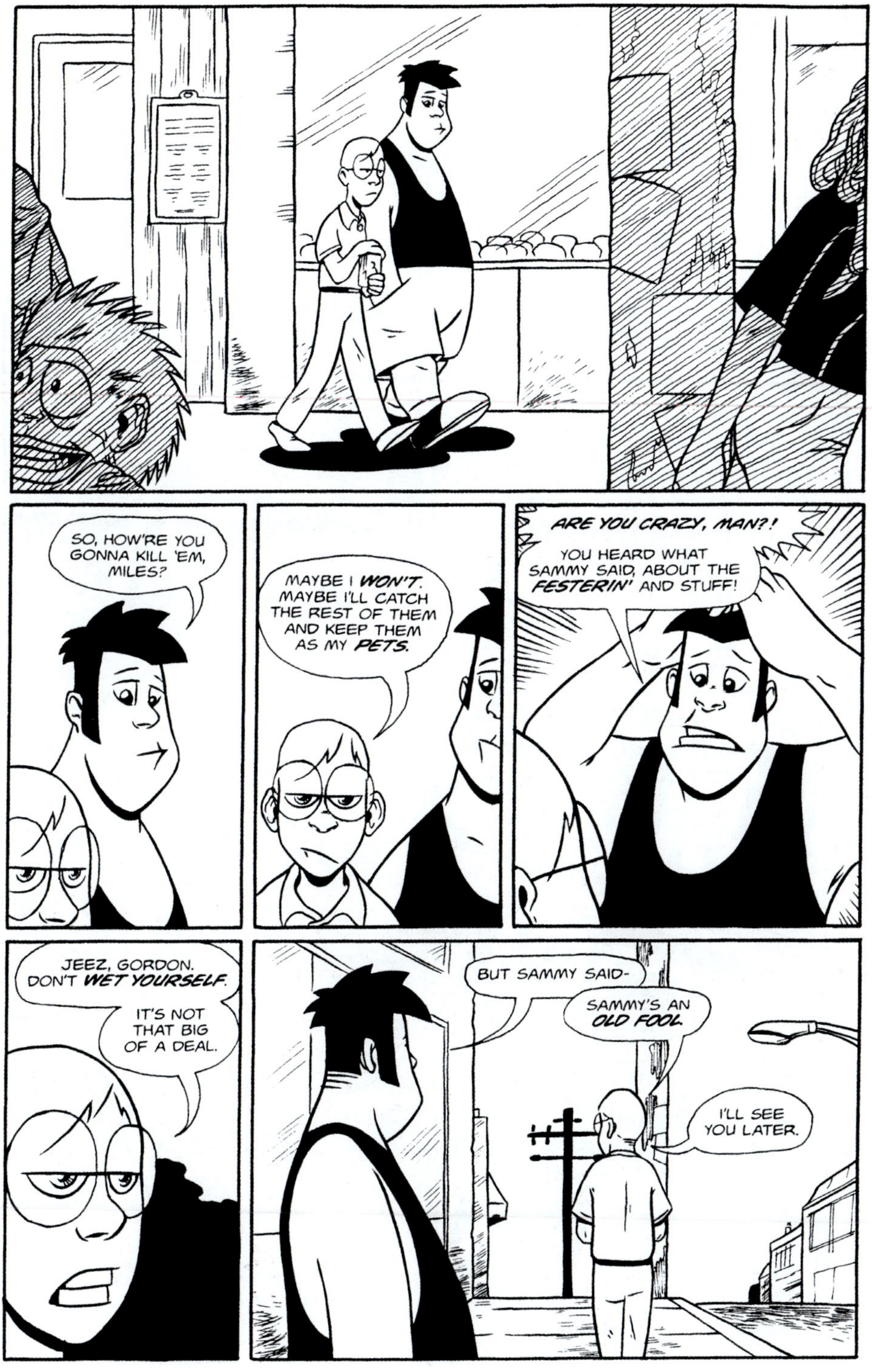
SO, HOW'RE YOU GONNA KILL 'EM, MILES?
MAYBE I WON'T. MAYBE I'LL CATCH THE REST OF THEM AND KEEP THEM AS MY PETS.
ARE YOU CRAZY, MAN?!
YOU HEARD WHAT SAMMY SAID, ABOUT THE FESTERIN' AND STUFF!
JEEZ, GORDON. DON'T WET YOURSELF.
IT'S NOT THAT BIG OF A DEAL.
BUT SAMMY SAID-
SAMMY'S AN OLD FOOL.
I'LL SEE YOU LATER.

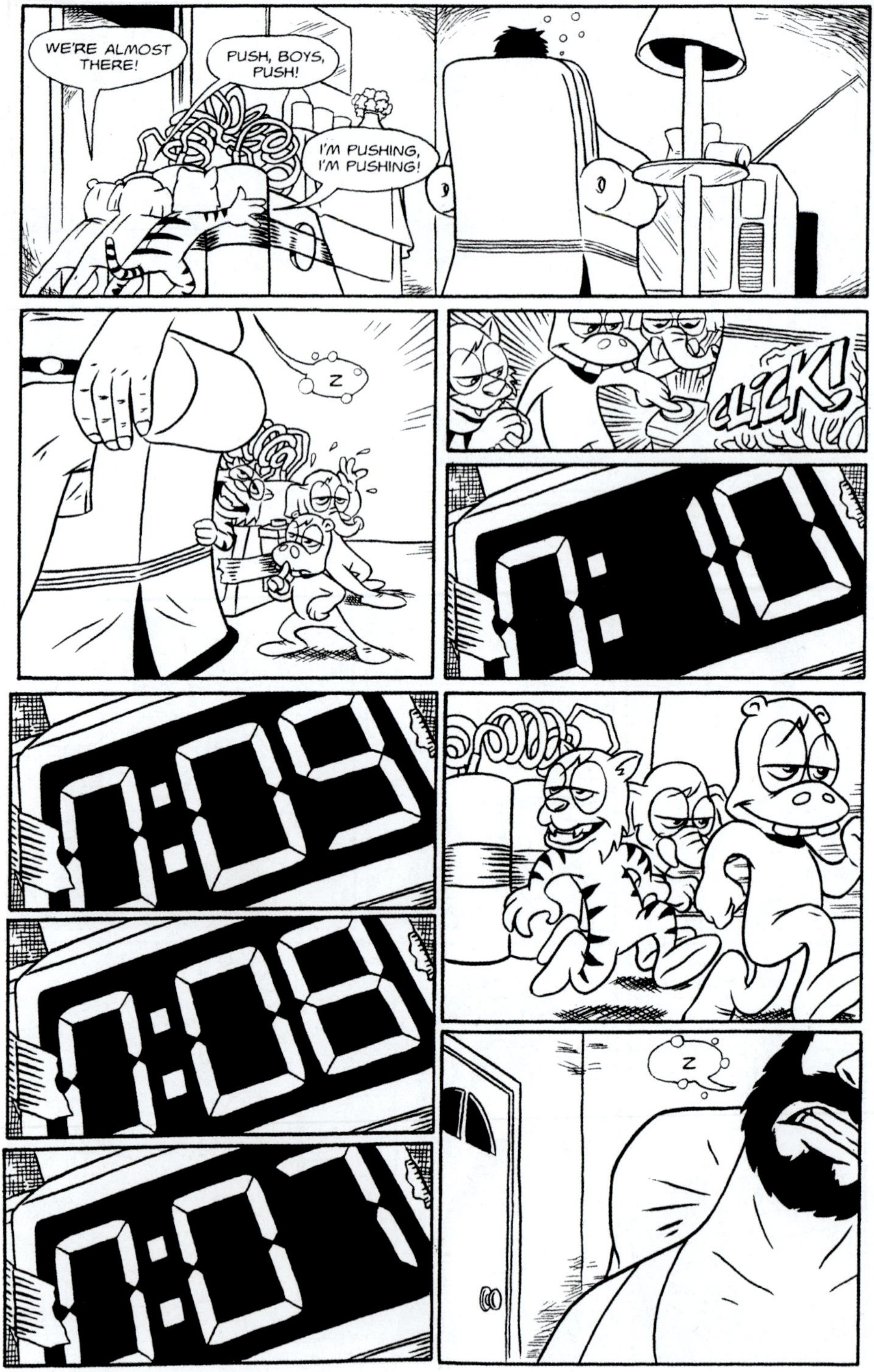
WE'RE ALMOST THERE!
PUSH, BOYS, PUSH!
I'M PUSHING, I'M PUSHING!
Z
CLICK!
Z

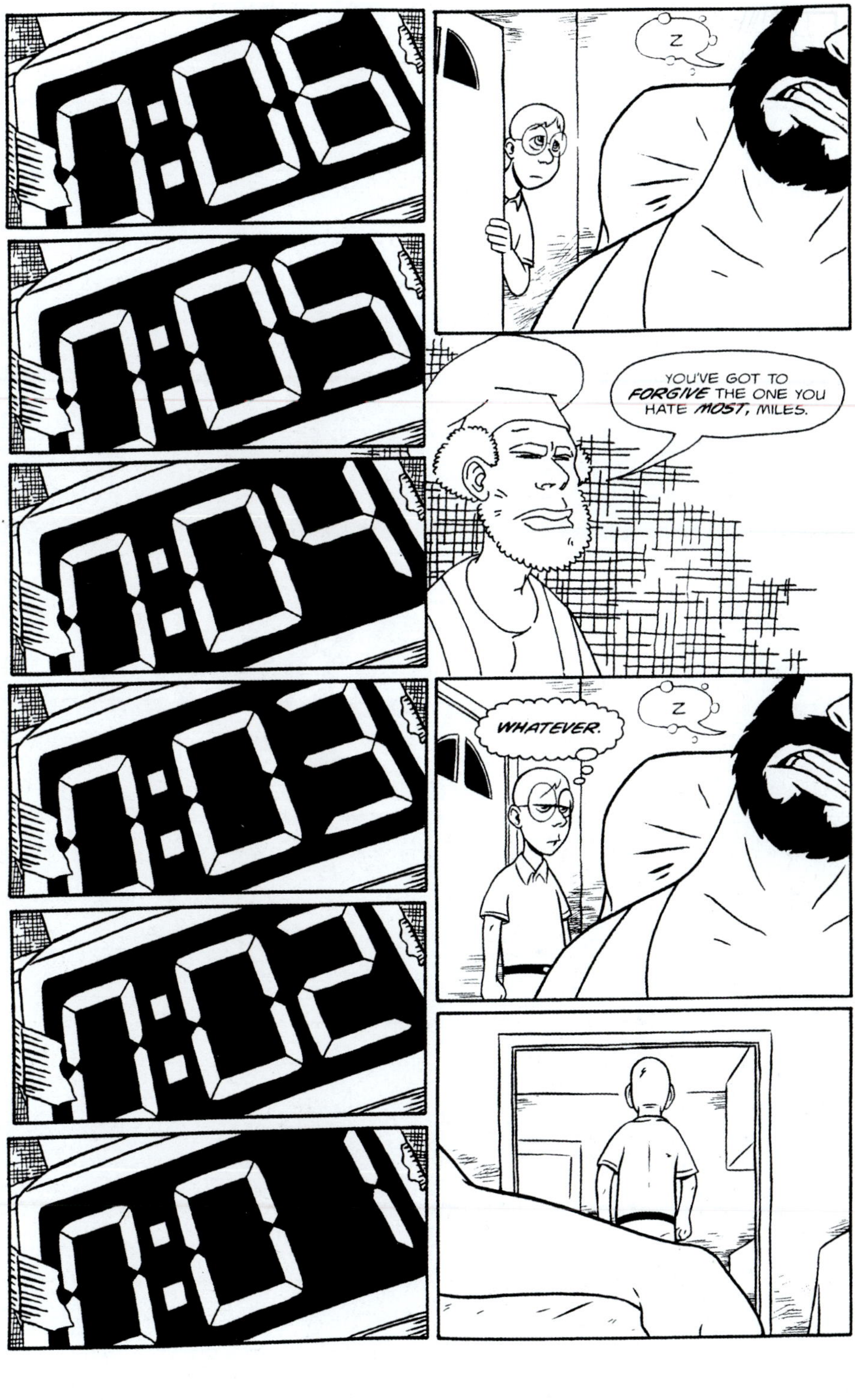

7:06
Z
7:05
YOU'VE GOT TO FORGIVE THE ONE YOU HATE MOST, MILES.
7:04
WHATEVER.
Z
7:03
7:02
7:01

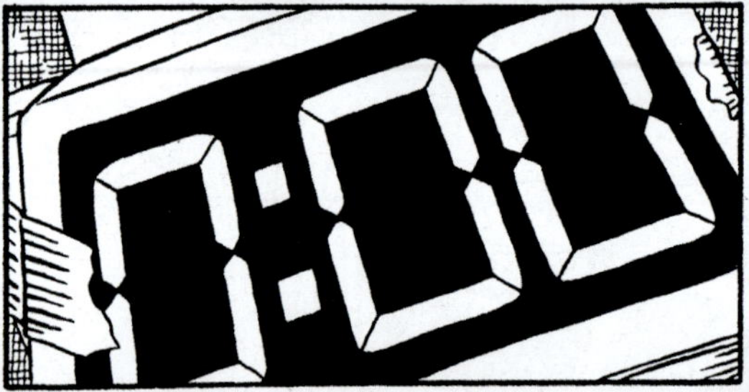

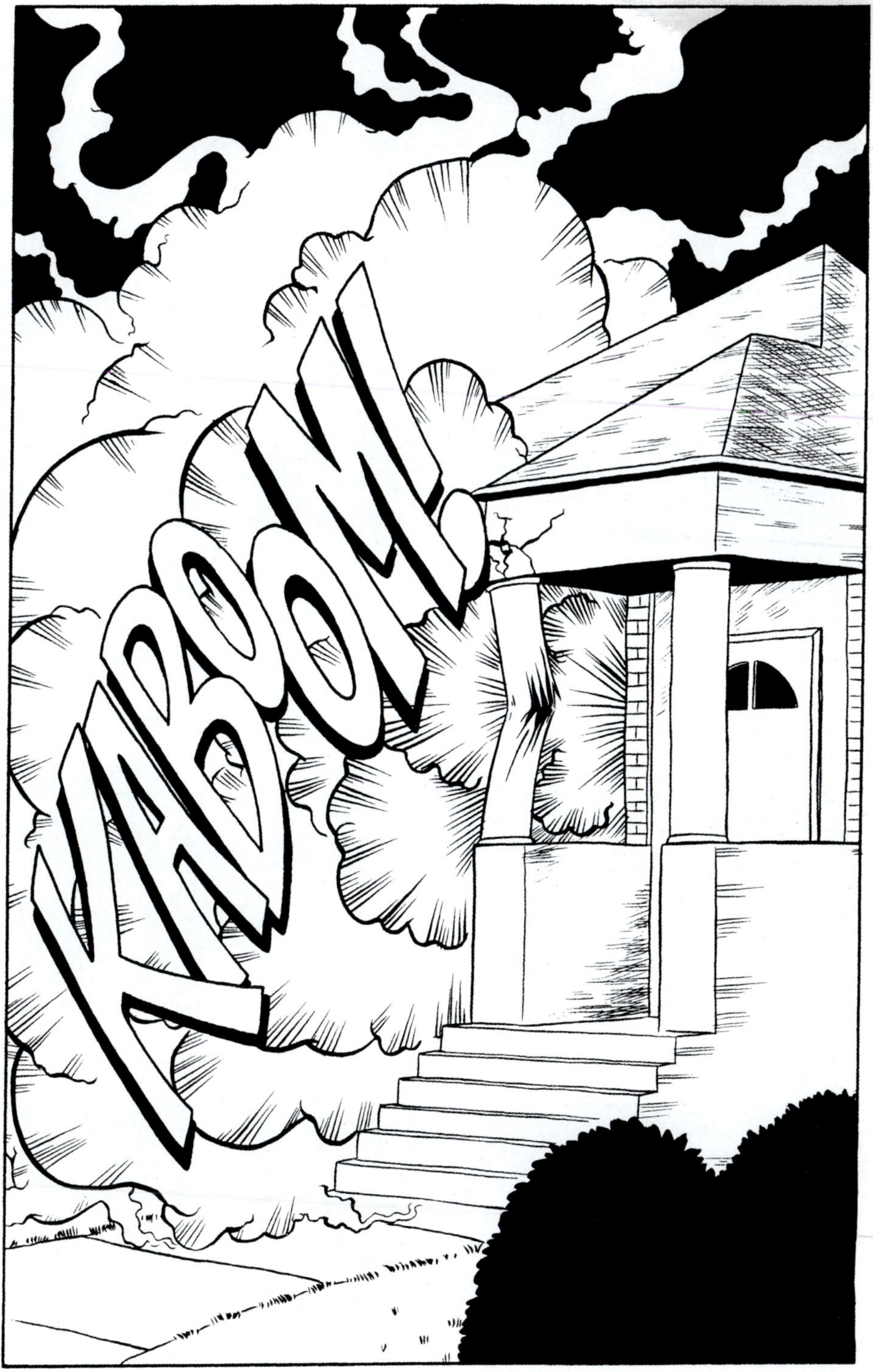
KABOOM!

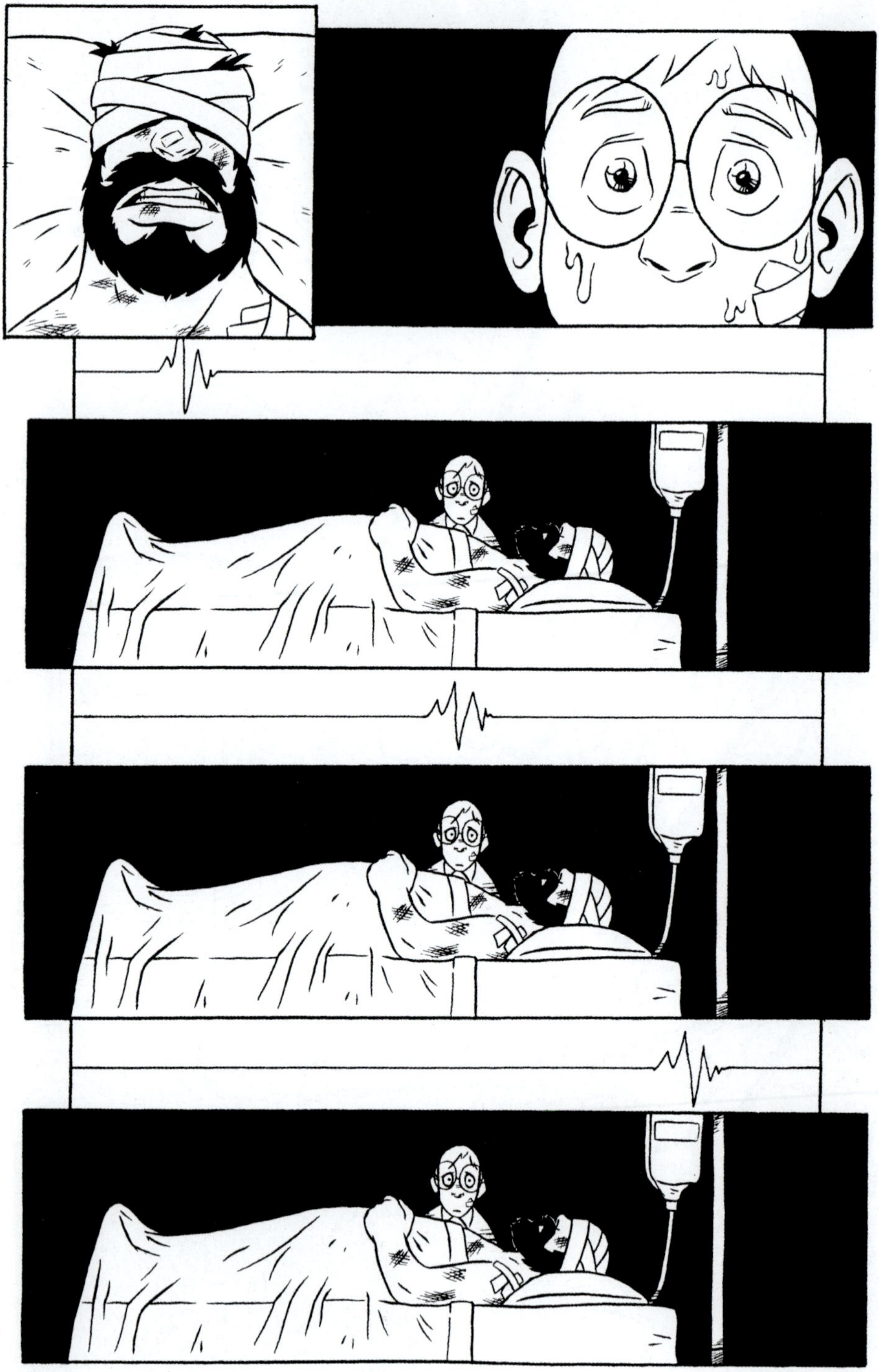

CHAPTER THREE

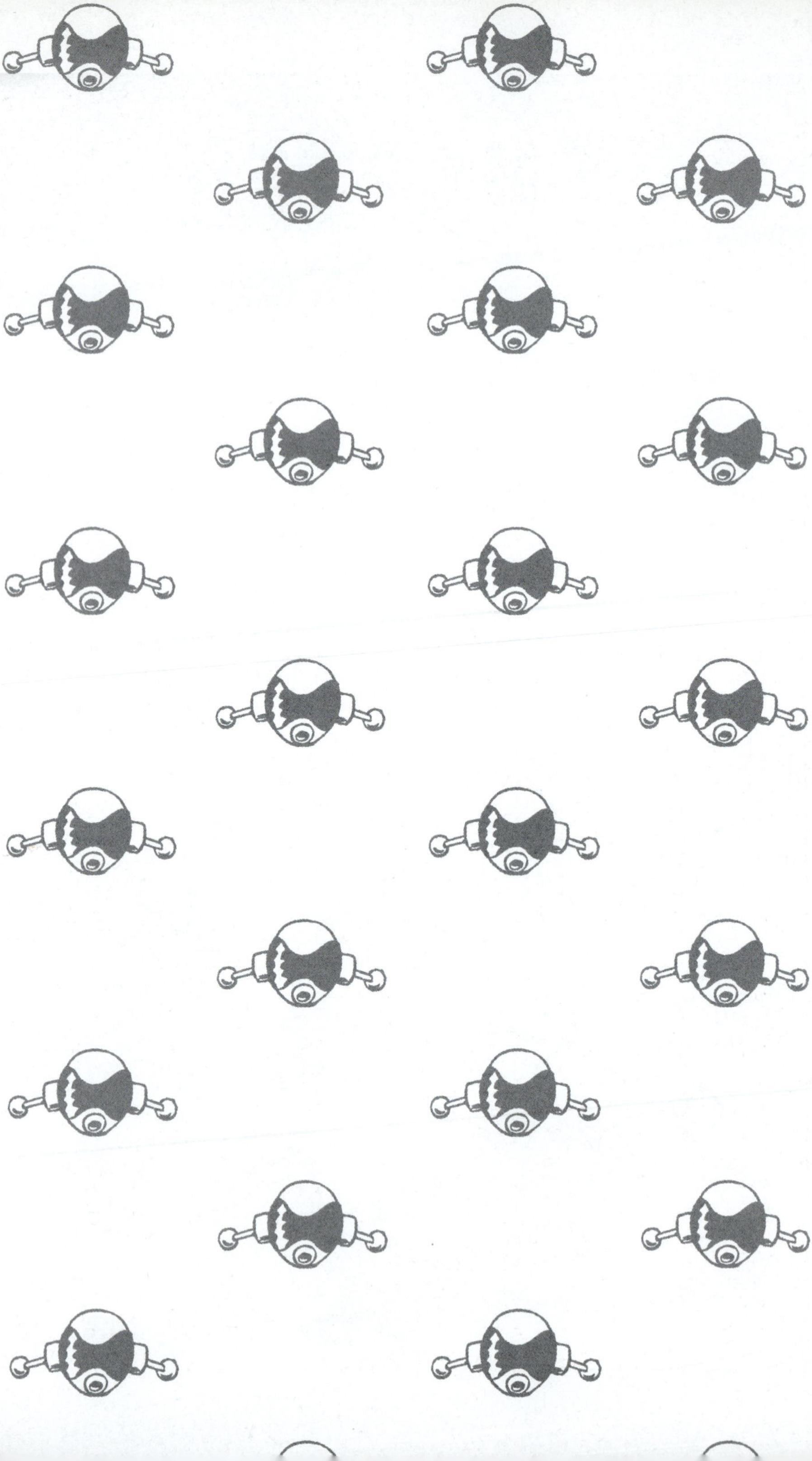

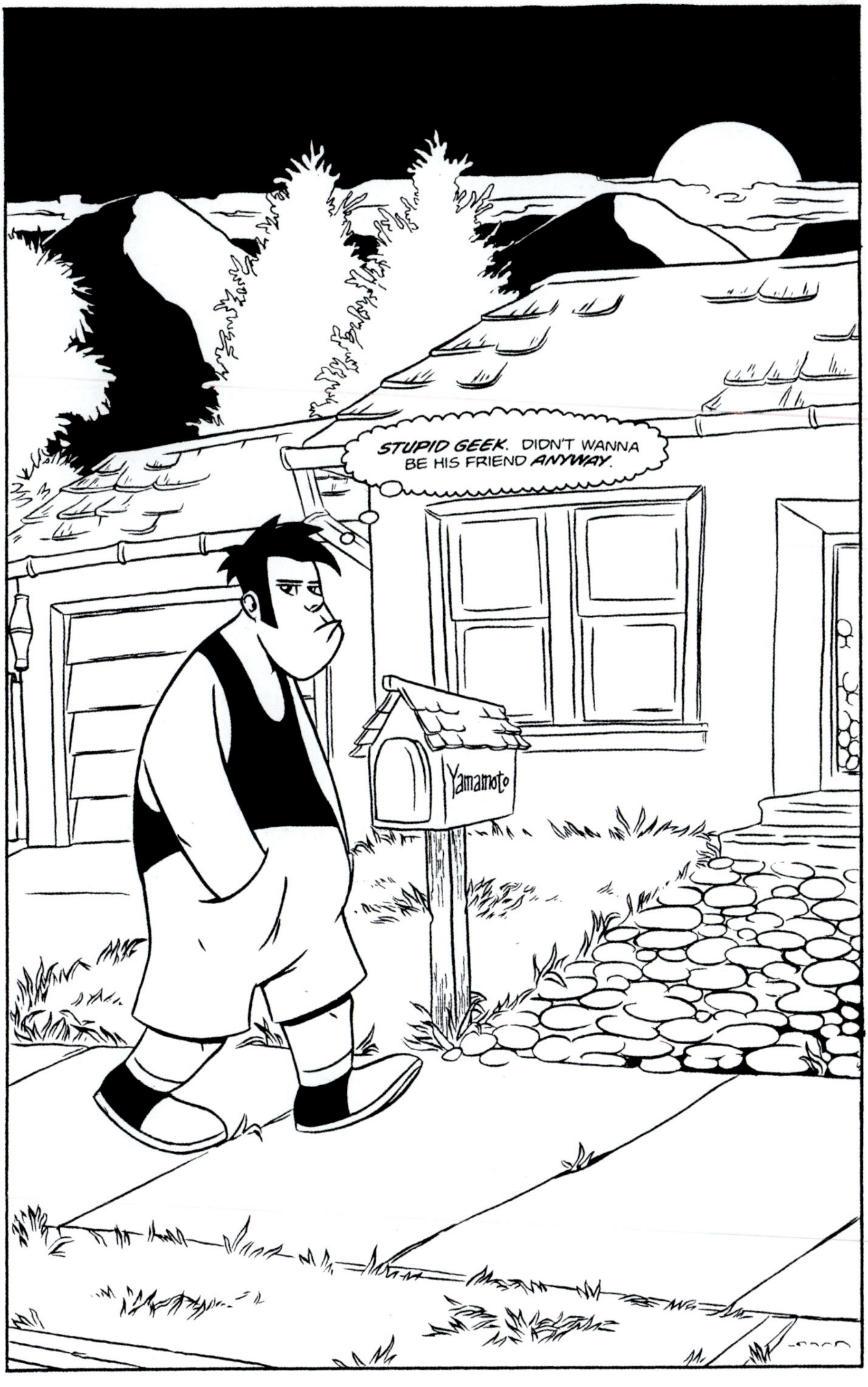
STUPID GEEK. DIDN'T WANNA BE HIS FRIEND ANYWAY.
Yamamoto

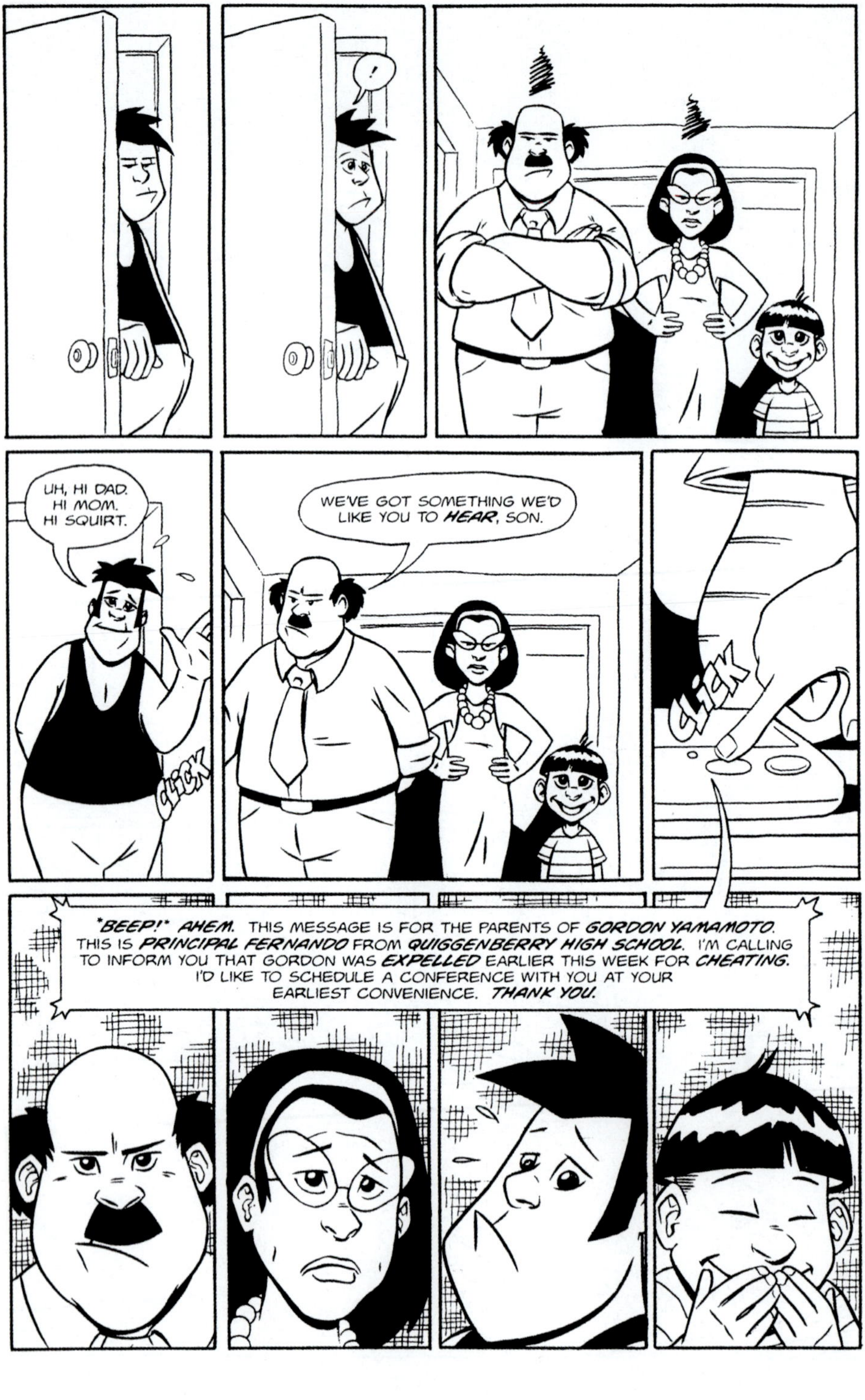
!
UH, HI DAD. HI MOM. HI SQUIRT.
CLICK
WE'VE GOT SOMETHING WE'D LIKE YOU TO HEAR, SON.
CLICK
BEEP! AHEM. THIS MESSAGE IS FOR THE PARENTS OF GORDON YAMAMOTO. THIS IS PRINCIPAL FERNANDO FROM QUIGGENBERRY HIGH SCHOOL. I'M CALLING TO INFORM YOU THAT GORDON WAS EXPELLED EARLIER THIS WEEK FOR CHEATING. I'D LIKE TO SCHEDULE A CONFERENCE WITH YOU AT YOUR EARLIEST CONVENIENCE. THANK YOU.

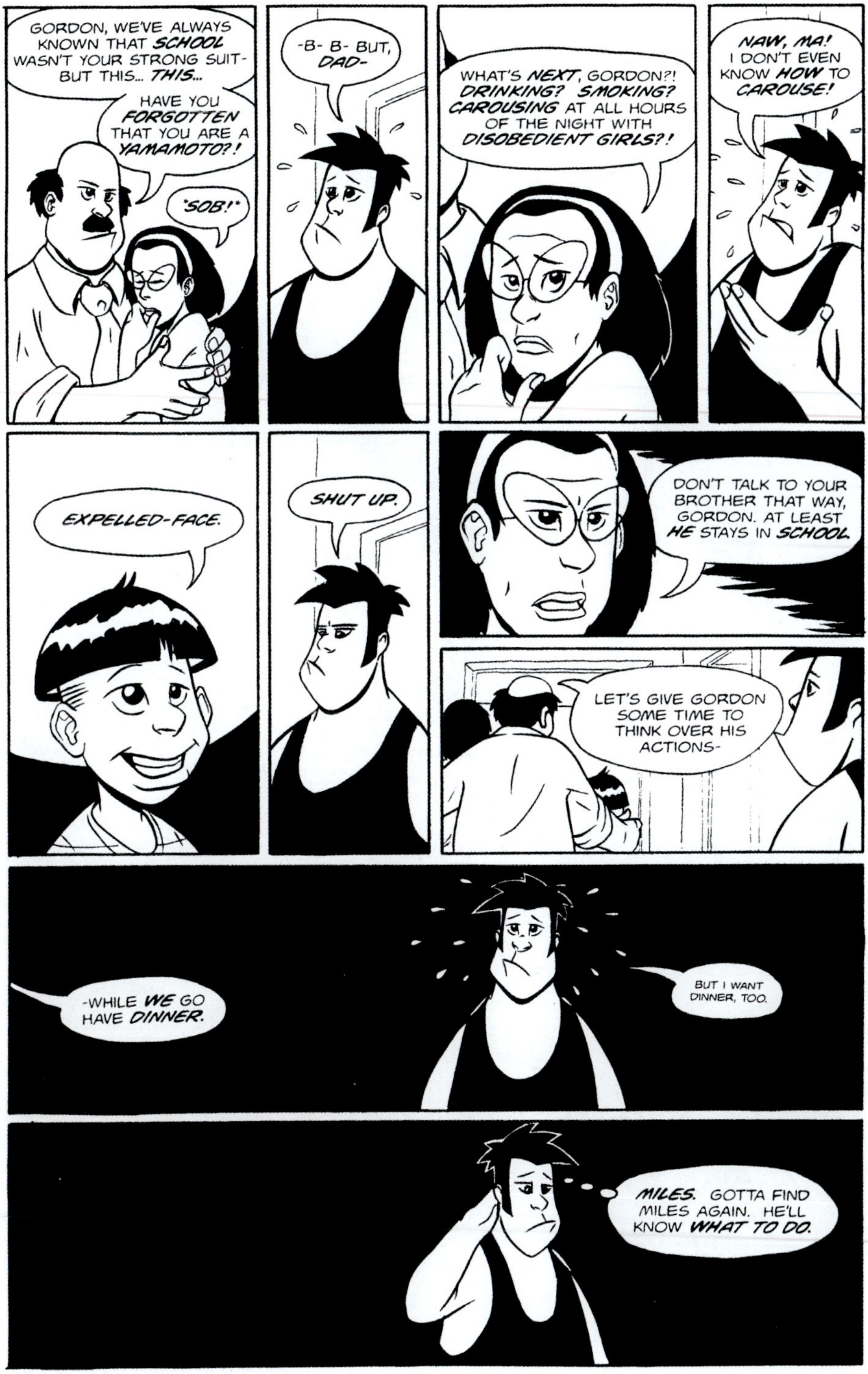
GORDON, WE'VE ALWAYS KNOWN THAT SCHOOL WASN'T YOUR STRONG SUIT- BUT THIS... THIS...
HAVE YOU FORGOTTEN THAT YOU ARE A YAMAMOTO?!
SOB!
-B- B- BUT, DAD-
WHAT'S NEXT, GORDON?! DRINKING? SMOKING? CAROUSING AT ALL HOURS OF THE NIGHT WITH DISOBEDIENT GIRLS?!
NAW, MA! I DON'T EVEN KNOW HOW TO CAROUSE!
EXPELLED-FACE.
SHUT UP.
DON'T TALK TO YOUR BROTHER THAT WAY, GORDON. AT LEAST HE STAYS IN SCHOOL.
LET'S GIVE GORDON SOME TIME TO THINK OVER HIS ACTIONS-
-WHILE WE GO HAVE DINNER.
BUT I WANT DINNER, TOO.
MILES. GOTTA FIND MILES AGAIN. HE'LL KNOW WHAT TO DO.

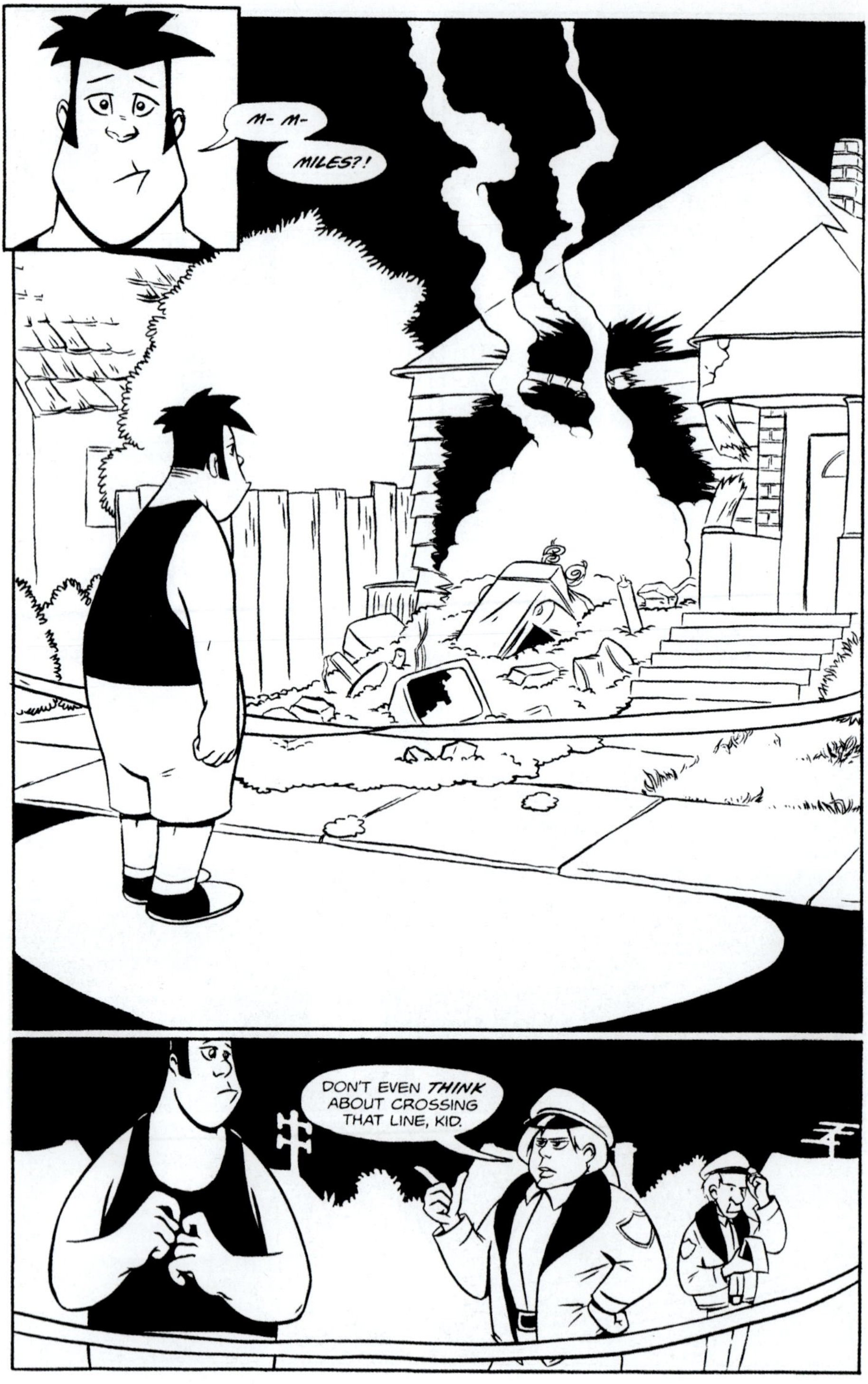
M- M-
MILES?!
DON'T EVEN THINK ABOUT CROSSING THAT LINE, KID.

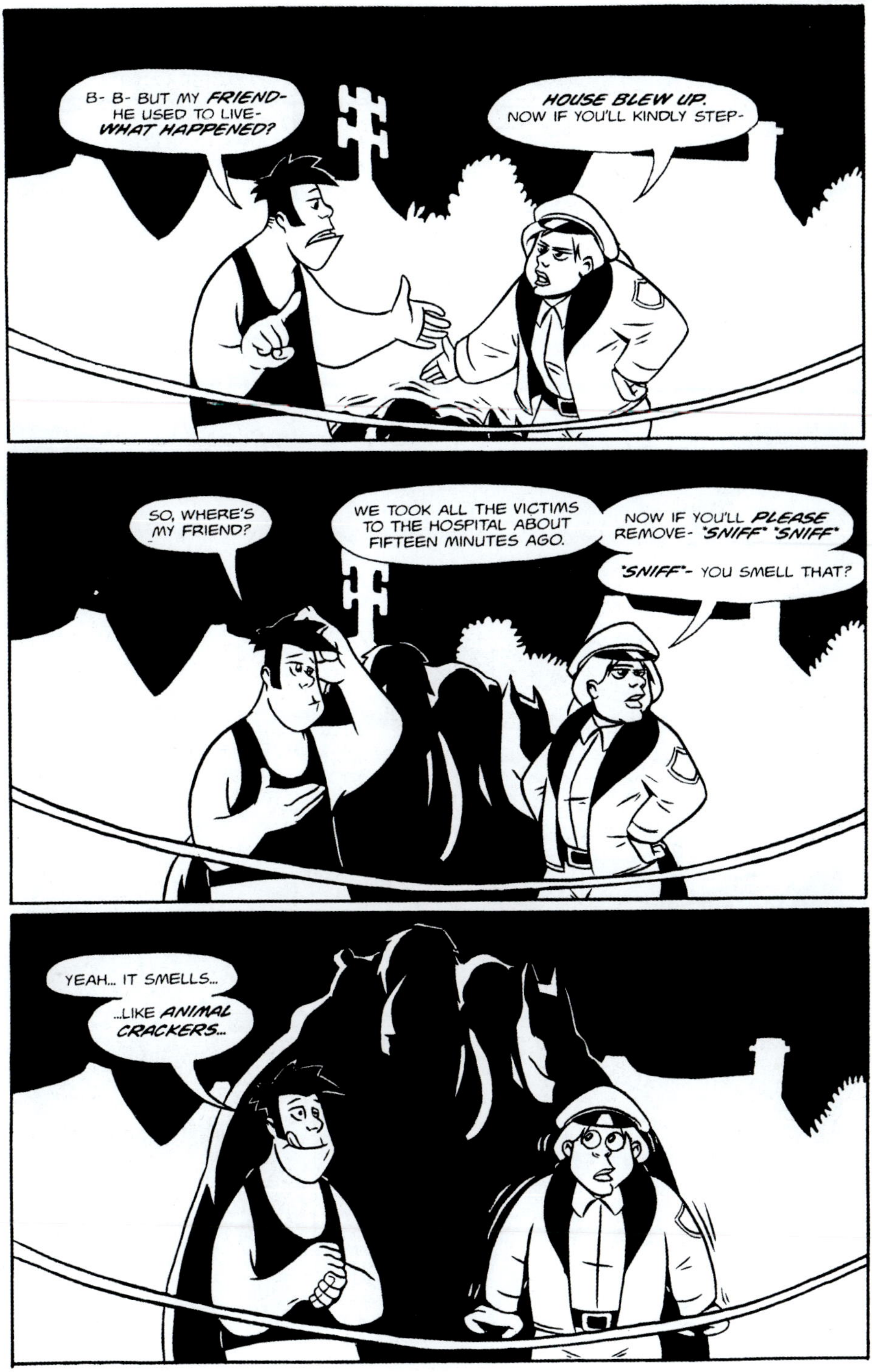
B- B- BUT MY FRIEND- HE USED TO LIVE- WHAT HAPPENED?
HOUSE BLEW UP. NOW IF YOU'LL KINDLY STEP-
SO, WHERE'S MY FRIEND?
WE TOOK ALL THE VICTIMS TO THE HOSPITAL ABOUT FIFTEEN MINUTES AGO.
NOW IF YOU'LL PLEASE REMOVE- *SNIFF* *SNIFF*
SNIFF- YOU SMELL THAT?
YEAH... IT SMELLS...
...LIKE ANIMAL CRACKERS...

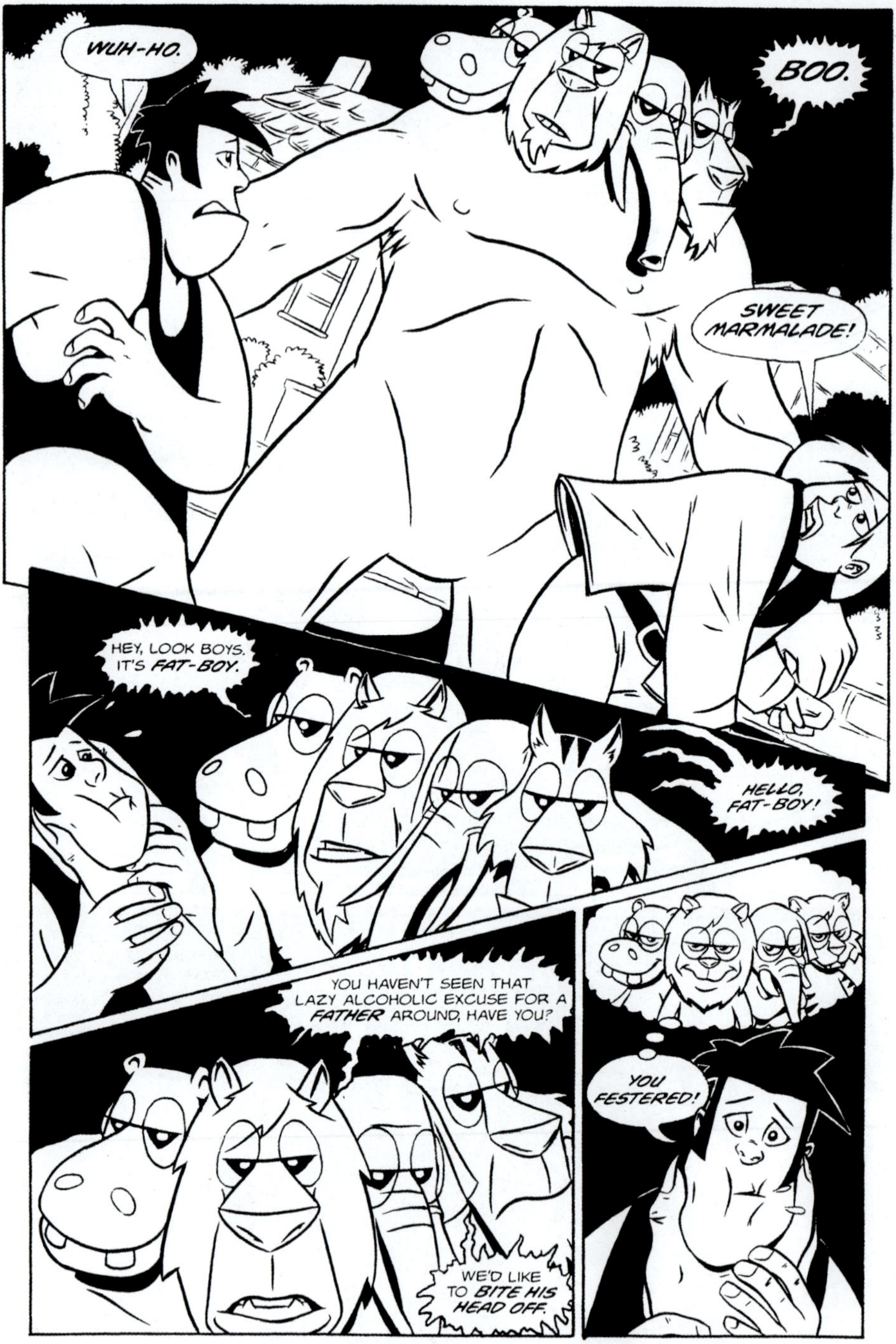
WUH-HO.
BOO.
SWEET MARMALADE!
HEY, LOOK BOYS. IT'S FAT-BOY.
HELLO, FAT-BOY!
YOU HAVEN'T SEEN THAT LAZY ALCOHOLIC EXCUSE FOR A FATHER AROUND, HAVE YOU?
WE'D LIKE TO BITE HIS HEAD OFF.
YOU FESTERED!

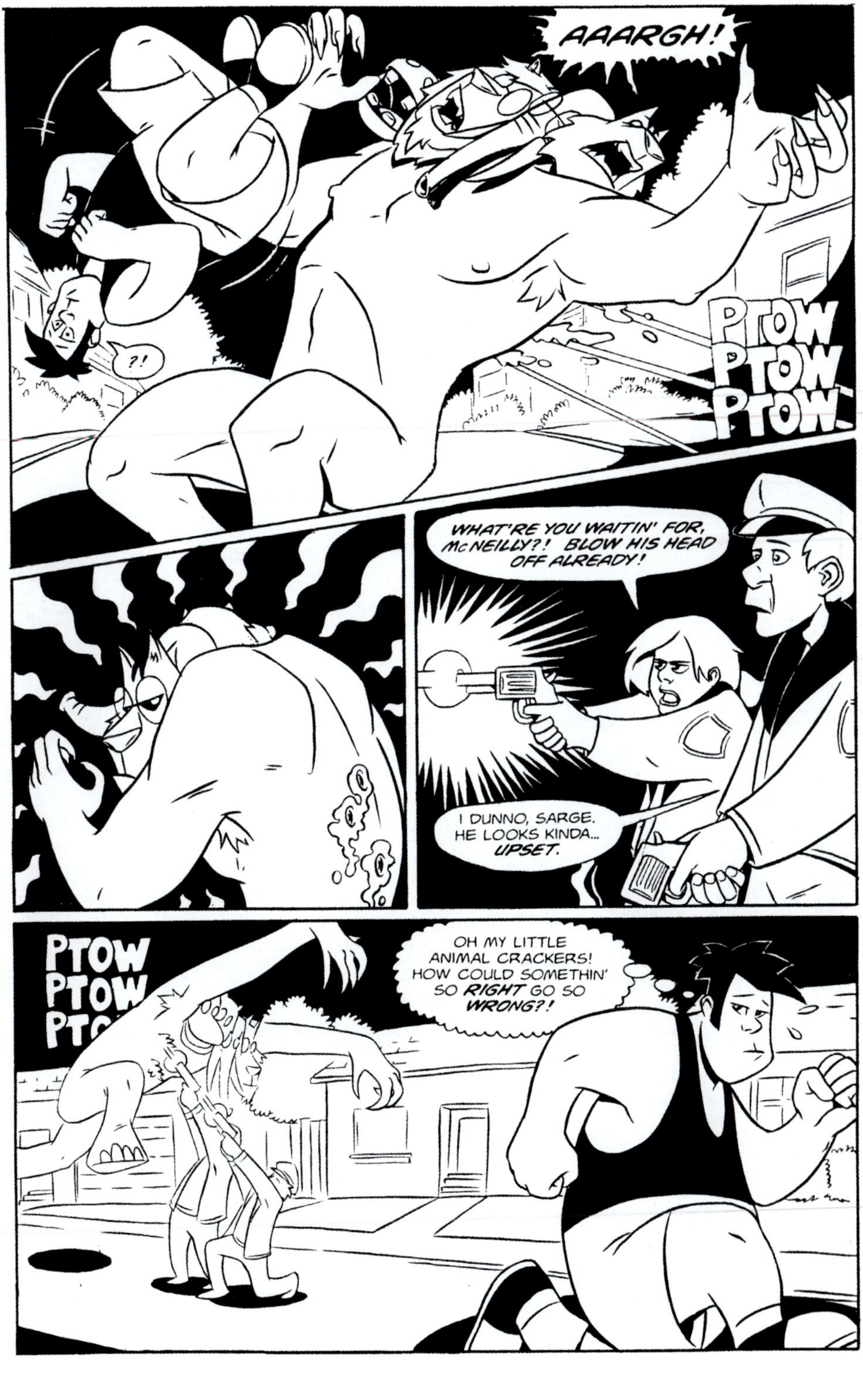
AAARGH!
?!
PTOW PTOW PTOW
WHAT'RE YOU WAITIN' FOR, McNEILLY?! BLOW HIS HEAD OFF ALREADY!
I DUNNO, SARGE. HE LOOKS KINDA... *UPSET*.
PTOW PTOW
OH MY LITTLE ANIMAL CRACKERS! HOW COULD SOMETHIN' SO *RIGHT* GO SO *WRONG*?!

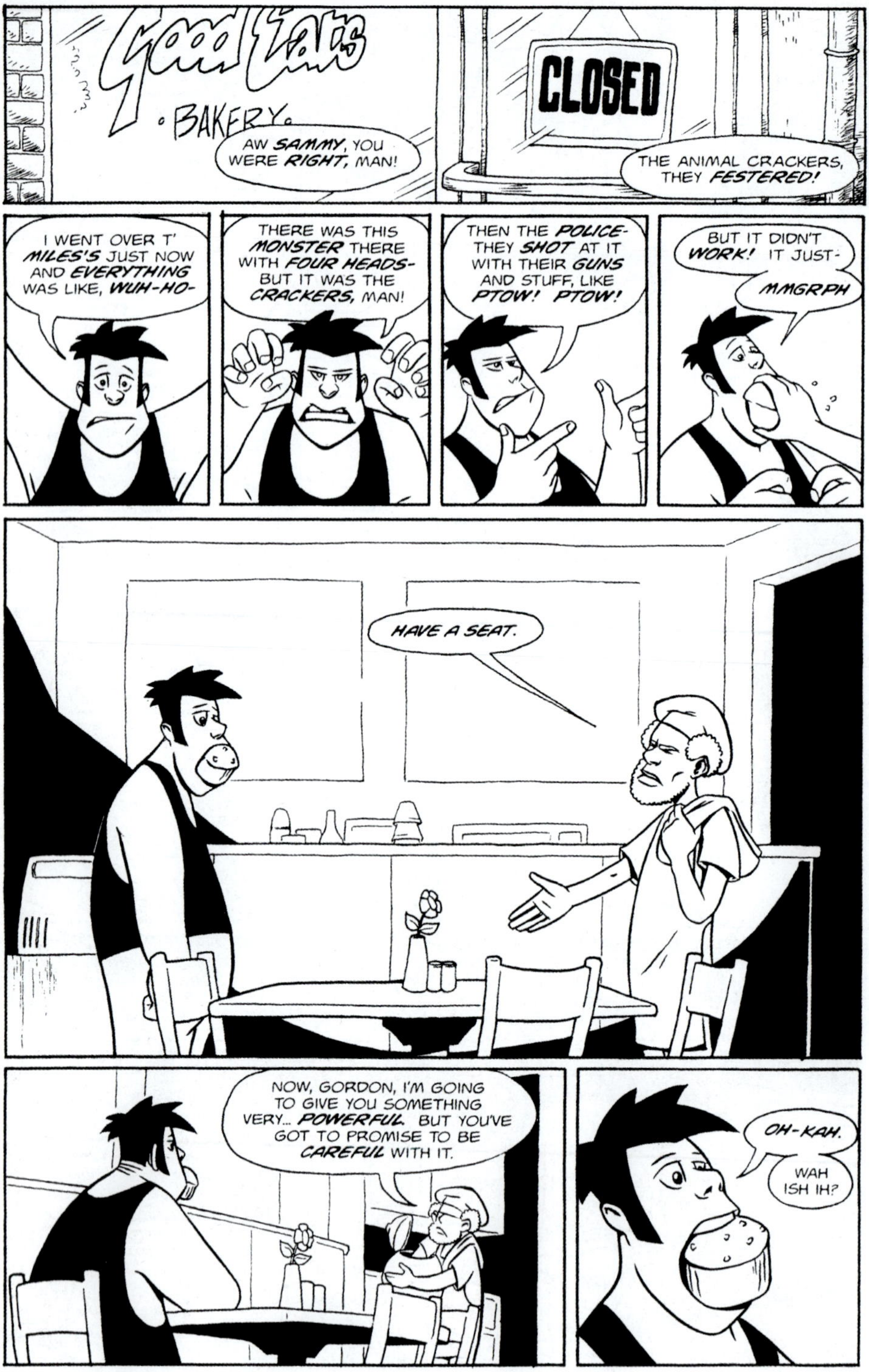
Good Eats
BAKERY
AW SAMMY, YOU WERE RIGHT, MAN!
CLOSED
THE ANIMAL CRACKERS, THEY FESTERED!
I WENT OVER T' MILES'S JUST NOW AND EVERYTHING WAS LIKE, WUH-HO-
THERE WAS THIS MONSTER THERE WITH FOUR HEADS- BUT IT WAS THE CRACKERS, MAN!
THEN THE POLICE- THEY SHOT AT IT WITH THEIR GUNS AND STUFF, LIKE PTOW! PTOW!
BUT IT DIDN'T WORK! IT JUST-
MMGRPH
HAVE A SEAT.
NOW, GORDON, I'M GOING TO GIVE YOU SOMETHING VERY... POWERFUL. BUT YOU'VE GOT TO PROMISE TO BE CAREFUL WITH IT.
OH-KAH.
WAH ISH IH?

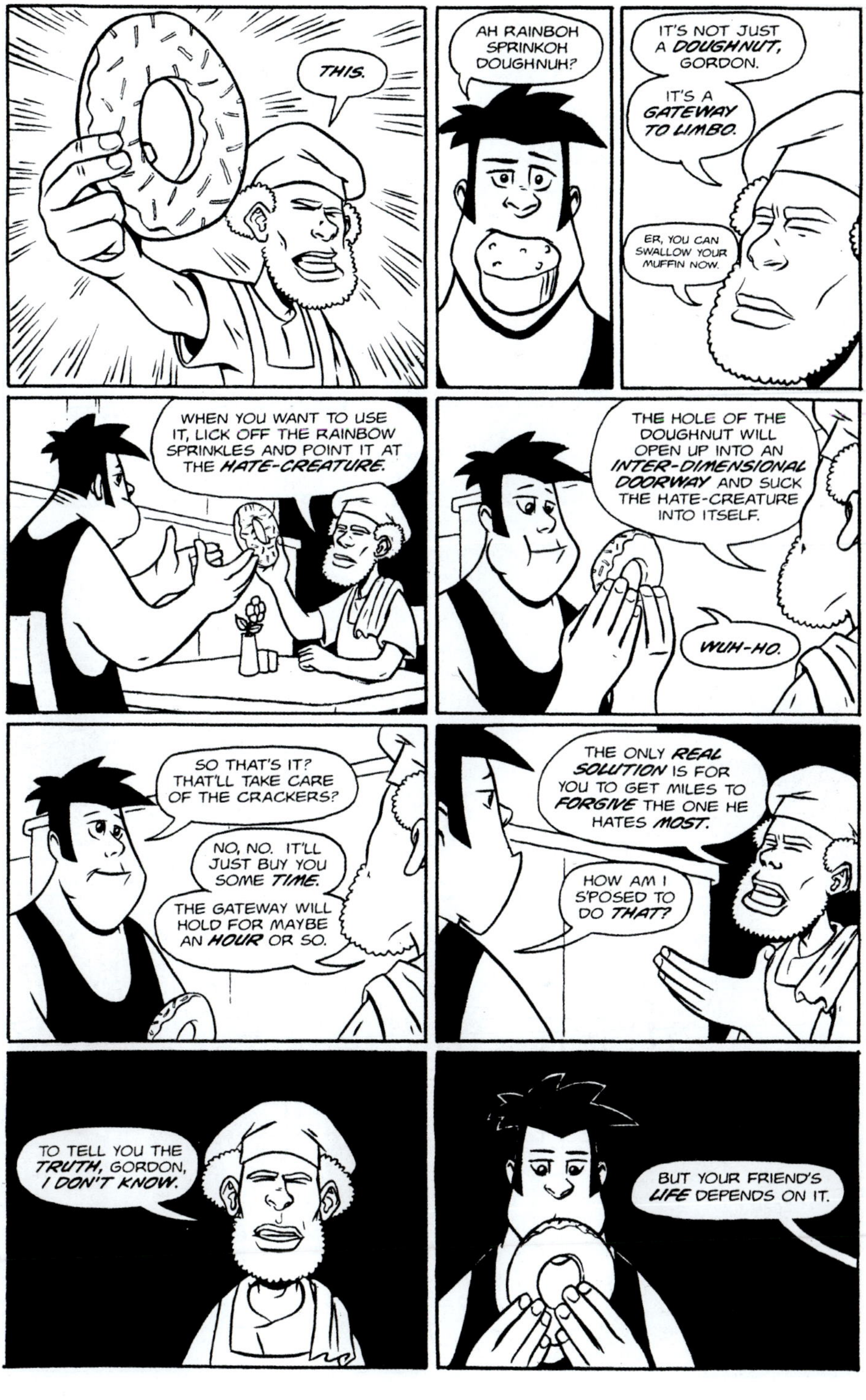
THIS.
AH RAINBOH SPRINKOH DOUGHNUH?
IT'S NOT JUST A DOUGHNUT, GORDON.
IT'S A GATEWAY TO LIMBO.
ER, YOU CAN SWALLOW YOUR MUFFIN NOW.
WHEN YOU WANT TO USE IT, LICK OFF THE RAINBOW SPRINKLES AND POINT IT AT THE HATE-CREATURE.
THE HOLE OF THE DOUGHNUT WILL OPEN UP INTO AN INTER-DIMENSIONAL DOORWAY AND SUCK THE HATE-CREATURE INTO ITSELF.
WUH-HO.
SO THAT'S IT? THAT'LL TAKE CARE OF THE CRACKERS?
NO, NO. IT'LL JUST BUY YOU SOME TIME.
THE GATEWAY WILL HOLD FOR MAYBE AN HOUR OR SO.
THE ONLY REAL SOLUTION IS FOR YOU TO GET MILES TO FORGIVE THE ONE HE HATES MOST.
HOW AM I S'POSED TO DO THAT?
TO TELL YOU THE TRUTH, GORDON, I DON'T KNOW.
BUT YOUR FRIEND'S LIFE DEPENDS ON IT.

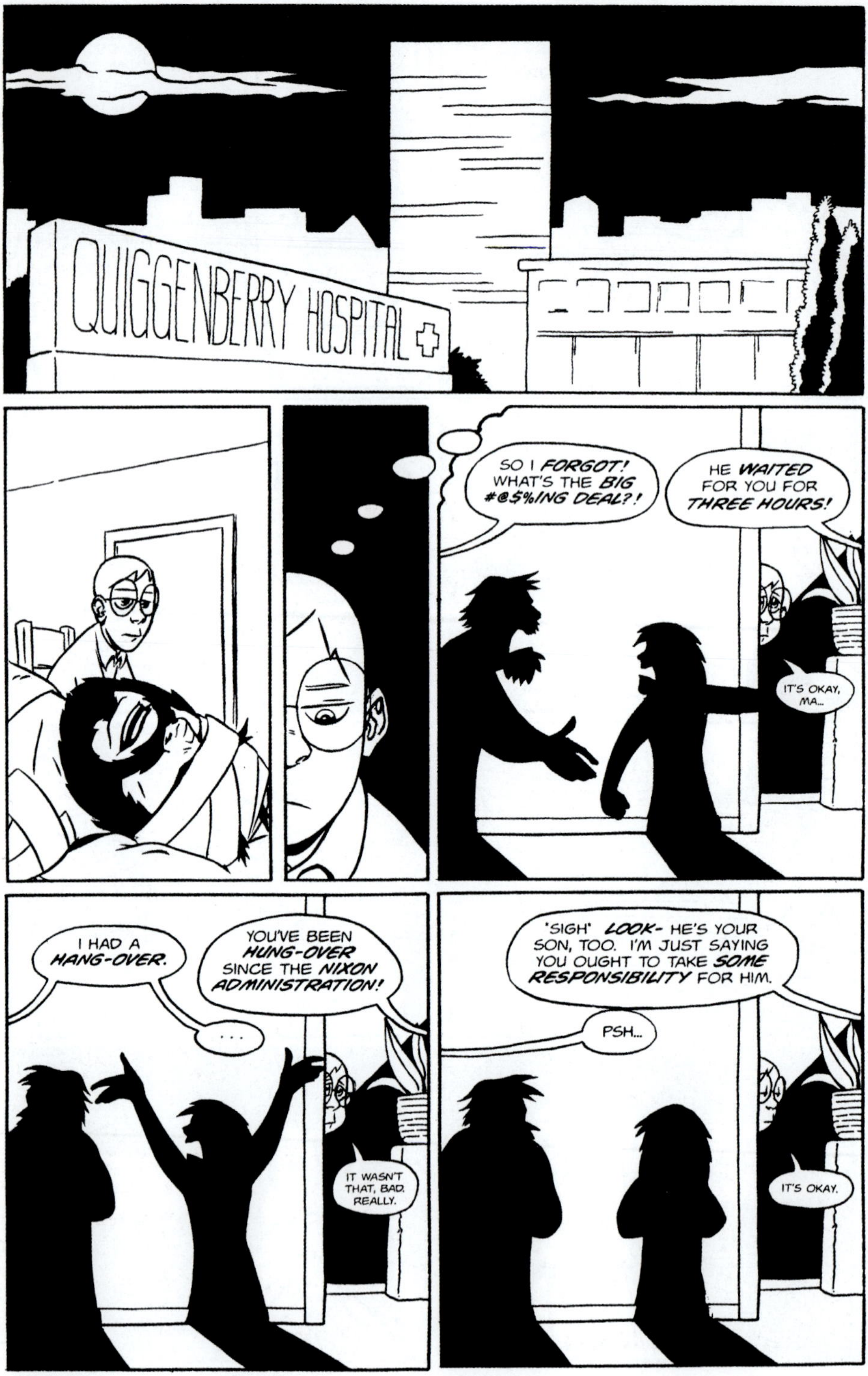
QUIGGENBERRY HOSPITAL
SO I FORGOT! WHAT'S THE BIG #@$%ING DEAL?!
HE WAITED FOR YOU FOR THREE HOURS!
IT'S OKAY, MA...
I HAD A HANG-OVER.
YOU'VE BEEN HUNG-OVER SINCE THE NIXON ADMINISTRATION!
. . .
IT WASN'T THAT, BAD. REALLY.
'SIGH' LOOK- HE'S YOUR SON, TOO. I'M JUST SAYING YOU OUGHT TO TAKE SOME RESPONSIBILITY FOR HIM.
PSH...
IT'S OKAY.

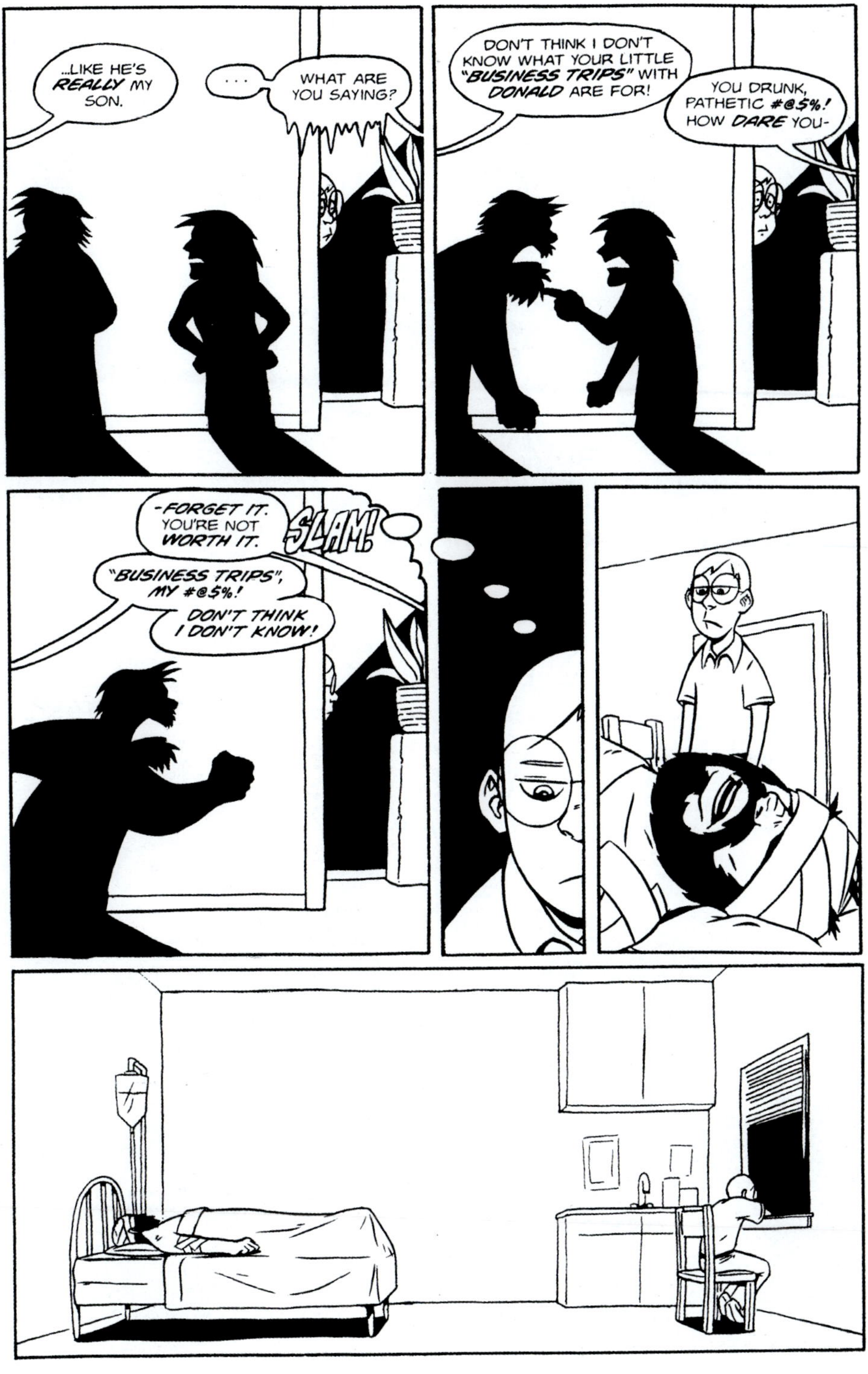
...LIKE HE'S *REALLY* MY SON.
. . .
WHAT ARE YOU SAYING?
DON'T THINK I DON'T KNOW WHAT YOUR LITTLE *"BUSINESS TRIPS"* WITH *DONALD* ARE FOR!
YOU DRUNK, PATHETIC *#@$%!* HOW *DARE* YOU-
-FORGET IT. YOU'RE NOT *WORTH IT.*
SLAM!
"BUSINESS TRIPS", MY #@$%!
DON'T THINK I DON'T KNOW!

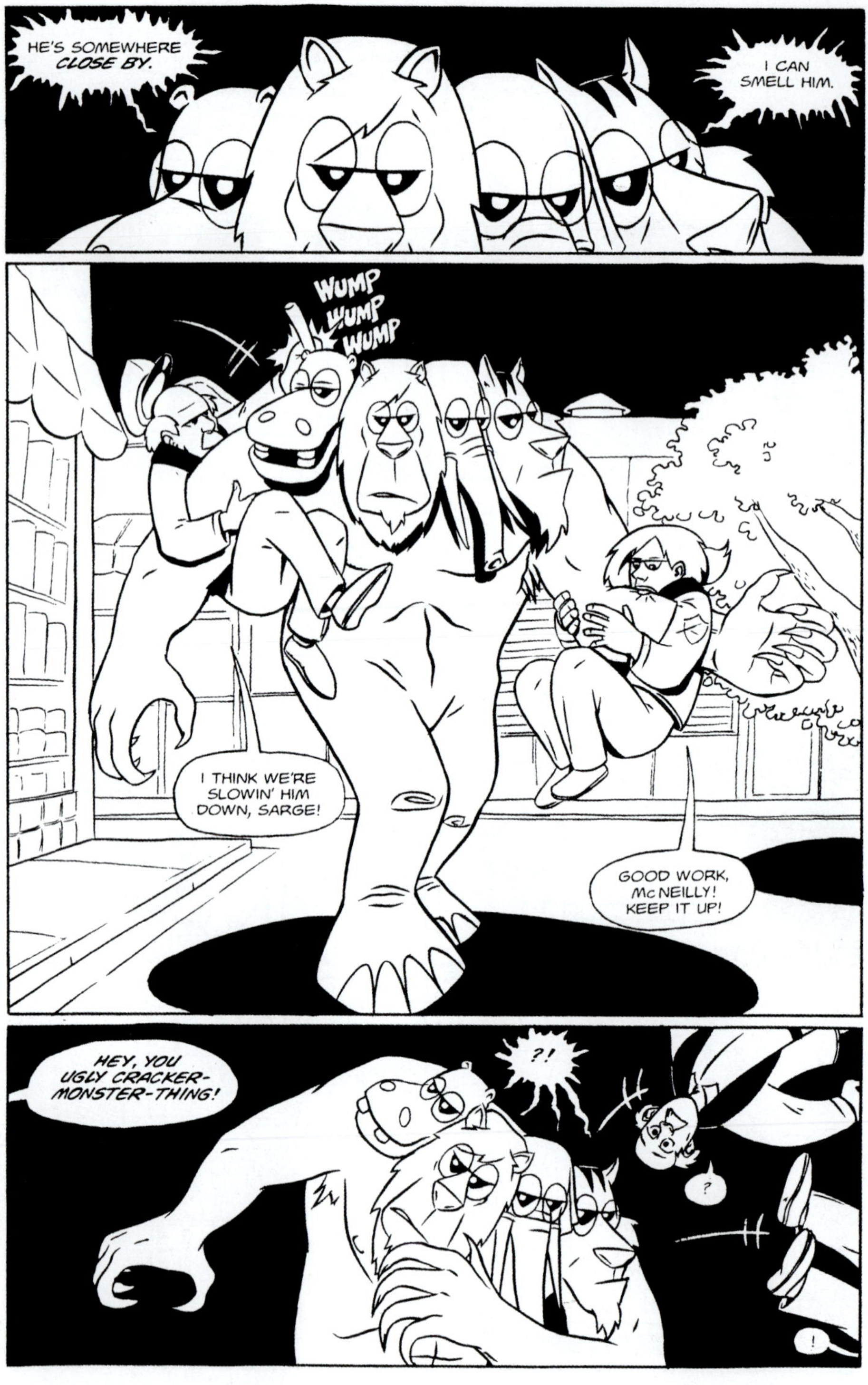
HE'S SOMEWHERE CLOSE BY.
I CAN SMELL HIM.
WUMP WUMP WUMP
I THINK WE'RE SLOWIN' HIM DOWN, SARGE!
GOOD WORK, McNEILLY! KEEP IT UP!
HEY, YOU UGLY CRACKER-MONSTER-THING!
?!
?
!

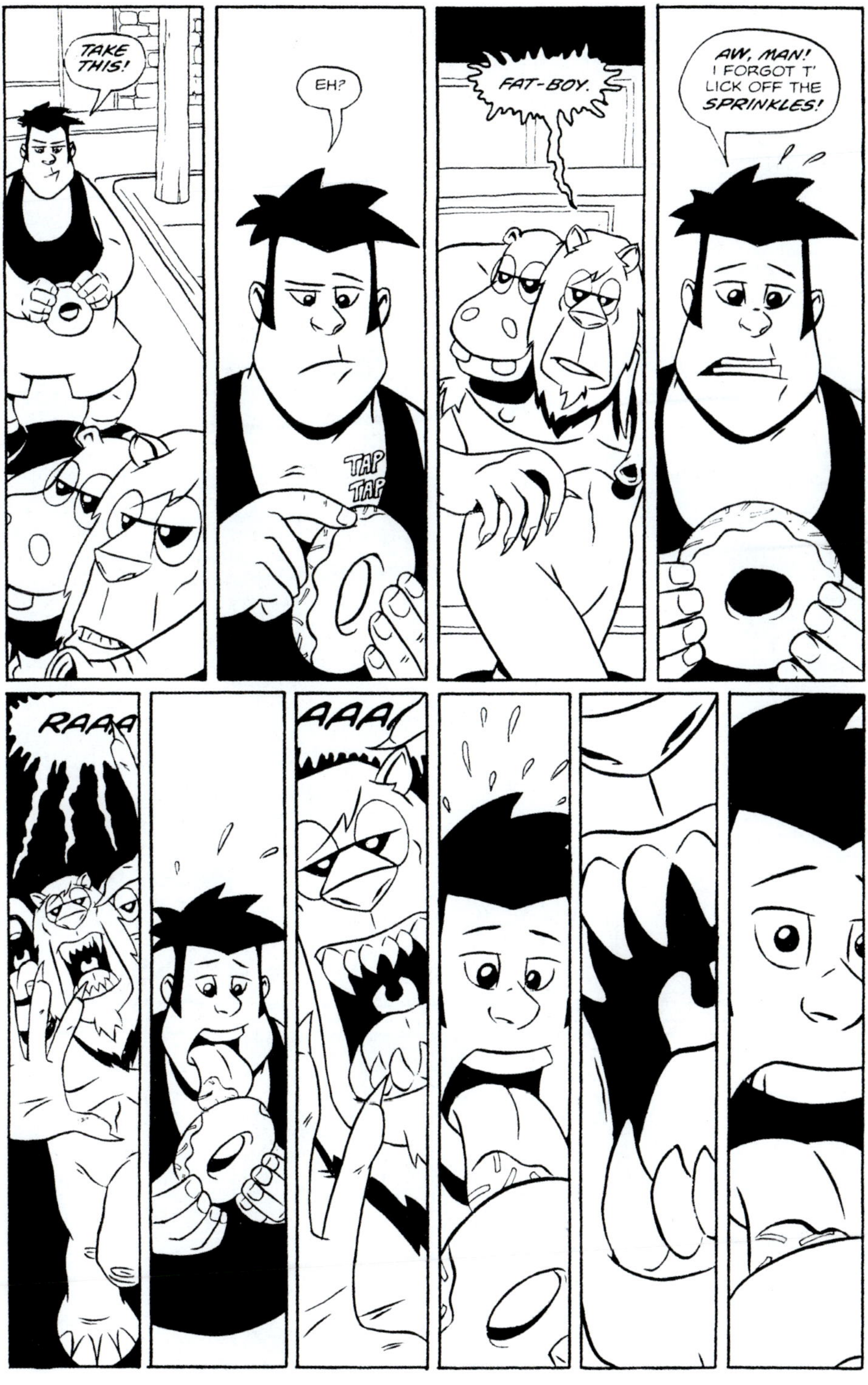
TAKE THIS!
EH?
TAP TAP
FAT-BOY.
AW, MAN! I FORGOT T' LICK OFF THE SPRINKLES!
RAAA
AAAA

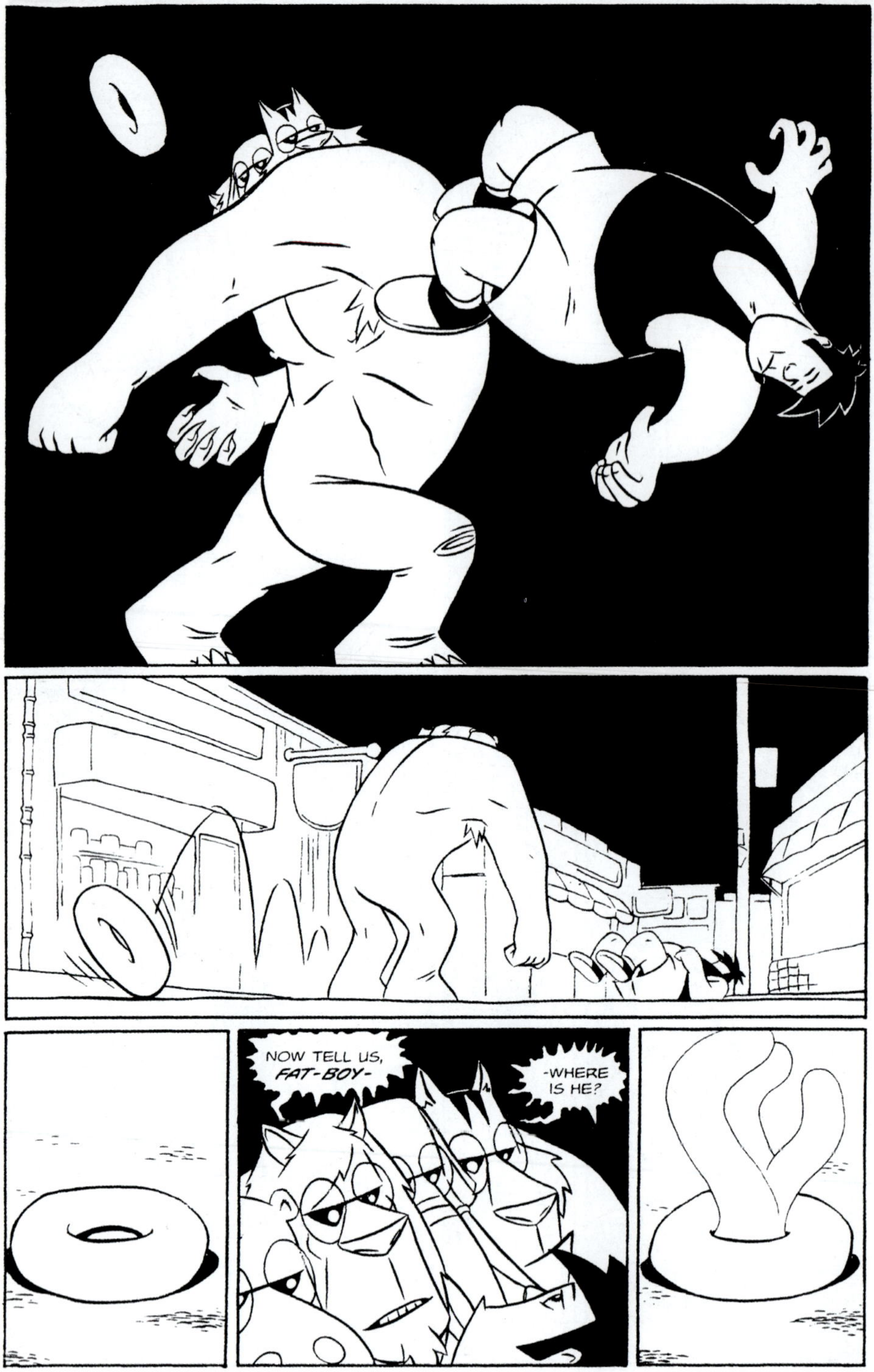
NOW TELL US, FAT-BOY-
-WHERE IS HE?

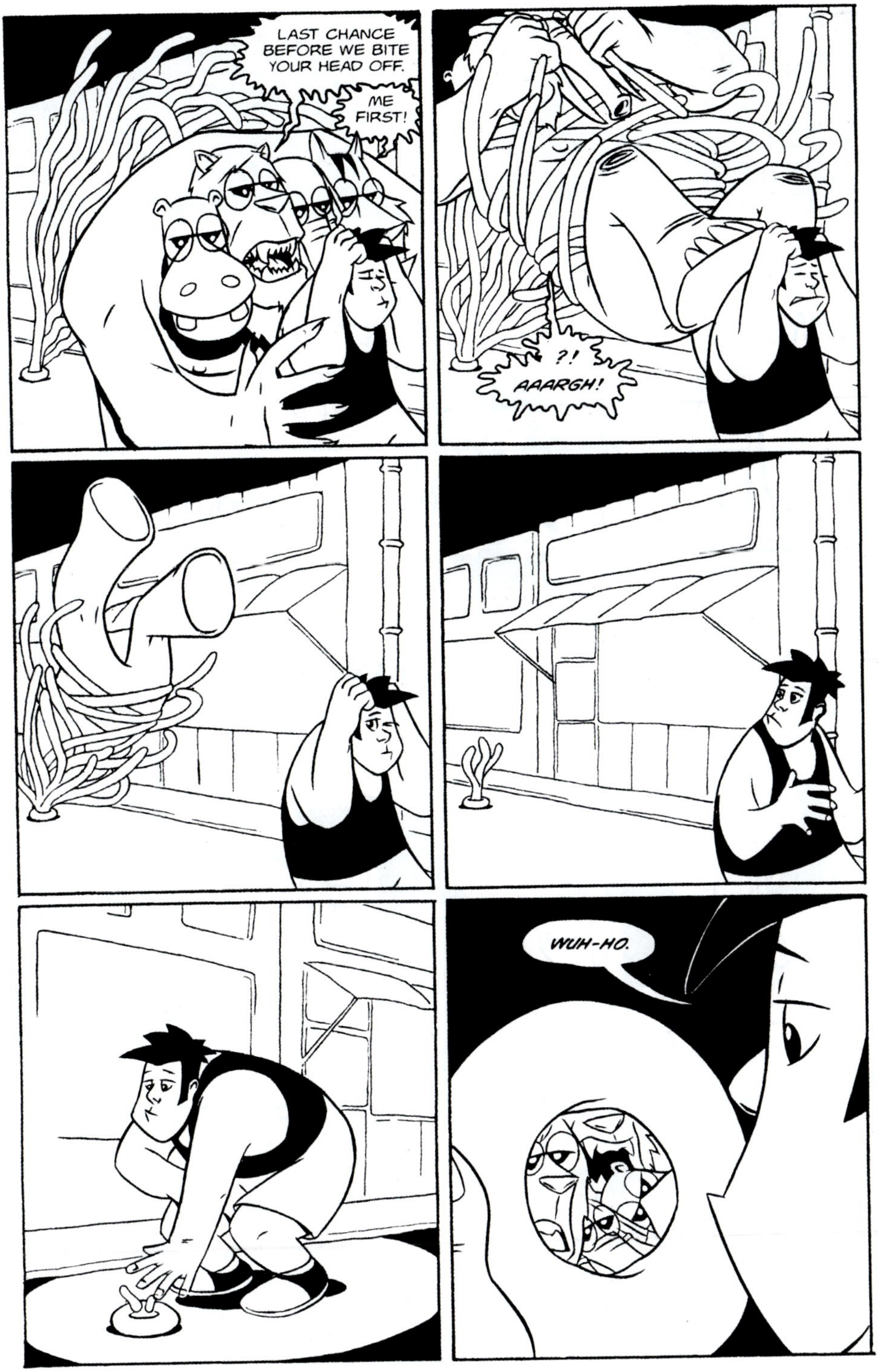
LAST CHANCE BEFORE WE BITE YOUR HEAD OFF.
ME FIRST!
?!
AAARGH!
WUH-HO.

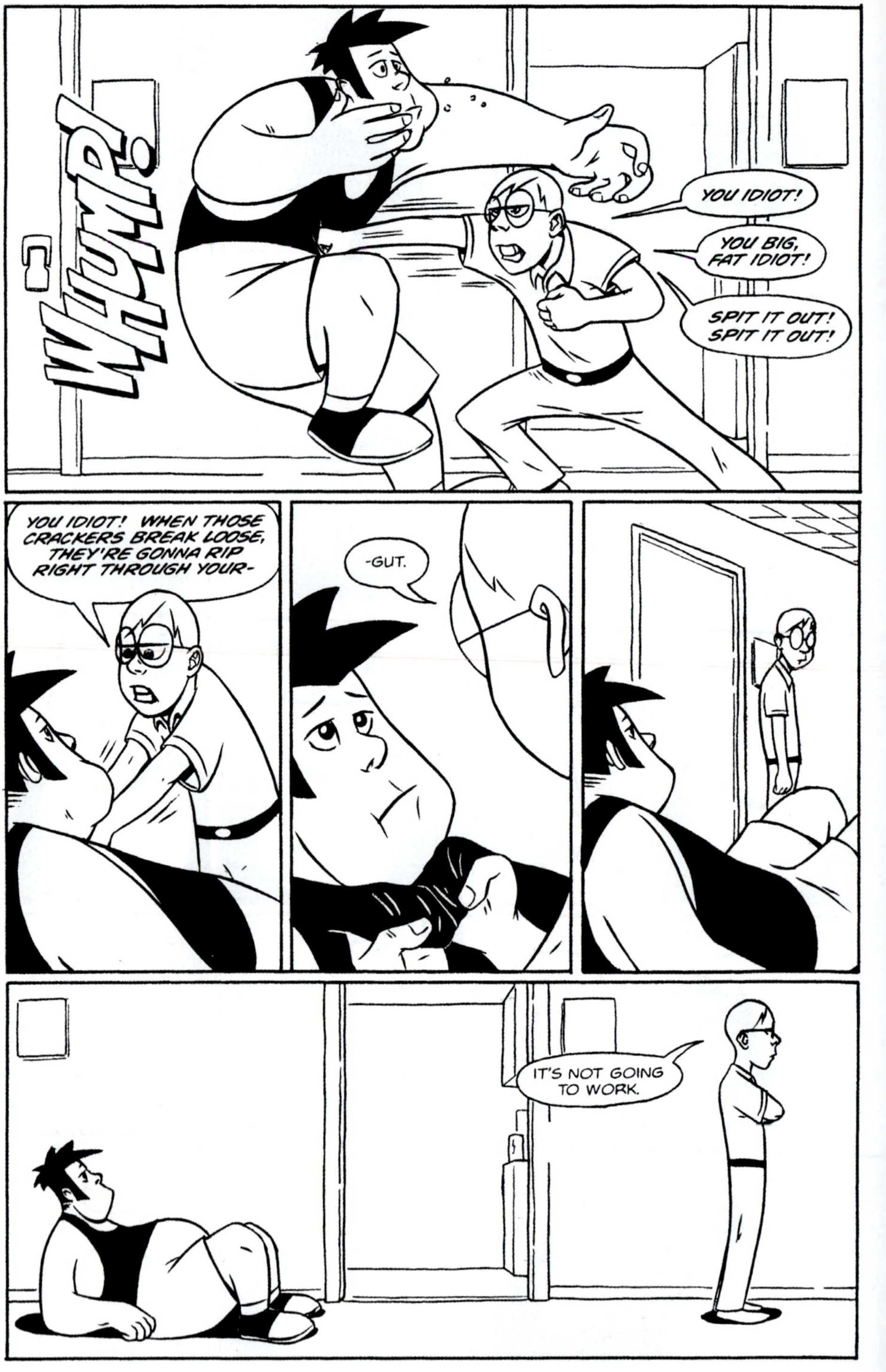
WHUMP!
YOU IDIOT!
YOU BIG, FAT IDIOT!
SPIT IT OUT! SPIT IT OUT!
YOU IDIOT! WHEN THOSE CRACKERS BREAK LOOSE, THEY'RE GONNA RIP RIGHT THROUGH YOUR-
-GUT.
IT'S NOT GOING TO WORK.

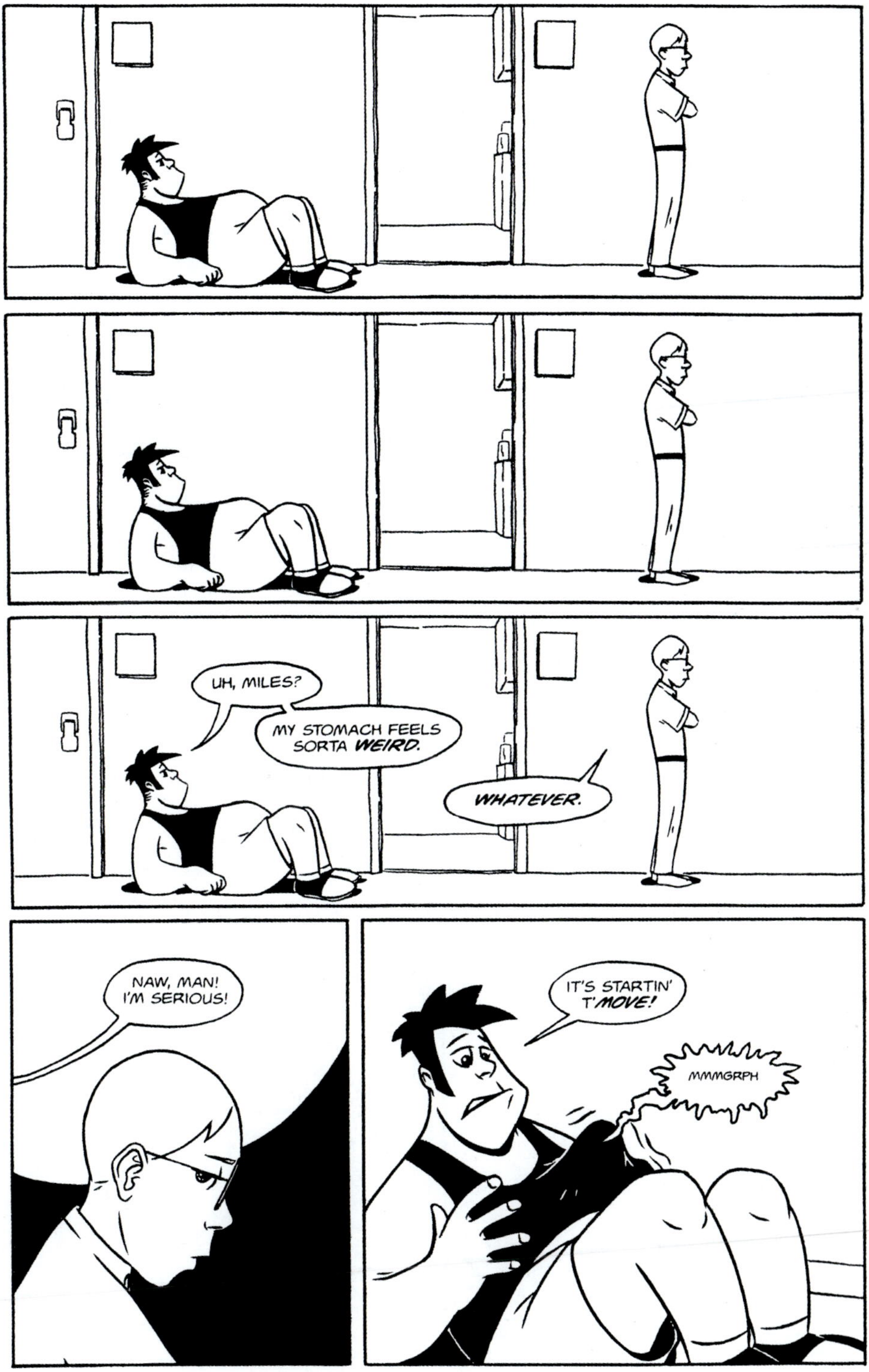
UH, MILES?
MY STOMACH FEELS SORTA WEIRD.
WHATEVER.
NAW, MAN! I'M SERIOUS!
IT'S STARTIN' T'MOVE!
MMMGRPH

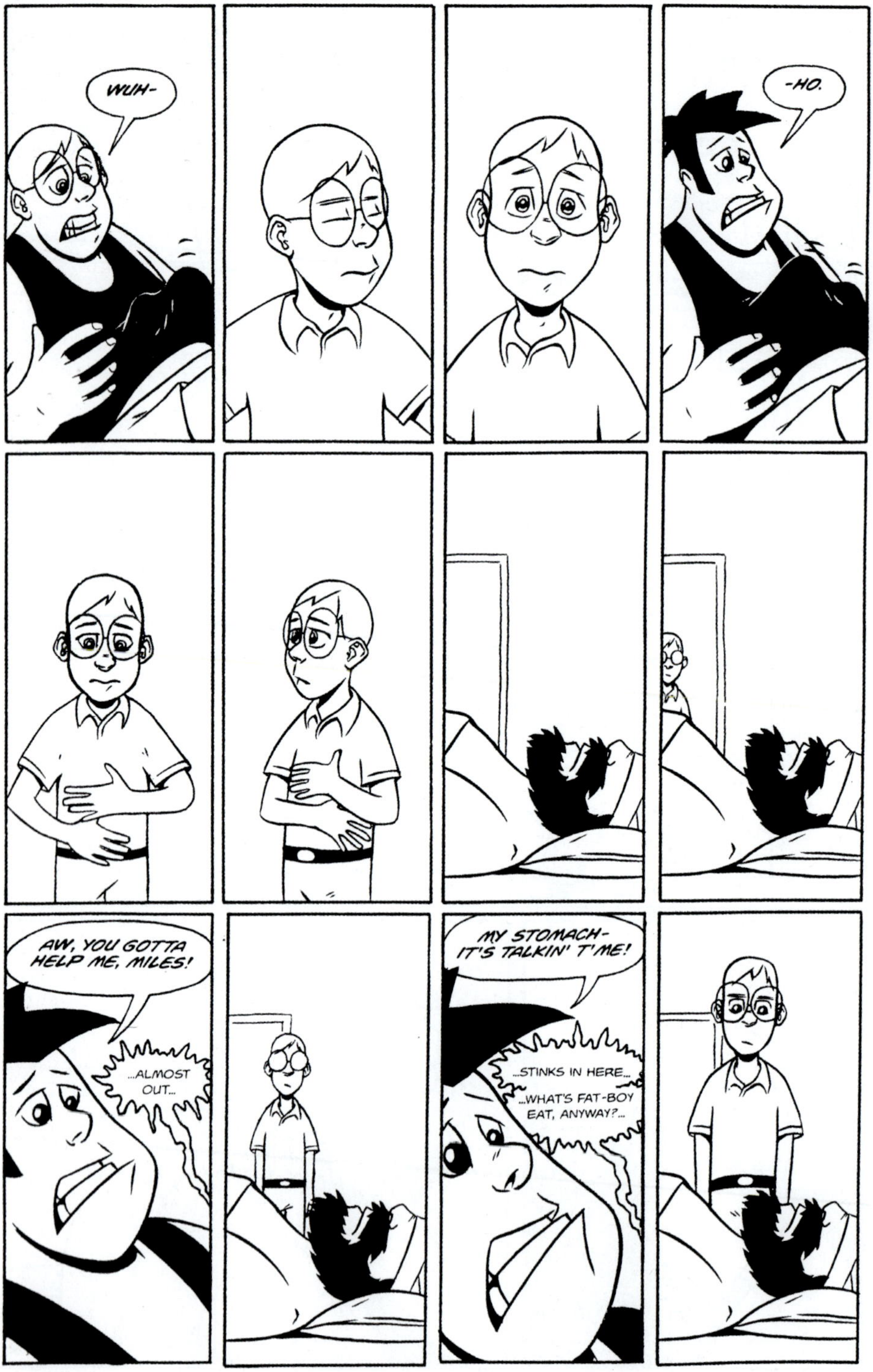
WUH-
-HO.
AW, YOU GOTTA HELP ME, MILES!
...ALMOST OUT...
MY STOMACH- IT'S TALKIN' T'ME!
...STINKS IN HERE...
...WHAT'S FAT-BOY EAT, ANYWAY?...

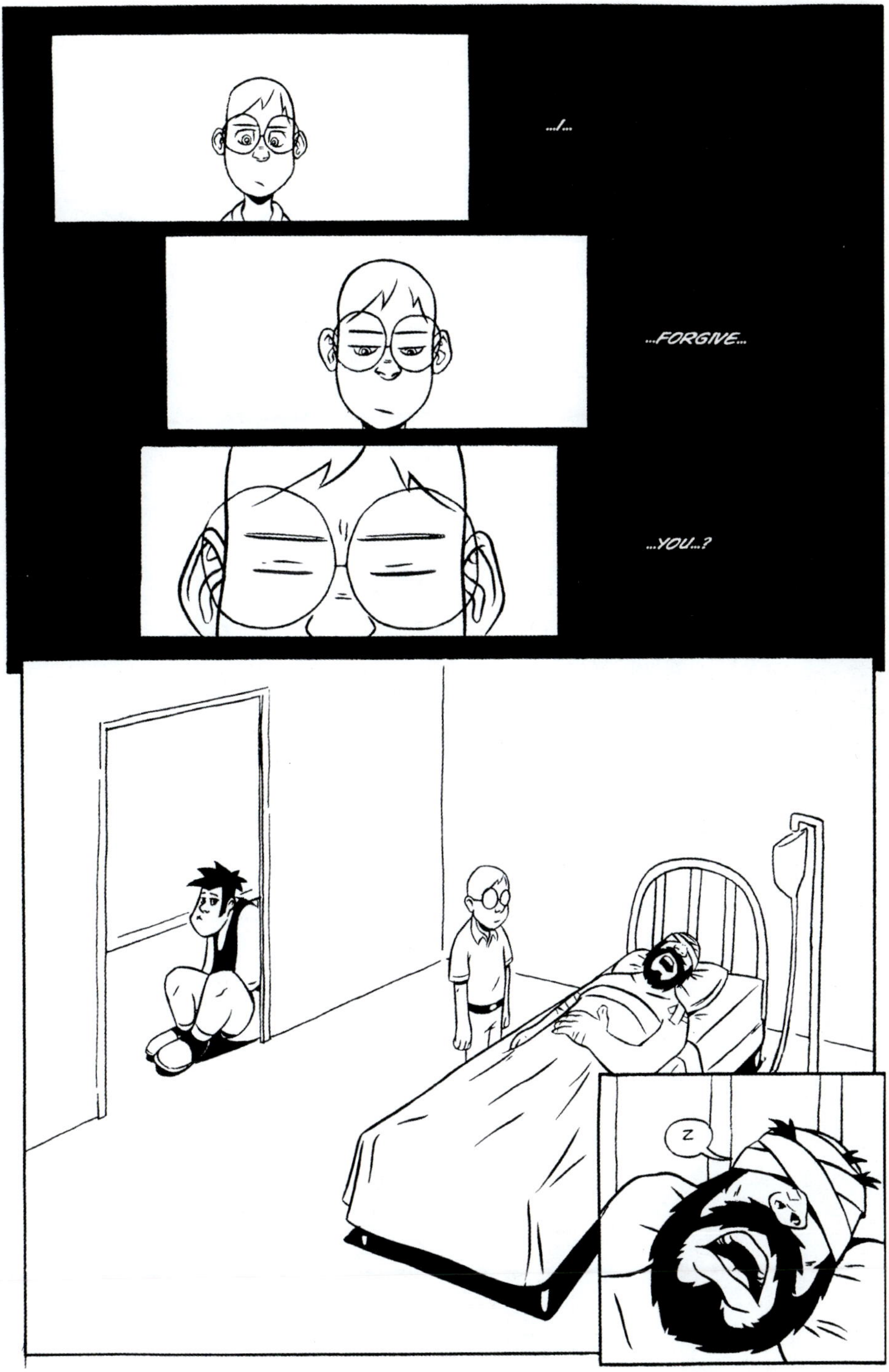

...I...
...FORGIVE...
...YOU...?
Z

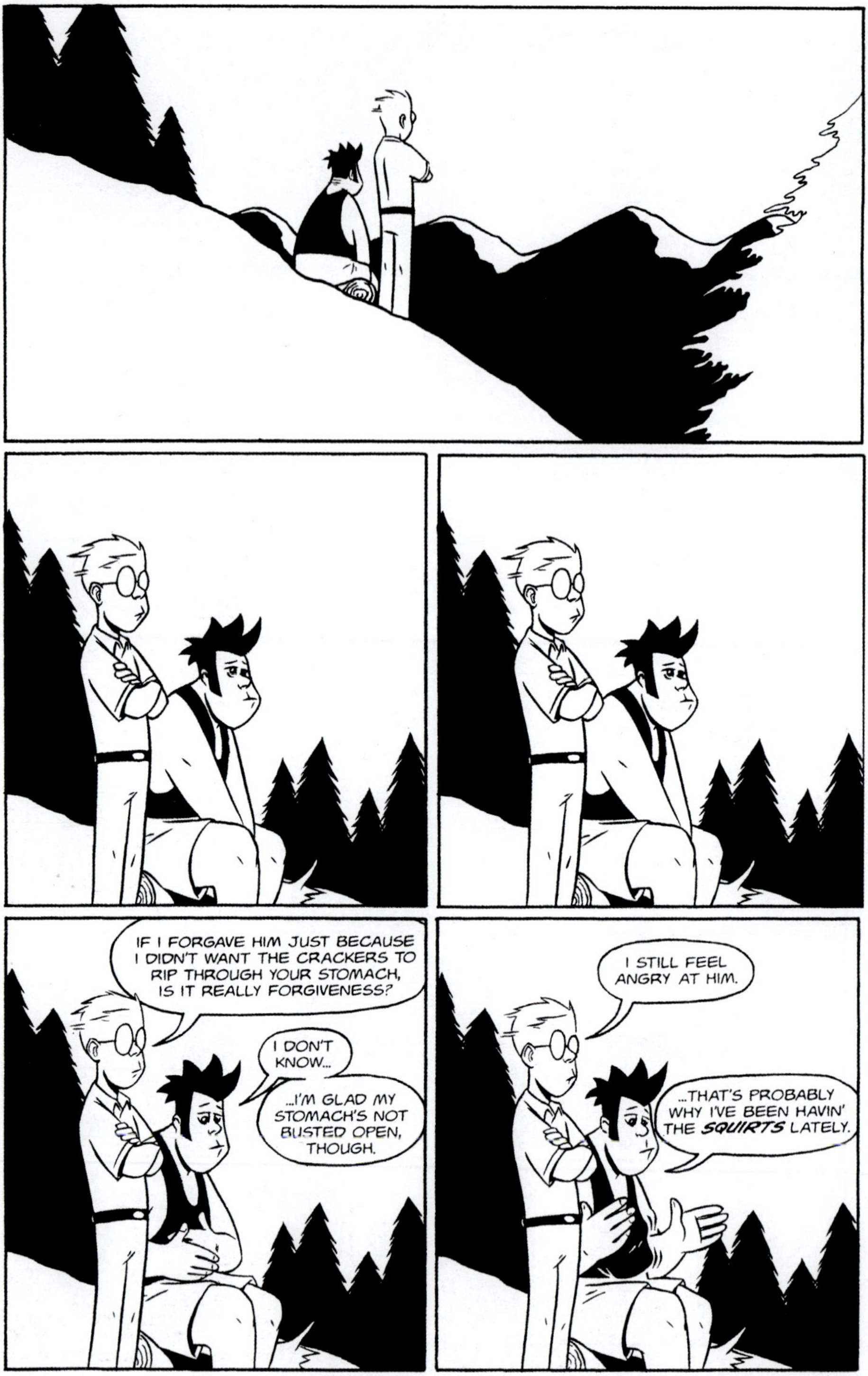
IF I FORGAVE HIM JUST BECAUSE I DIDN'T WANT THE CRACKERS TO RIP THROUGH YOUR STOMACH, IS IT REALLY FORGIVENESS?
I DON'T KNOW...
...I'M GLAD MY STOMACH'S NOT BUSTED OPEN, THOUGH.
I STILL FEEL ANGRY AT HIM.
...THAT'S PROBABLY WHY I'VE BEEN HAVIN' THE *SQUIRTS* LATELY.

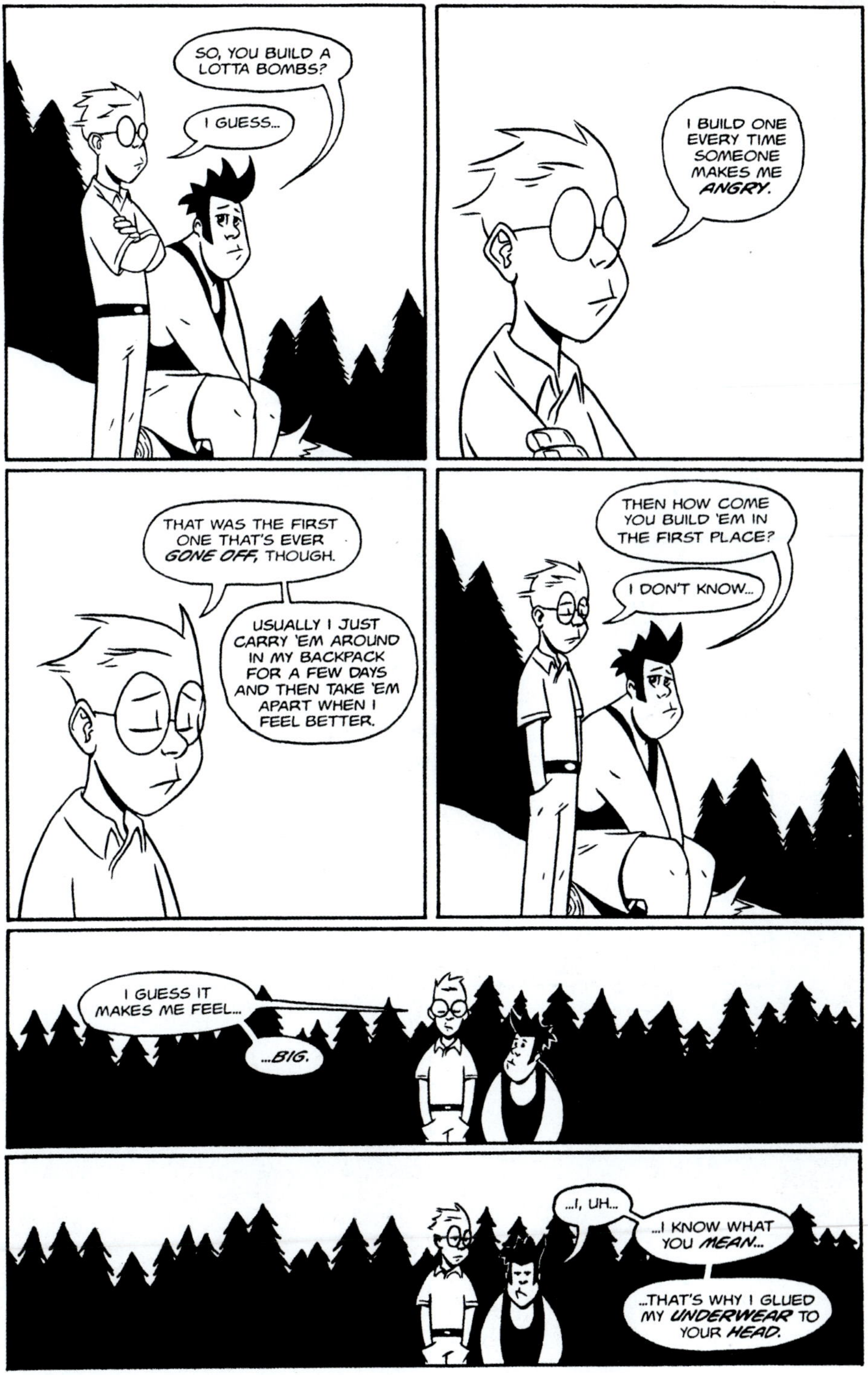
SO, YOU BUILD A LOTTA BOMBS?
I GUESS...
I BUILD ONE EVERY TIME SOMEONE MAKES ME ANGRY.
THAT WAS THE FIRST ONE THAT'S EVER GONE OFF, THOUGH.
USUALLY I JUST CARRY 'EM AROUND IN MY BACKPACK FOR A FEW DAYS AND THEN TAKE 'EM APART WHEN I FEEL BETTER.
THEN HOW COME YOU BUILD 'EM IN THE FIRST PLACE?
I DON'T KNOW...
I GUESS IT MAKES ME FEEL...
...BIG.
...I, UH...
...I KNOW WHAT YOU MEAN...
...THAT'S WHY I GLUED MY UNDERWEAR TO YOUR HEAD.

SAMMY THE BAKER AND THE M.A.C.

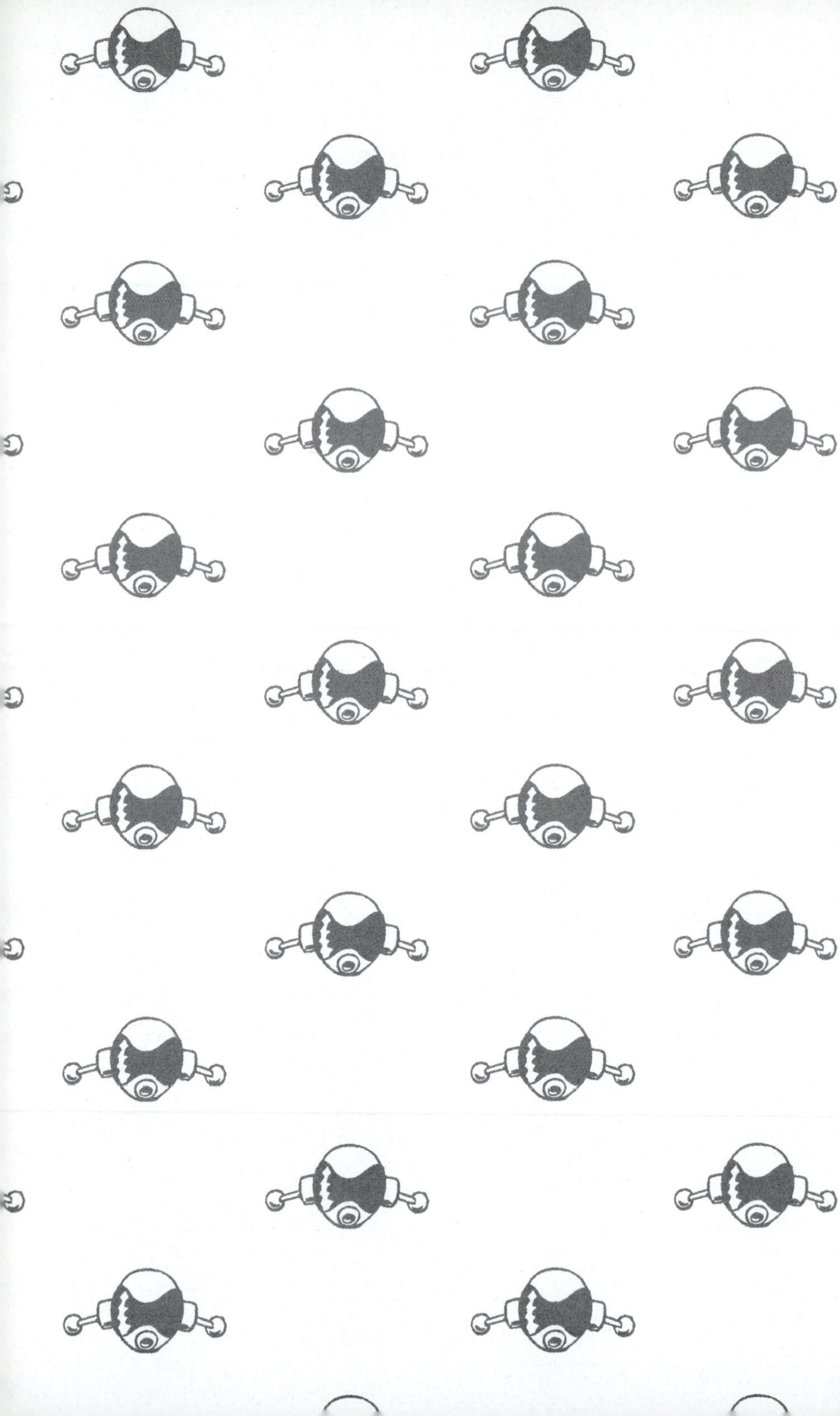

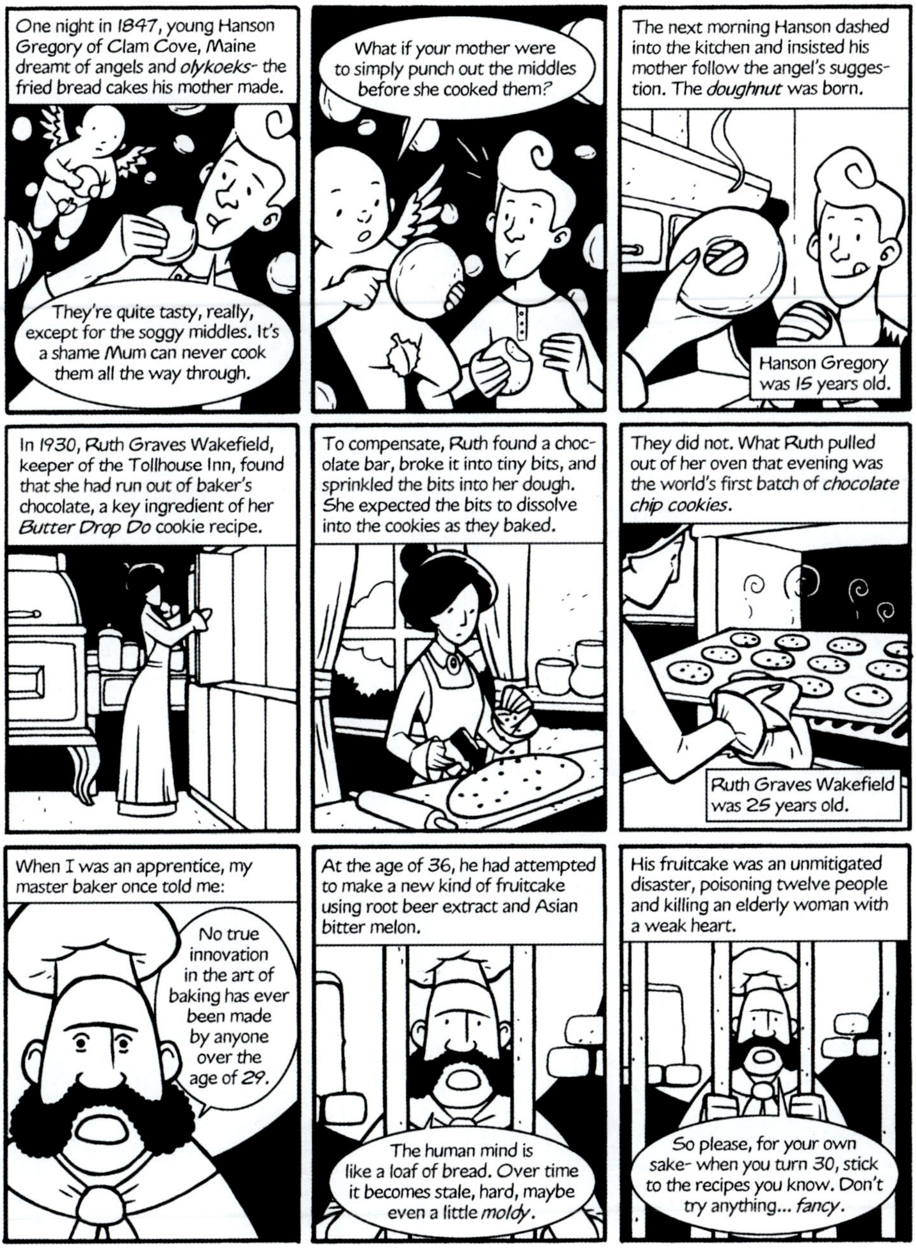

One night in 1847, young Hanson Gregory of Clam Cove, Maine dreamt of angels and *olykoeks*- the fried bread cakes his mother made.
They're quite tasty, really, except for the soggy middles. It's a shame Mum can never cook them all the way through.
What if your mother were to simply punch out the middles before she cooked them?
The next morning Hanson dashed into the kitchen and insisted his mother follow the angel's suggestion. The *doughnut* was born.
Hanson Gregory was 15 years old.
In 1930, Ruth Graves Wakefield, keeper of the Tollhouse Inn, found that she had run out of baker's chocolate, a key ingredient of her *Butter Drop Do* cookie recipe.
To compensate, Ruth found a chocolate bar, broke it into tiny bits, and sprinkled the bits into her dough. She expected the bits to dissolve into the cookies as they baked.
They did not. What Ruth pulled out of her oven that evening was the world's first batch of *chocolate chip cookies*.
Ruth Graves Wakefield was 25 years old.
When I was an apprentice, my master baker once told me:
No true innovation in the art of baking has ever been made by anyone over the age of 29.
At the age of 36, he had attempted to make a new kind of fruitcake using root beer extract and Asian bitter melon.
The human mind is like a loaf of bread. Over time it becomes stale, hard, maybe even a little *moldy*.
His fruitcake was an unmitigated disaster, poisoning twelve people and killing an elderly woman with a weak heart.
So please, for your own sake- when you turn 30, stick to the recipes you know. Don't try anything... *fancy*.

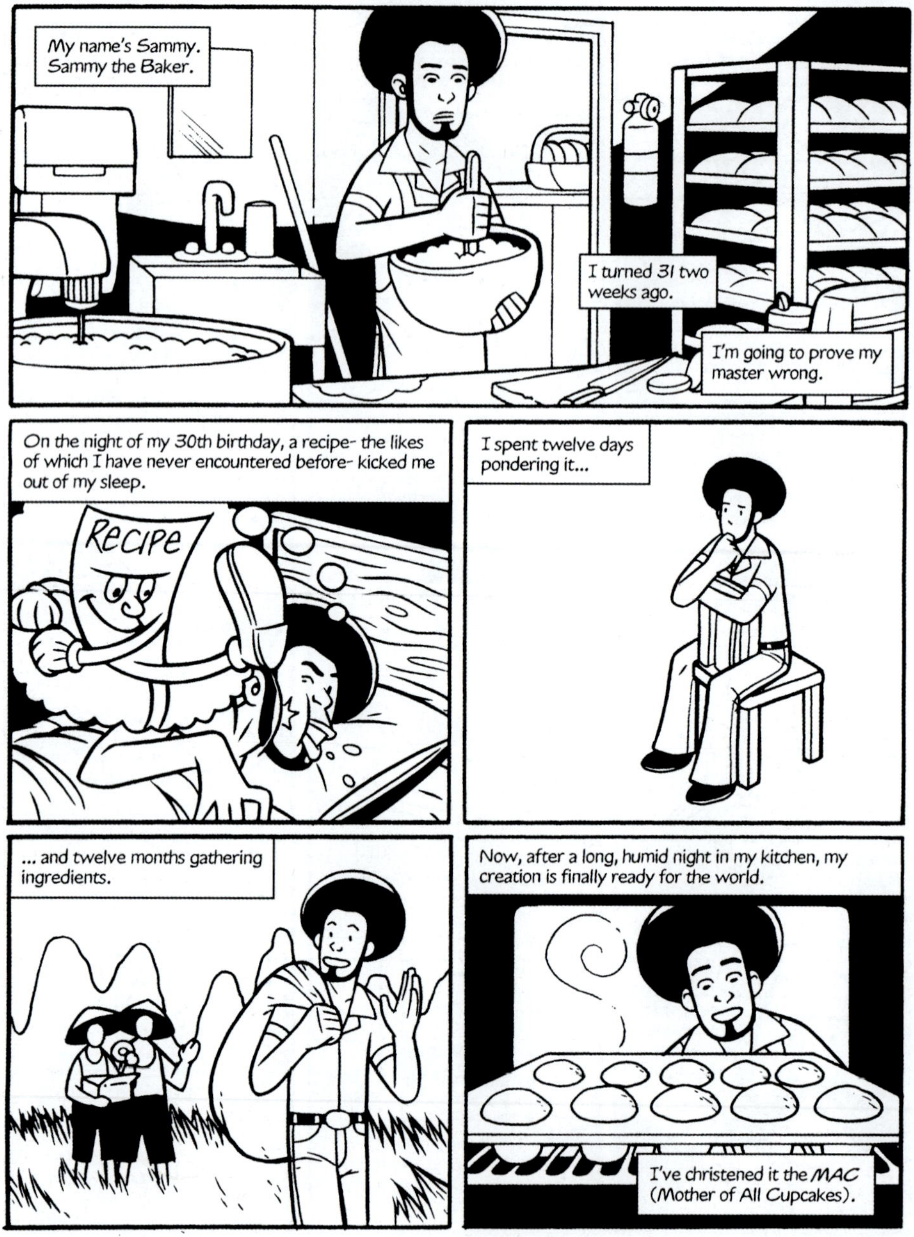
My name's Sammy. Sammy the Baker.
I turned 31 two weeks ago.
I'm going to prove my master wrong.
On the night of my 30th birthday, a recipe- the likes of which I have never encountered before- kicked me out of my sleep.
RECIPE
I spent twelve days pondering it...
... and twelve months gathering ingredients.
Now, after a long, humid night in my kitchen, my creation is finally ready for the world.
I've christened it the *MAC* (Mother of All Cupcakes).

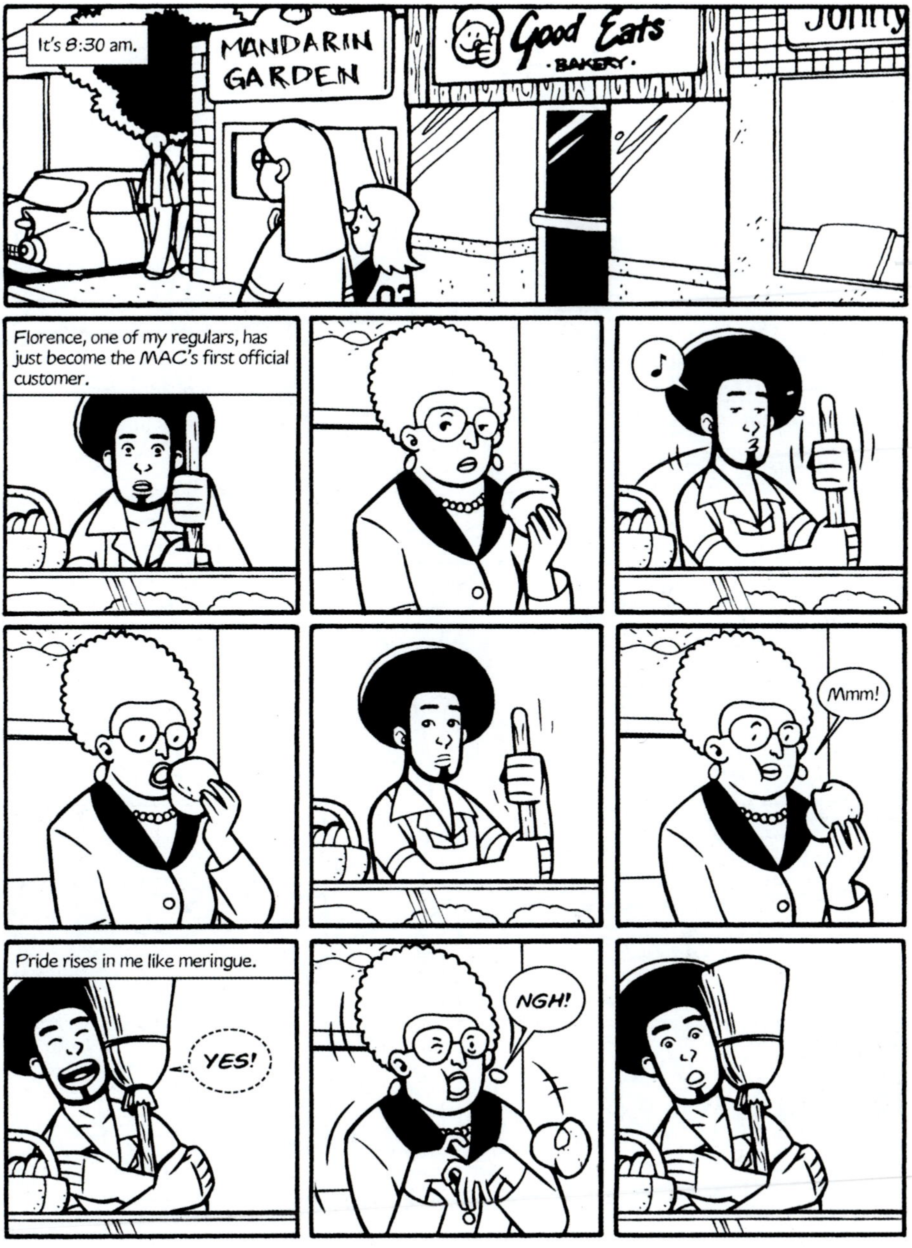
It's 8:30 am.
MANDARIN GARDEN
Good Eats
BAKERY
Florence, one of my regulars, has just become the MAC's first official customer.
♪
Mmm!
Pride rises in me like meringue.
YES!
NGH!

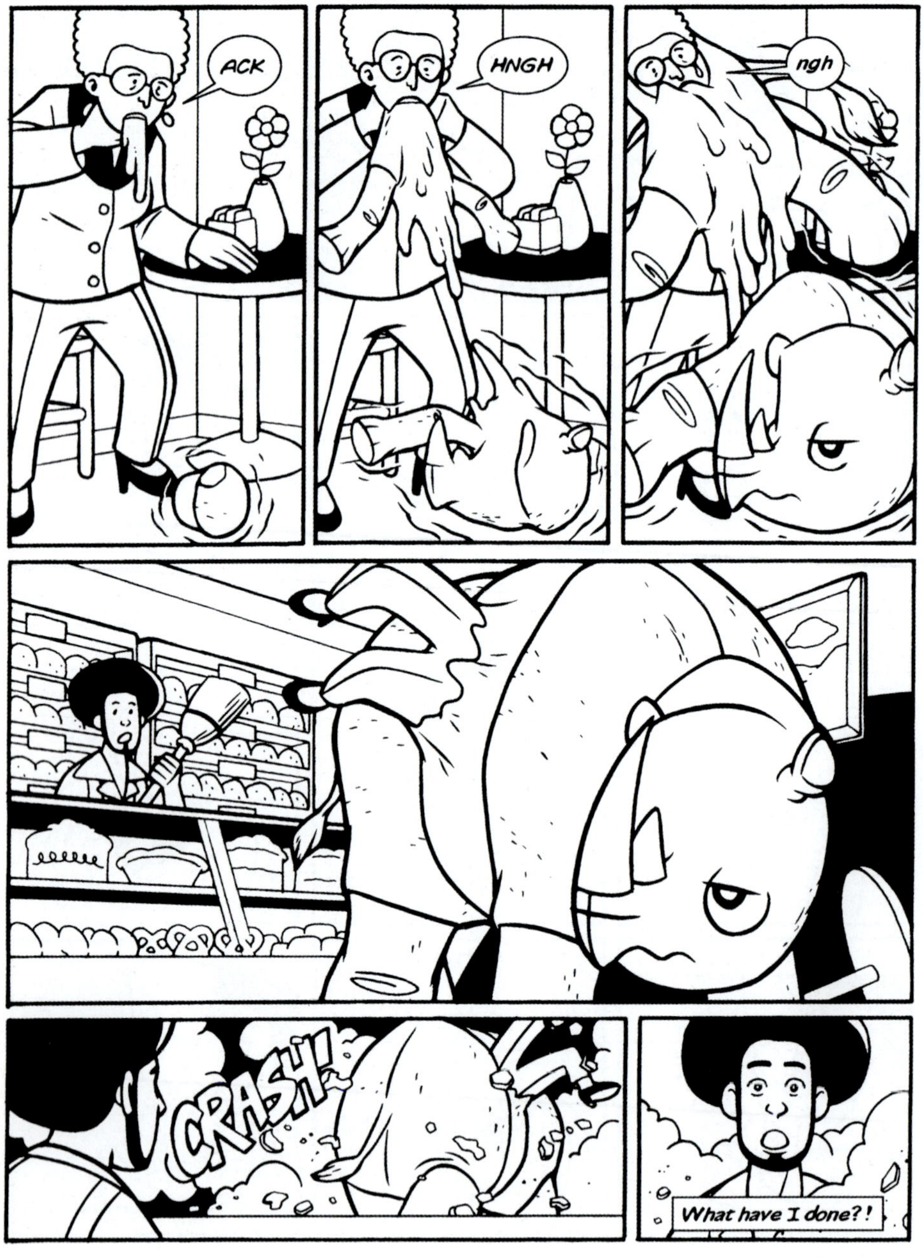
ACK
HNGH
ngh
CRASH!
What have I done?!

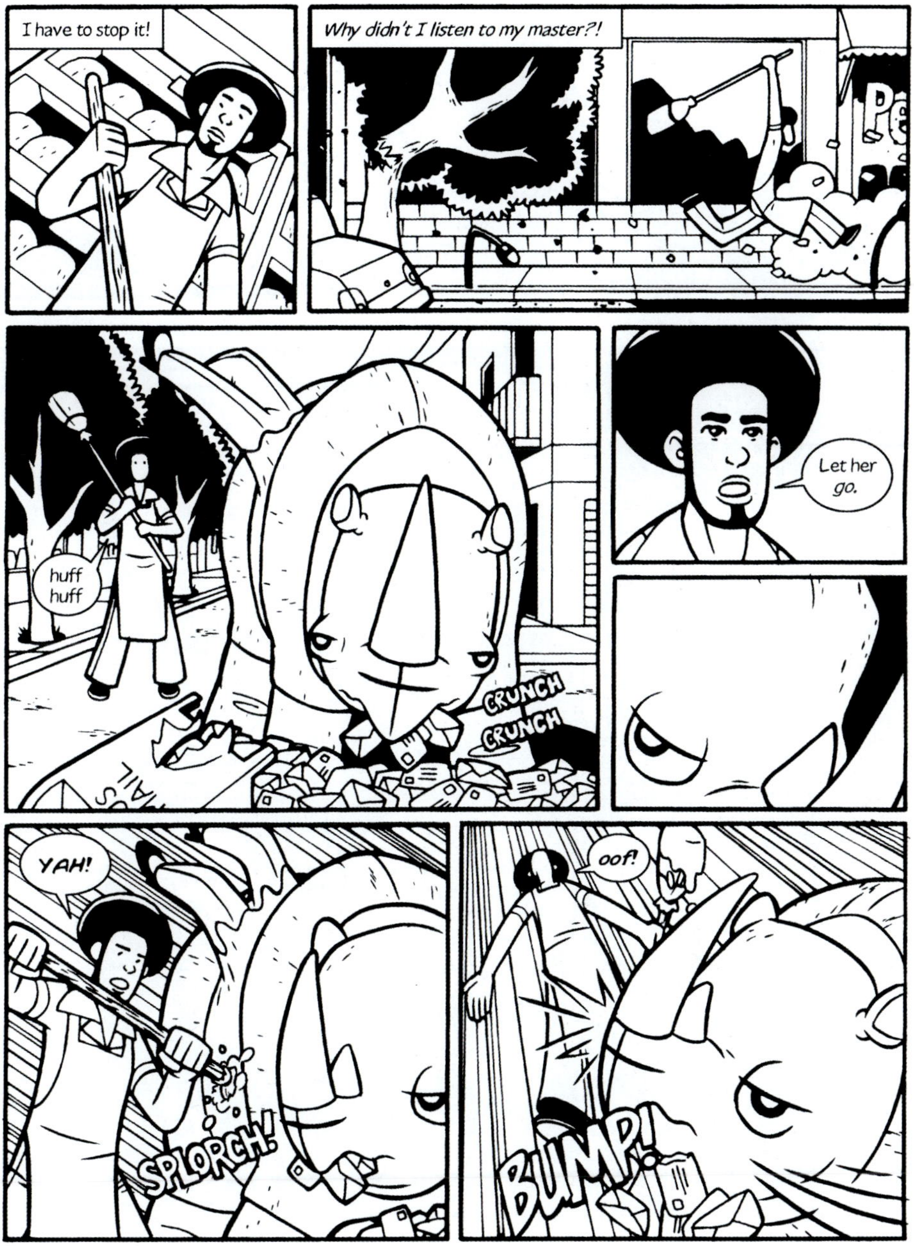
I have to stop it!
Why didn't I listen to my master?!
huff huff
CRUNCH
CRUNCH
Let her go.
YAH!
SPLORCH!
oof!
BUMP!

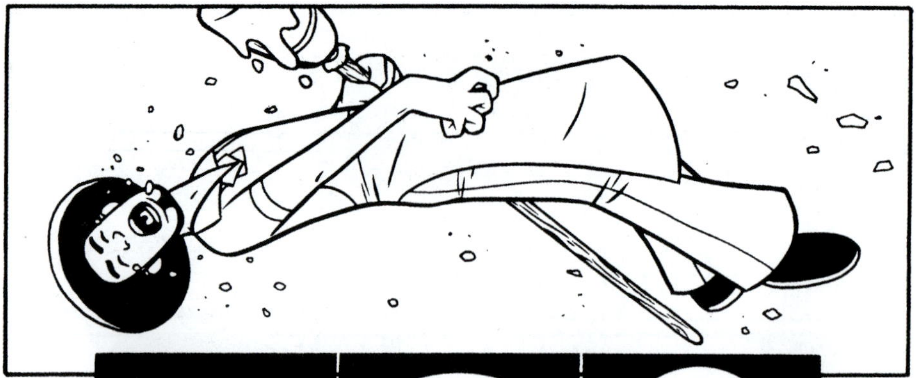

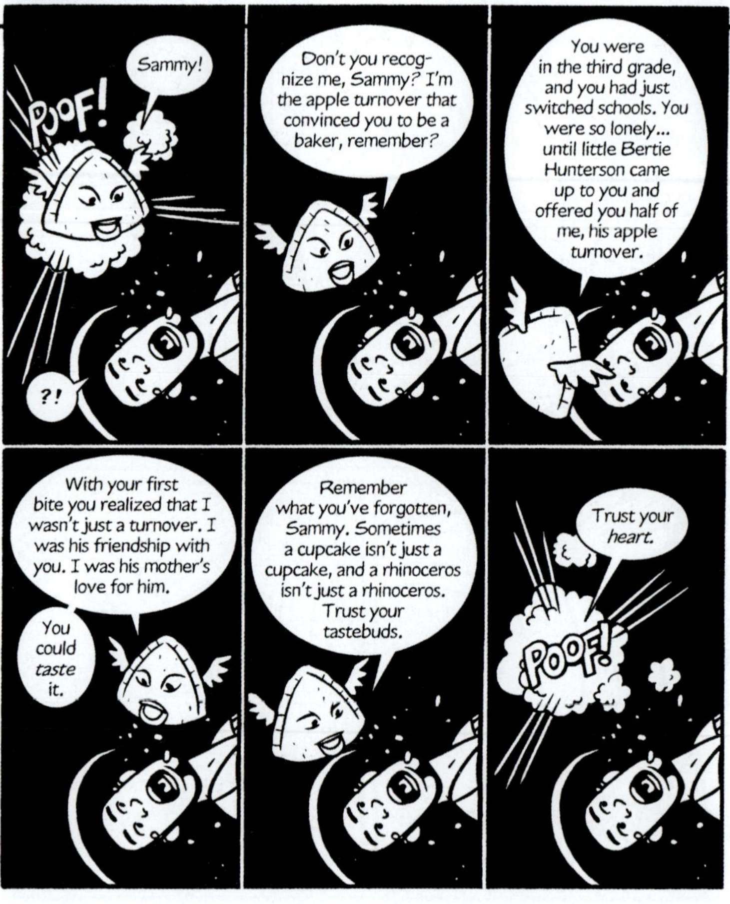
POOF!
Sammy!
?!
Don't you recognize me, Sammy? I'm the apple turnover that convinced you to be a baker, remember?
You were in the third grade, and you had just switched schools. You were so lonely... until little Bertie Hunterson came up to you and offered you half of me, his apple turnover.
With your first bite you realized that I wasn't just a turnover. I was his friendship with you. I was his mother's love for him.
You could *taste* it.
Remember what you've forgotten, Sammy. Sometimes a cupcake isn't just a cupcake, and a rhinoceros isn't just a rhinoceros. Trust your tastebuds.
Trust your *heart.*
POOF!

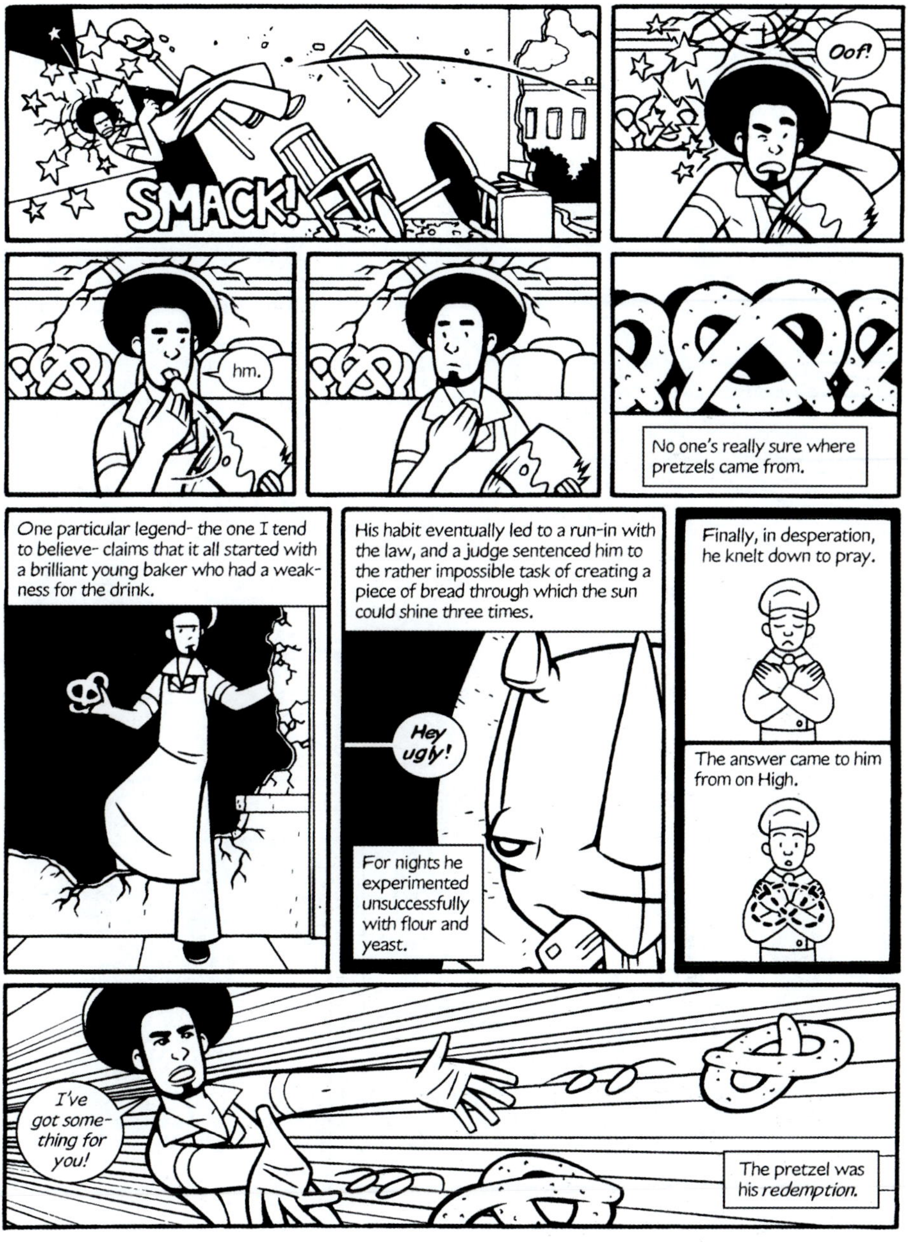
SMACK!
Oof!
hm.
No one's really sure where pretzels came from.
One particular legend- the one I tend to believe- claims that it all started with a brilliant young baker who had a weakness for the drink.
His habit eventually led to a run-in with the law, and a judge sentenced him to the rather impossible task of creating a piece of bread through which the sun could shine three times.
Hey ugly!
For nights he experimented unsuccessfully with flour and yeast.
Finally, in desperation, he knelt down to pray.
The answer came to him from on High.
I've got something for you!
The pretzel was his *redemption.*

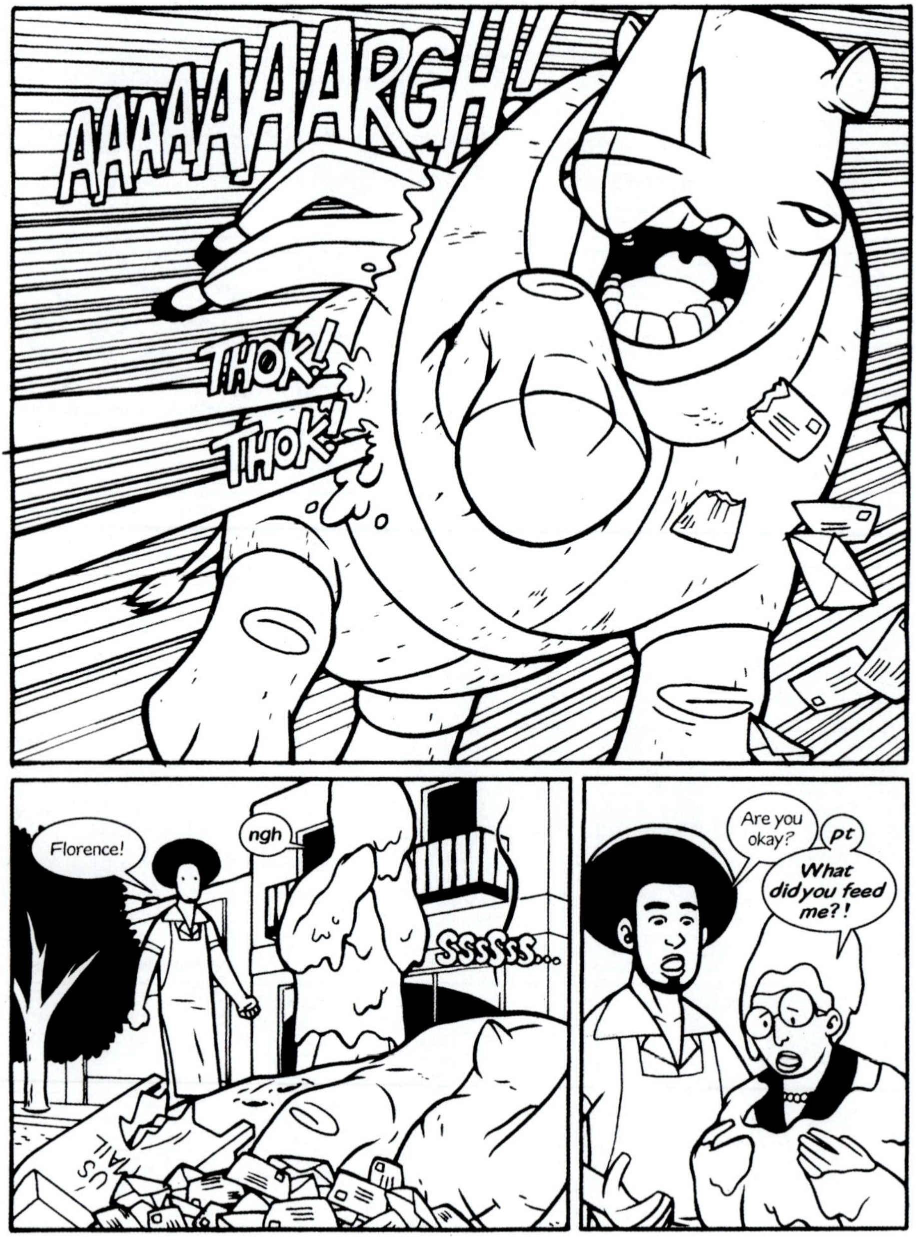
AAAAAAARGH!!
THOK!
THOK!
Florence!
ngh
SSSSSS...
US MAIL
Are you okay?
pt
What did you feed me?!

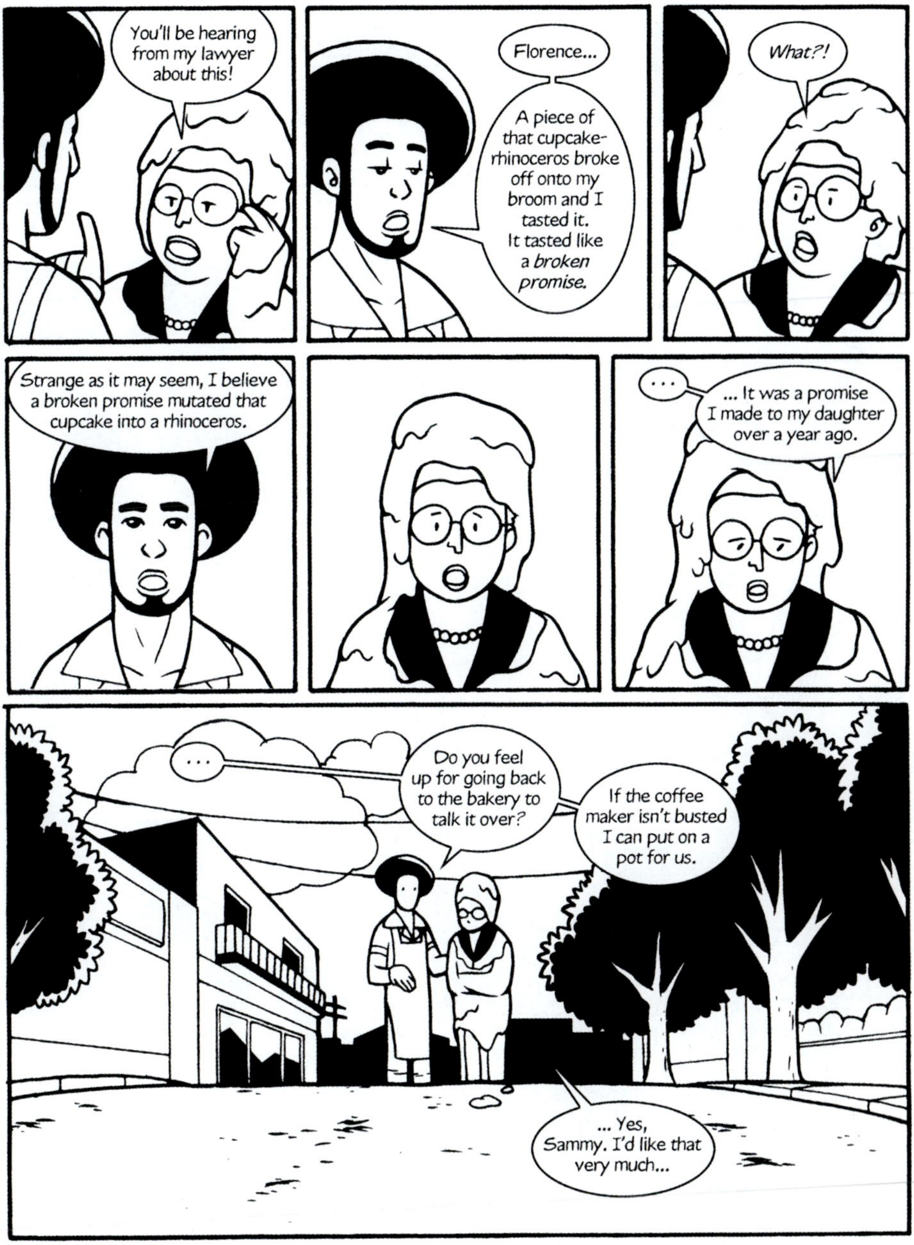
You'll be hearing from my lawyer about this!
Florence...
A piece of that cupcake-rhinoceros broke off onto my broom and I tasted it. It tasted like a *broken promise.*
What?!
Strange as it may seem, I believe a broken promise mutated that cupcake into a rhinoceros.
...
... It was a promise I made to my daughter over a year ago.
...
Do you feel up for going back to the bakery to talk it over?
If the coffee maker isn't busted I can put on a pot for us.
... Yes, Sammy. I'd like that very much...

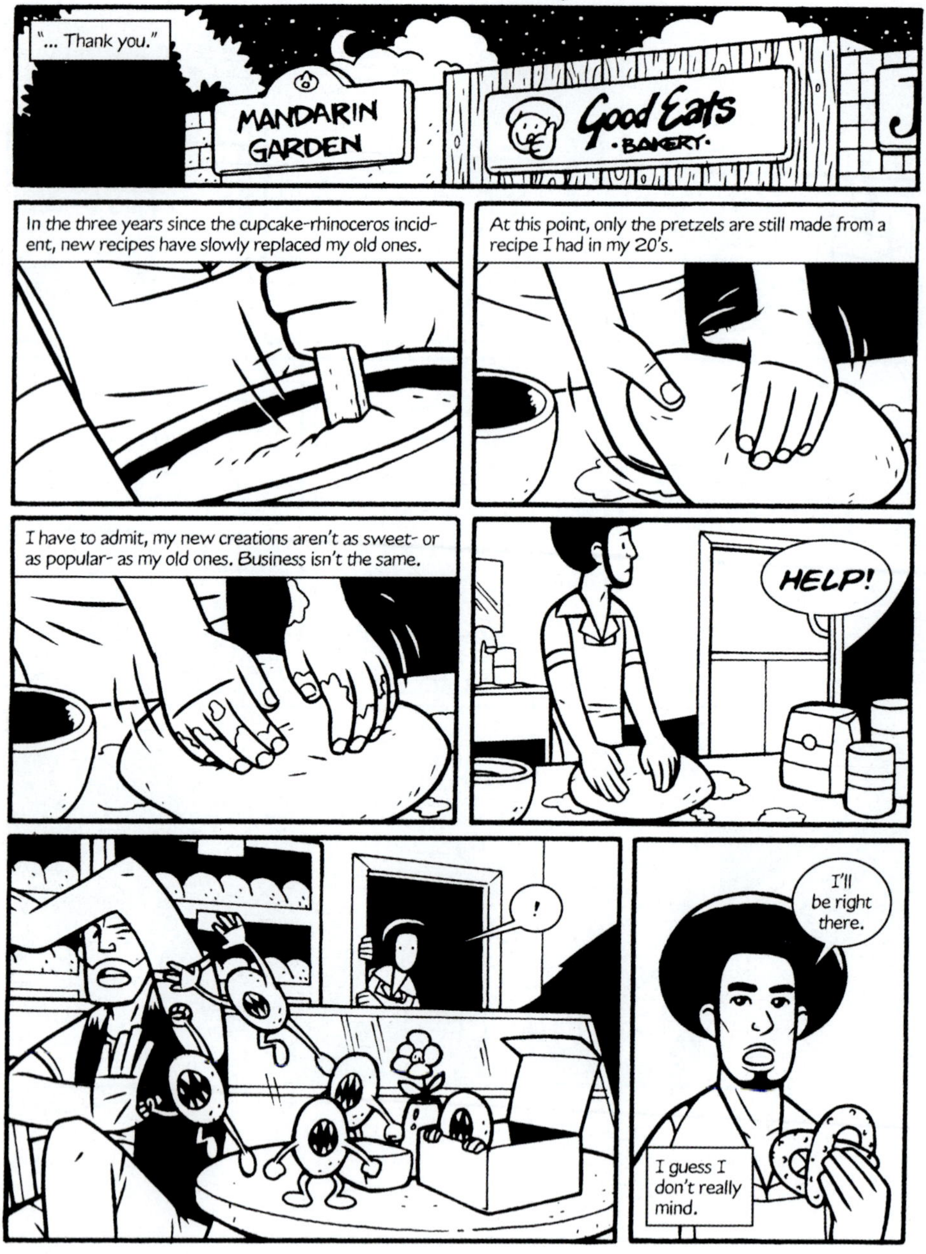
"... Thank you."
MANDARIN GARDEN
Good Eats
·BAKERY·
In the three years since the cupcake-rhinoceros incident, new recipes have slowly replaced my old ones.
At this point, only the pretzels are still made from a recipe I had in my 20's.
I have to admit, my new creations aren't as sweet- or as popular- as my old ones. Business isn't the same.
HELP!
!
I'll be right there.
I guess I don't really mind.

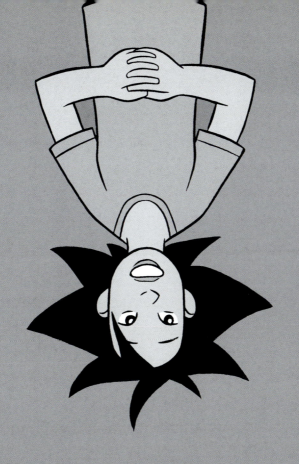

LOYOLA CHIN
and THE SAN PELIGRAN ORDER

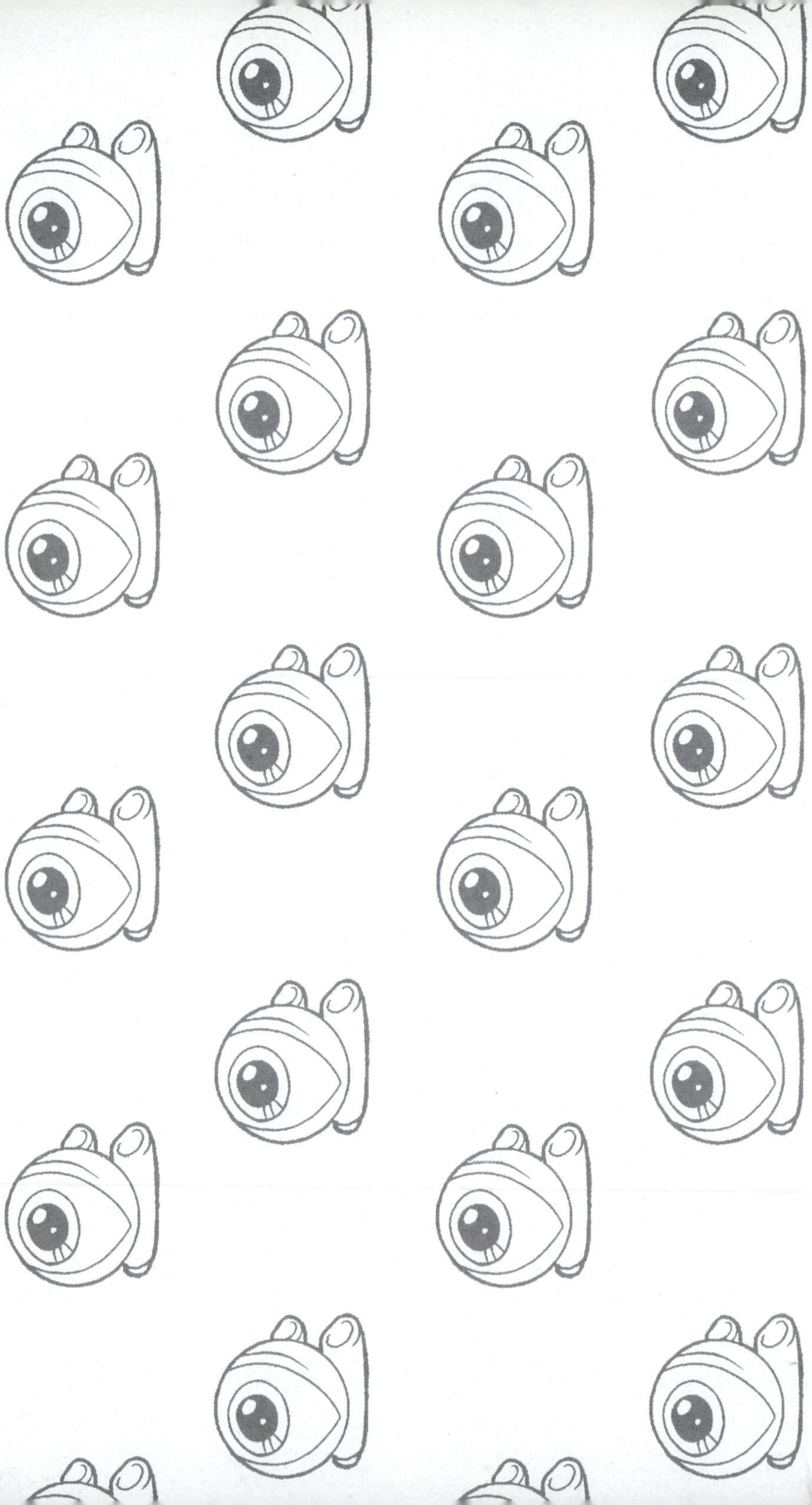

CHAPTER ONE

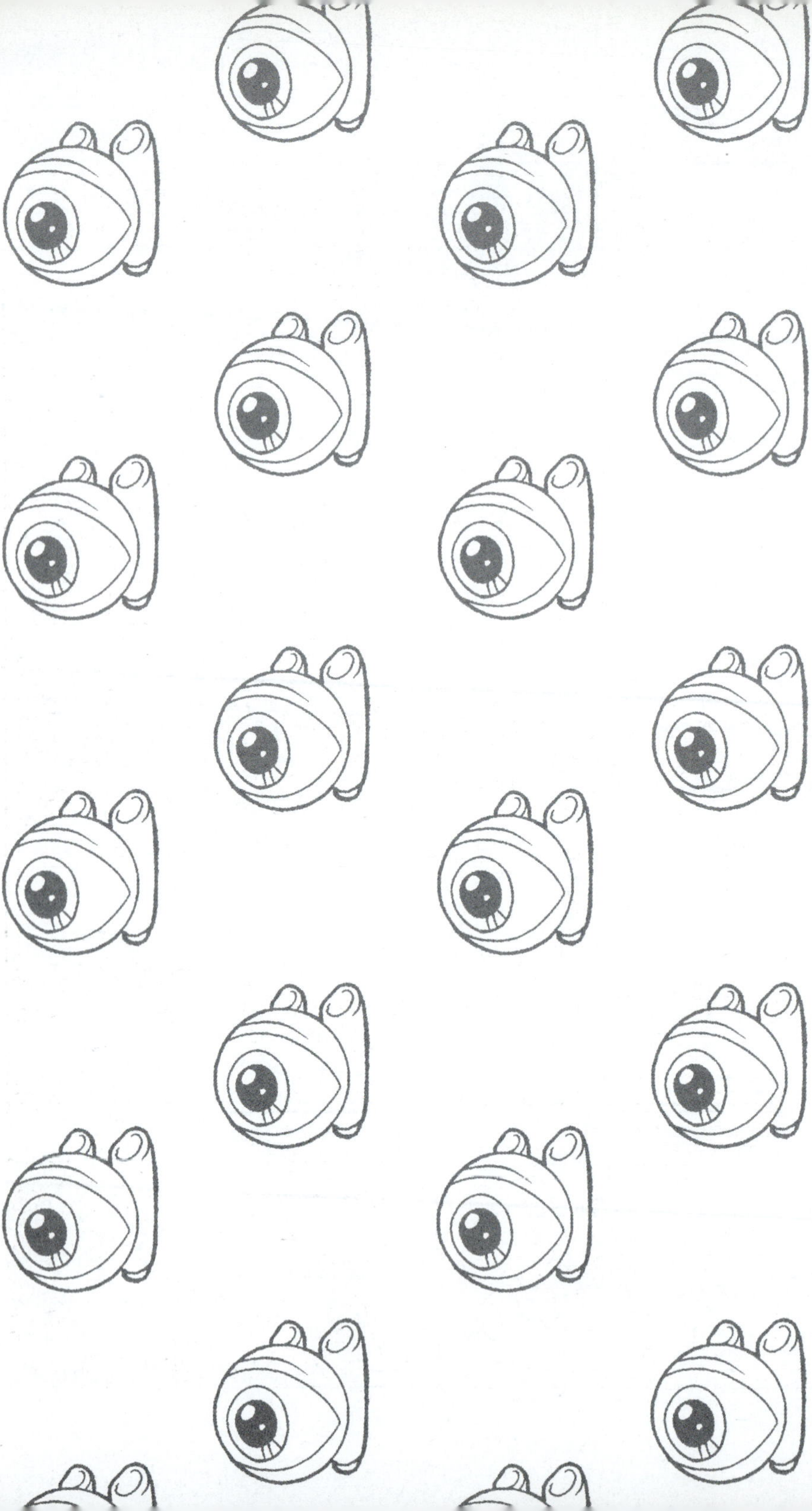

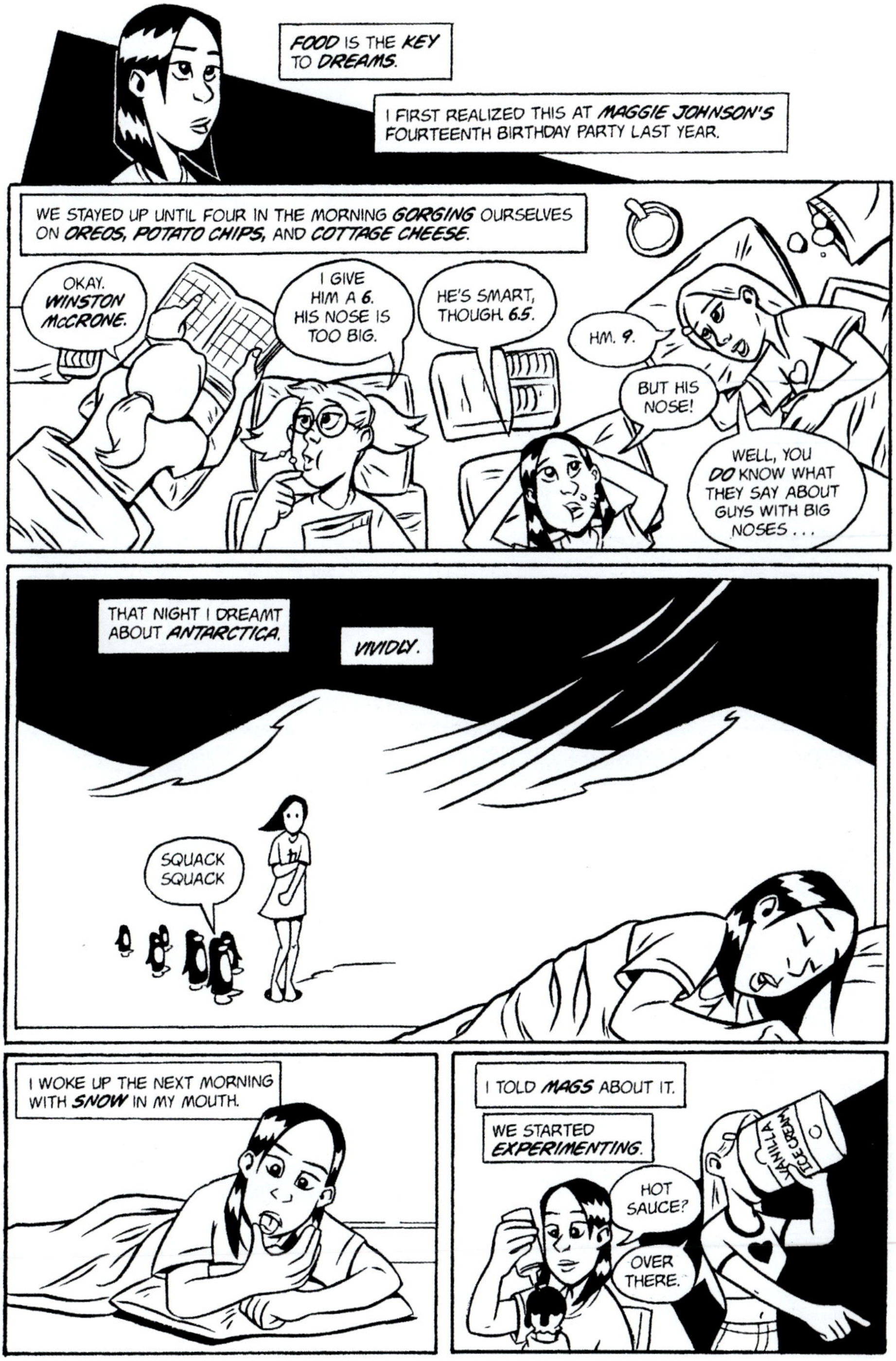

FOOD IS THE KEY TO DREAMS.
I FIRST REALIZED THIS AT MAGGIE JOHNSON'S FOURTEENTH BIRTHDAY PARTY LAST YEAR.
WE STAYED UP UNTIL FOUR IN THE MORNING GORGING OURSELVES ON OREOS, POTATO CHIPS, AND COTTAGE CHEESE.
OKAY. WINSTON McCRONE.
I GIVE HIM A 6. HIS NOSE IS TOO BIG.
HE'S SMART, THOUGH. 6.5.
HM. 9.
BUT HIS NOSE!
WELL, YOU DO KNOW WHAT THEY SAY ABOUT GUYS WITH BIG NOSES . . .
THAT NIGHT I DREAMT ABOUT ANTARCTICA.
VIVIDLY.
SQUACK SQUACK
I WOKE UP THE NEXT MORNING WITH SNOW IN MY MOUTH.
I TOLD MAGS ABOUT IT.
WE STARTED EXPERIMENTING.
VANILLA ICE CREAM
HOT SAUCE?
OVER THERE.

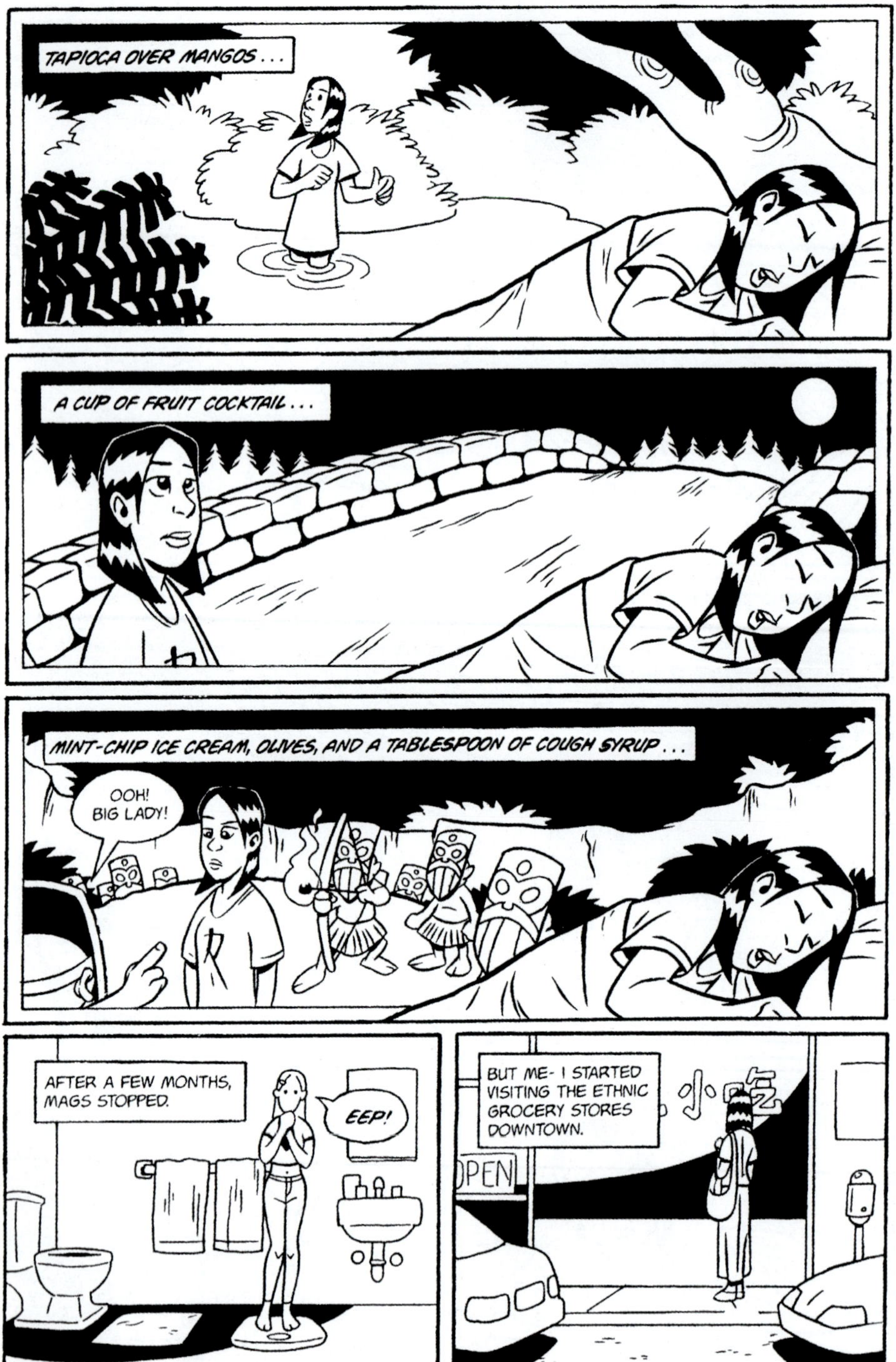
TAPIOCA OVER MANGOS...
A CUP OF FRUIT COCKTAIL...
MINT-CHIP ICE CREAM, OLIVES, AND A TABLESPOON OF COUGH SYRUP...
OOH! BIG LADY!
AFTER A FEW MONTHS, MAGS STOPPED.
EEP!
BUT ME- I STARTED VISITING THE ETHNIC GROCERY STORES DOWNTOWN.
OPEN

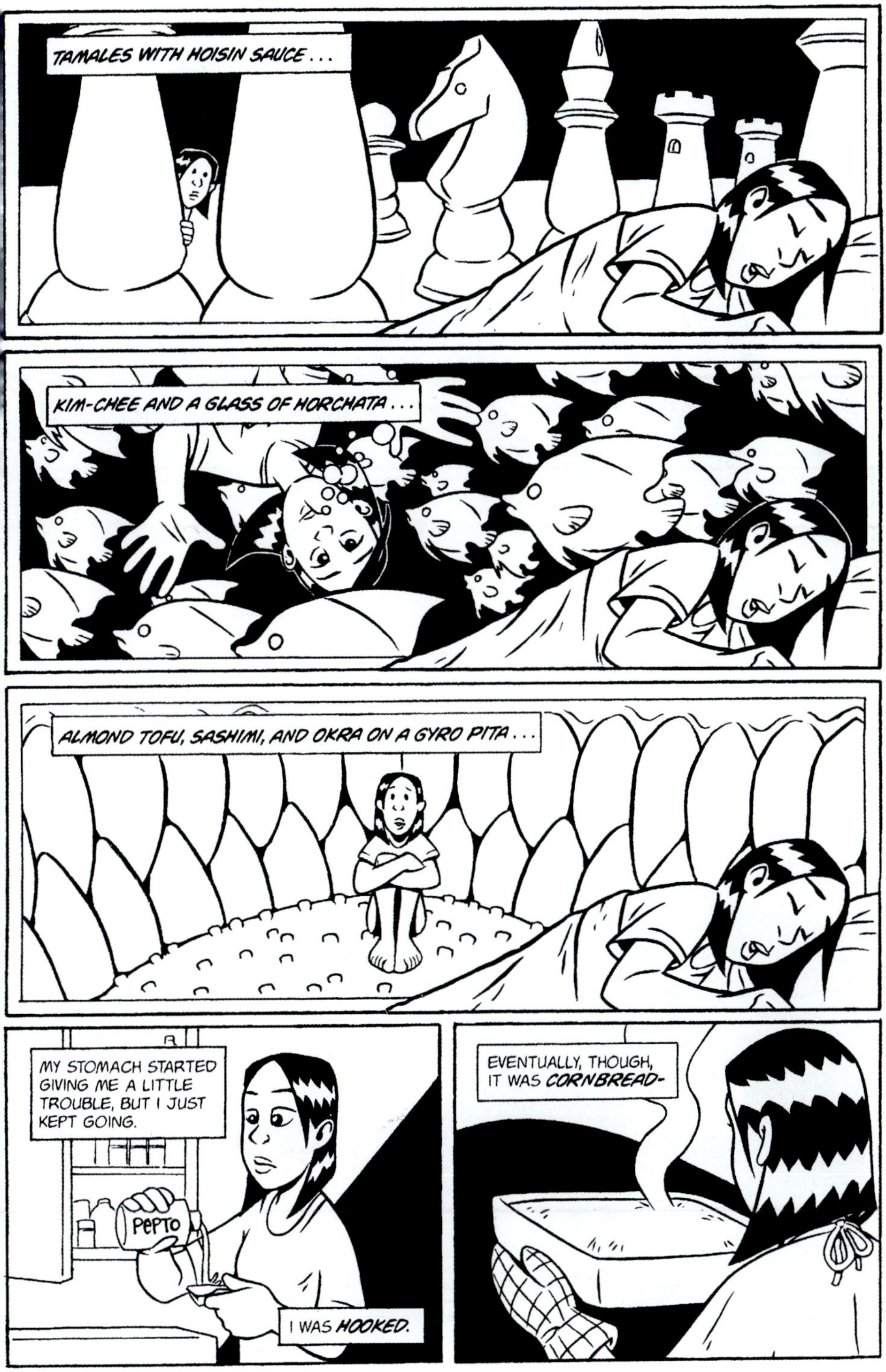

TAMALES WITH HOISIN SAUCE . . .
KIM-CHEE AND A GLASS OF HORCHATA . . .
ALMOND TOFU, SASHIMI, AND OKRA ON A GYRO PITA . . .
MY STOMACH STARTED GIVING ME A LITTLE TROUBLE, BUT I JUST KEPT GOING.
PEPTO
I WAS HOOKED.
EVENTUALLY, THOUGH, IT WAS CORNBREAD-

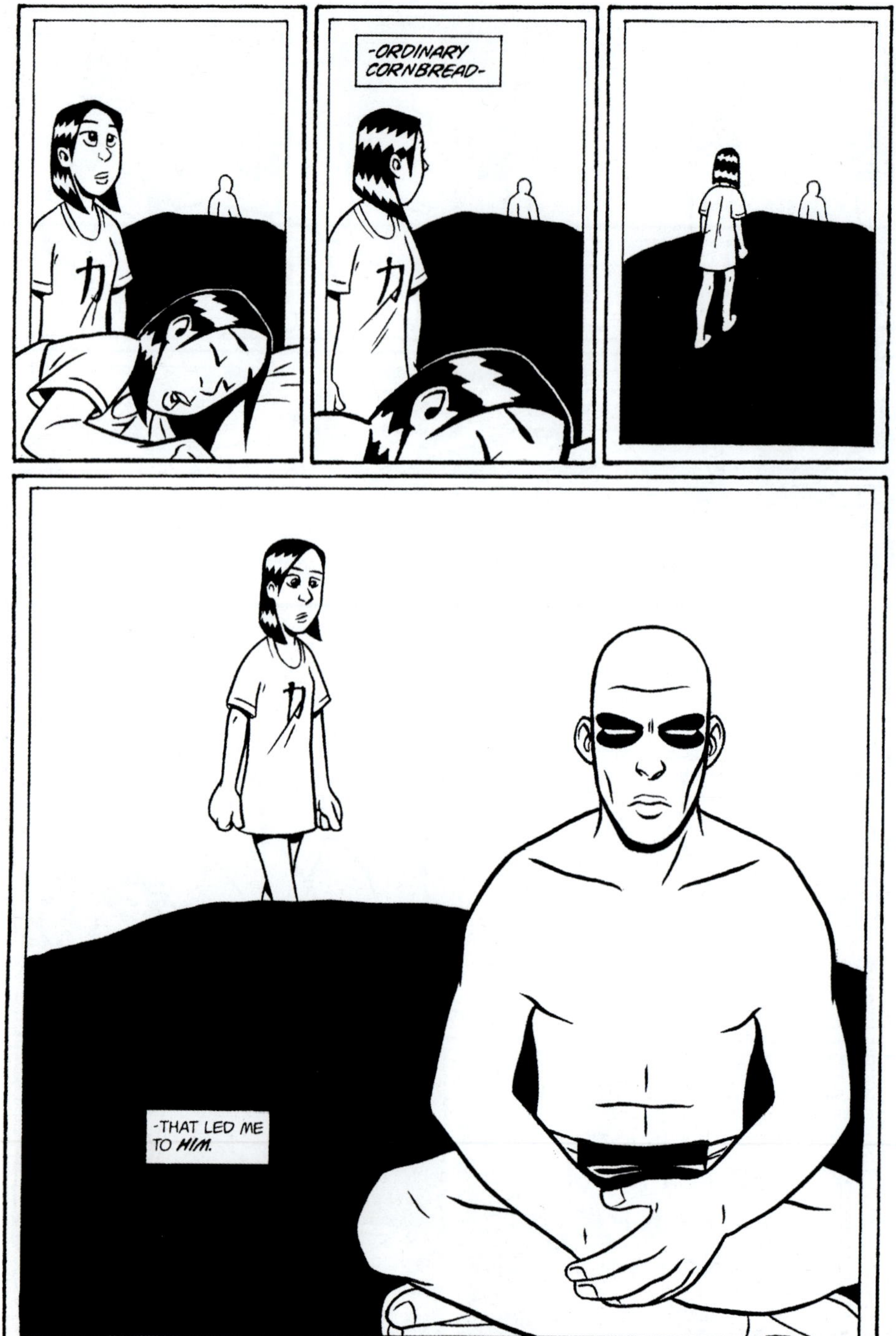
-ORDINARY CORNBREAD-
-THAT LED ME TO HIM.

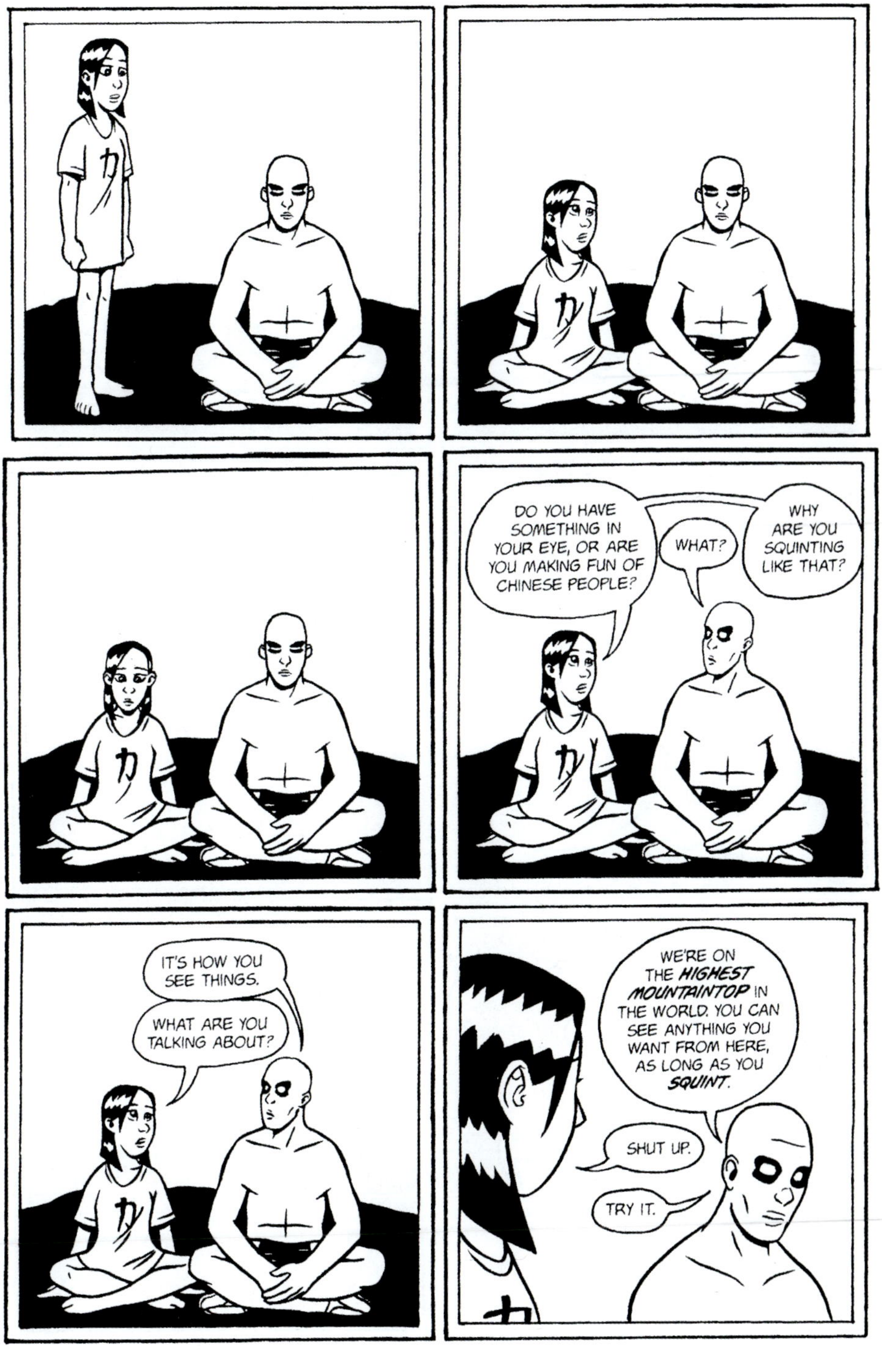
DO YOU HAVE SOMETHING IN YOUR EYE, OR ARE YOU MAKING FUN OF CHINESE PEOPLE?
WHAT?
WHY ARE YOU SQUINTING LIKE THAT?
IT'S HOW YOU SEE THINGS.
WHAT ARE YOU TALKING ABOUT?
WE'RE ON THE HIGHEST MOUNTAINTOP IN THE WORLD. YOU CAN SEE ANYTHING YOU WANT FROM HERE, AS LONG AS YOU SQUINT.
SHUT UP.
TRY IT.

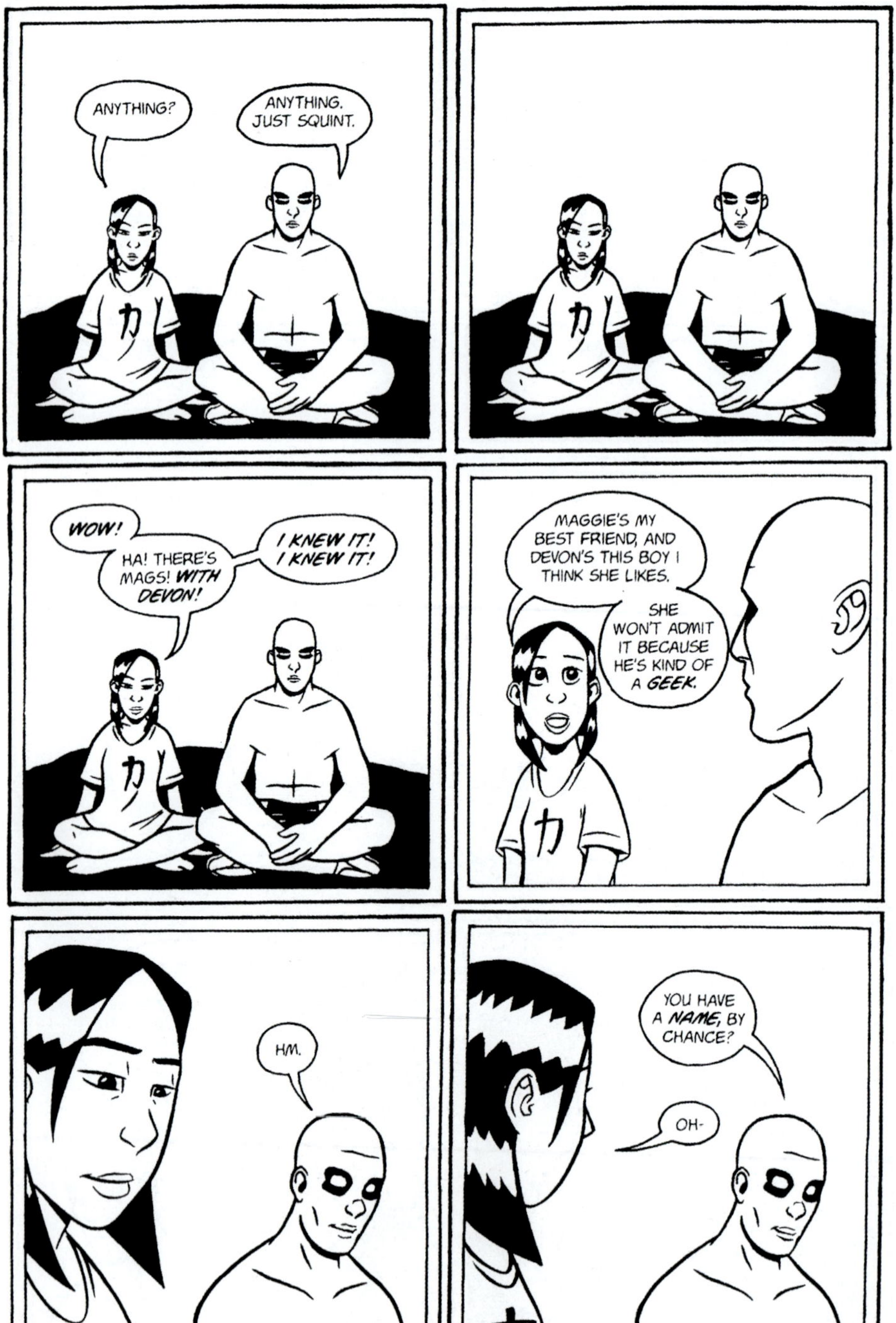
ANYTHING?
ANYTHING. JUST SQUINT.
WOW!
HA! THERE'S MAGS! **WITH DEVON!**
I KNEW IT! I KNEW IT!
MAGGIE'S MY BEST FRIEND, AND DEVON'S THIS BOY I THINK SHE LIKES.
SHE WON'T ADMIT IT BECAUSE HE'S KIND OF A **GEEK.**
HM.
YOU HAVE A **NAME**, BY CHANCE?
OH-

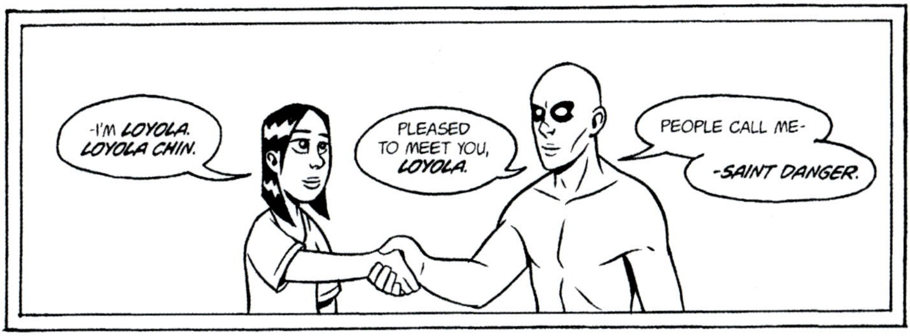
-I'M LOYOLA. LOYOLA CHIN.
PLEASED TO MEET YOU, LOYOLA.
PEOPLE CALL ME-
-SAINT DANGER.

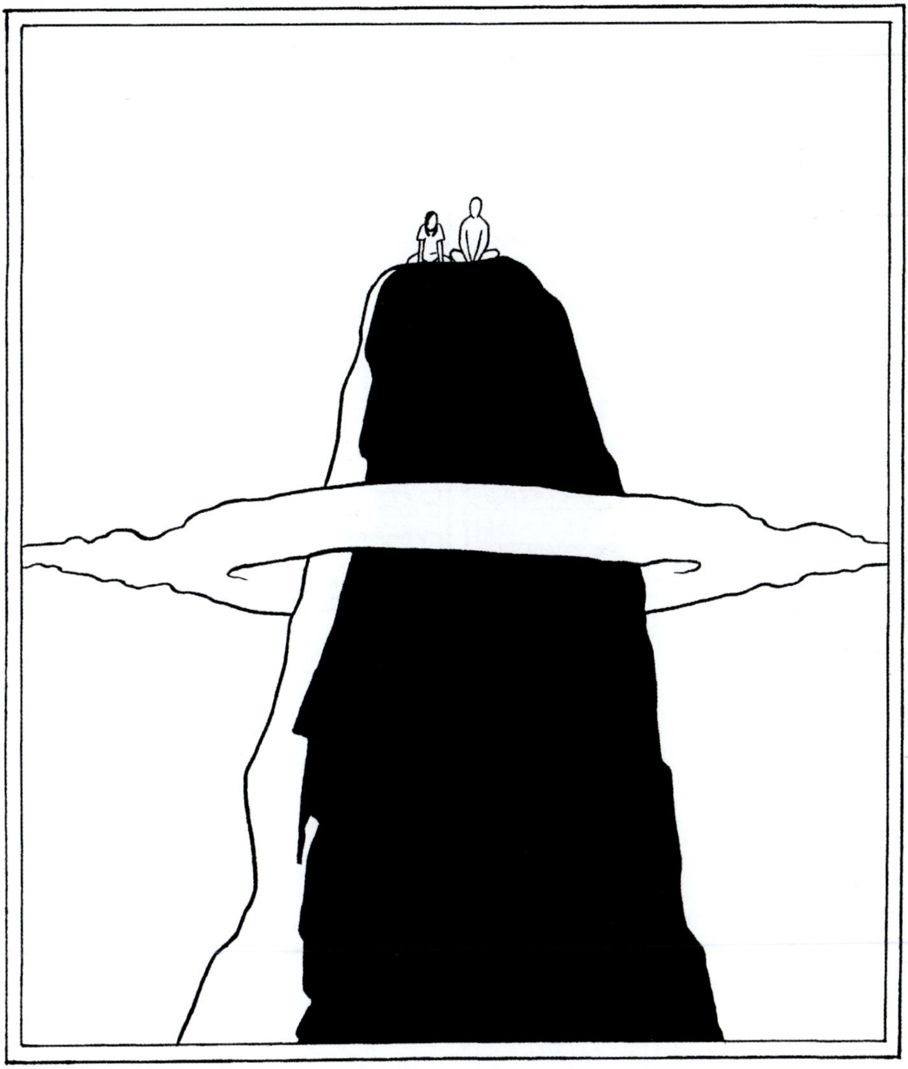

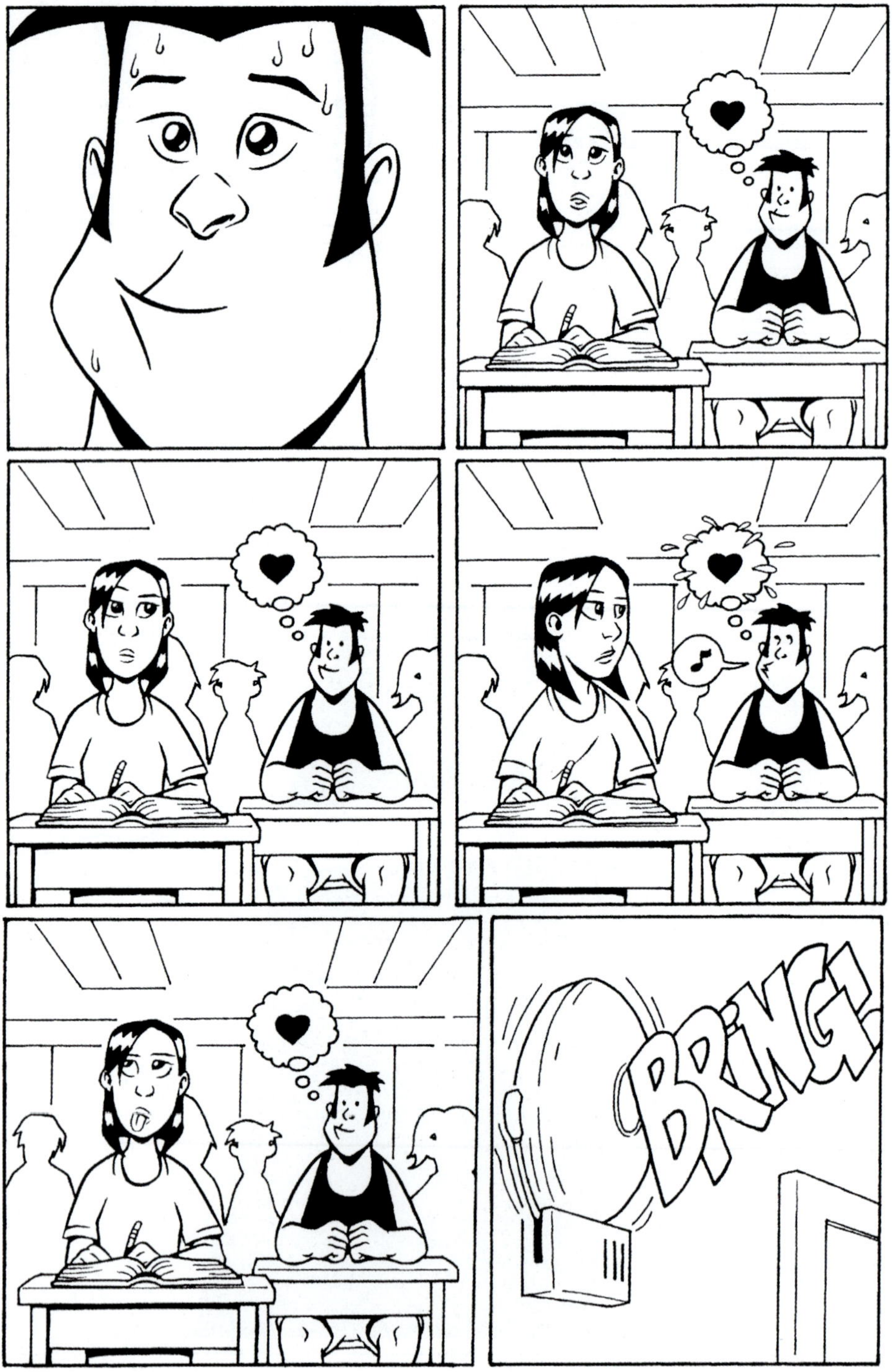
BRING!

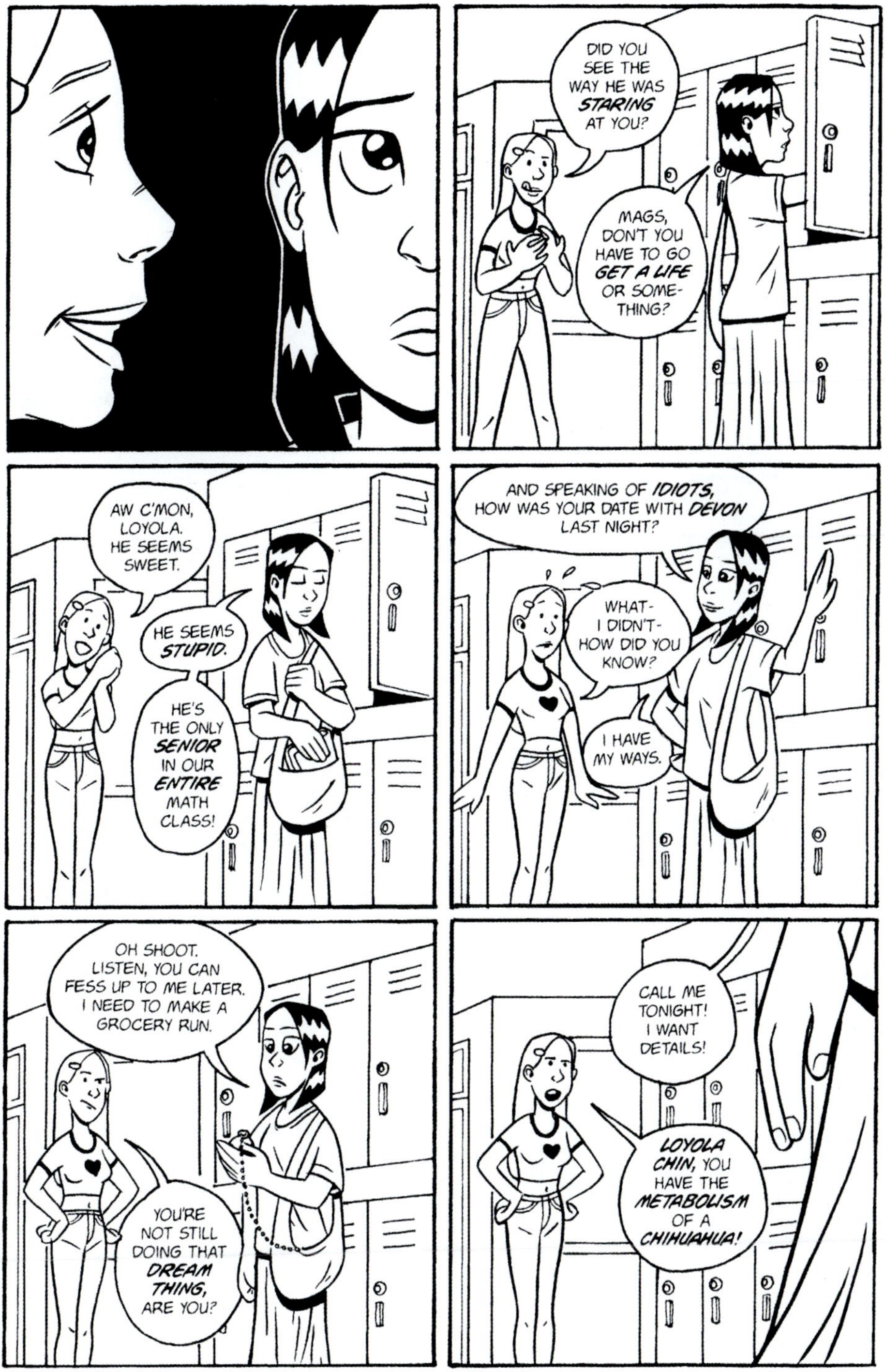
DID YOU SEE THE WAY HE WAS STARING AT YOU?
MAGS, DON'T YOU HAVE TO GO GET A LIFE OR SOME-THING?
AW C'MON, LOYOLA. HE SEEMS SWEET.
HE SEEMS STUPID.
HE'S THE ONLY SENIOR IN OUR ENTIRE MATH CLASS!
AND SPEAKING OF IDIOTS, HOW WAS YOUR DATE WITH DEVON LAST NIGHT?
WHAT- I DIDN'T- HOW DID YOU KNOW?
I HAVE MY WAYS.
OH SHOOT. LISTEN, YOU CAN FESS UP TO ME LATER. I NEED TO MAKE A GROCERY RUN.
YOU'RE NOT STILL DOING THAT DREAM THING, ARE YOU?
CALL ME TONIGHT! I WANT DETAILS!
LOYOLA CHIN, YOU HAVE THE METABOLISM OF A CHIHUAHUA!

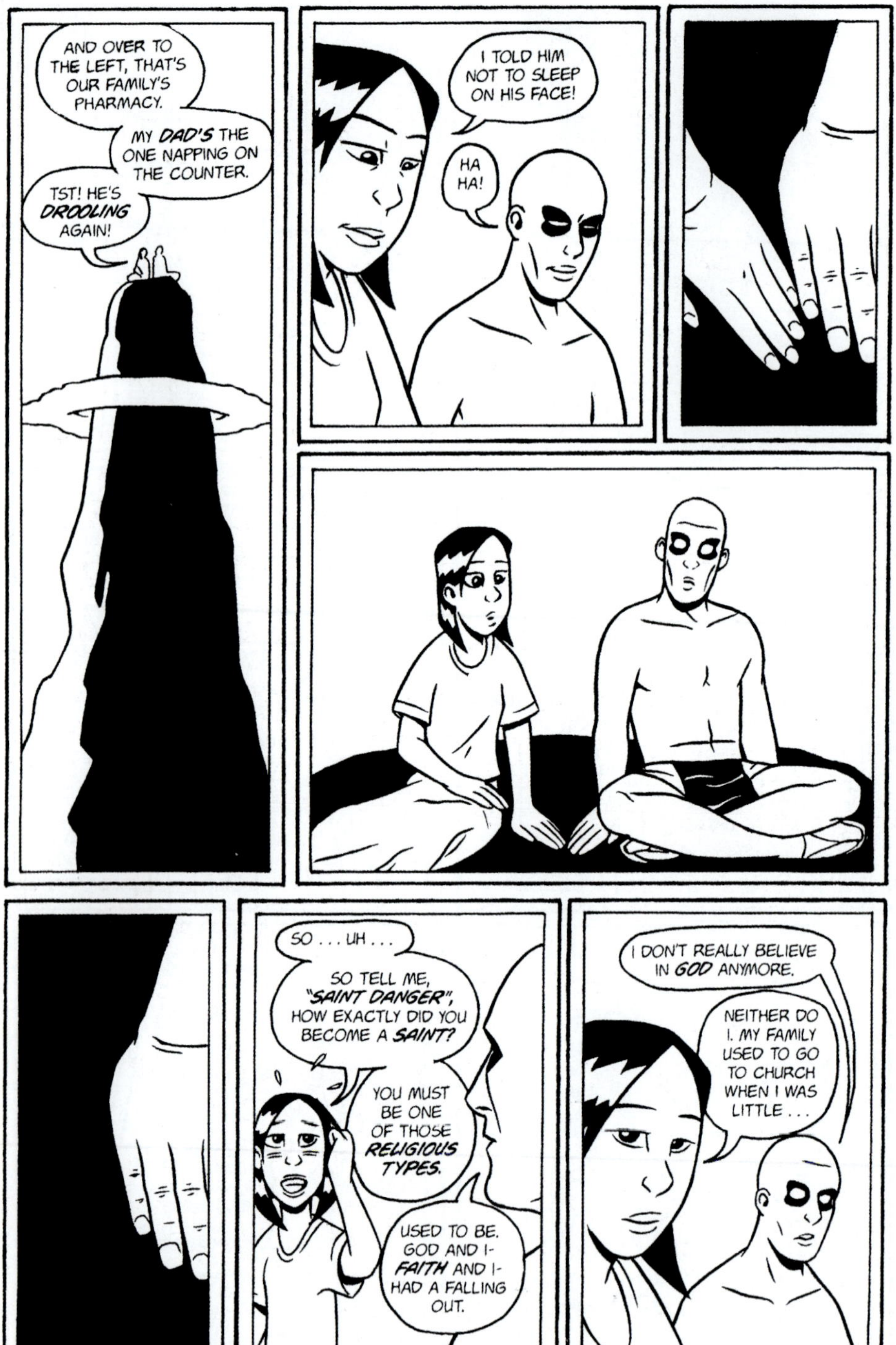
AND OVER TO THE LEFT, THAT'S OUR FAMILY'S PHARMACY.
MY ***DAD'S*** THE ONE NAPPING ON THE COUNTER.
TST! HE'S ***DROOLING*** AGAIN!
I TOLD HIM NOT TO SLEEP ON HIS FACE!
HA HA!
SO . . . UH . . .
SO TELL ME, ***"SAINT DANGER"***, HOW EXACTLY DID YOU BECOME A ***SAINT?***
YOU MUST BE ONE OF THOSE ***RELIGIOUS TYPES.***
USED TO BE. GOD AND I- ***FAITH*** AND I- HAD A FALLING OUT.
I DON'T REALLY BELIEVE IN ***GOD*** ANYMORE.
NEITHER DO I. MY FAMILY USED TO GO TO CHURCH WHEN I WAS LITTLE . . .

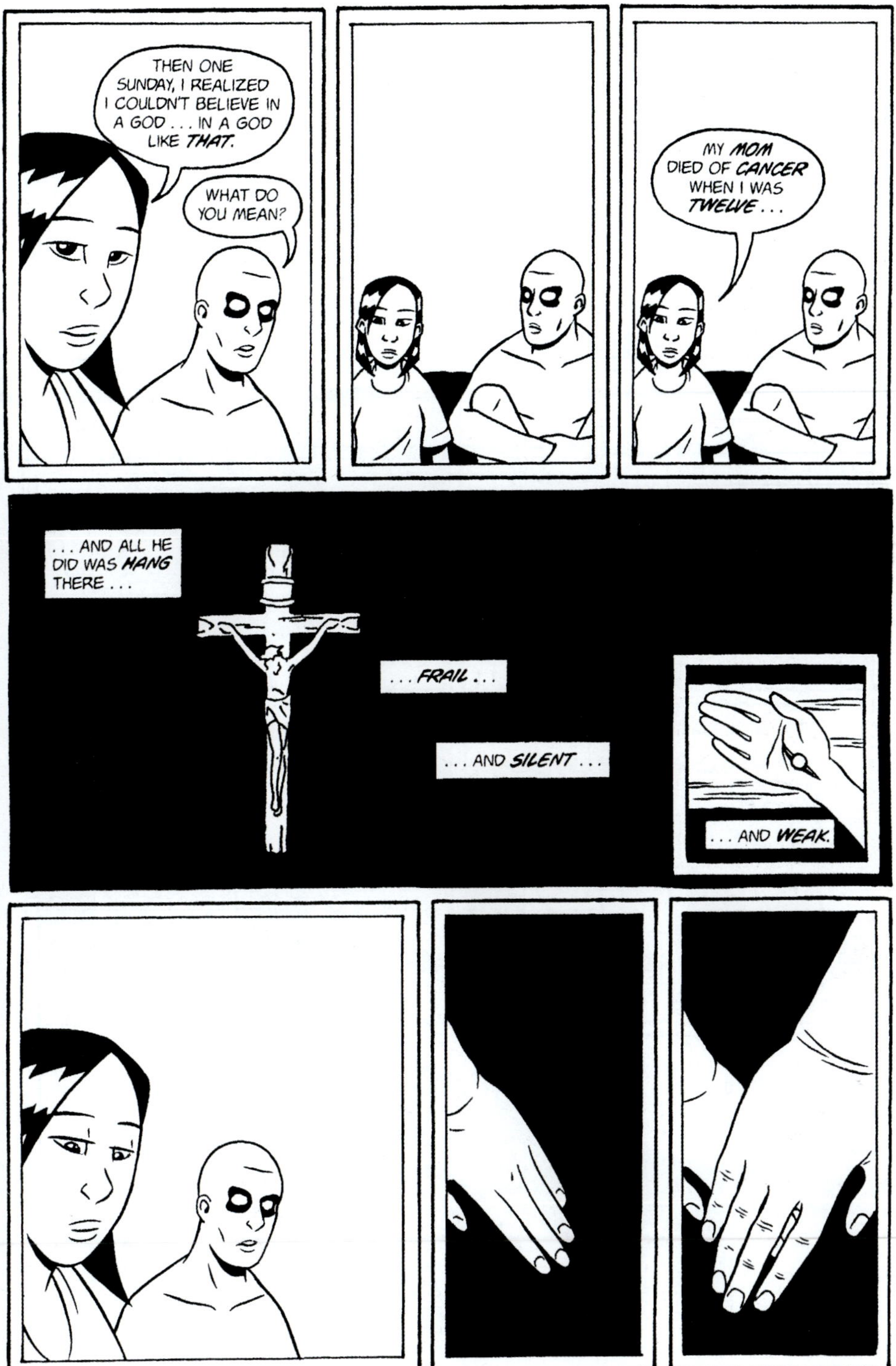
THEN ONE SUNDAY, I REALIZED I COULDN'T BELIEVE IN A GOD . . . IN A GOD LIKE THAT.
WHAT DO YOU MEAN?
MY MOM DIED OF CANCER WHEN I WAS TWELVE . . .
. . . AND ALL HE DID WAS HANG THERE . . .
. . . FRAIL . . .
. . . AND SILENT . . .
. . . AND WEAK.

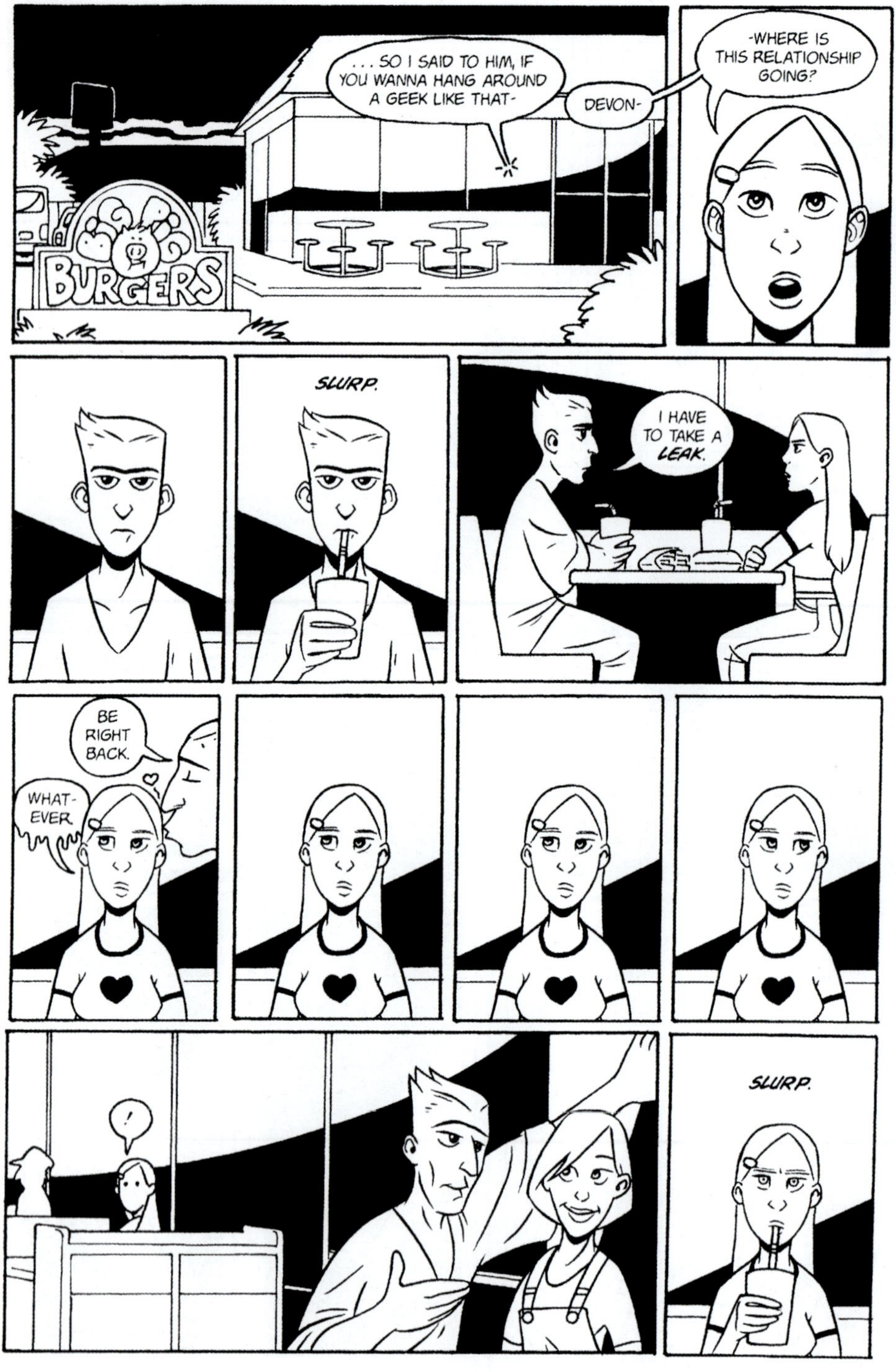
. . . SO I SAID TO HIM, IF YOU WANNA HANG AROUND A GEEK LIKE THAT-
BURGERS
DEVON-
-WHERE IS THIS RELATIONSHIP GOING?
SLURP.
I HAVE TO TAKE A LEAK.
BE RIGHT BACK.
WHAT-EVER.
!
SLURP.

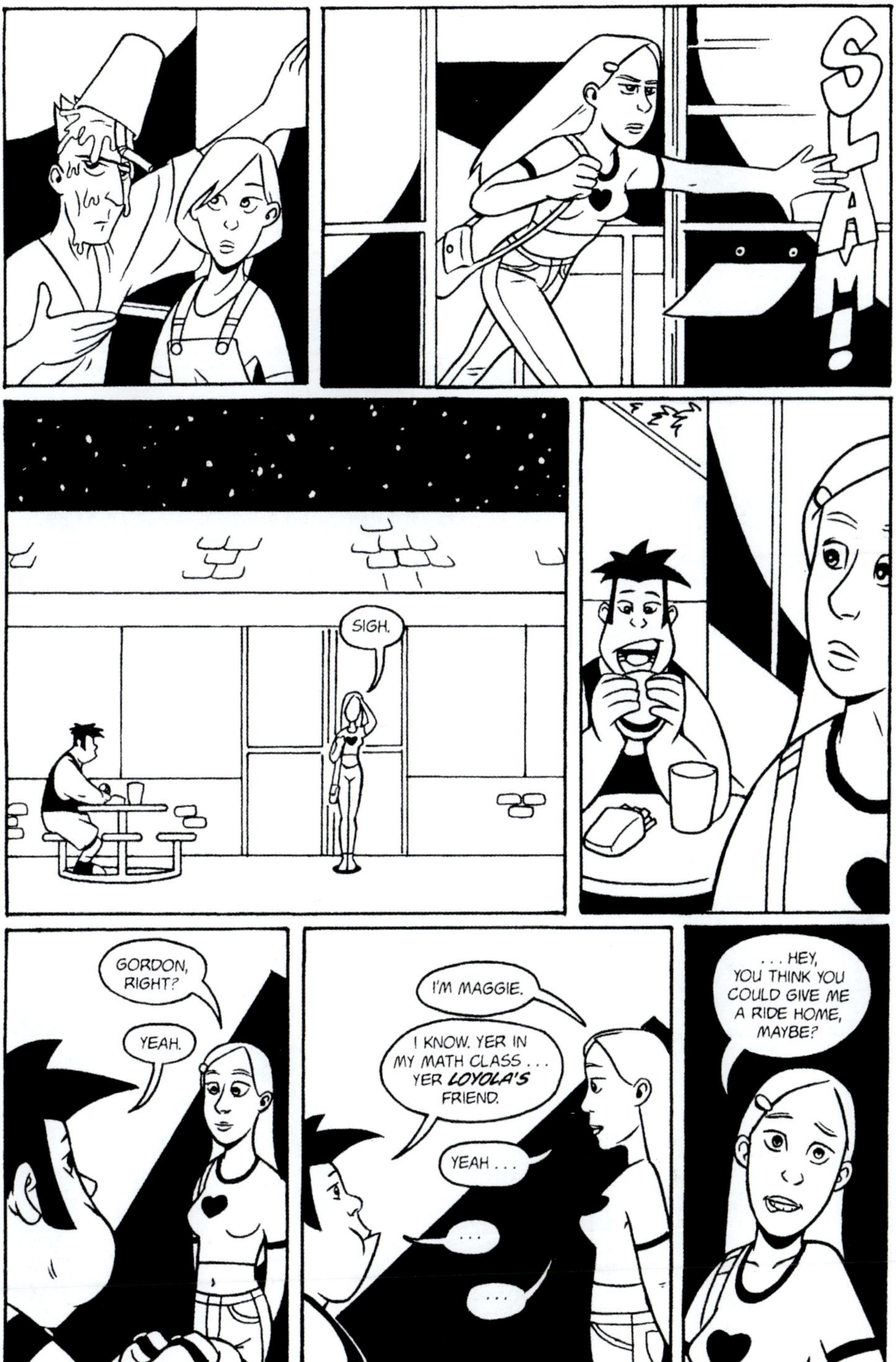
SLAM!
SIGH.
GORDON, RIGHT?
YEAH.
I'M MAGGIE.
I KNOW. YER IN MY MATH CLASS . . . YER *LOYOLA'S* FRIEND.
YEAH . . .
. . .
. . .
. . . HEY, YOU THINK YOU COULD GIVE ME A RIDE HOME, MAYBE?

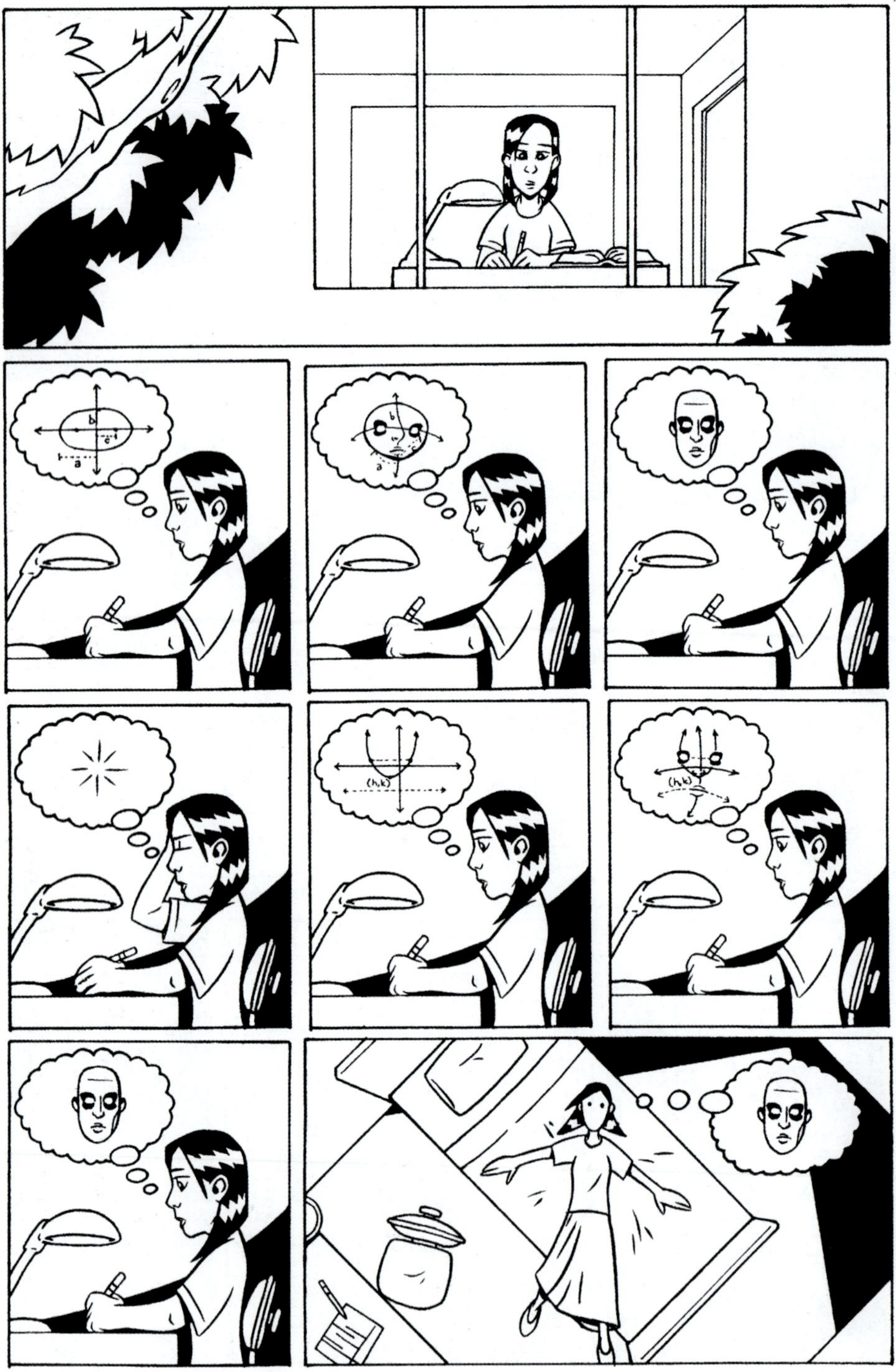
b
c
a
b
a
(h,k)
(h,k)

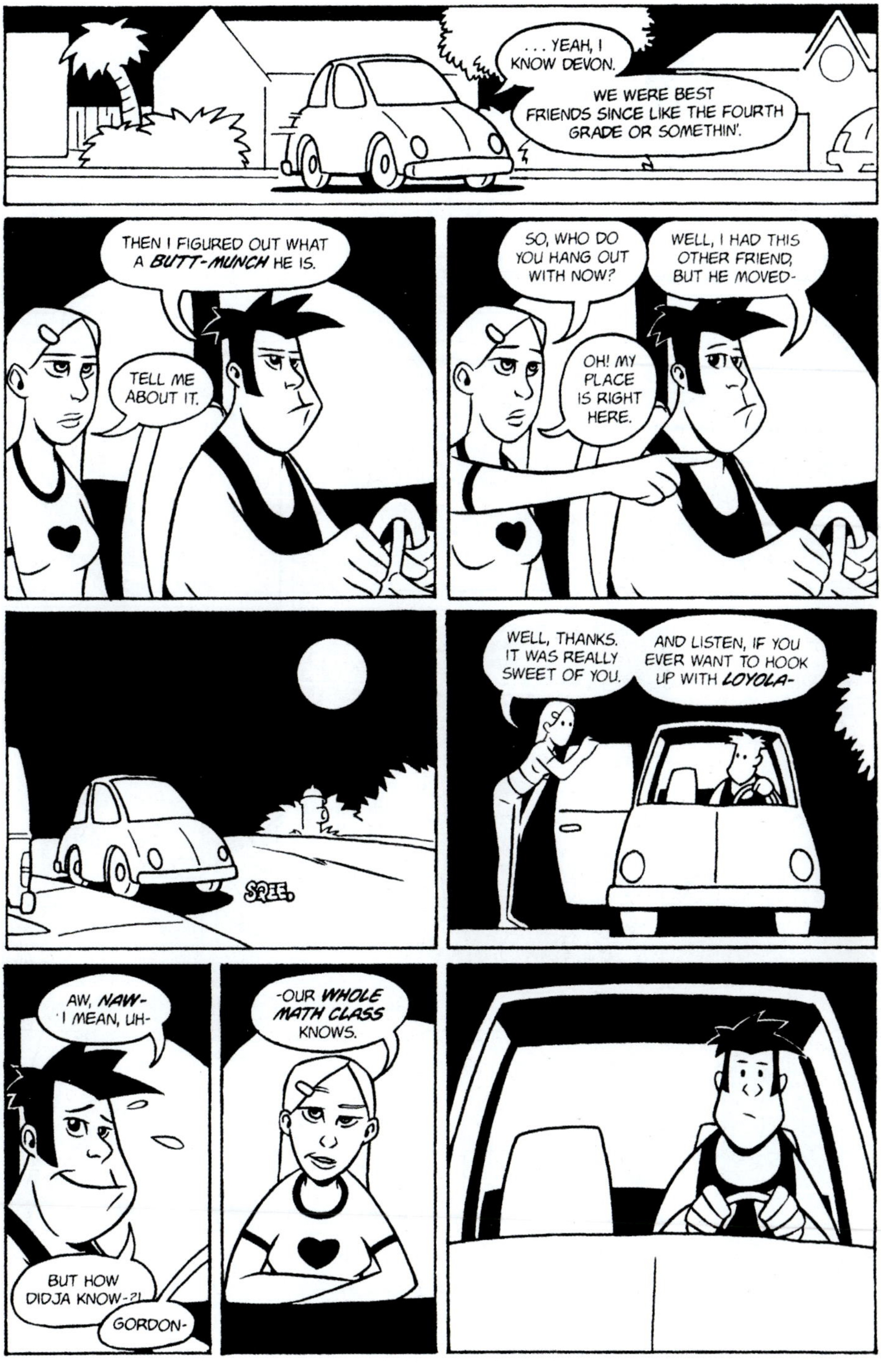
. . . YEAH, I KNOW DEVON.
WE WERE BEST FRIENDS SINCE LIKE THE FOURTH GRADE OR SOMETHIN'.
THEN I FIGURED OUT WHAT A BUTT-MUNCH HE IS.
TELL ME ABOUT IT.
SO, WHO DO YOU HANG OUT WITH NOW?
WELL, I HAD THIS OTHER FRIEND, BUT HE MOVED-
OH! MY PLACE IS RIGHT HERE.
SQEE.
WELL, THANKS. IT WAS REALLY SWEET OF YOU.
AND LISTEN, IF YOU EVER WANT TO HOOK UP WITH LOYOLA-
AW, NAW- I MEAN, UH-
BUT HOW DIDJA KNOW-?!
GORDON-
-OUR WHOLE MATH CLASS KNOWS.

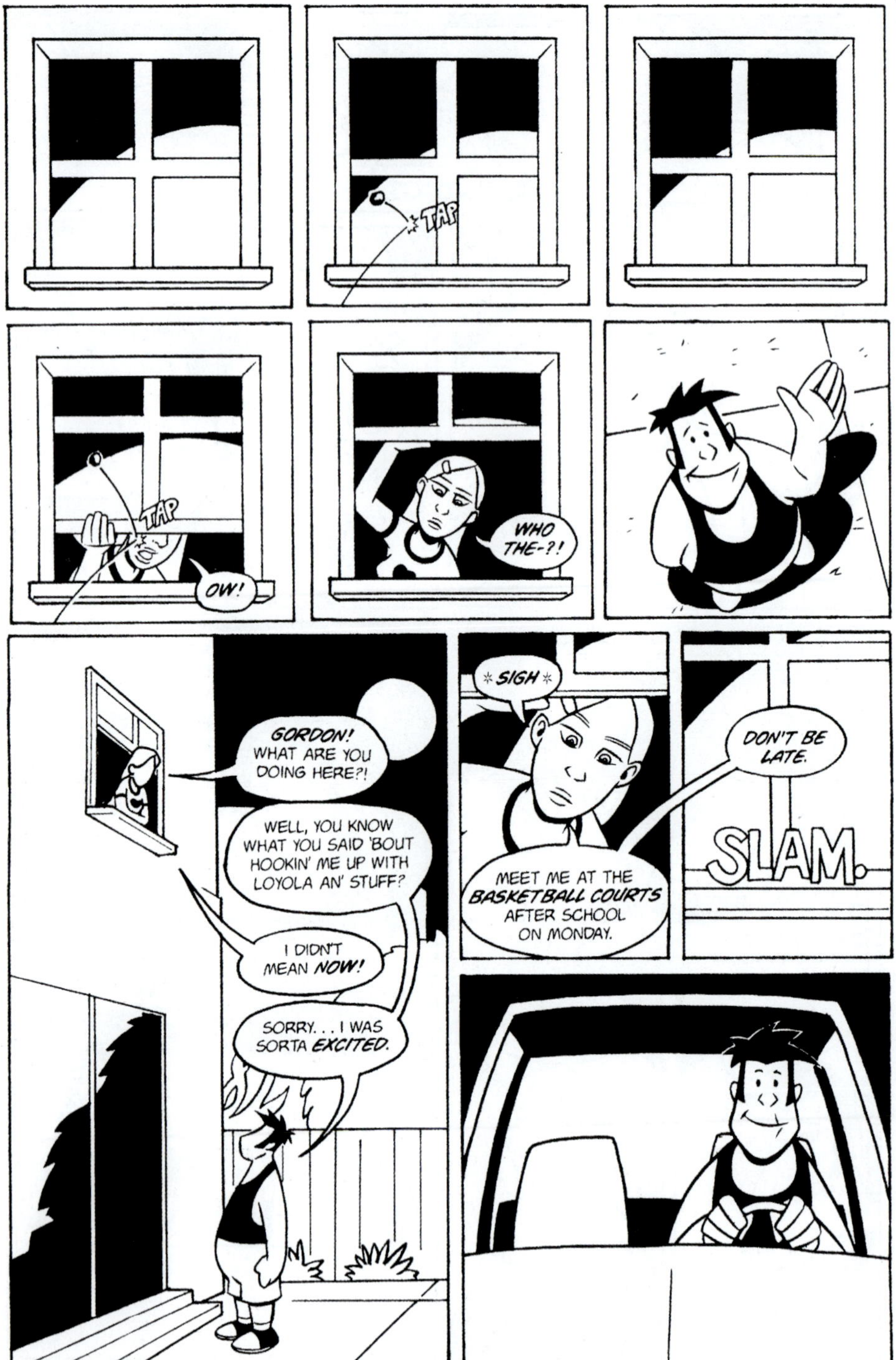
TAP
TAP
OW!
WHO THE-?!
GORDON! WHAT ARE YOU DOING HERE?!
WELL, YOU KNOW WHAT YOU SAID 'BOUT HOOKIN' ME UP WITH LOYOLA AN' STUFF?
I DIDN'T MEAN NOW!
SORRY. . . I WAS SORTA EXCITED.
SIGH
MEET ME AT THE BASKETBALL COURTS AFTER SCHOOL ON MONDAY.
DON'T BE LATE.
SLAM.

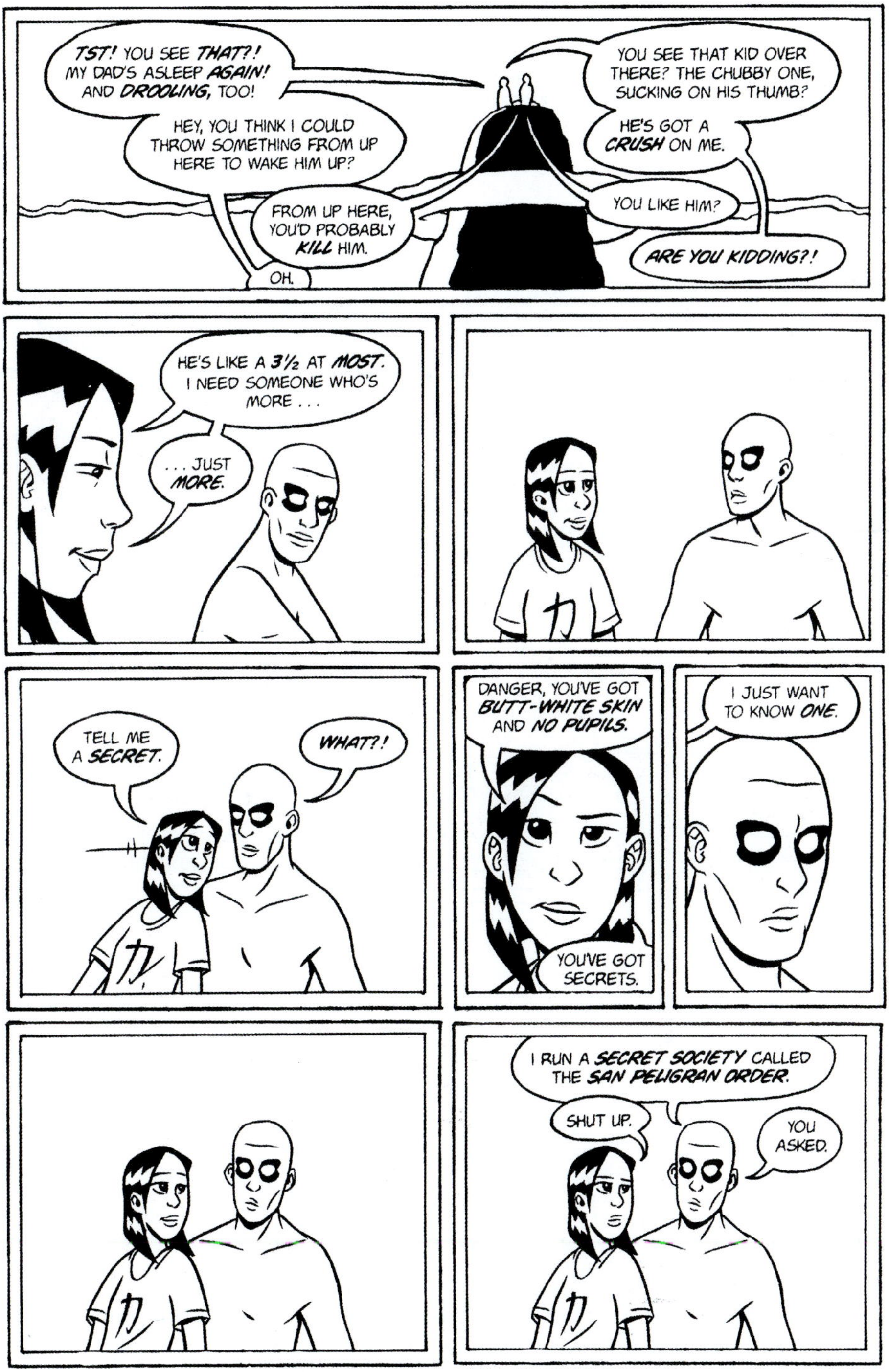
TST! YOU SEE THAT?! MY DAD'S ASLEEP AGAIN! AND DROOLING, TOO!
YOU SEE THAT KID OVER THERE? THE CHUBBY ONE, SUCKING ON HIS THUMB?
HE'S GOT A CRUSH ON ME.
HEY, YOU THINK I COULD THROW SOMETHING FROM UP HERE TO WAKE HIM UP?
FROM UP HERE, YOU'D PROBABLY KILL HIM.
OH.
YOU LIKE HIM?
ARE YOU KIDDING?!
HE'S LIKE A 3½ AT MOST. I NEED SOMEONE WHO'S MORE . . .
. . . JUST MORE.
TELL ME A SECRET.
WHAT?!
DANGER, YOU'VE GOT BUTT-WHITE SKIN AND NO PUPILS.
YOU'VE GOT SECRETS.
I JUST WANT TO KNOW ONE.
I RUN A SECRET SOCIETY CALLED THE SAN PELIGRAN ORDER.
SHUT UP.
YOU ASKED.

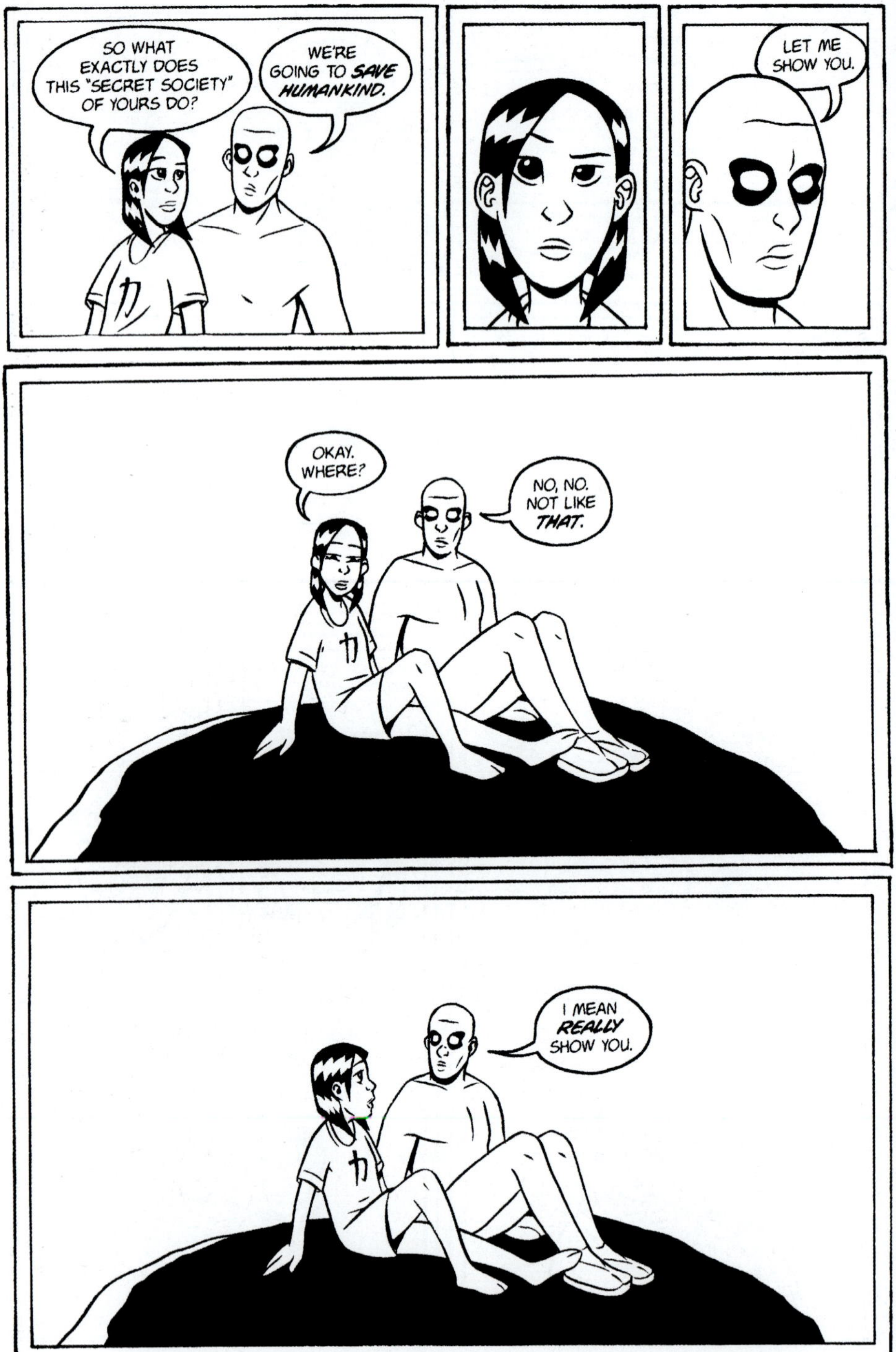
SO WHAT EXACTLY DOES THIS "SECRET SOCIETY" OF YOURS DO?
WE'RE GOING TO SAVE HUMANKIND.
LET ME SHOW YOU.
OKAY. WHERE?
NO, NO. NOT LIKE THAT.
I MEAN REALLY SHOW YOU.

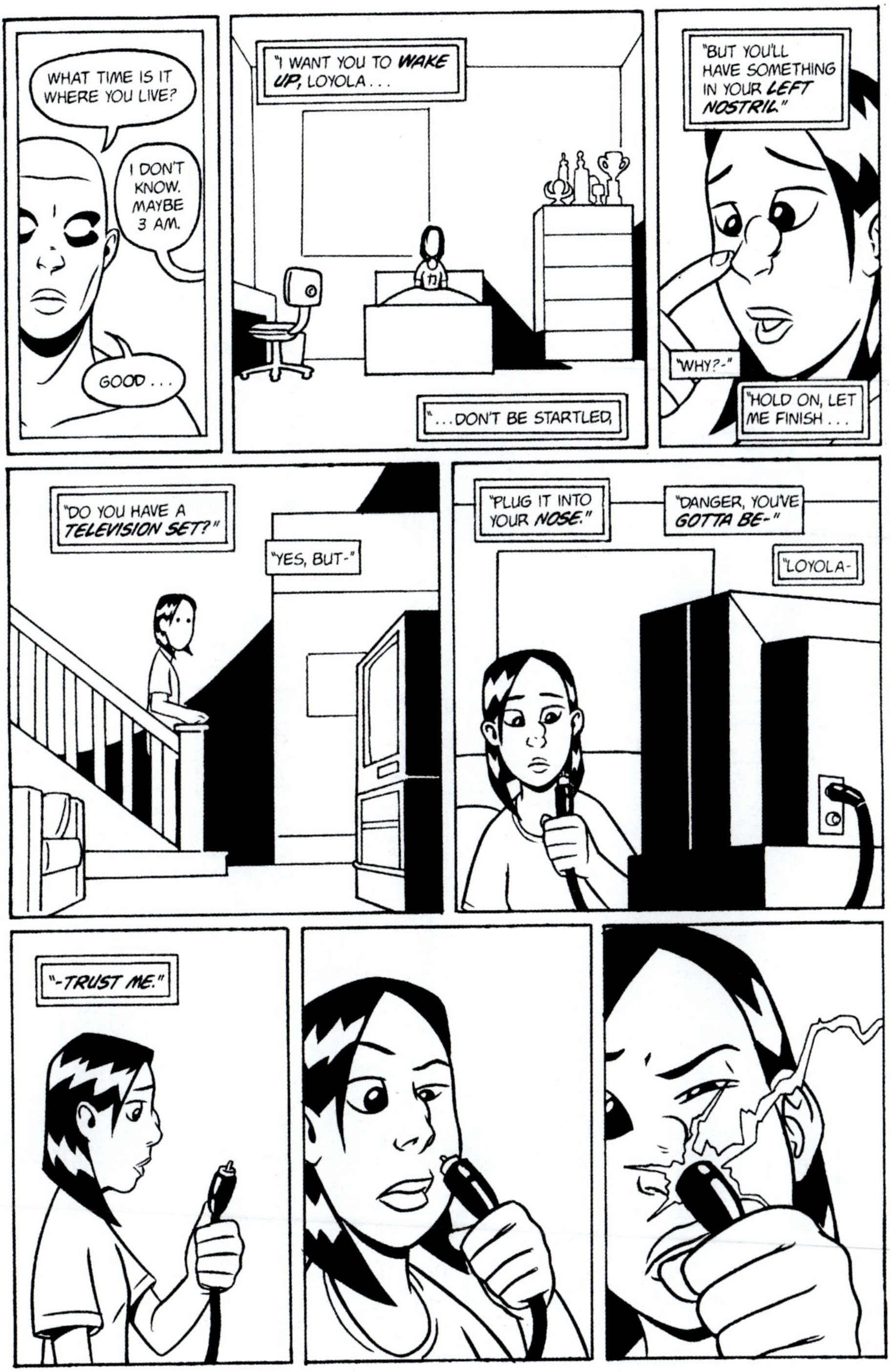
WHAT TIME IS IT WHERE YOU LIVE?
I DON'T KNOW. MAYBE 3 AM.
GOOD . . .
"I WANT YOU TO WAKE UP, LOYOLA . . .
". . . DON'T BE STARTLED,
"BUT YOU'LL HAVE SOMETHING IN YOUR LEFT NOSTRIL."
"WHY?-"
"HOLD ON, LET ME FINISH . . .
"DO YOU HAVE A TELEVISION SET?"
"YES, BUT-"
"PLUG IT INTO YOUR NOSE."
"DANGER, YOU'VE GOTTA BE-"
"LOYOLA-
"-TRUST ME."

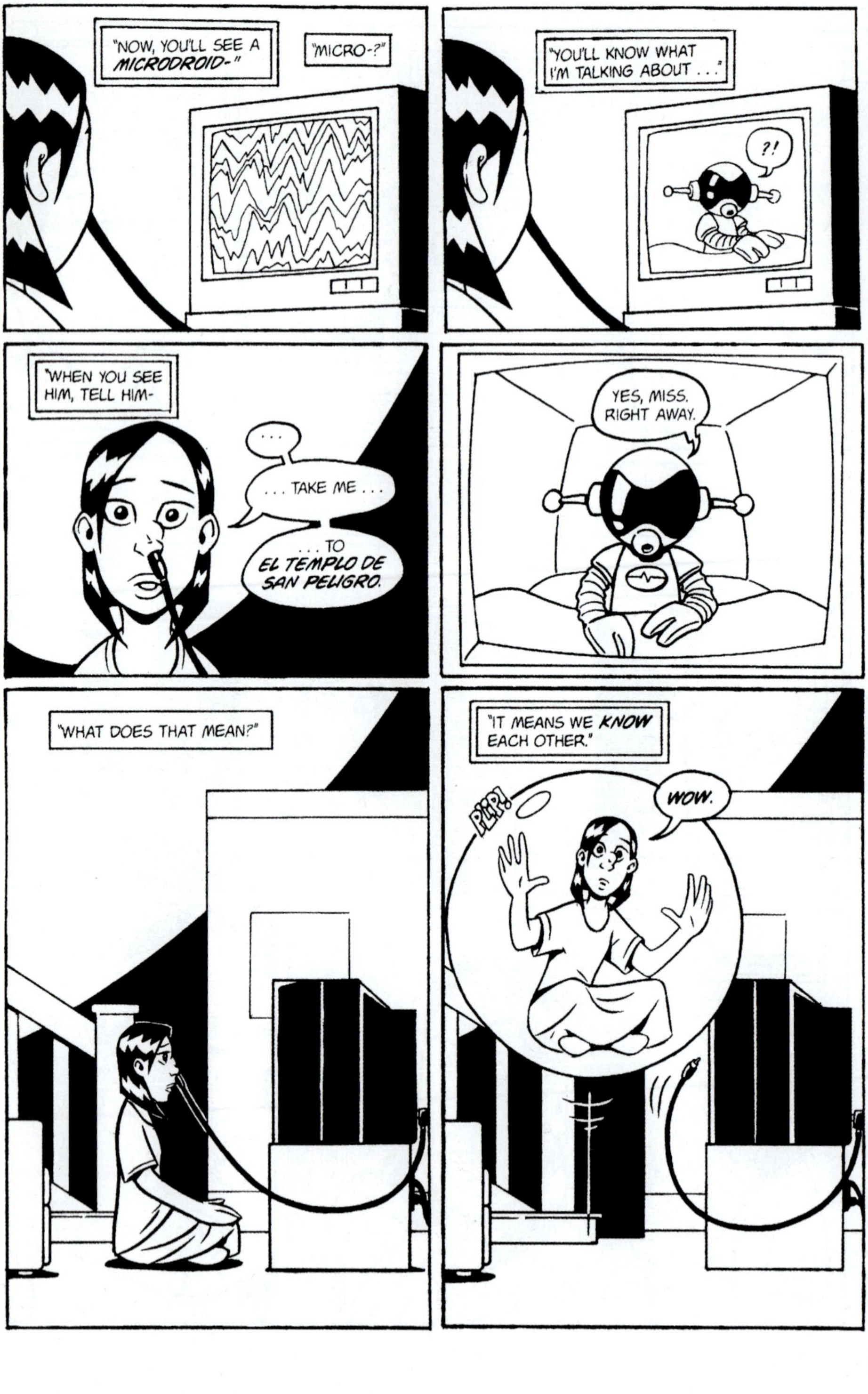
"NOW, YOU'LL SEE A MICRODROID-"
"MICRO-?"
"YOU'LL KNOW WHAT I'M TALKING ABOUT . . ."
?!
"WHEN YOU SEE HIM, TELL HIM-
. . .
. . . TAKE ME . . .
. . . TO EL TEMPLO DE SAN PELIGRO.
YES, MISS. RIGHT AWAY.
"WHAT DOES THAT MEAN?"
"IT MEANS WE KNOW EACH OTHER."
PLIP!
WOW.

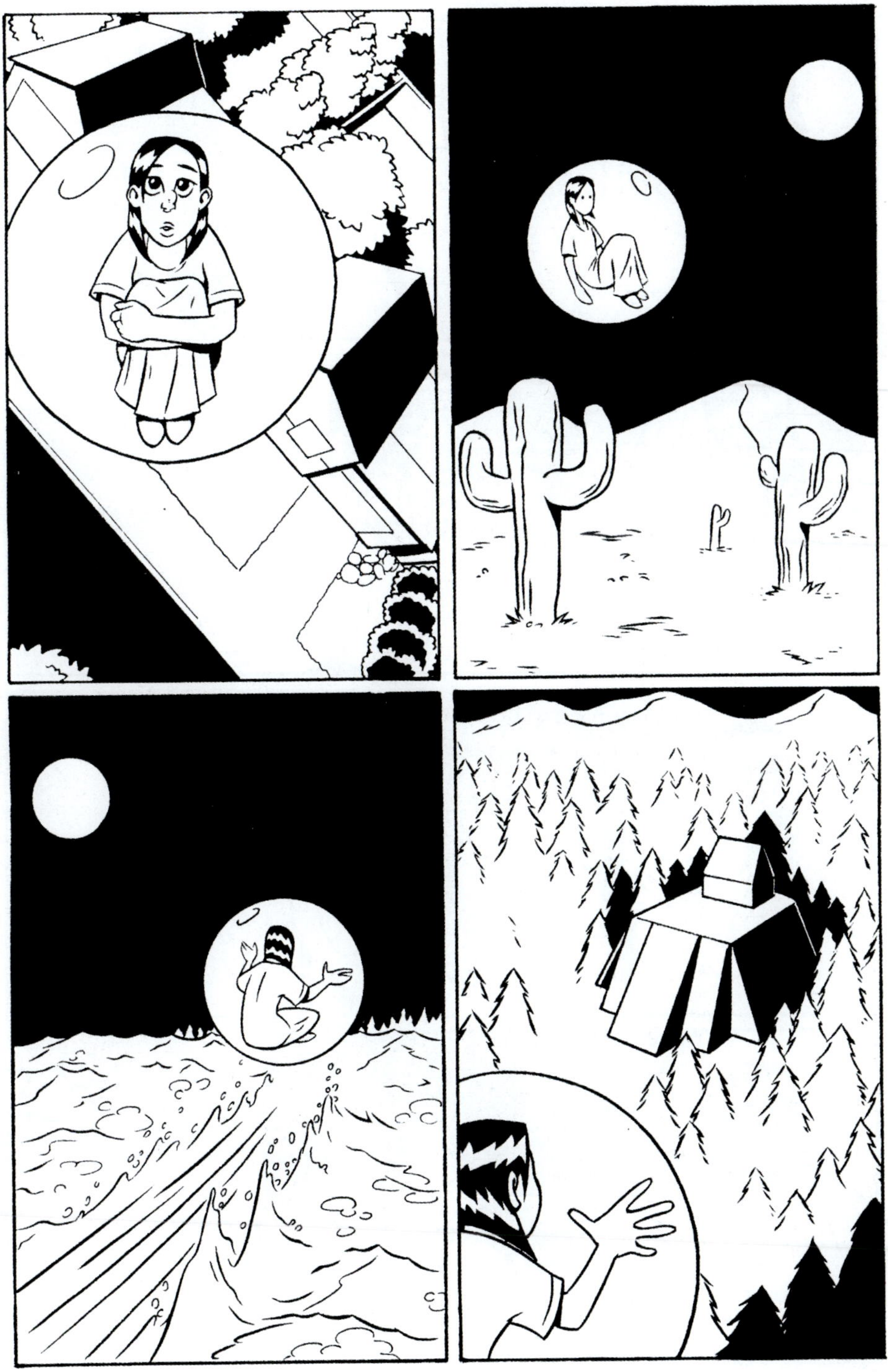

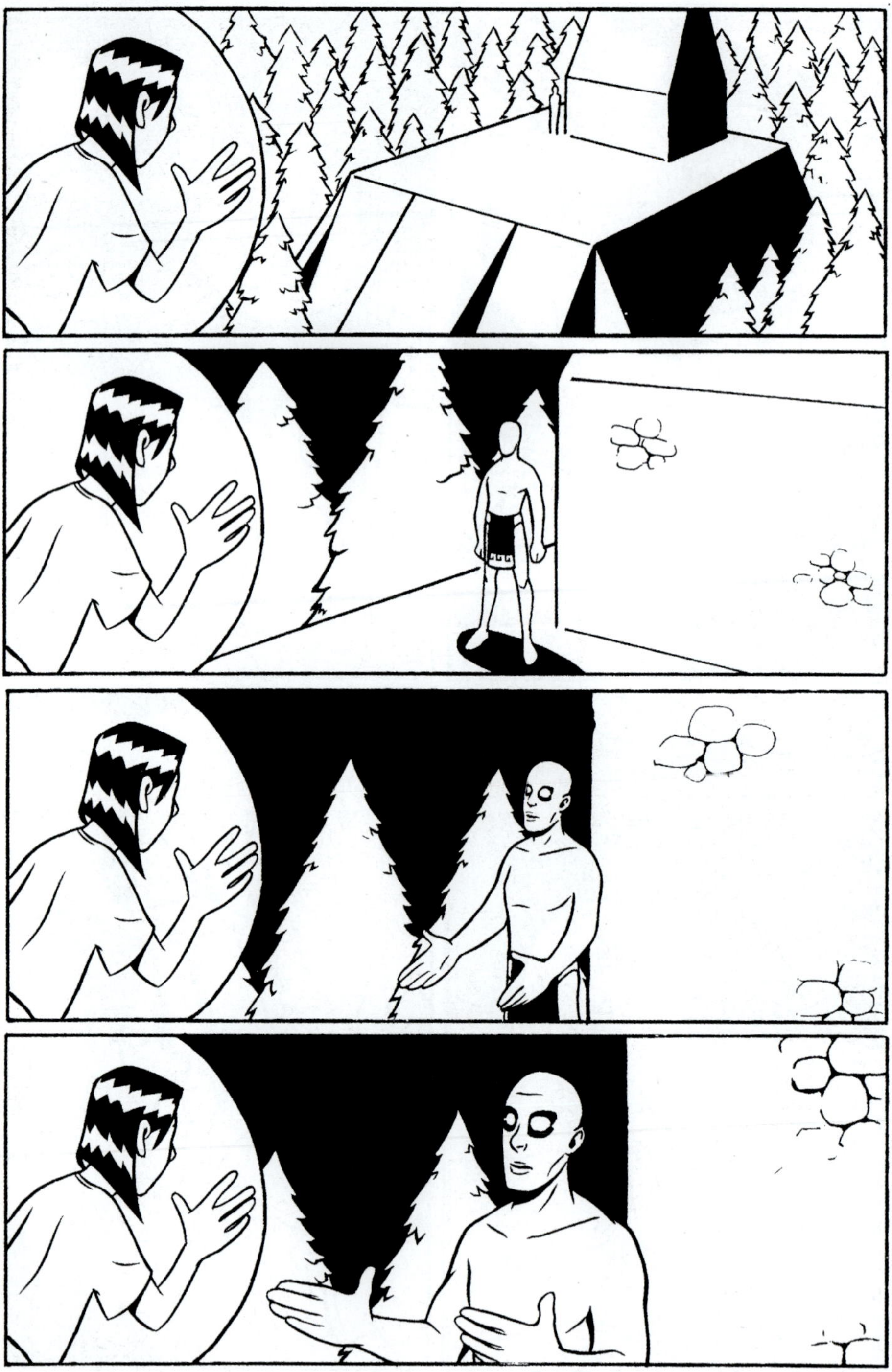

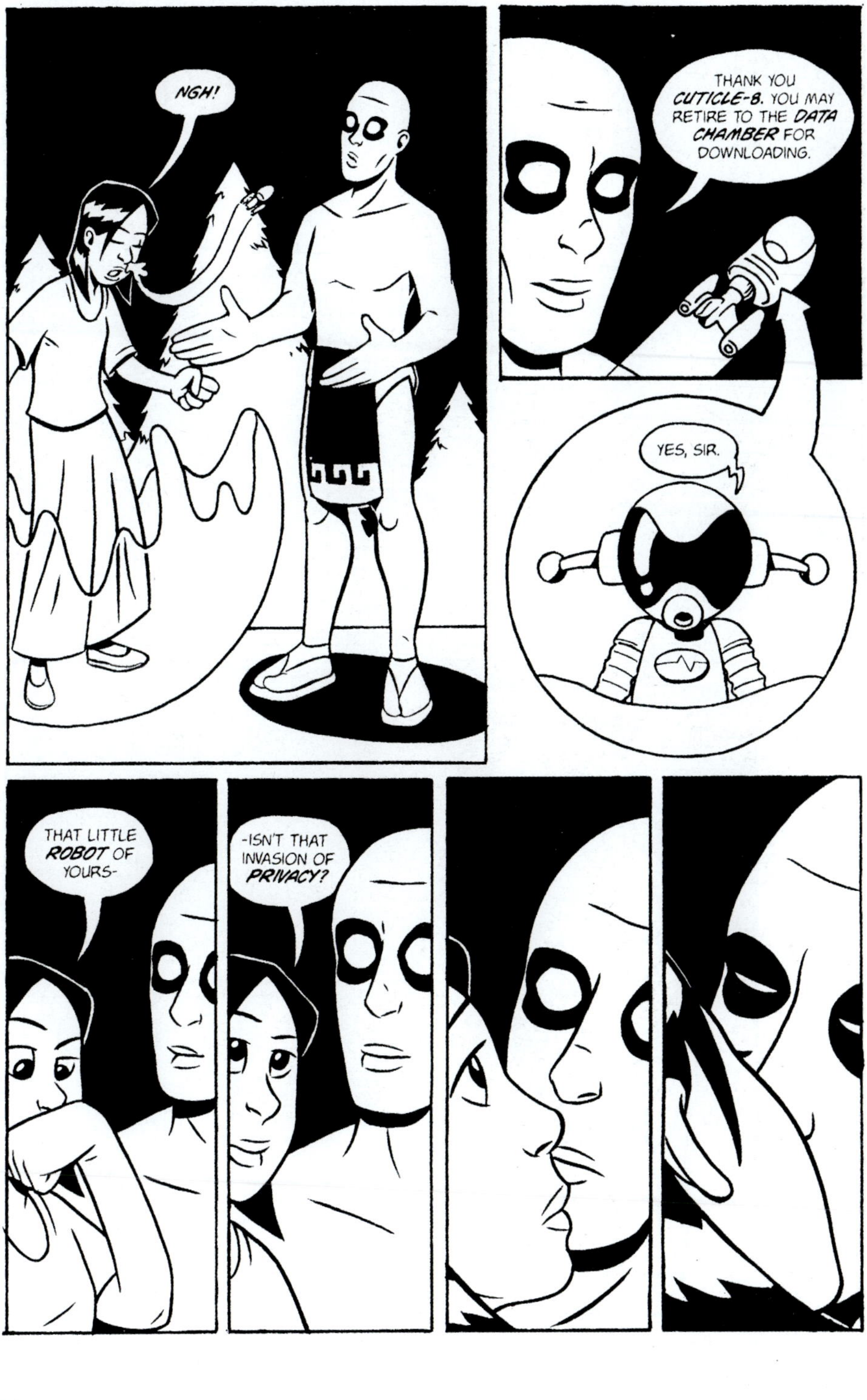
NGH!
THANK YOU CUTICLE-8. YOU MAY RETIRE TO THE DATA CHAMBER FOR DOWNLOADING.
YES, SIR.
THAT LITTLE ROBOT OF YOURS-
-ISN'T THAT INVASION OF PRIVACY?

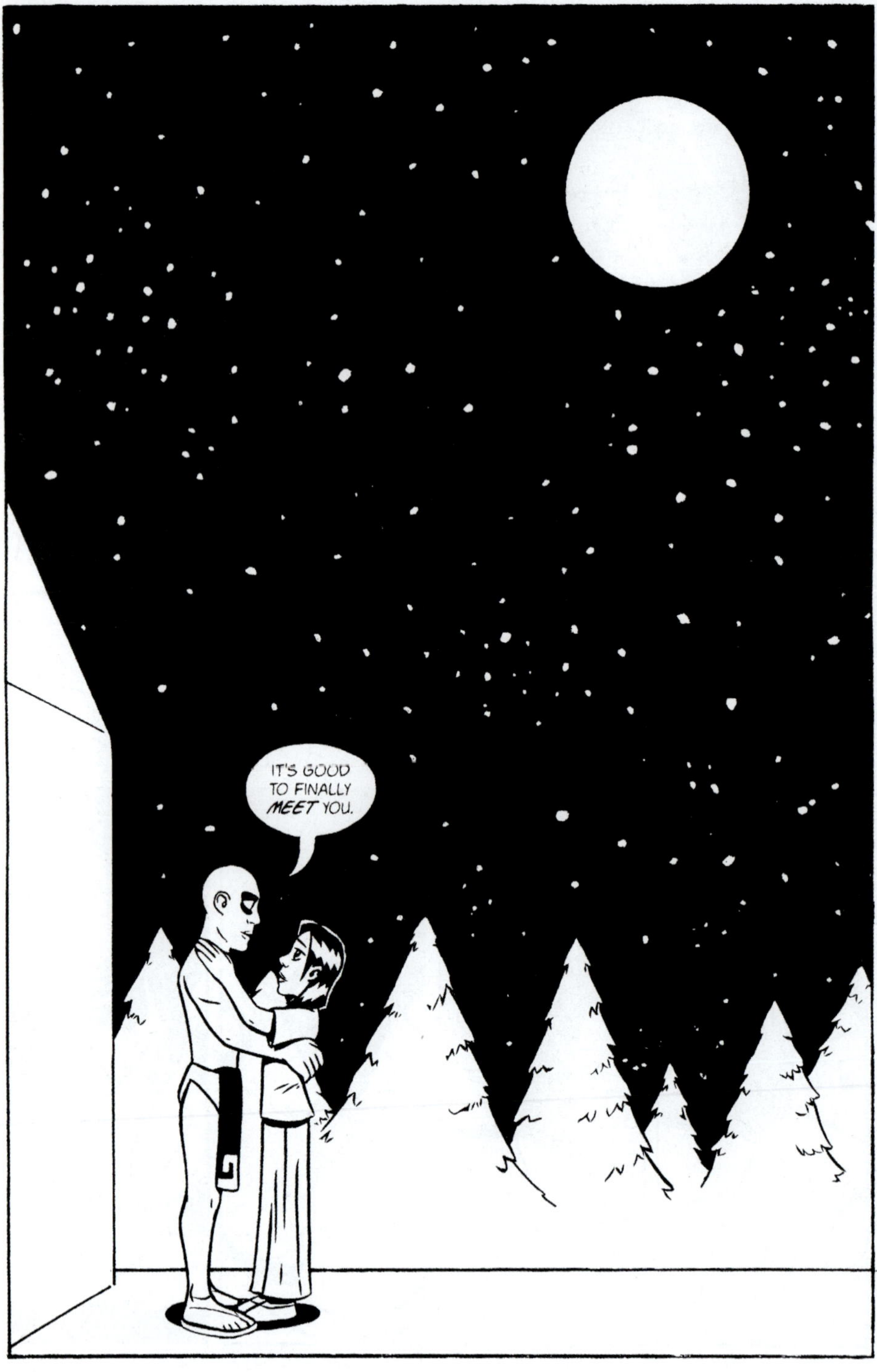
IT'S GOOD TO FINALLY *MEET* YOU.

CHAPTER TWO

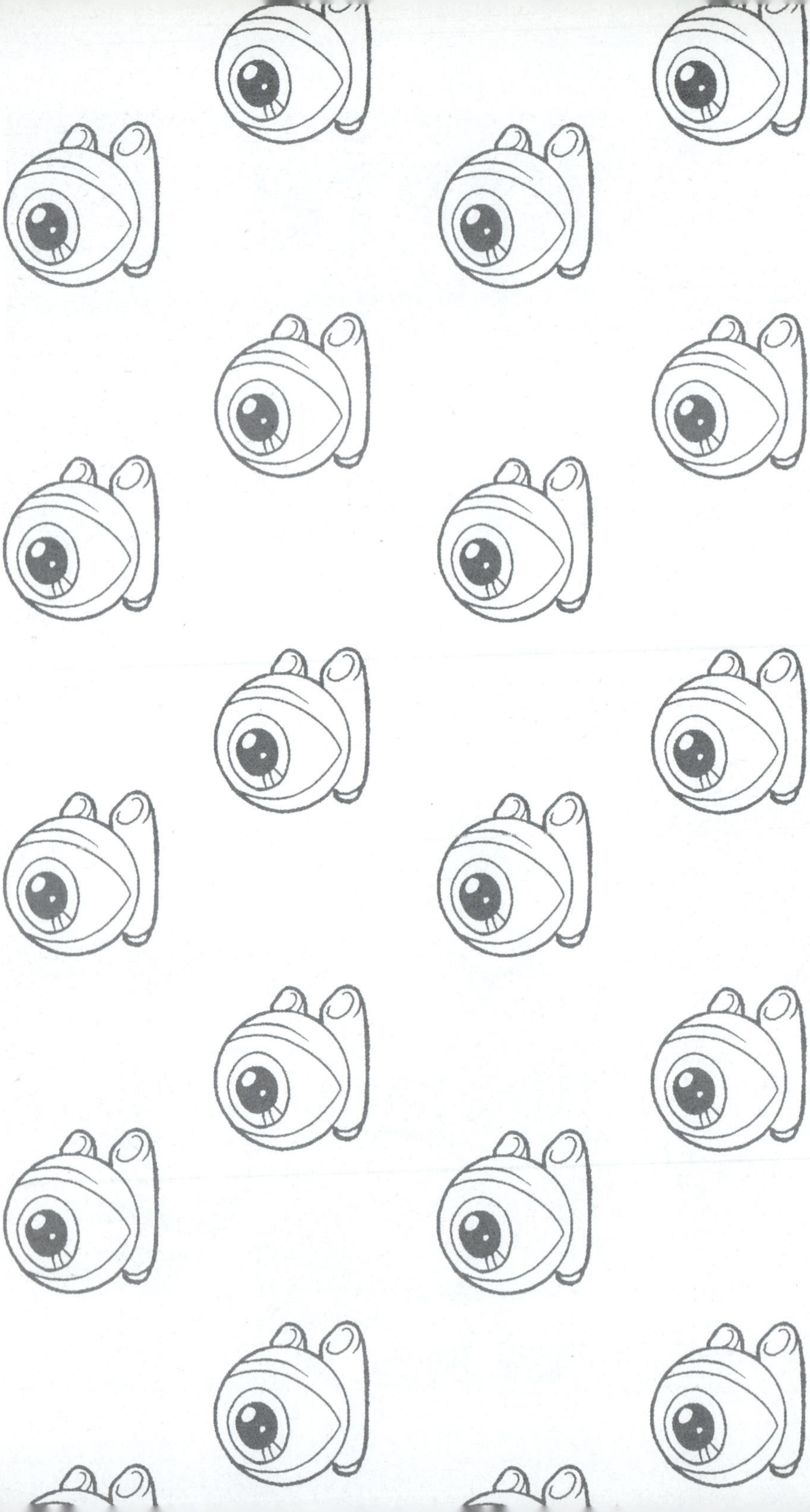

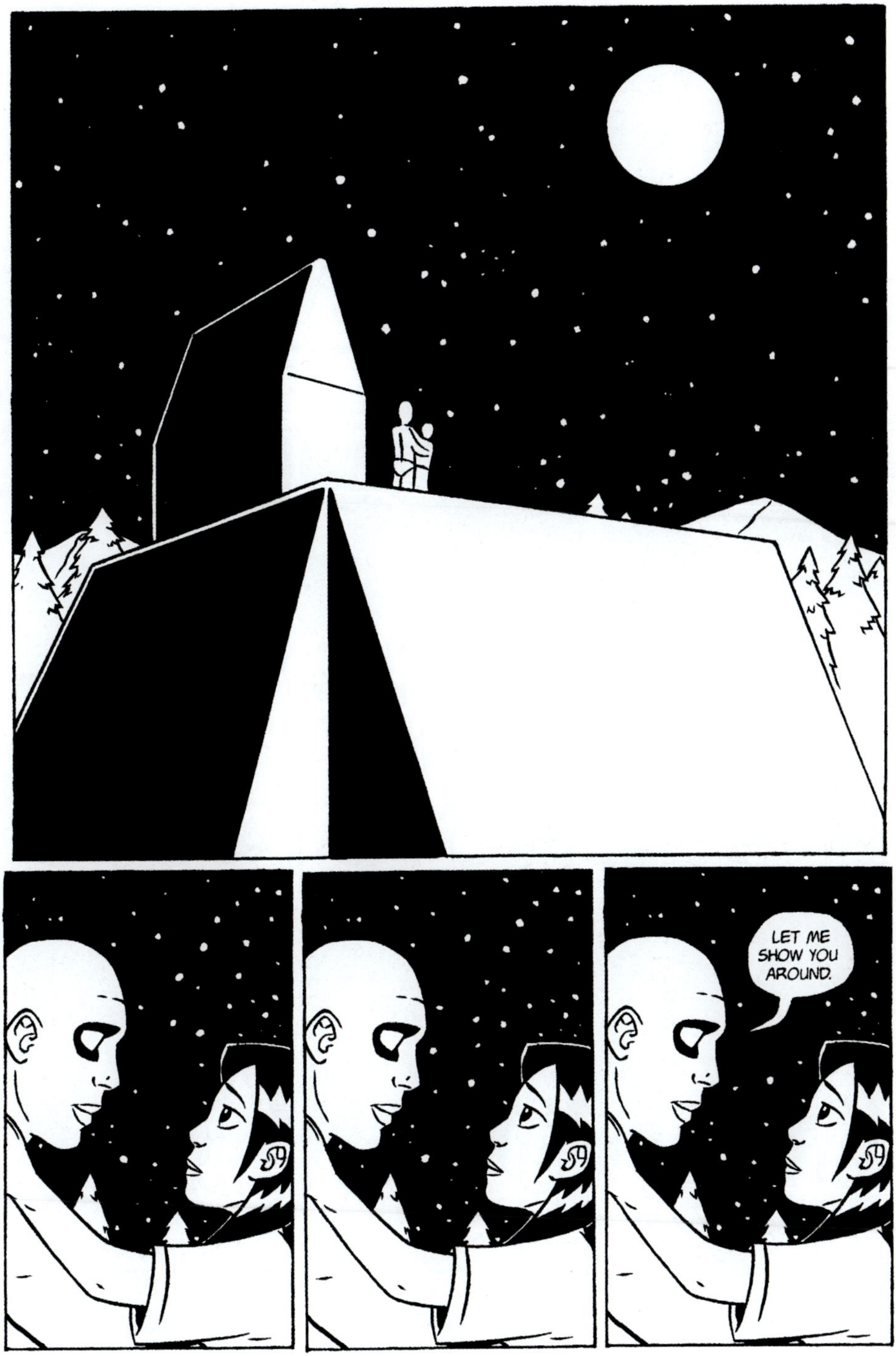
LET ME SHOW YOU AROUND.

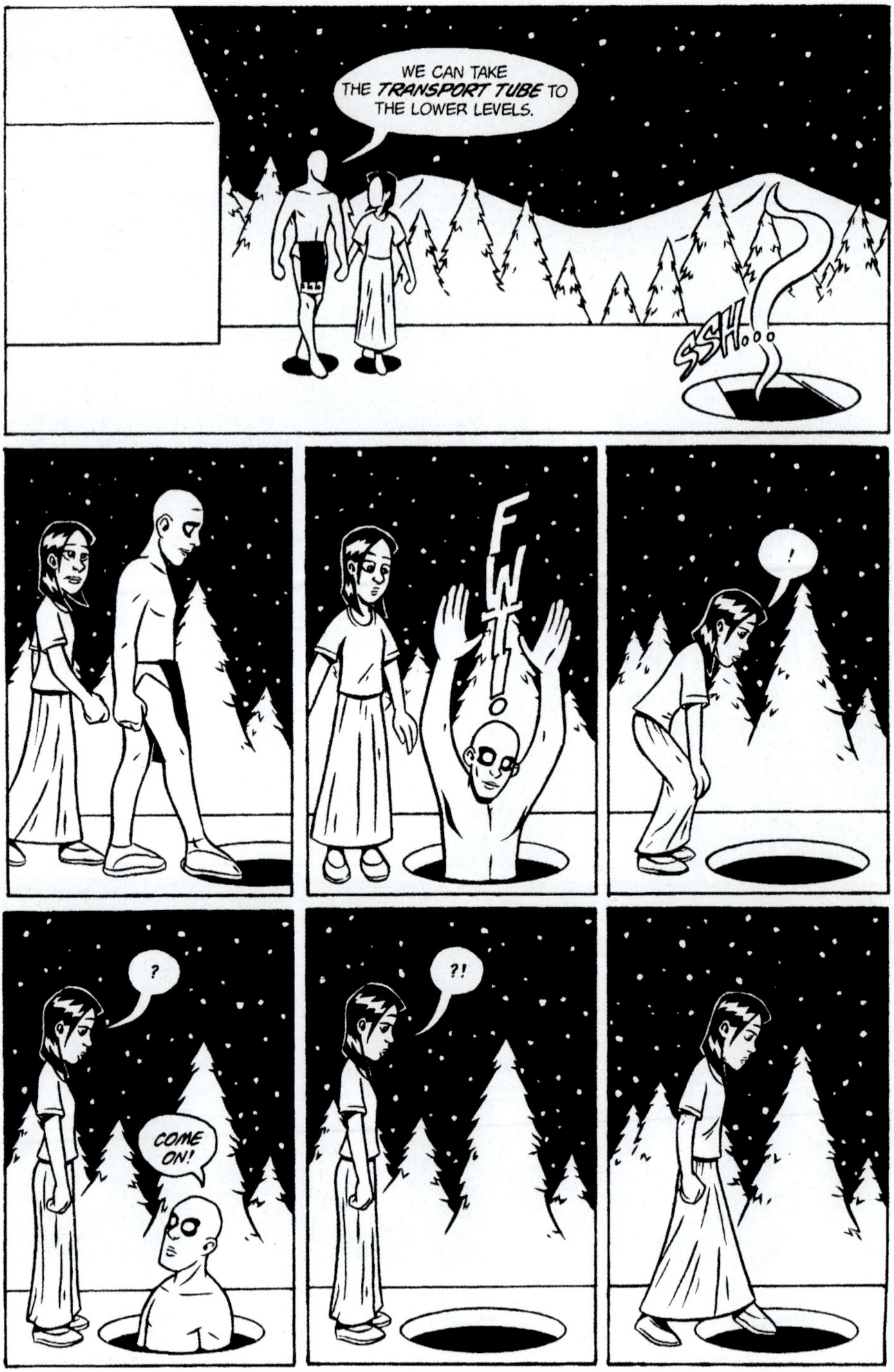
WE CAN TAKE THE TRANSPORT TUBE TO THE LOWER LEVELS.
SSH...
FWT!
!
?
COME ON!
?!

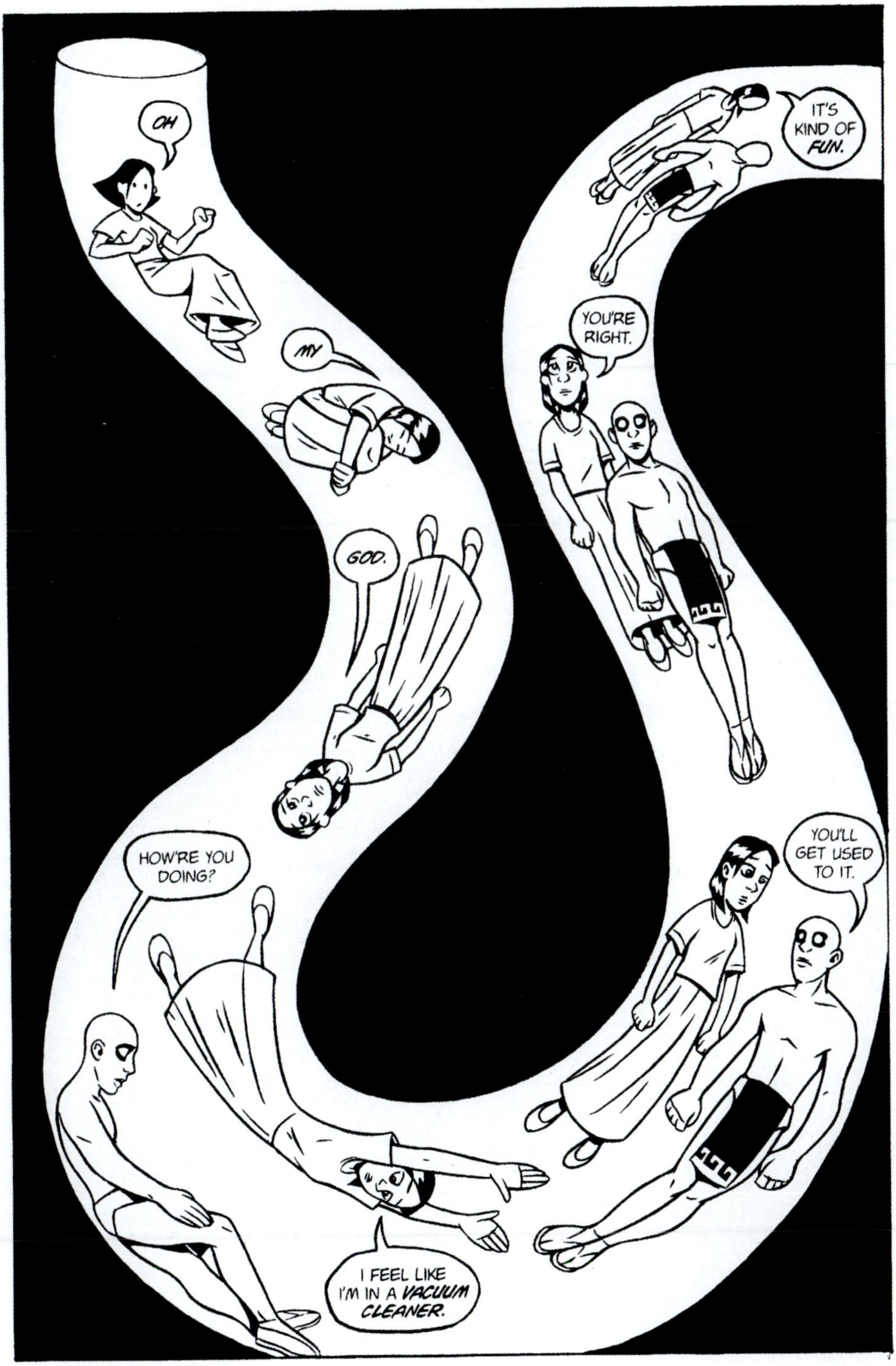
OH
MY
GOD.
HOW'RE YOU DOING?
I FEEL LIKE I'M IN A VACUUM CLEANER.
YOU'LL GET USED TO IT.
YOU'RE RIGHT.
IT'S KIND OF FUN.

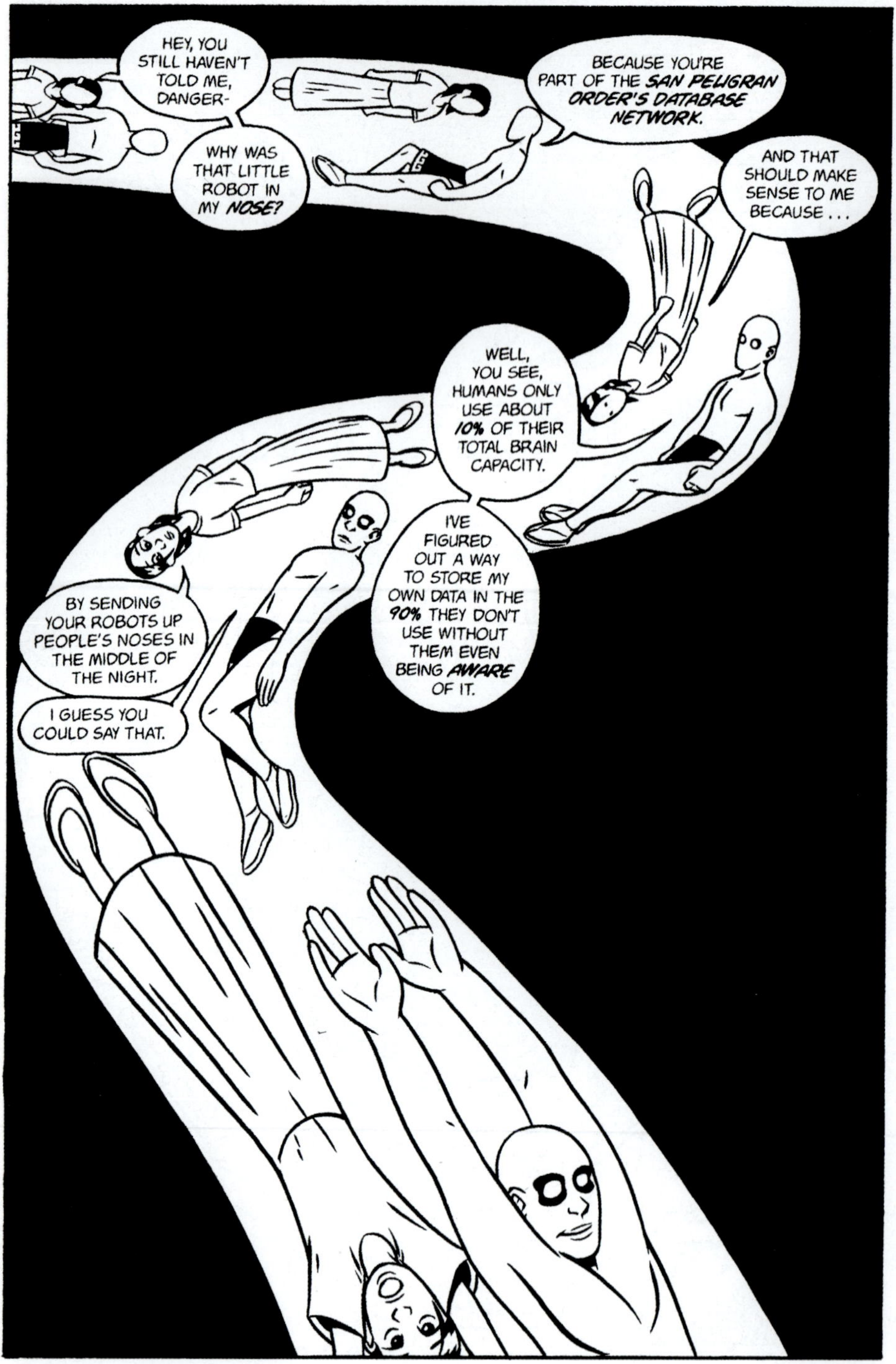
HEY, YOU STILL HAVEN'T TOLD ME, DANGER-
WHY WAS THAT LITTLE ROBOT IN MY *NOSE?*
BECAUSE YOU'RE PART OF THE *SAN PELIGRAN ORDER'S DATABASE NETWORK.*
AND THAT SHOULD MAKE SENSE TO ME BECAUSE . . .
WELL, YOU SEE, HUMANS ONLY USE ABOUT *10%* OF THEIR TOTAL BRAIN CAPACITY.
I'VE FIGURED OUT A WAY TO STORE MY OWN DATA IN THE *90%* THEY DON'T USE WITHOUT THEM EVEN BEING *AWARE* OF IT.
BY SENDING YOUR ROBOTS UP PEOPLE'S NOSES IN THE MIDDLE OF THE NIGHT.
I GUESS YOU COULD SAY THAT.

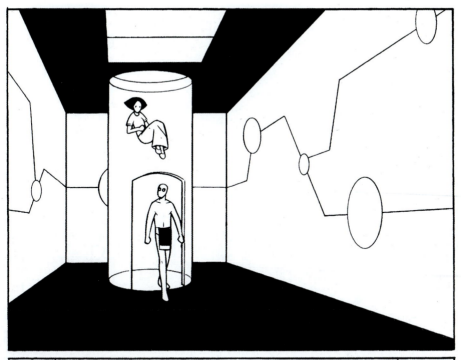

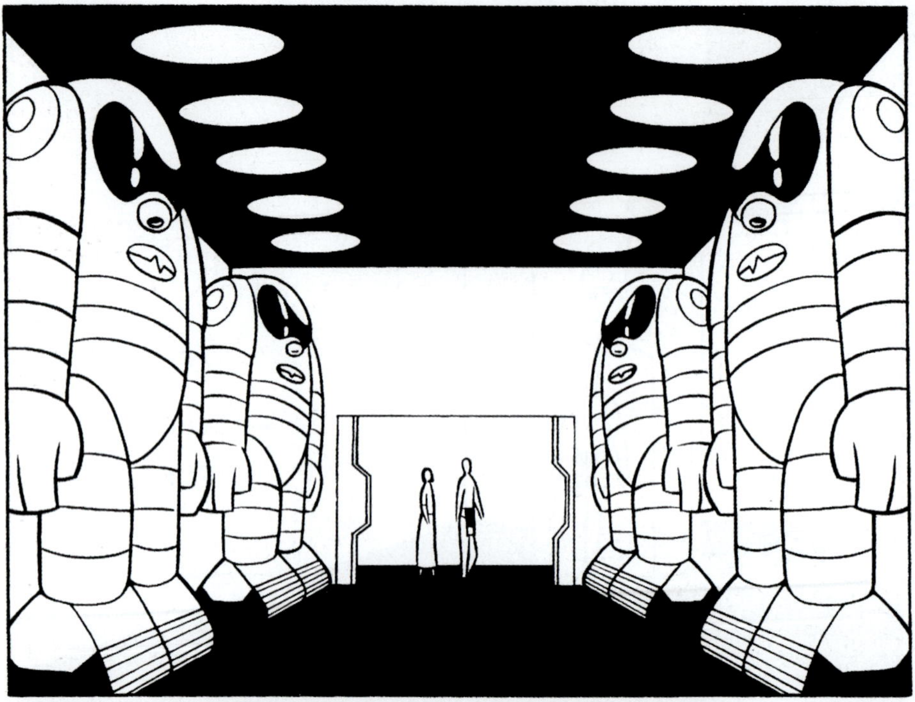

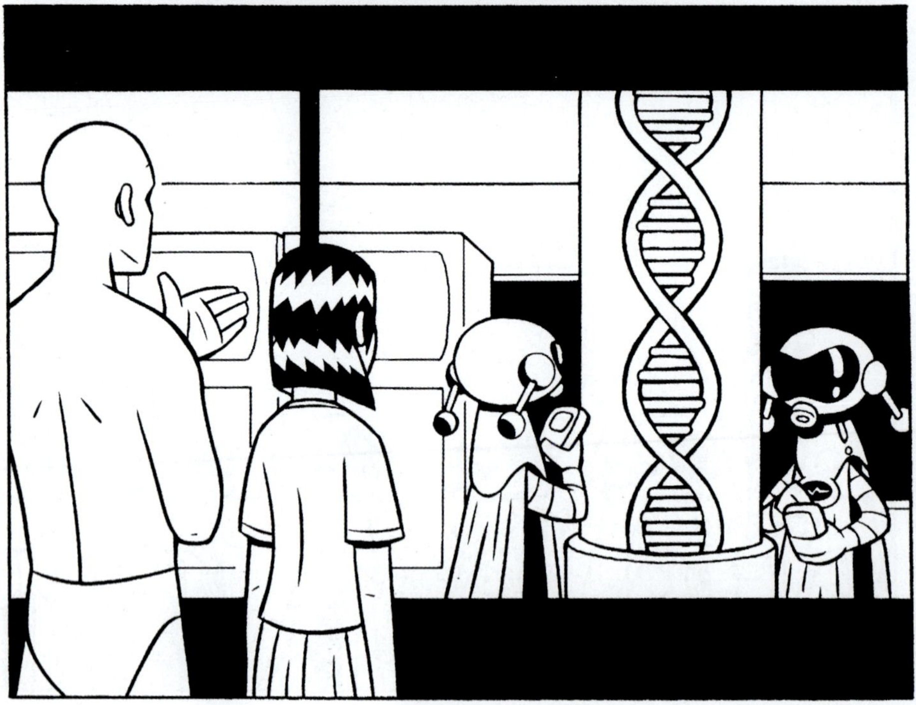

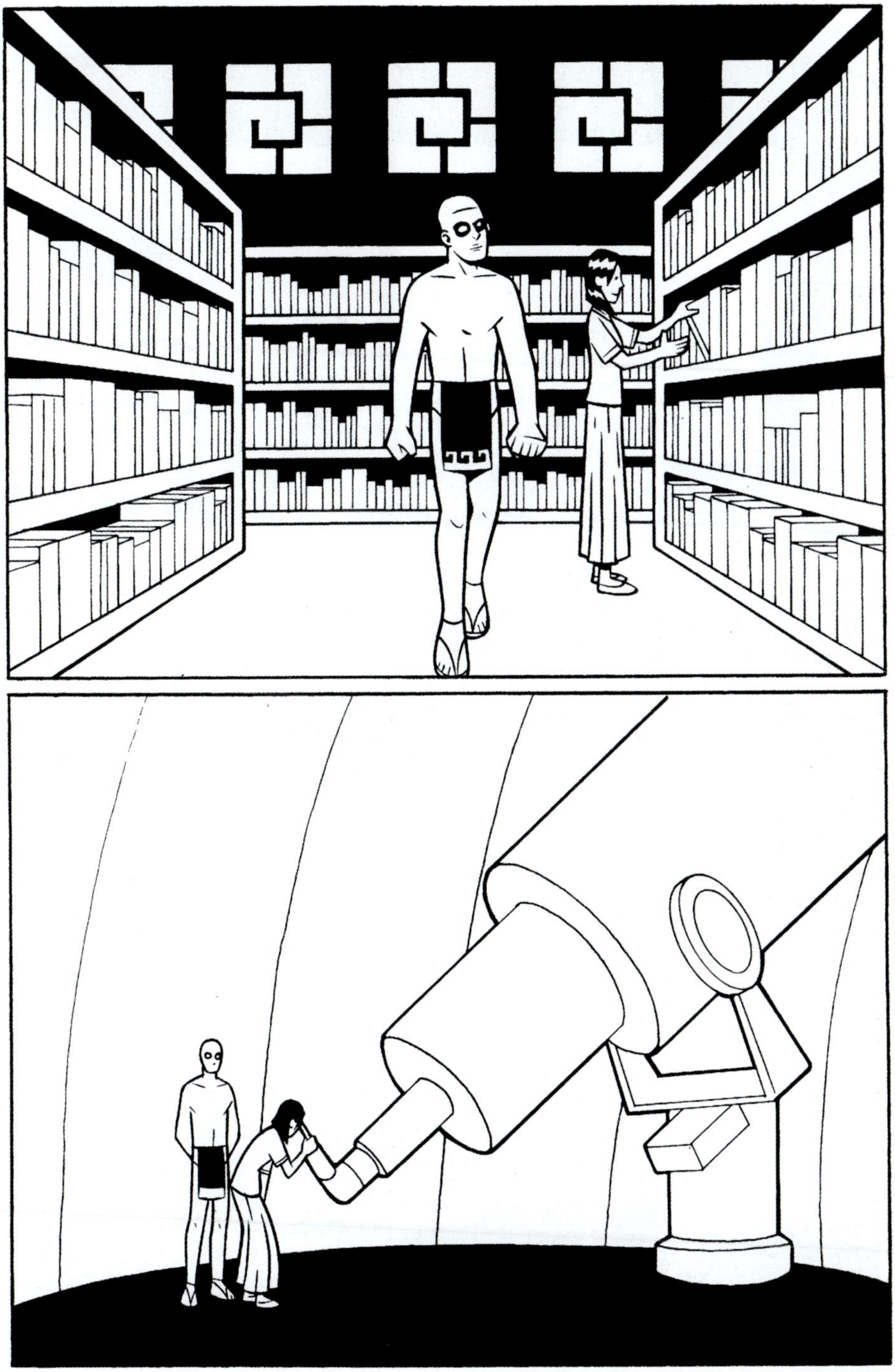

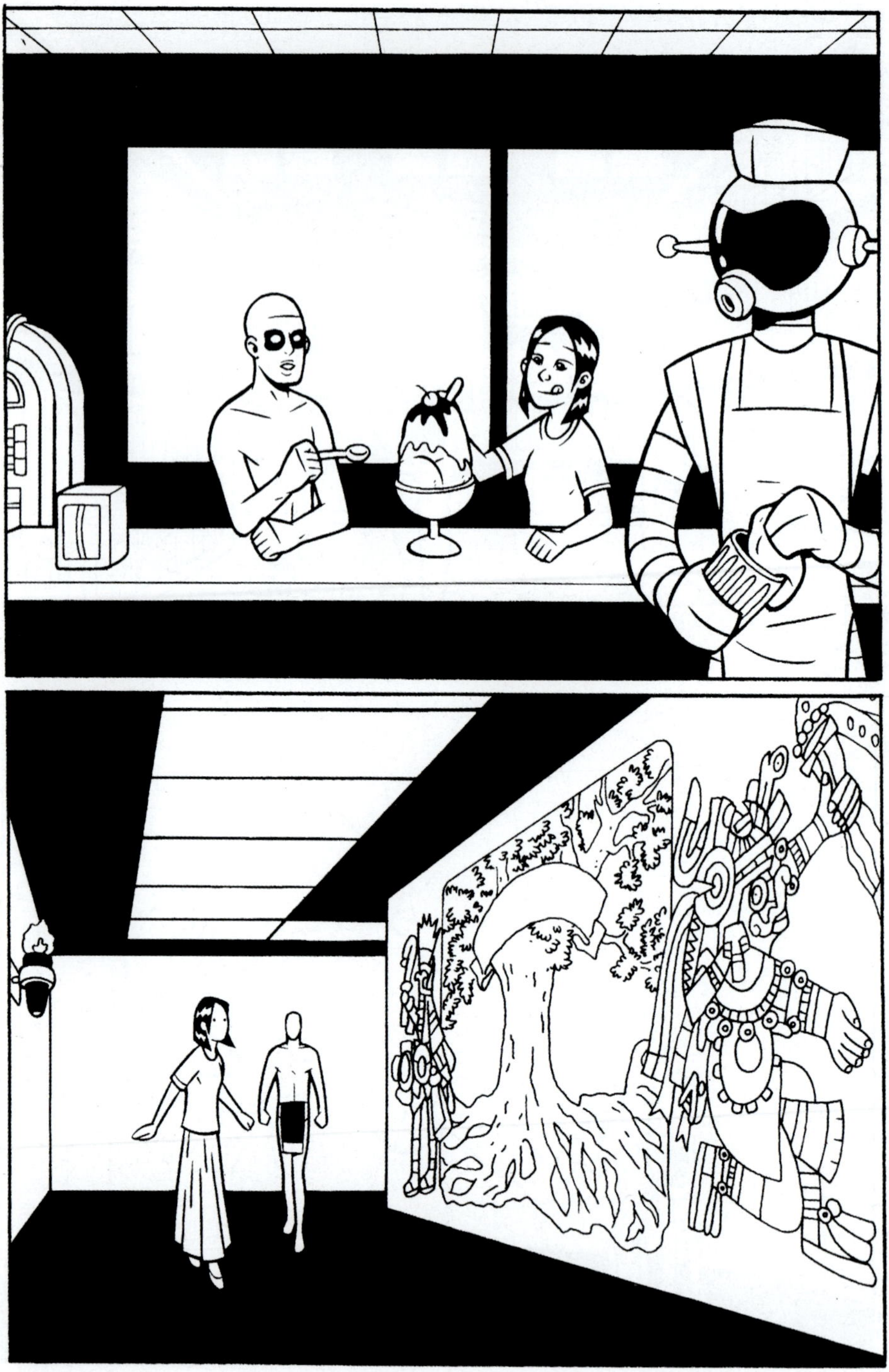

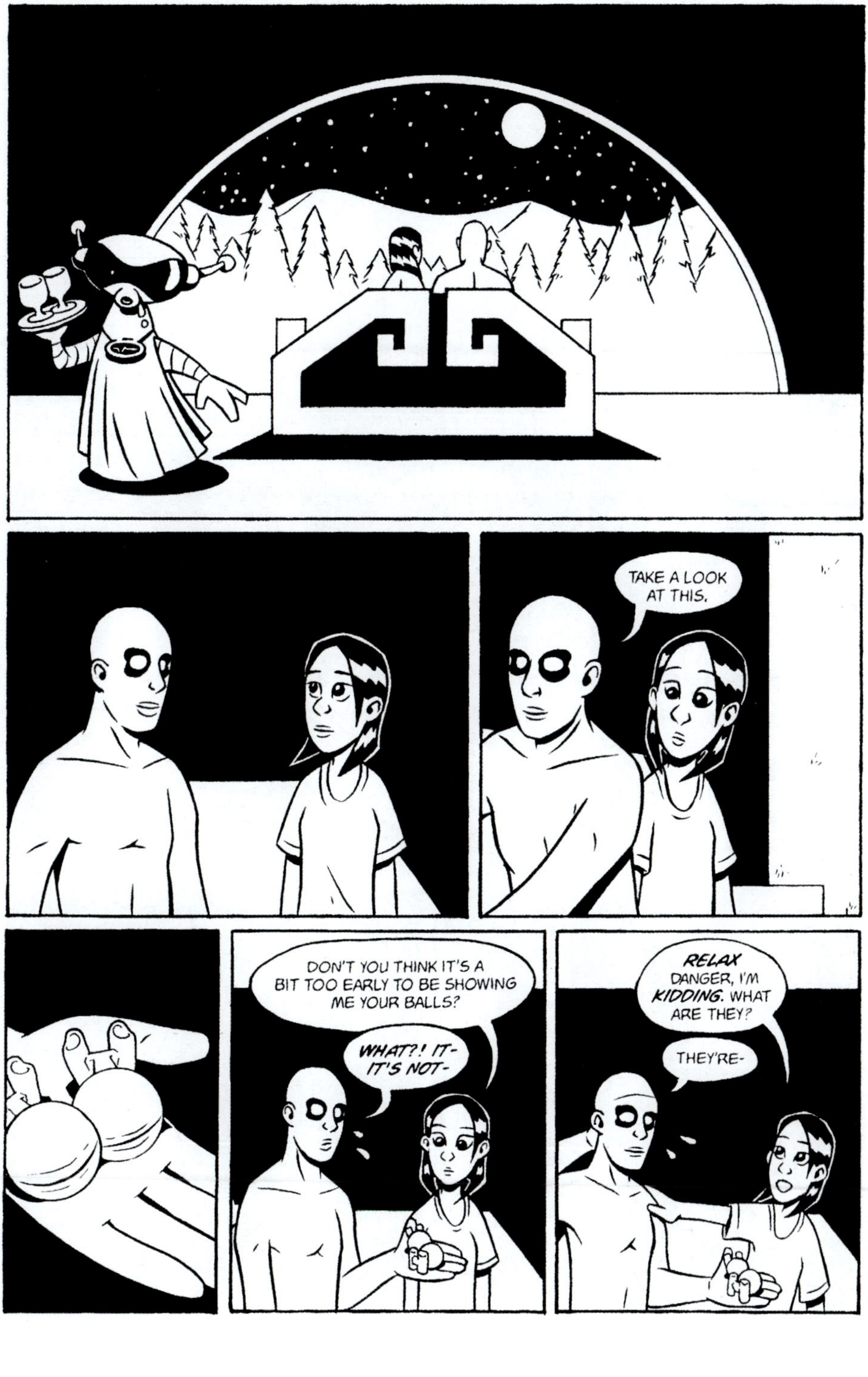
TAKE A LOOK AT THIS.
DON'T YOU THINK IT'S A BIT TOO EARLY TO BE SHOWING ME YOUR BALLS?
WHAT?! IT- IT'S NOT-
RELAX DANGER, I'M KIDDING. WHAT ARE THEY?
THEY'RE-

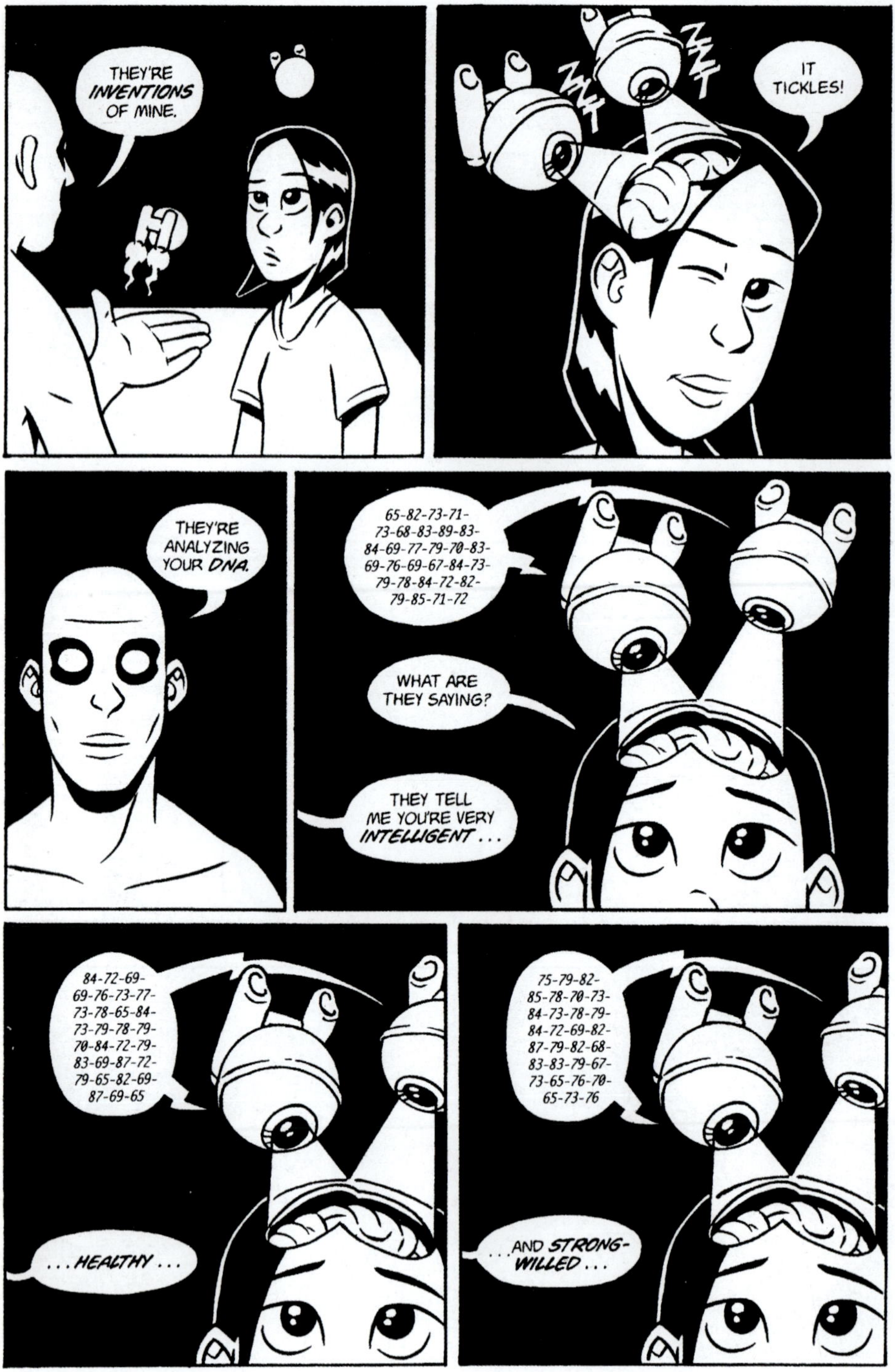
THEY'RE INVENTIONS OF MINE.
IT TICKLES!
THEY'RE ANALYZING YOUR DNA.
65-82-73-71-73-68-83-89-83-84-69-77-79-70-83-69-76-69-67-84-73-79-78-84-72-82-79-85-71-72
WHAT ARE THEY SAYING?
THEY TELL ME YOU'RE VERY INTELLIGENT . . .
84-72-69-69-76-73-77-73-78-65-84-73-79-78-79-70-84-72-79-83-69-87-72-79-65-82-69-87-69-65
. . . HEALTHY . . .
75-79-82-85-78-70-73-84-73-78-79-84-72-69-82-87-79-82-68-83-83-79-67-73-65-76-70-65-73-76
. . . AND STRONG-WILLED . . .

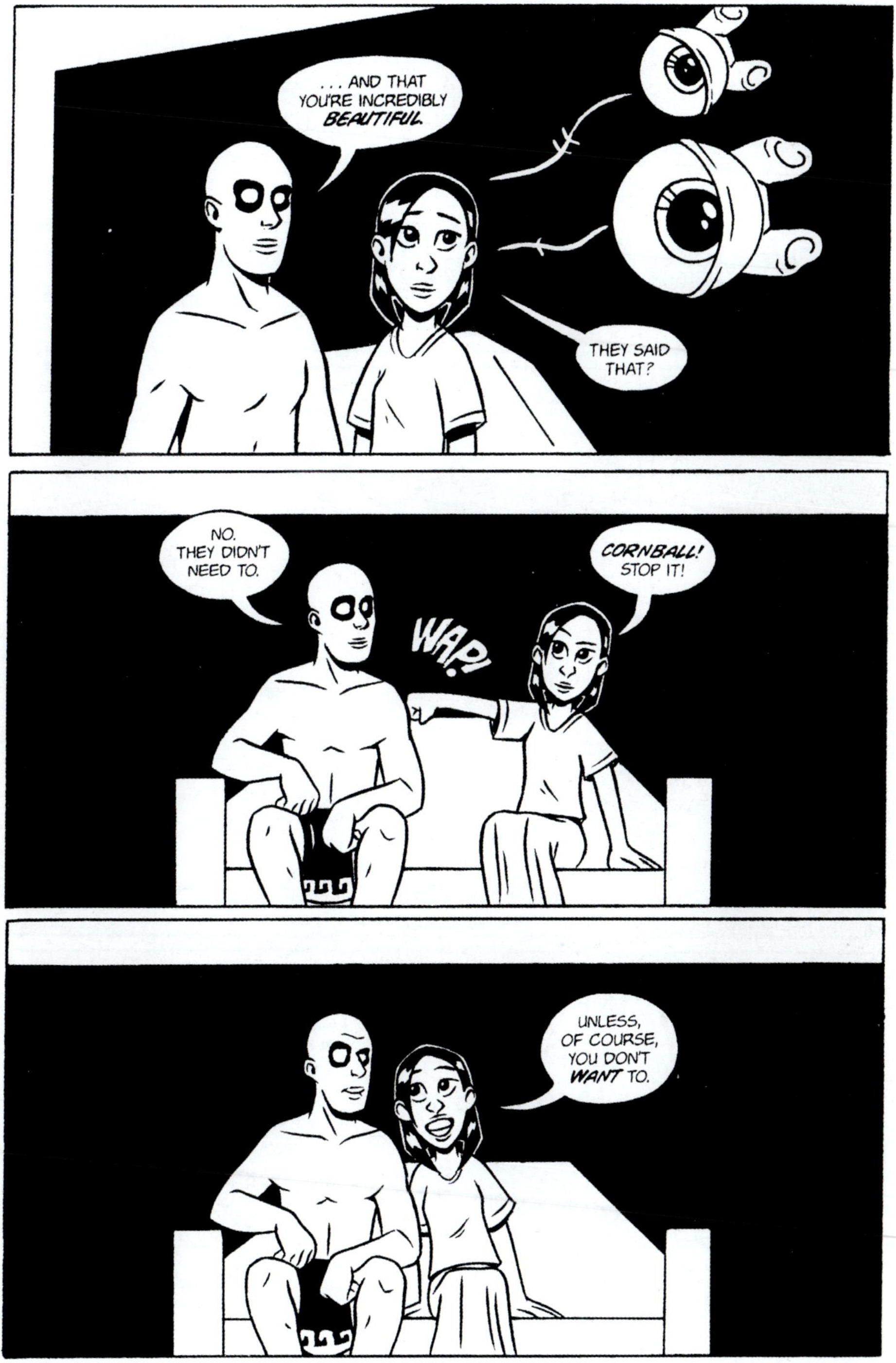
. . . AND THAT YOU'RE INCREDIBLY BEAUTIFUL.
THEY SAID THAT?
NO. THEY DIDN'T NEED TO.
WAP!
CORNBALL! STOP IT!
UNLESS, OF COURSE, YOU DON'T WANT TO.

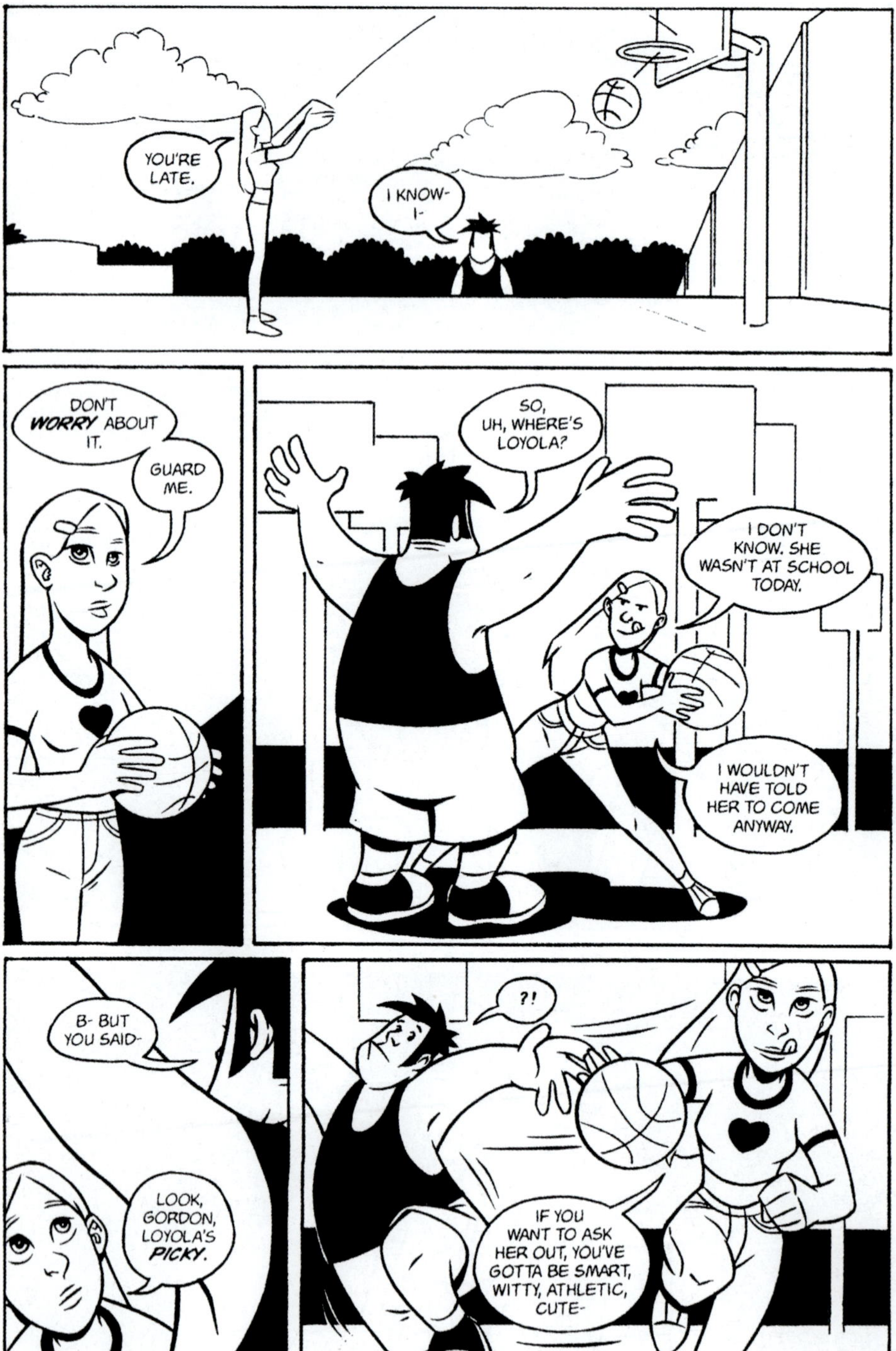
YOU'RE LATE.
I KNOW- I-
DON'T WORRY ABOUT IT.
GUARD ME.
SO, UH, WHERE'S LOYOLA?
I DON'T KNOW. SHE WASN'T AT SCHOOL TODAY.
I WOULDN'T HAVE TOLD HER TO COME ANYWAY.
B- BUT YOU SAID-
LOOK, GORDON, LOYOLA'S PICKY.
?!
IF YOU WANT TO ASK HER OUT, YOU'VE GOTTA BE SMART, WITTY, ATHLETIC, CUTE-

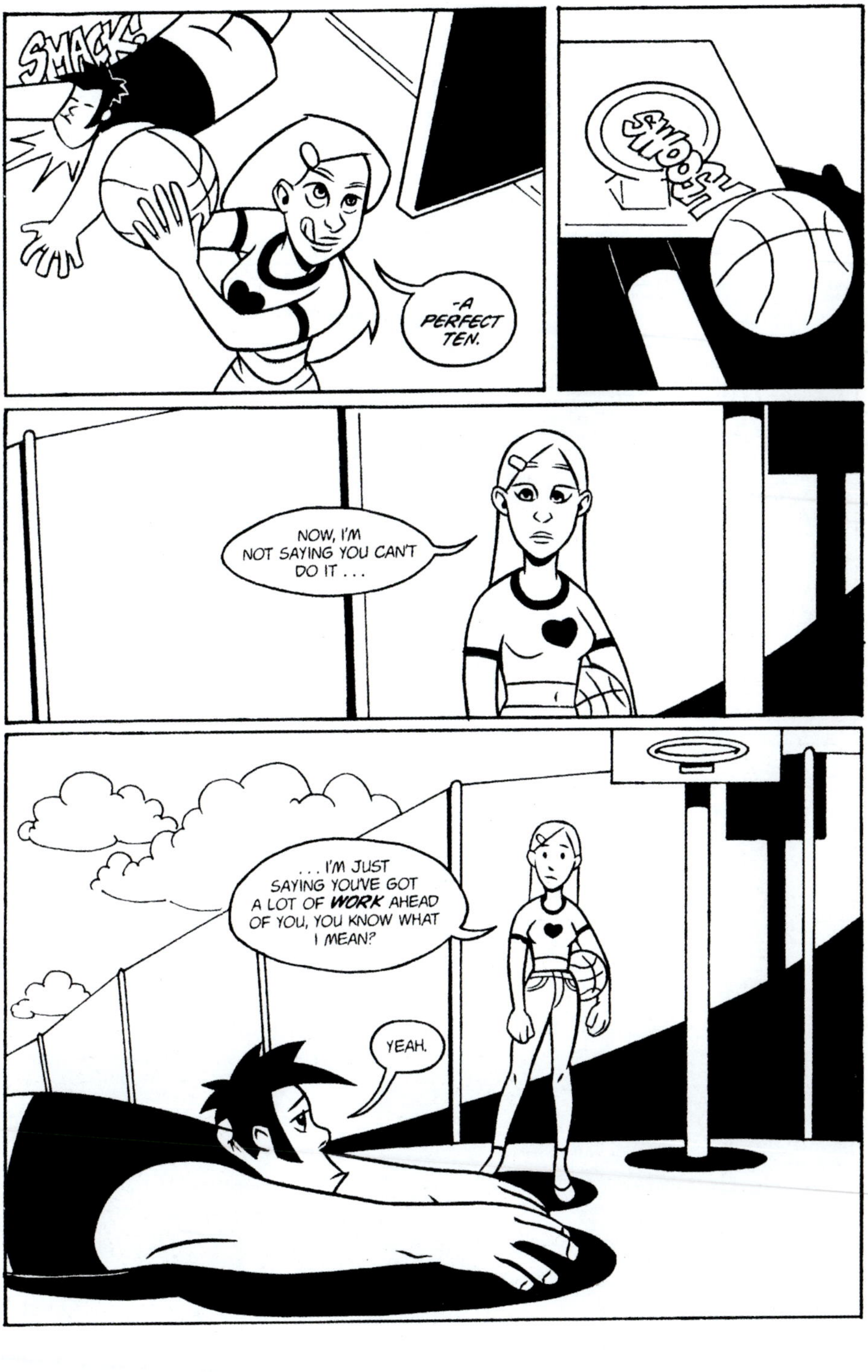
SMACK!
-A PERFECT TEN.
NOW, I'M NOT SAYING YOU CAN'T DO IT . . .
. . . I'M JUST SAYING YOU'VE GOT A LOT OF **WORK** AHEAD OF YOU, YOU KNOW WHAT I MEAN?
YEAH.

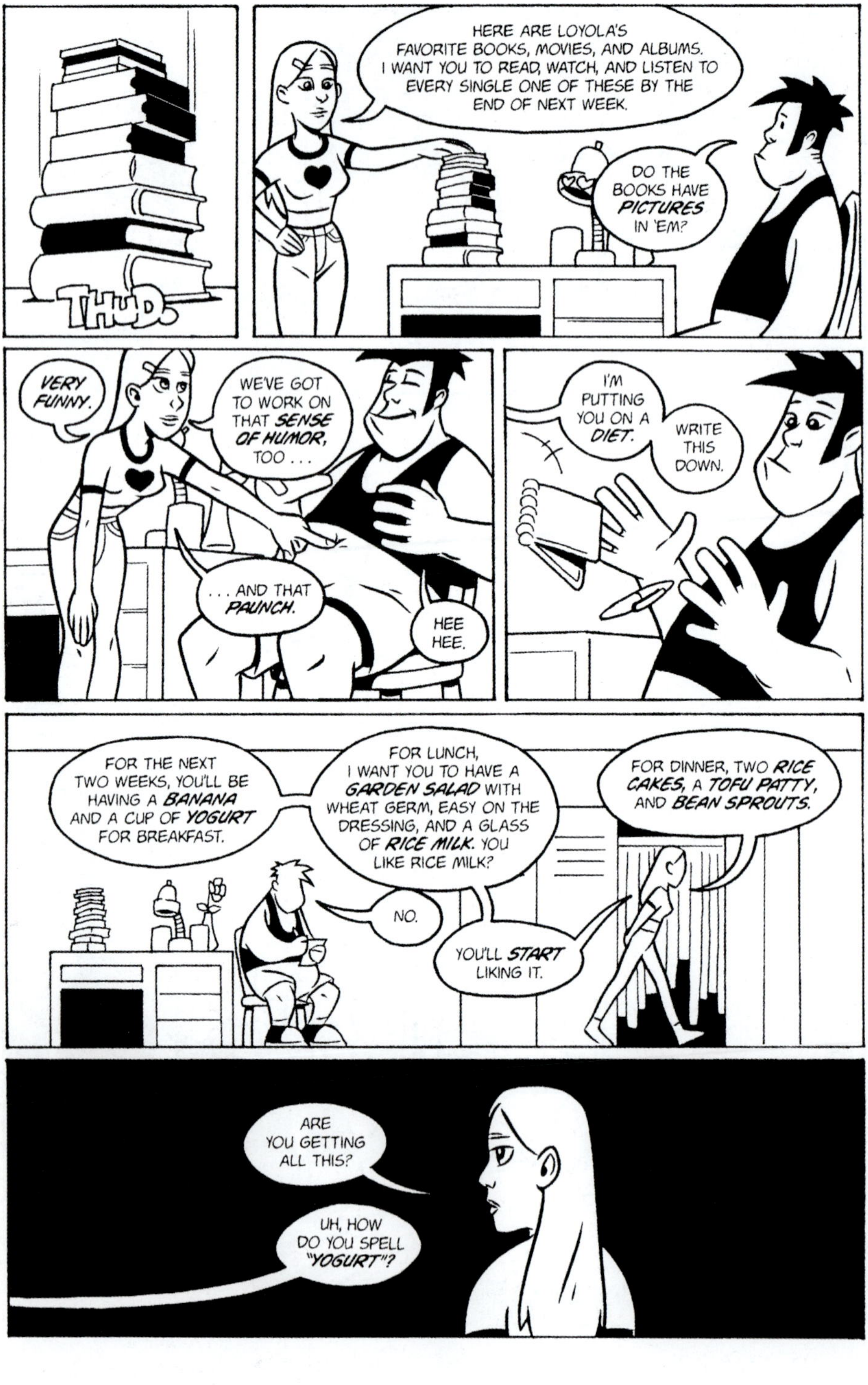
THUD.
HERE ARE LOYOLA'S FAVORITE BOOKS, MOVIES, AND ALBUMS. I WANT YOU TO READ, WATCH, AND LISTEN TO EVERY SINGLE ONE OF THESE BY THE END OF NEXT WEEK.
DO THE BOOKS HAVE *PICTURES* IN 'EM?
VERY FUNNY.
WE'VE GOT TO WORK ON THAT *SENSE OF HUMOR,* TOO . . .
. . . AND THAT *PAUNCH.*
HEE HEE.
I'M PUTTING YOU ON A *DIET.*
WRITE THIS DOWN.
FOR THE NEXT TWO WEEKS, YOU'LL BE HAVING A *BANANA* AND A CUP OF *YOGURT* FOR BREAKFAST.
FOR LUNCH, I WANT YOU TO HAVE A *GARDEN SALAD* WITH WHEAT GERM, EASY ON THE DRESSING, AND A GLASS OF *RICE MILK.* YOU LIKE RICE MILK?
NO.
YOU'LL *START* LIKING IT.
FOR DINNER, TWO *RICE CAKES,* A *TOFU PATTY,* AND *BEAN SPROUTS.*
ARE YOU GETTING ALL THIS?
UH, HOW DO YOU SPELL *"YOGURT"?*

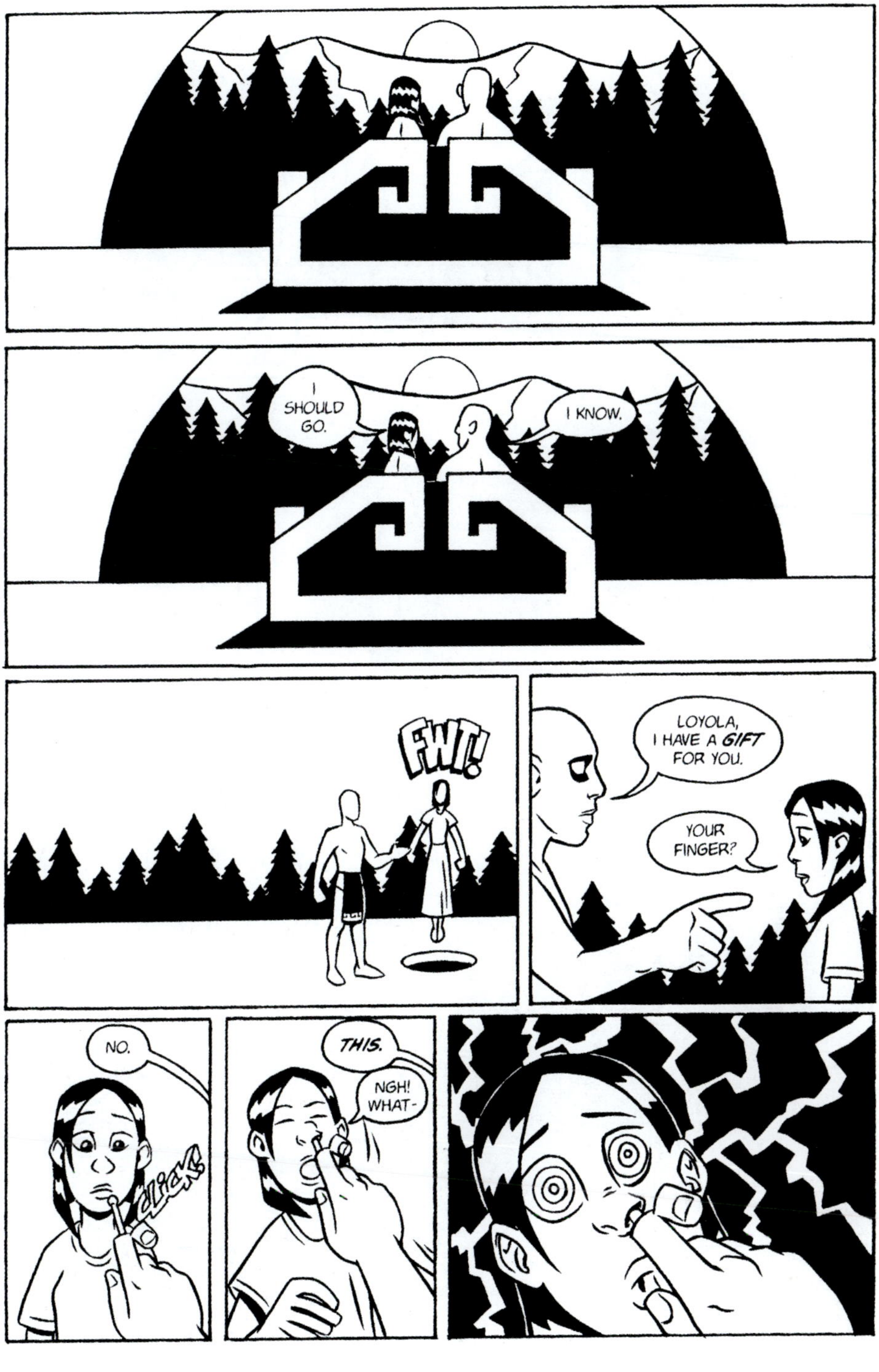
I SHOULD GO.
I KNOW.
FWT!
LOYOLA, I HAVE A GIFT FOR YOU.
YOUR FINGER?
NO.
CLICK!
THIS.
NGH! WHAT-

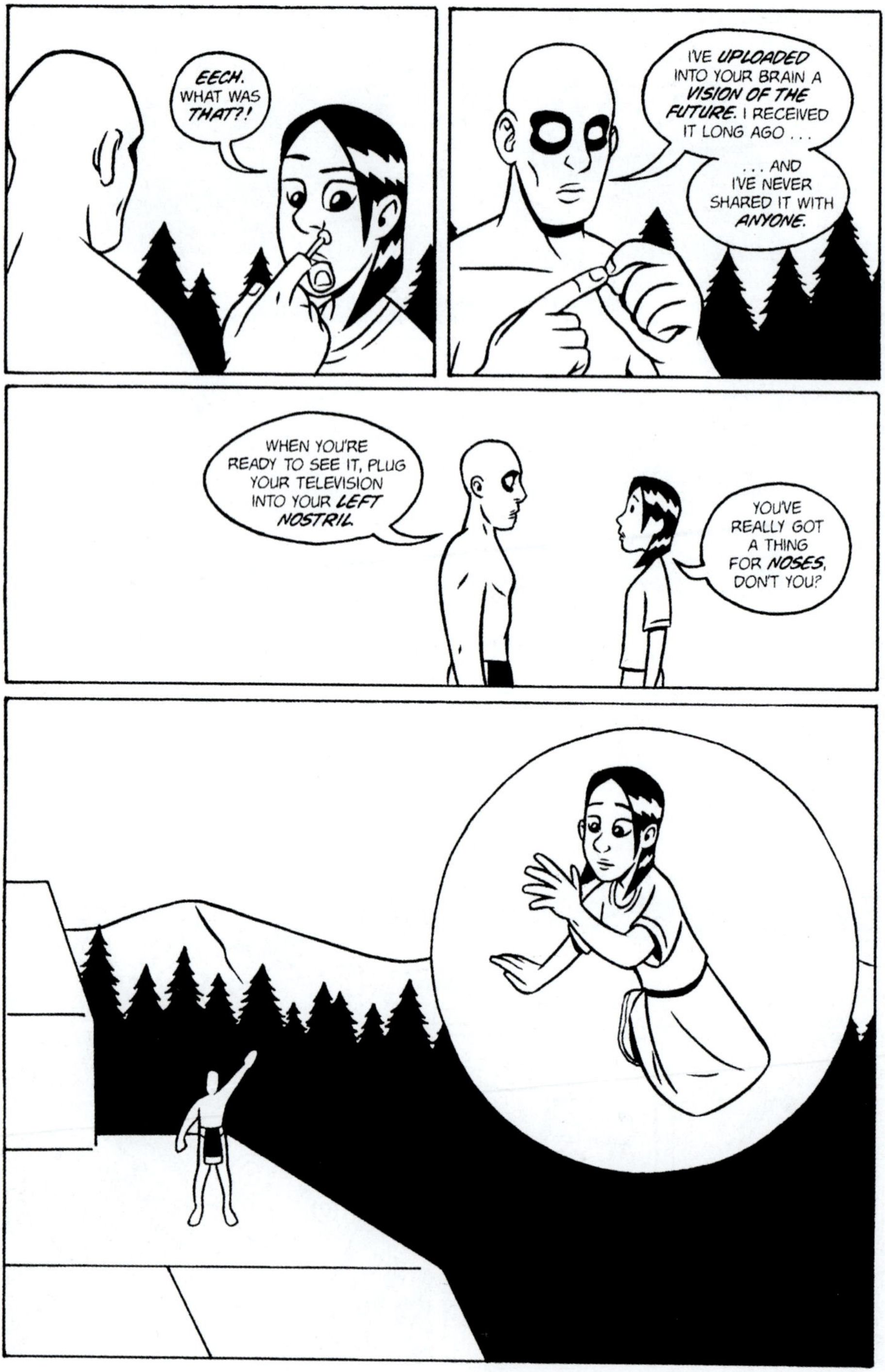
EECH. WHAT WAS THAT?!
I'VE UPLOADED INTO YOUR BRAIN A VISION OF THE FUTURE. I RECEIVED IT LONG AGO . . .
. . . AND I'VE NEVER SHARED IT WITH ANYONE.
WHEN YOU'RE READY TO SEE IT, PLUG YOUR TELEVISION INTO YOUR LEFT NOSTRIL.
YOU'VE REALLY GOT A THING FOR NOSES, DON'T YOU?

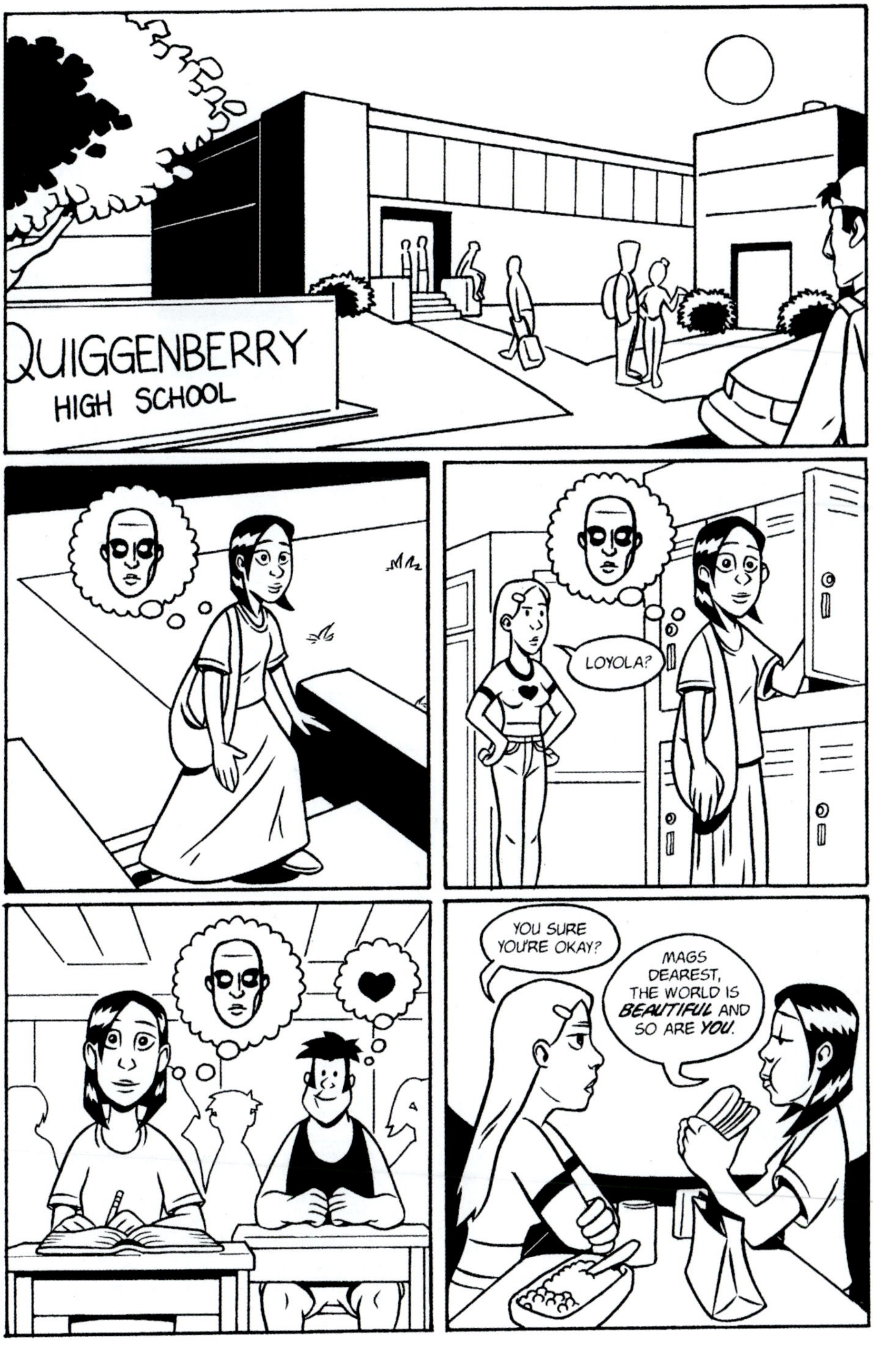

QUIGGENBERRY
HIGH SCHOOL
LOYOLA?
YOU SURE YOU'RE OKAY?
MAGS DEAREST, THE WORLD IS BEAUTIFUL AND SO ARE YOU.

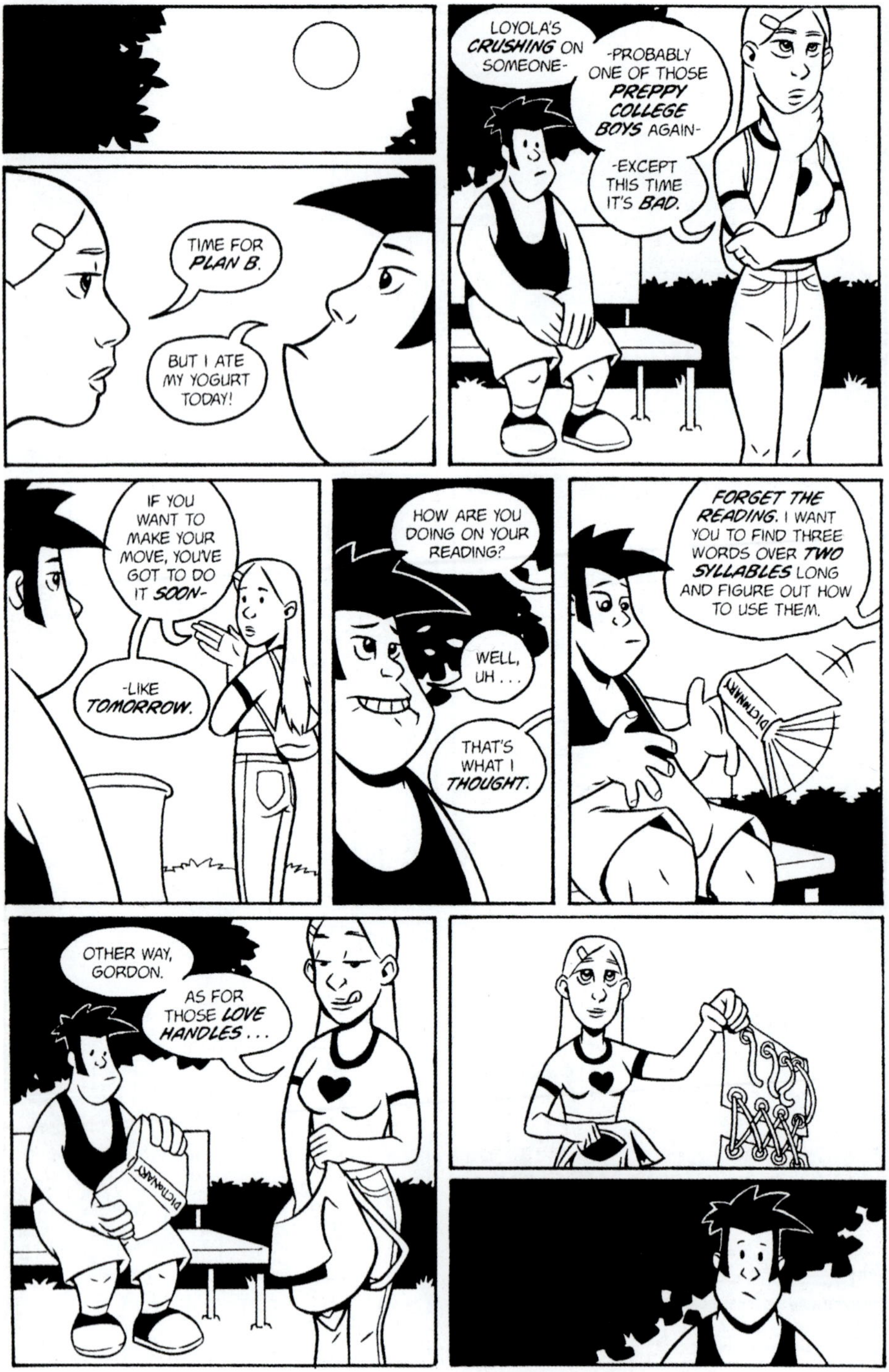

TIME FOR PLAN B.
BUT I ATE MY YOGURT TODAY!
LOYOLA'S CRUSHING ON SOMEONE-
-PROBABLY ONE OF THOSE PREPPY COLLEGE BOYS AGAIN-
-EXCEPT THIS TIME IT'S BAD.
IF YOU WANT TO MAKE YOUR MOVE, YOU'VE GOT TO DO IT SOON-
-LIKE TOMORROW.
HOW ARE YOU DOING ON YOUR READING?
WELL, UH . . .
THAT'S WHAT I THOUGHT.
FORGET THE READING. I WANT YOU TO FIND THREE WORDS OVER TWO SYLLABLES LONG AND FIGURE OUT HOW TO USE THEM.
DICTIONARY
OTHER WAY, GORDON.
AS FOR THOSE LOVE HANDLES . . .
DICTIONARY

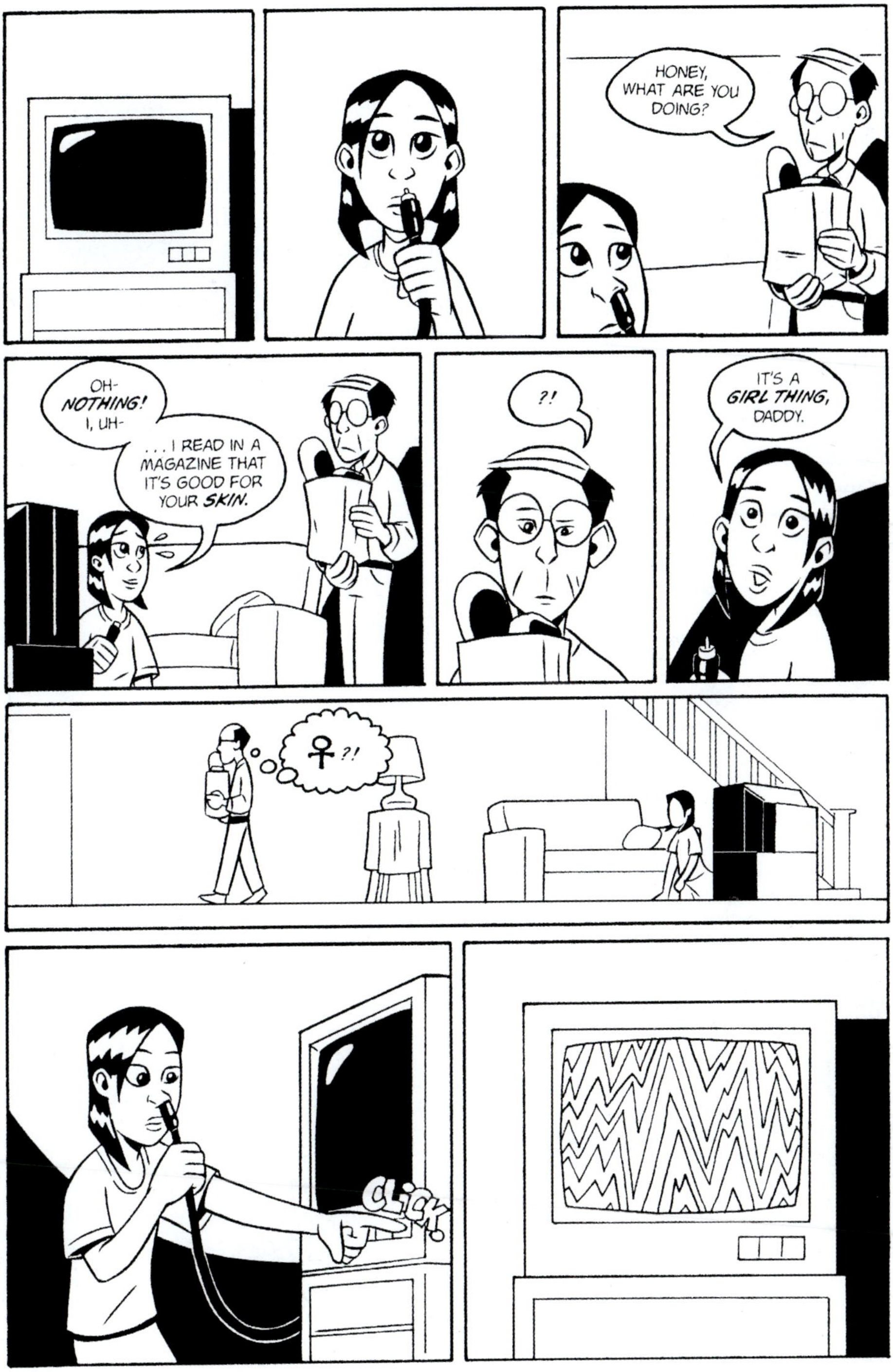
HONEY, WHAT ARE YOU DOING?
OH- NOTHING! I, UH-
. . . I READ IN A MAGAZINE THAT IT'S GOOD FOR YOUR SKIN.
?!
IT'S A GIRL THING, DADDY.
♀?!
CLICK!

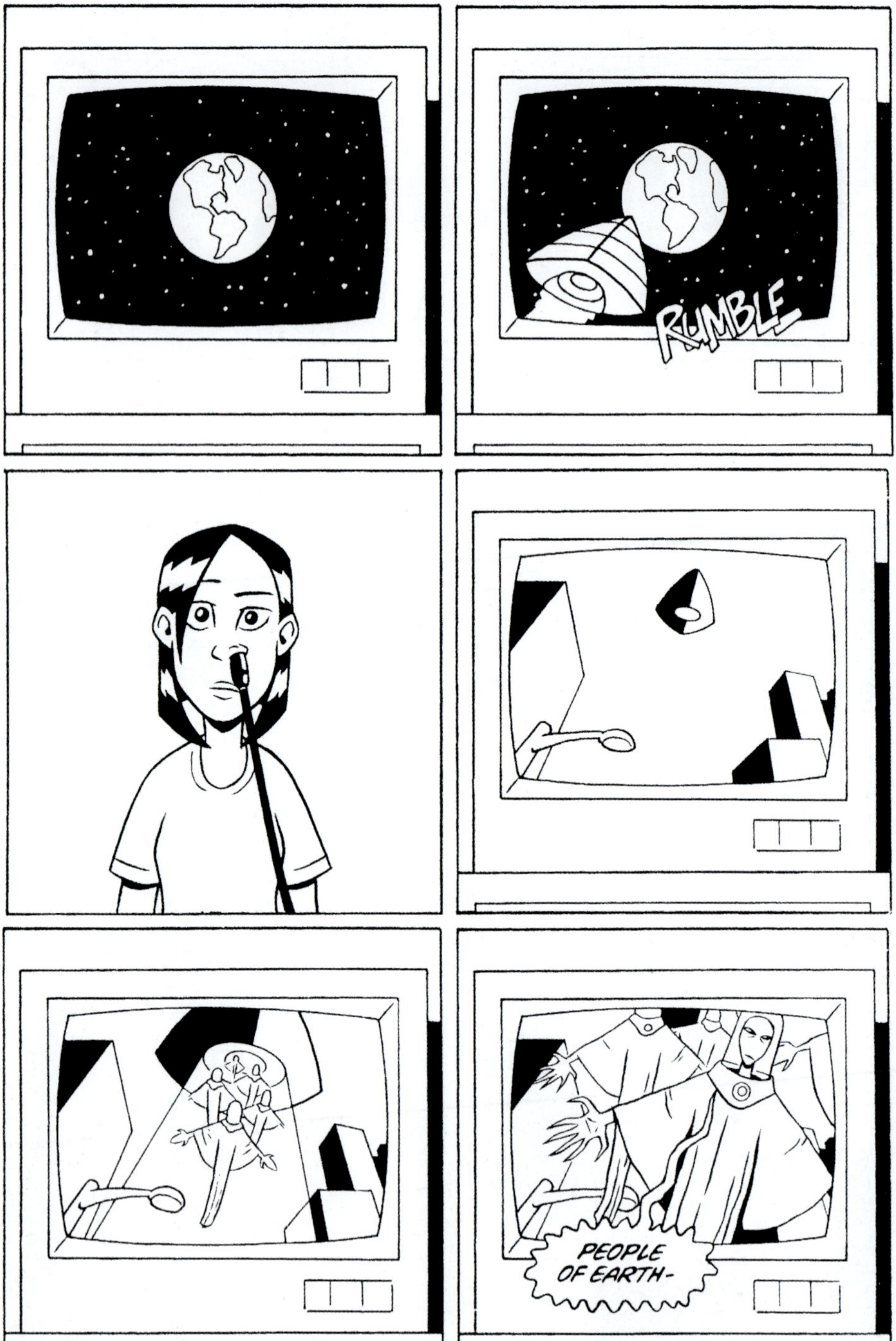
RUMBLE
PEOPLE OF EARTH-

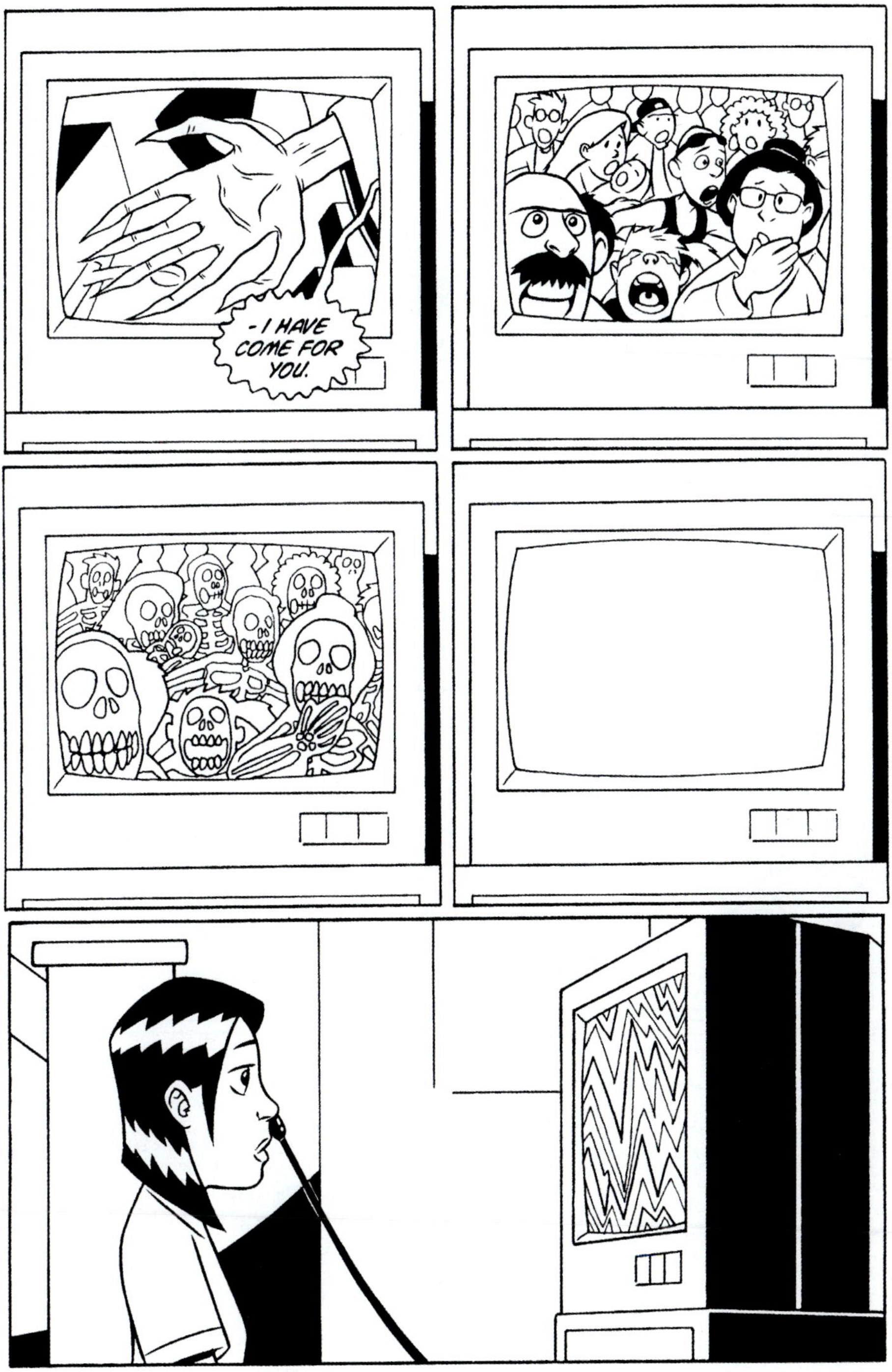
-I HAVE COME FOR YOU.

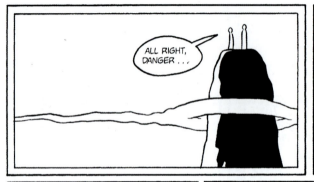

ALL RIGHT, DANGER...

WHAT *STRAIGHT-TO-VIDEO* SCI-FI FLICK DID YOU *INFLICT* ON MY *BRAIN?*

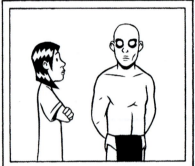

WHEN I RECEIVED THAT VISION, IT *CHANGED* ME- INTELLECTUALLY, EMOTIONALLY, EVEN *PHYSICALLY.* IT MADE ME *WHO I AM.*

I THOUGHT YOU WOULD *UNDERSTAND.* I'M *SORRY.*

NO, NO- I *DO!* ...WELL, I *WANT* TO.

PLEASE, DANGER. EXPLAIN.

...

I THINK IT'S A *WARNING*...OF HOW THINGS MAY *END* FOR *HUMANKIND.*

DO YOU KNOW WHY I'M UP HERE SO OFTEN, LOYOLA? I LOVE WATCHING *HUMANKIND.* WE ARE SUCH AN INTRICATE, BEAUTIFUL SPECIES- IT'S NO WONDER THAT WE *DOMINATE* OUR PLANET.

BUT THERE *ARE* OTHER PLANETS.

FROM THOSE OTHER PLANETS WILL COME OTHER *SPECIES,* MORE *EVOLVED* THAN OUR OWN-

-SPECIES CAPABLE OF *DOMINATING* US.

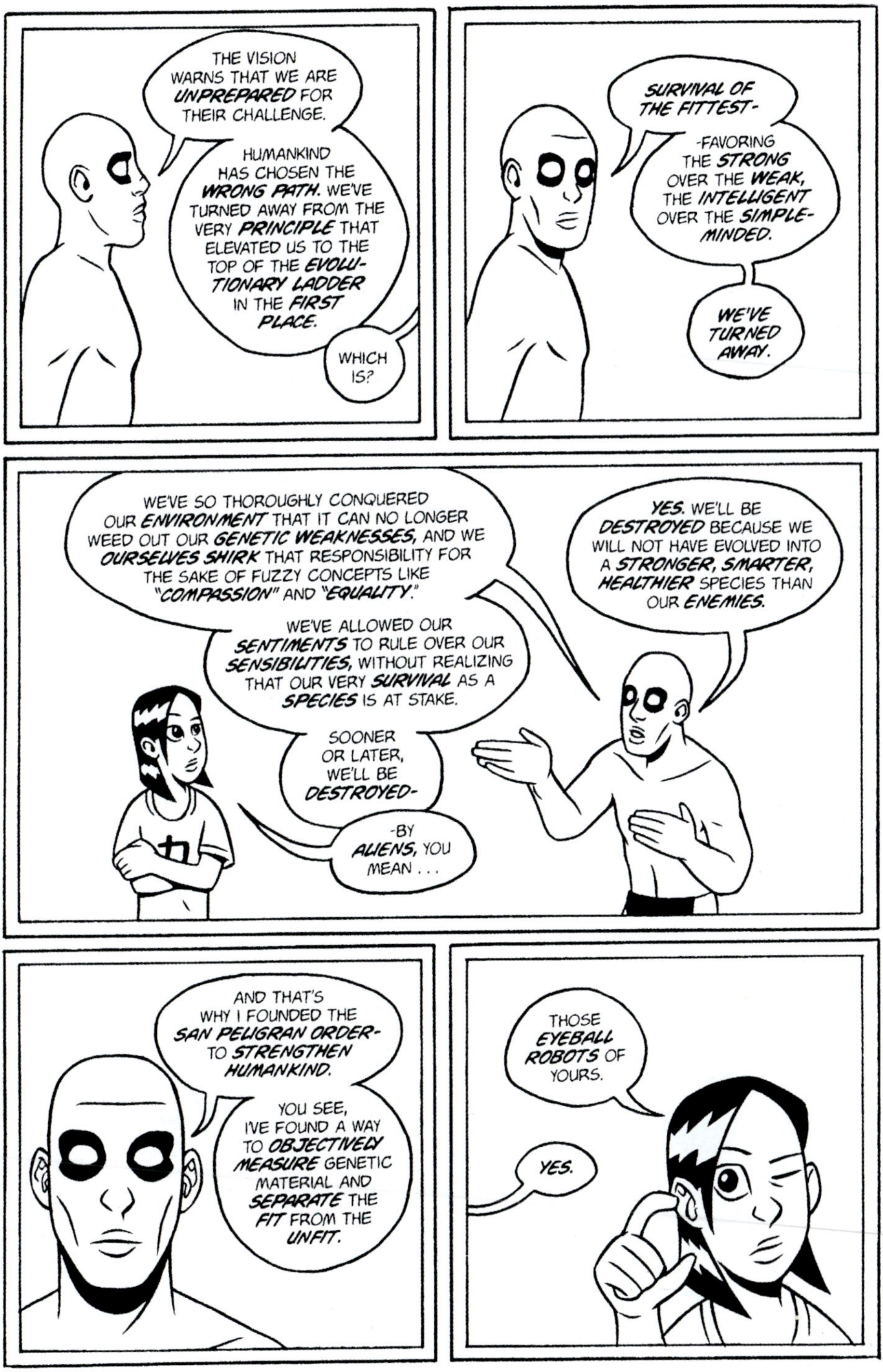
THE VISION WARNS THAT WE ARE UNPREPARED FOR THEIR CHALLENGE.
HUMANKIND HAS CHOSEN THE WRONG PATH. WE'VE TURNED AWAY FROM THE VERY PRINCIPLE THAT ELEVATED US TO THE TOP OF THE EVOLUTIONARY LADDER IN THE FIRST PLACE.
WHICH IS?
SURVIVAL OF THE FITTEST-
-FAVORING THE STRONG OVER THE WEAK, THE INTELLIGENT OVER THE SIMPLE-MINDED.
WE'VE TURNED AWAY.
WE'VE SO THOROUGHLY CONQUERED OUR ENVIRONMENT THAT IT CAN NO LONGER WEED OUT OUR GENETIC WEAKNESSES, AND WE OURSELVES SHIRK THAT RESPONSIBILITY FOR THE SAKE OF FUZZY CONCEPTS LIKE "COMPASSION" AND "EQUALITY."
WE'VE ALLOWED OUR SENTIMENTS TO RULE OVER OUR SENSIBILITIES, WITHOUT REALIZING THAT OUR VERY SURVIVAL AS A SPECIES IS AT STAKE.
SOONER OR LATER, WE'LL BE DESTROYED-
-BY ALIENS, YOU MEAN . . .
YES. WE'LL BE DESTROYED BECAUSE WE WILL NOT HAVE EVOLVED INTO A STRONGER, SMARTER, HEALTHIER SPECIES THAN OUR ENEMIES.
AND THAT'S WHY I FOUNDED THE SAN PELIGRAN ORDER-TO STRENGTHEN HUMANKIND.
YOU SEE, I'VE FOUND A WAY TO OBJECTIVELY MEASURE GENETIC MATERIAL AND SEPARATE THE FIT FROM THE UNFIT.
THOSE EYEBALL ROBOTS OF YOURS.
YES.

...SO DANGER, WHAT *EXACTLY* ARE YOU TRYING TO SAY?

WHAT HAPPENS TO THE "*UNFIT?*"

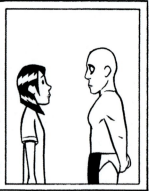

I CAN IMAGINE HOW *CALLOUS* THIS MUST SOUND TO YOU, LOYOLA.

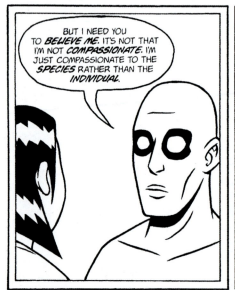

BUT I NEED YOU TO *BELIEVE ME.* IT'S NOT THAT I'M NOT *COMPASSIONATE.* I'M JUST COMPASSIONATE TO THE *SPECIES* RATHER THAN THE *INDIVIDUAL.*

I'VE RESEARCHED *THOUSANDS* OF OTHER *SOLUTIONS*... I MEAN, WHAT DO YOU THINK IT IS THAT I STORE IN THAT ENORMOUS *NETWORK* OF *BRAINS?* IF THERE WAS ANOTHER *WAY*...

...*BUT THERE ISN'T.*

I WANT TO *SAVE OUR SPECIES*— AND THIS IS THE *ONLY WAY I KNOW HOW.*

BELIEVE ME.

PLEASE.

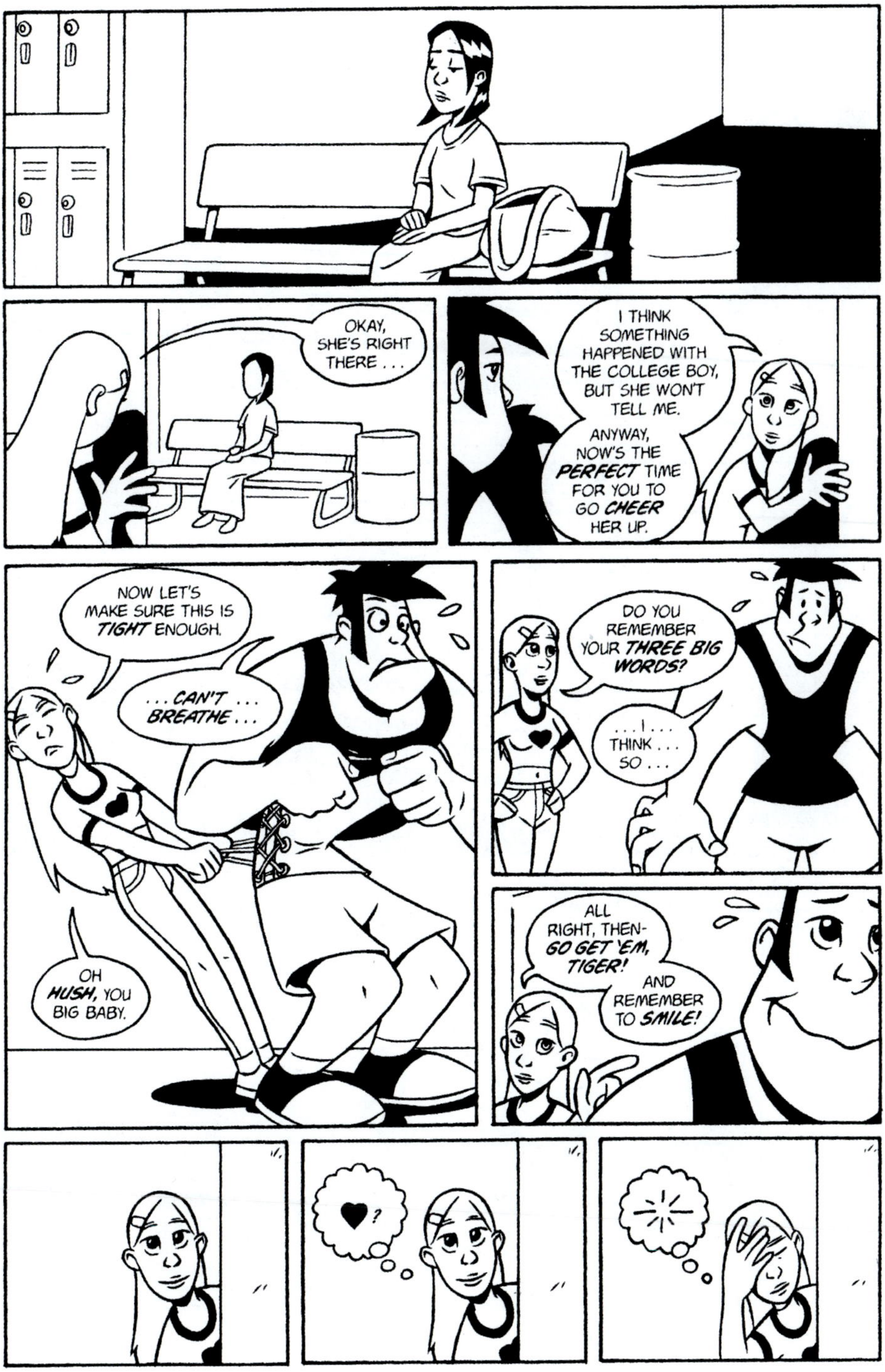
OKAY, SHE'S RIGHT THERE . . .
I THINK SOMETHING HAPPENED WITH THE COLLEGE BOY, BUT SHE WON'T TELL ME.
ANYWAY, NOW'S THE **PERFECT** TIME FOR YOU TO GO **CHEER** HER UP.
NOW LET'S MAKE SURE THIS IS **TIGHT** ENOUGH.
. . . **CAN'T** . . . **BREATHE** . . .
OH **HUSH,** YOU BIG BABY.
DO YOU REMEMBER YOUR **THREE BIG WORDS?**
. . . I . . . THINK . . . SO . . .
ALL RIGHT, THEN- **GO GET 'EM, TIGER!**
AND REMEMBER TO **SMILE!**

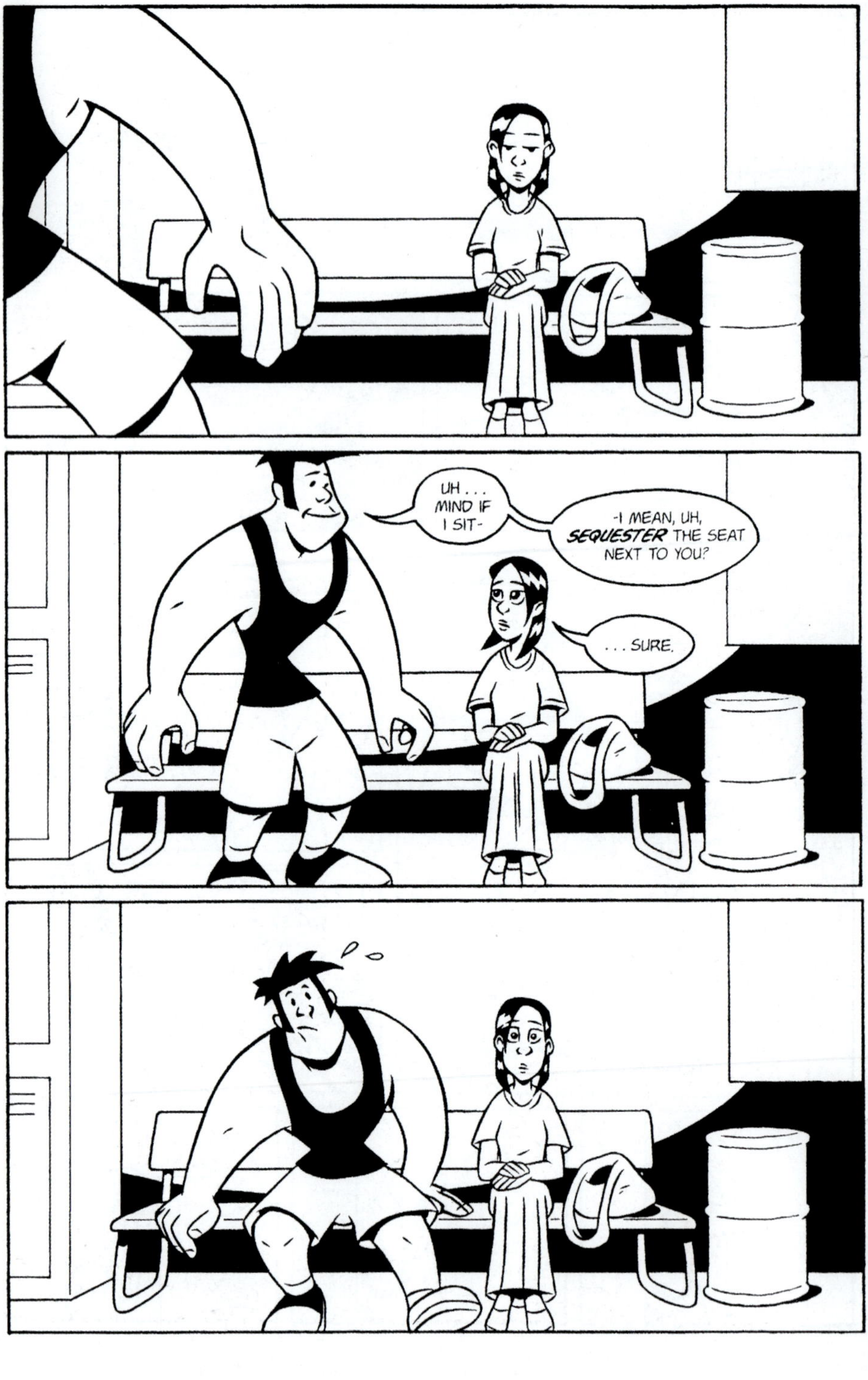
UH . . . MIND IF I SIT-
-I MEAN, UH, SEQUESTER THE SEAT NEXT TO YOU?
. . . SURE.

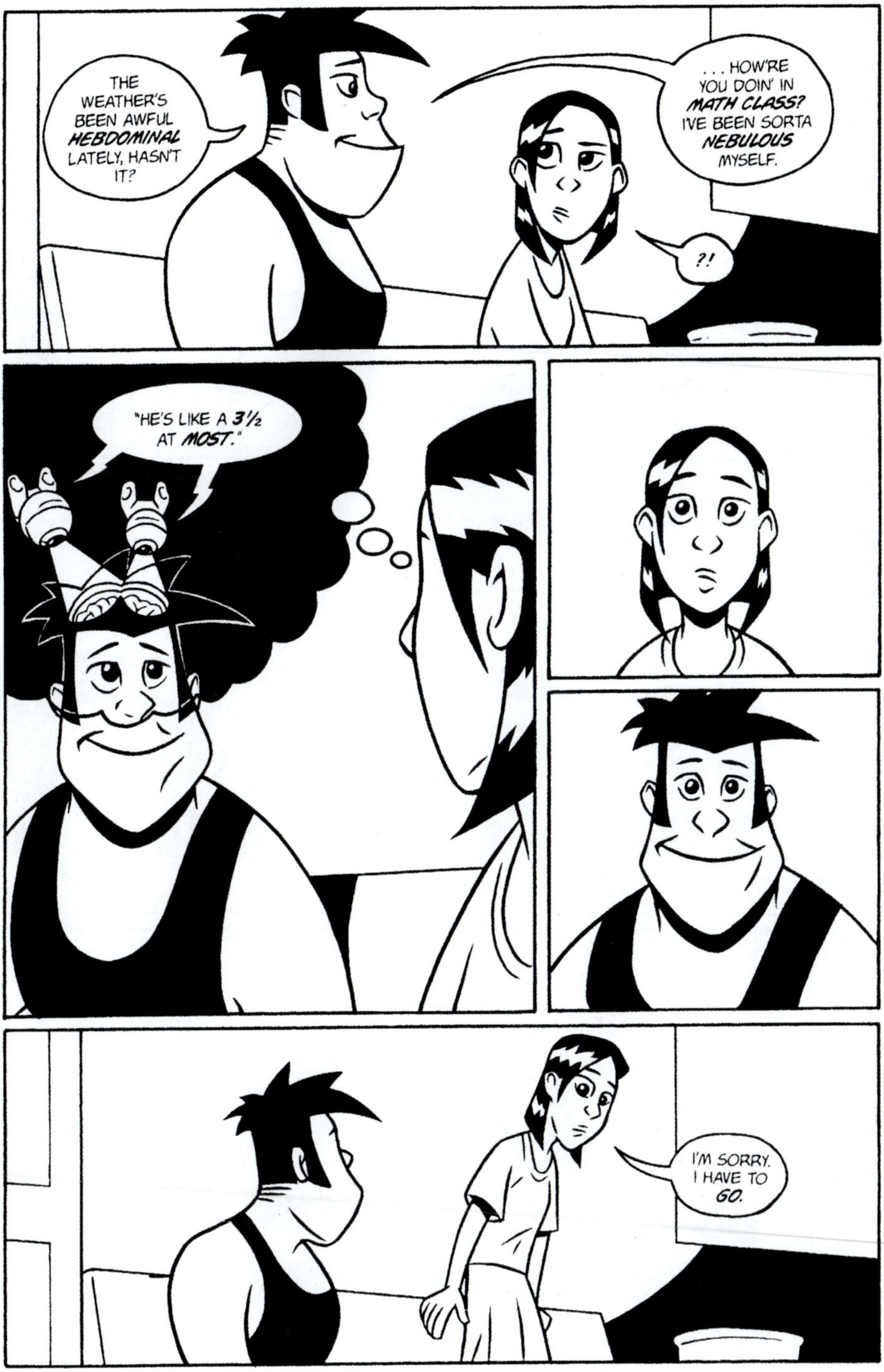

THE WEATHER'S BEEN AWFUL HEBDOMINAL LATELY, HASN'T IT?
. . . HOW'RE YOU DOIN' IN MATH CLASS? I'VE BEEN SORTA NEBULOUS MYSELF.
?!
"HE'S LIKE A 3½ AT MOST."
I'M SORRY. I HAVE TO GO.

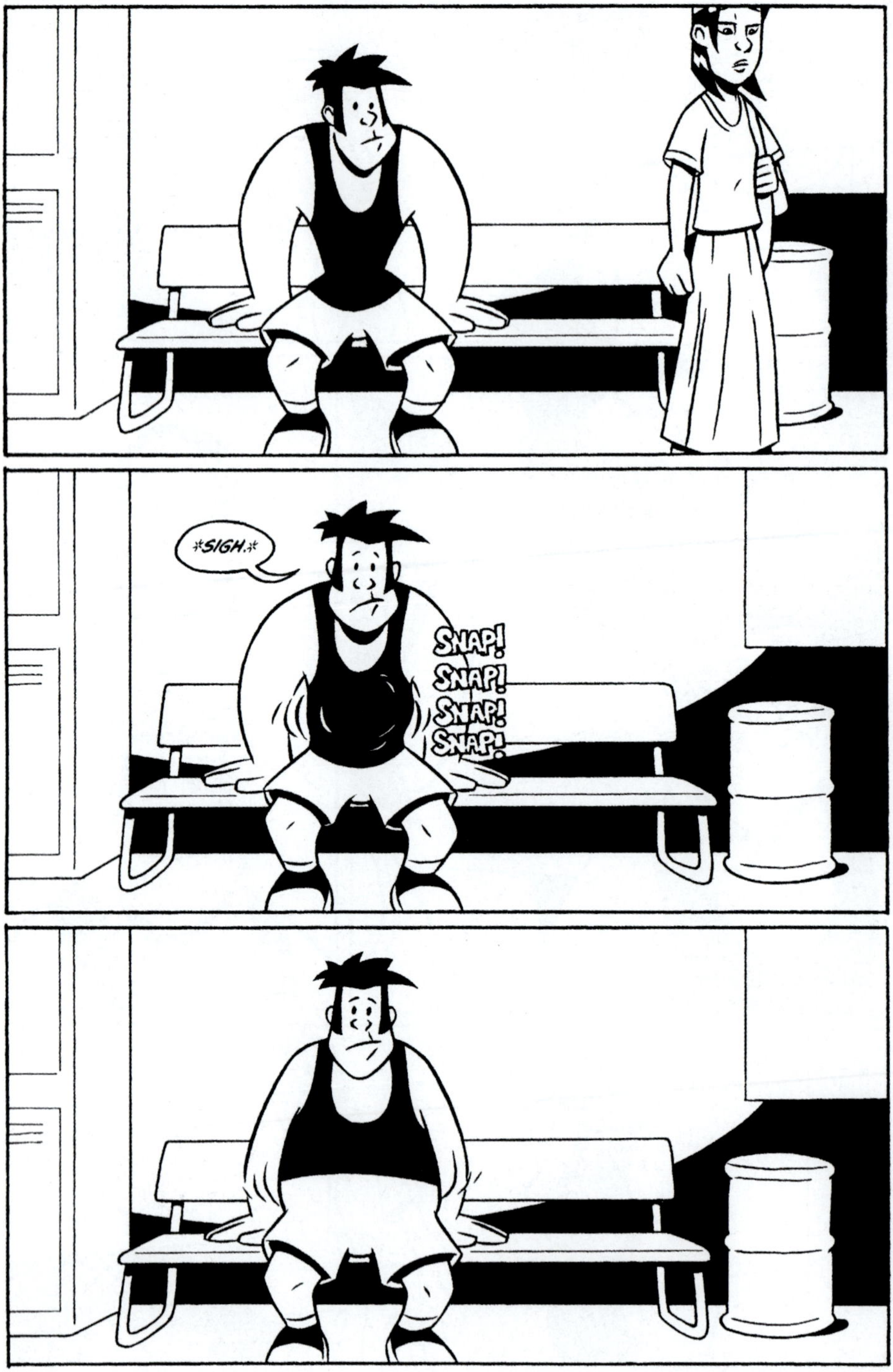

SIGH.
SNAP!
SNAP!
SNAP!
SNAP!

CHAPTER THREE

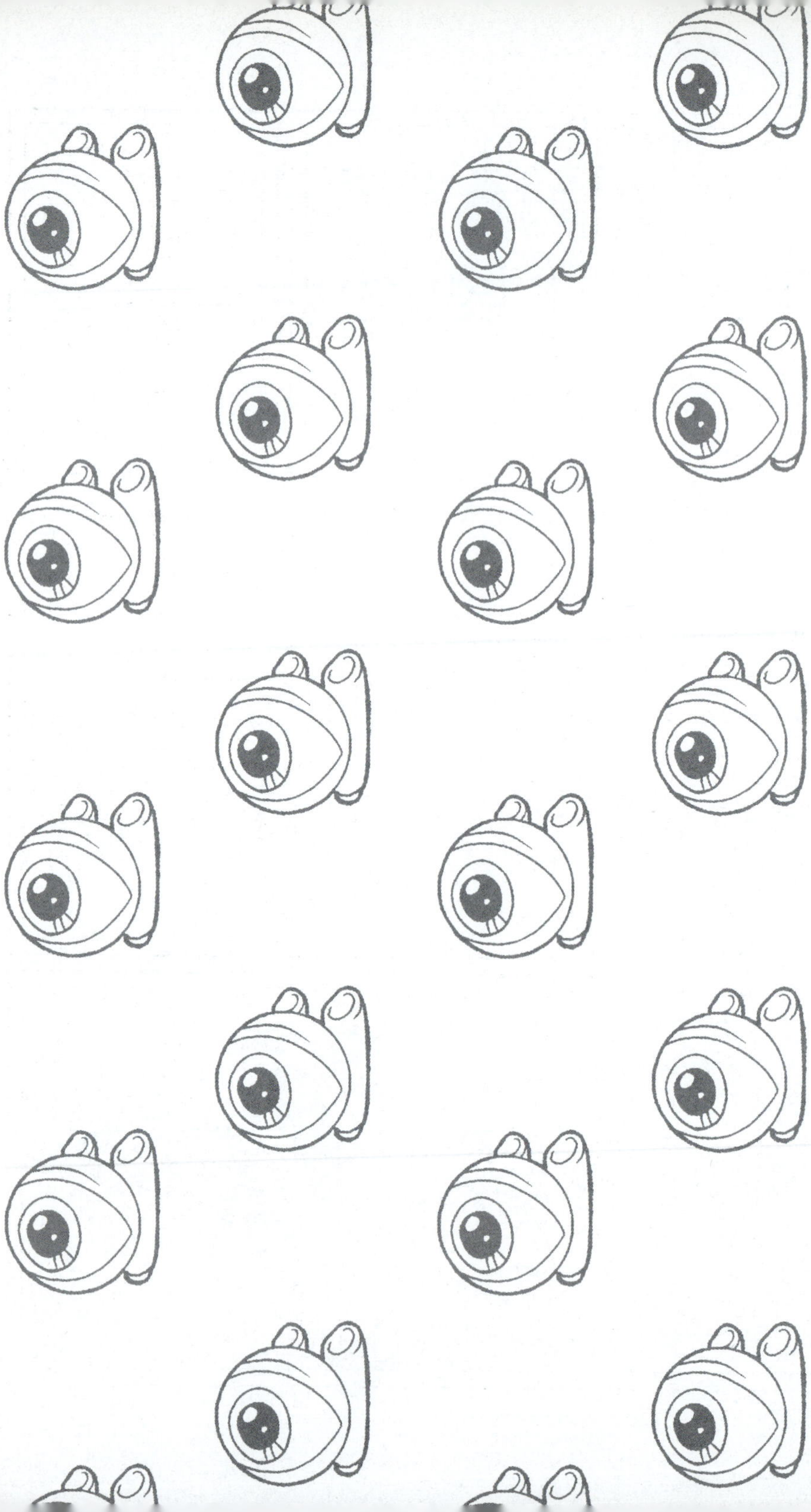

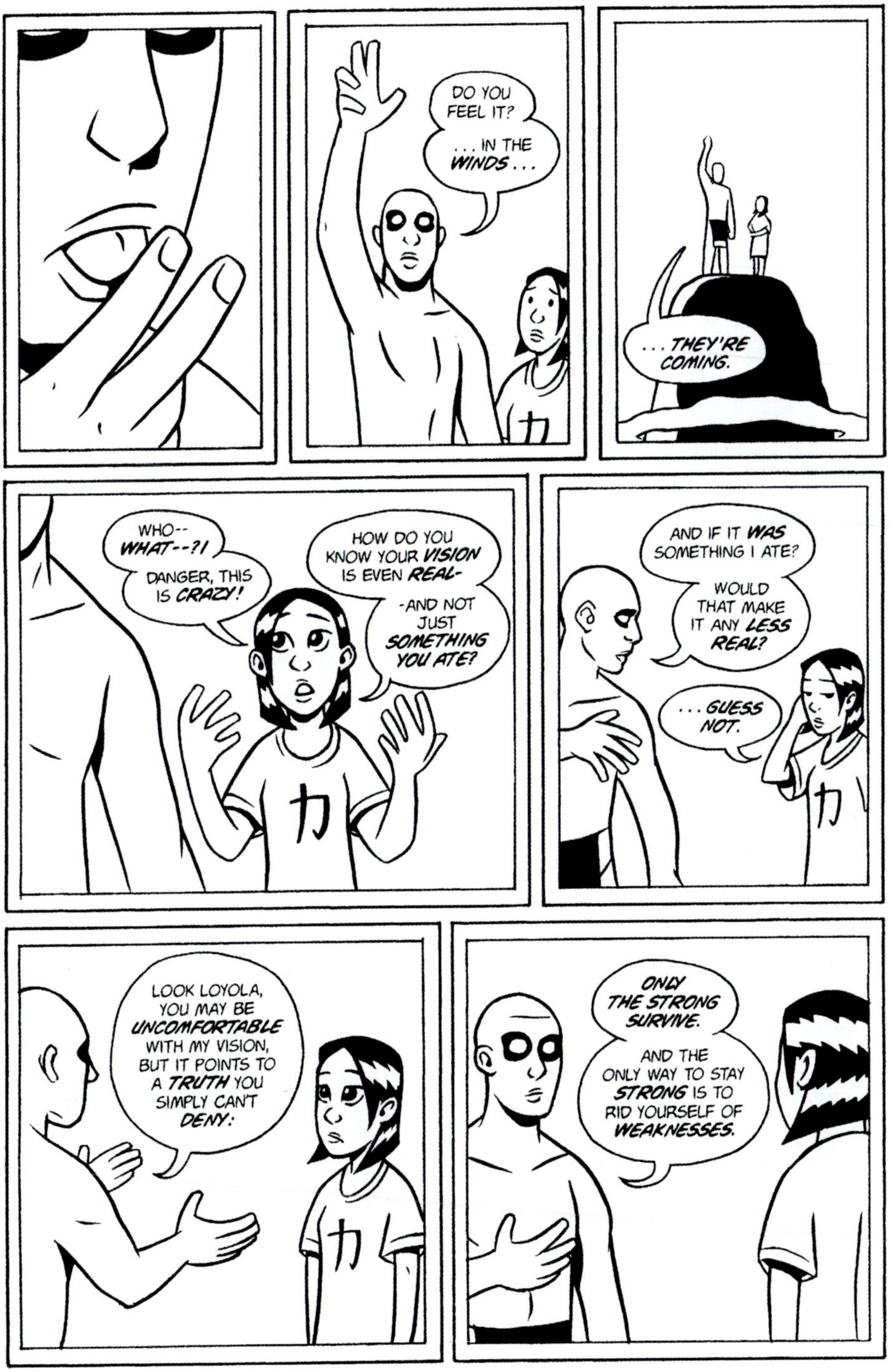
DO YOU FEEL IT?
. . . IN THE WINDS . . .
. . . THEY'RE COMING.
WHO-- WHAT--?!
DANGER, THIS IS CRAZY!
HOW DO YOU KNOW YOUR VISION IS EVEN REAL-
-AND NOT JUST SOMETHING YOU ATE?
AND IF IT WAS SOMETHING I ATE?
WOULD THAT MAKE IT ANY LESS REAL?
. . . GUESS NOT.
LOOK LOYOLA, YOU MAY BE UNCOMFORTABLE WITH MY VISION, BUT IT POINTS TO A TRUTH YOU SIMPLY CAN'T DENY:
ONLY THE STRONG SURVIVE.
AND THE ONLY WAY TO STAY STRONG IS TO RID YOURSELF OF WEAKNESSES.

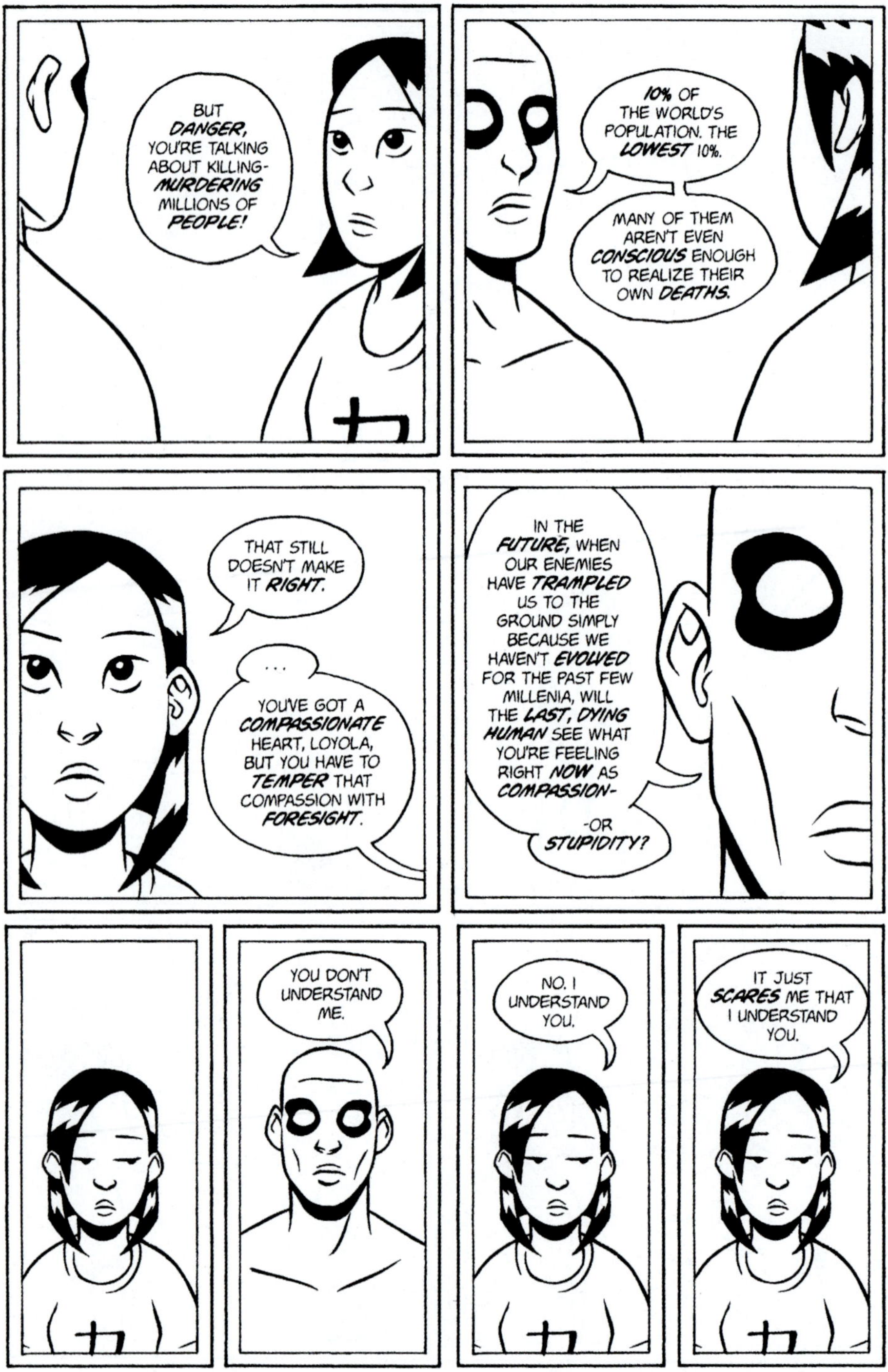
BUT DANGER, YOU'RE TALKING ABOUT KILLING- MURDERING MILLIONS OF PEOPLE!
10% OF THE WORLD'S POPULATION. THE LOWEST 10%.
MANY OF THEM AREN'T EVEN CONSCIOUS ENOUGH TO REALIZE THEIR OWN DEATHS.
THAT STILL DOESN'T MAKE IT RIGHT.
. . .
YOU'VE GOT A COMPASSIONATE HEART, LOYOLA, BUT YOU HAVE TO TEMPER THAT COMPASSION WITH FORESIGHT.
IN THE FUTURE, WHEN OUR ENEMIES HAVE TRAMPLED US TO THE GROUND SIMPLY BECAUSE WE HAVEN'T EVOLVED FOR THE PAST FEW MILLENIA, WILL THE LAST, DYING HUMAN SEE WHAT YOU'RE FEELING RIGHT NOW AS COMPASSION-
-OR STUPIDITY?
YOU DON'T UNDERSTAND ME.
NO. I UNDERSTAND YOU.
IT JUST SCARES ME THAT I UNDERSTAND YOU.

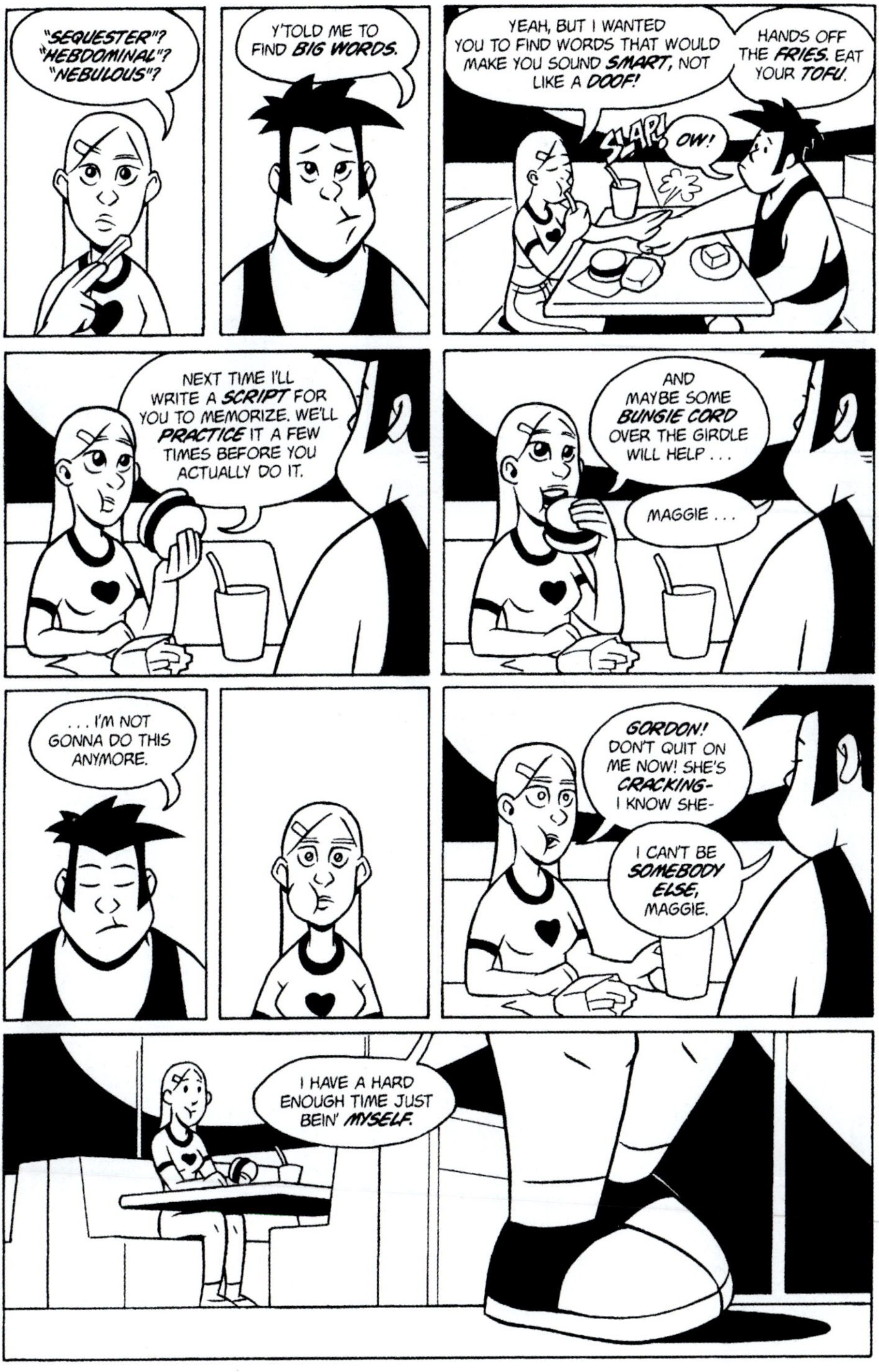
"SEQUESTER"? "HEBDOMINAL"? "NEBULOUS"?
Y'TOLD ME TO FIND BIG WORDS.
YEAH, BUT I WANTED YOU TO FIND WORDS THAT WOULD MAKE YOU SOUND SMART, NOT LIKE A DOOF!
HANDS OFF THE FRIES. EAT YOUR TOFU.
SLAP!
OW!
NEXT TIME I'LL WRITE A SCRIPT FOR YOU TO MEMORIZE. WE'LL PRACTICE IT A FEW TIMES BEFORE YOU ACTUALLY DO IT.
AND MAYBE SOME BUNGIE CORD OVER THE GIRDLE WILL HELP . . .
MAGGIE . . .
. . . I'M NOT GONNA DO THIS ANYMORE.
GORDON! DON'T QUIT ON ME NOW! SHE'S CRACKING- I KNOW SHE-
I CAN'T BE SOMEBODY ELSE, MAGGIE.
I HAVE A HARD ENOUGH TIME JUST BEIN' MYSELF.

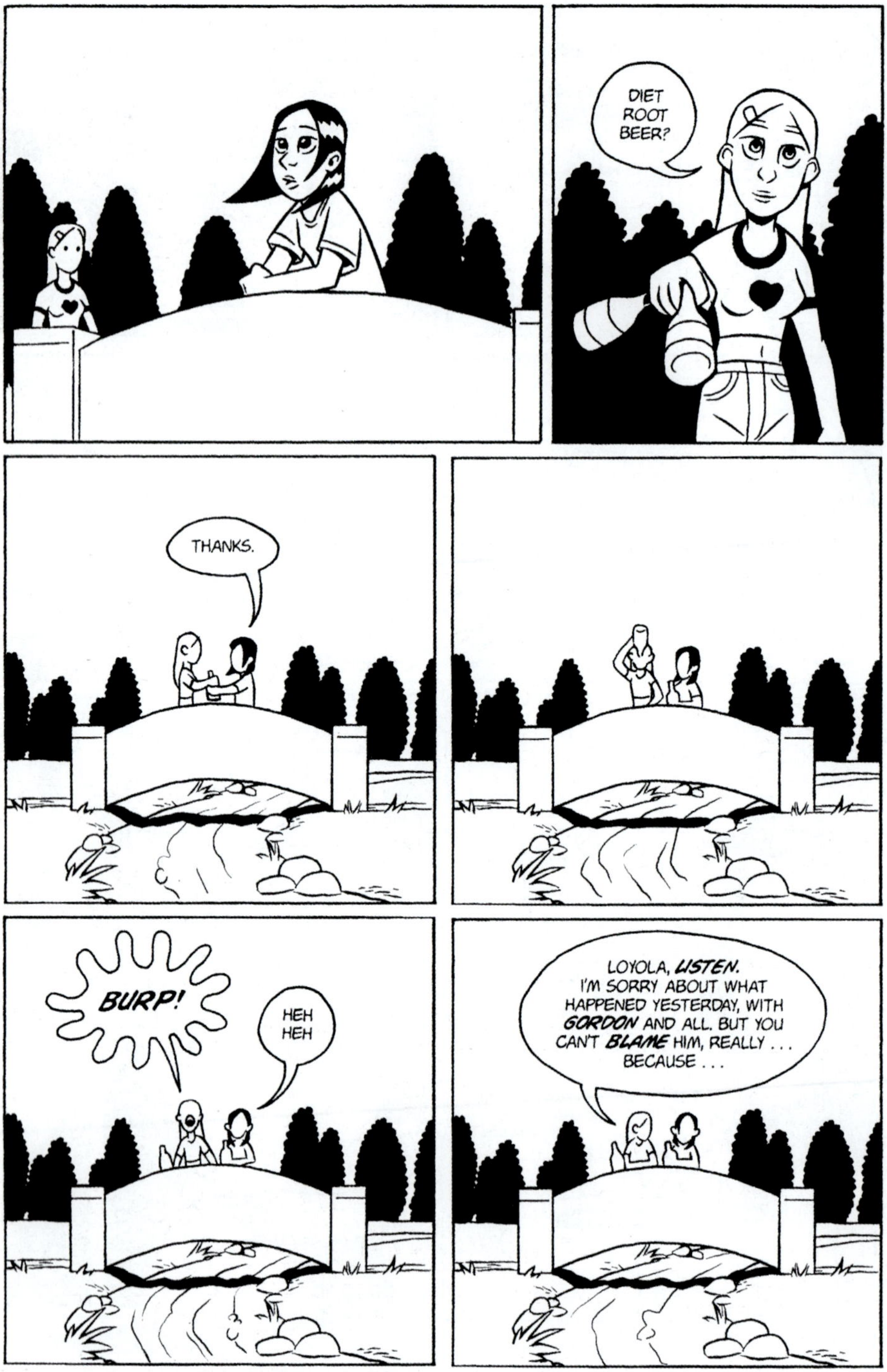
DIET
ROOT
BEER?
THANKS.
BURP!
HEH
HEH
LOYOLA, LISTEN.
I'M SORRY ABOUT WHAT
HAPPENED YESTERDAY, WITH
GORDON AND ALL. BUT YOU
CAN'T BLAME HIM, REALLY . . .
BECAUSE . . .

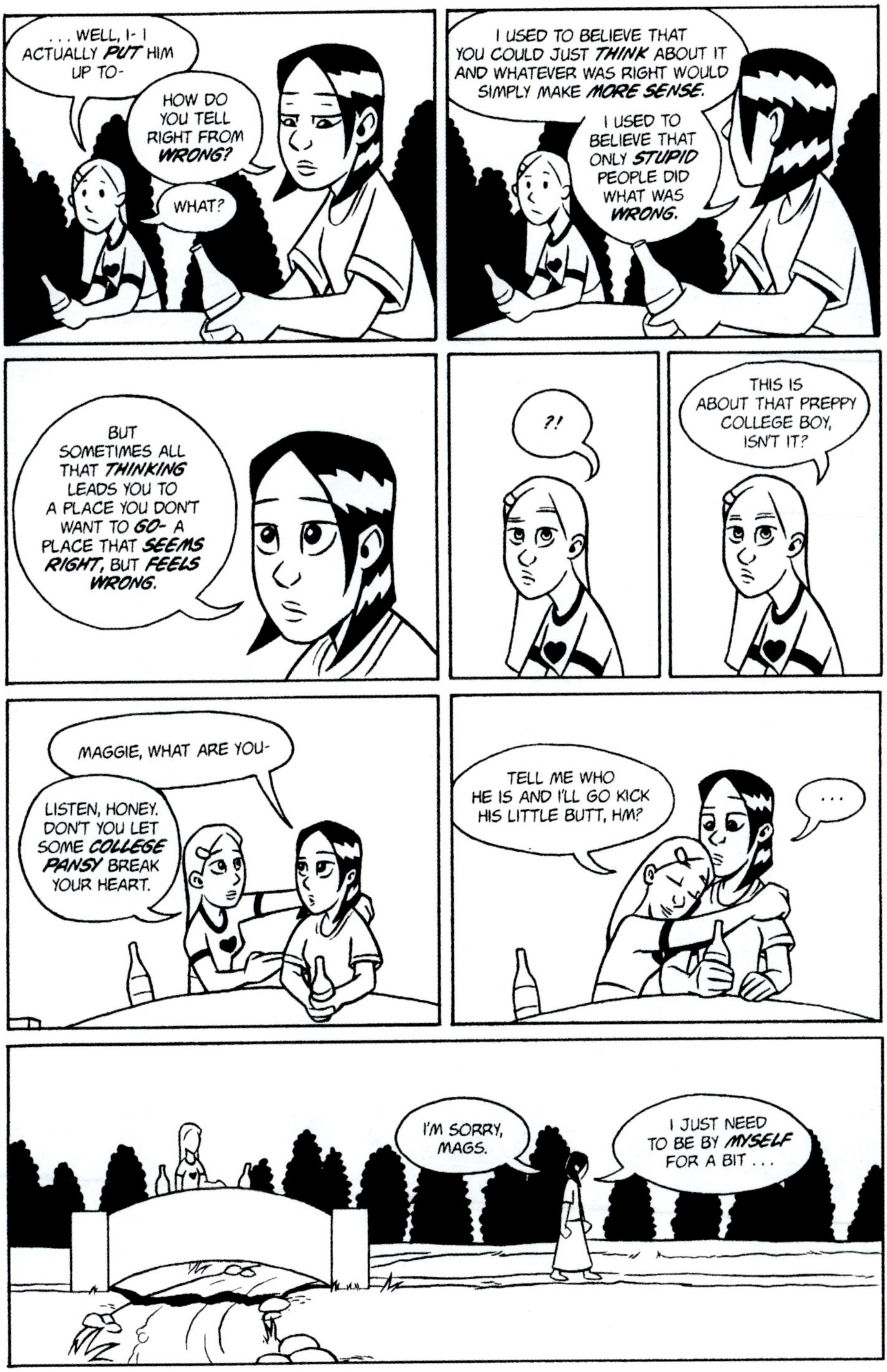
. . . WELL, I- I ACTUALLY PUT HIM UP TO-
HOW DO YOU TELL RIGHT FROM WRONG?
WHAT?
I USED TO BELIEVE THAT YOU COULD JUST THINK ABOUT IT AND WHATEVER WAS RIGHT WOULD SIMPLY MAKE MORE SENSE.
I USED TO BELIEVE THAT ONLY STUPID PEOPLE DID WHAT WAS WRONG.
BUT SOMETIMES ALL THAT THINKING LEADS YOU TO A PLACE YOU DON'T WANT TO GO- A PLACE THAT SEEMS RIGHT, BUT FEELS WRONG.
?!
THIS IS ABOUT THAT PREPPY COLLEGE BOY, ISN'T IT?
MAGGIE, WHAT ARE YOU-
LISTEN, HONEY. DON'T YOU LET SOME COLLEGE PANSY BREAK YOUR HEART.
TELL ME WHO HE IS AND I'LL GO KICK HIS LITTLE BUTT, HM?
. . .
I'M SORRY, MAGS.
I JUST NEED TO BE BY MYSELF FOR A BIT . . .

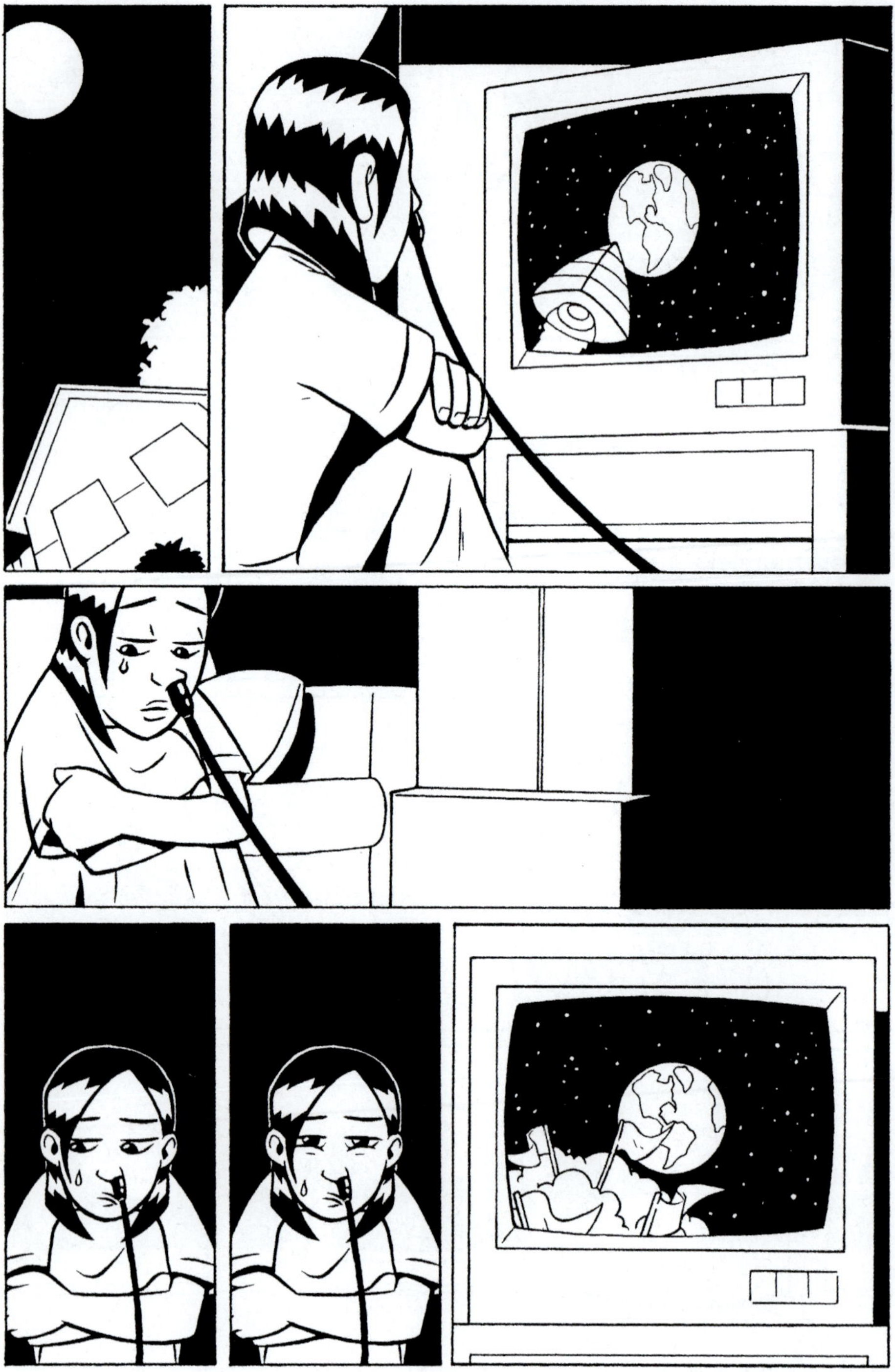

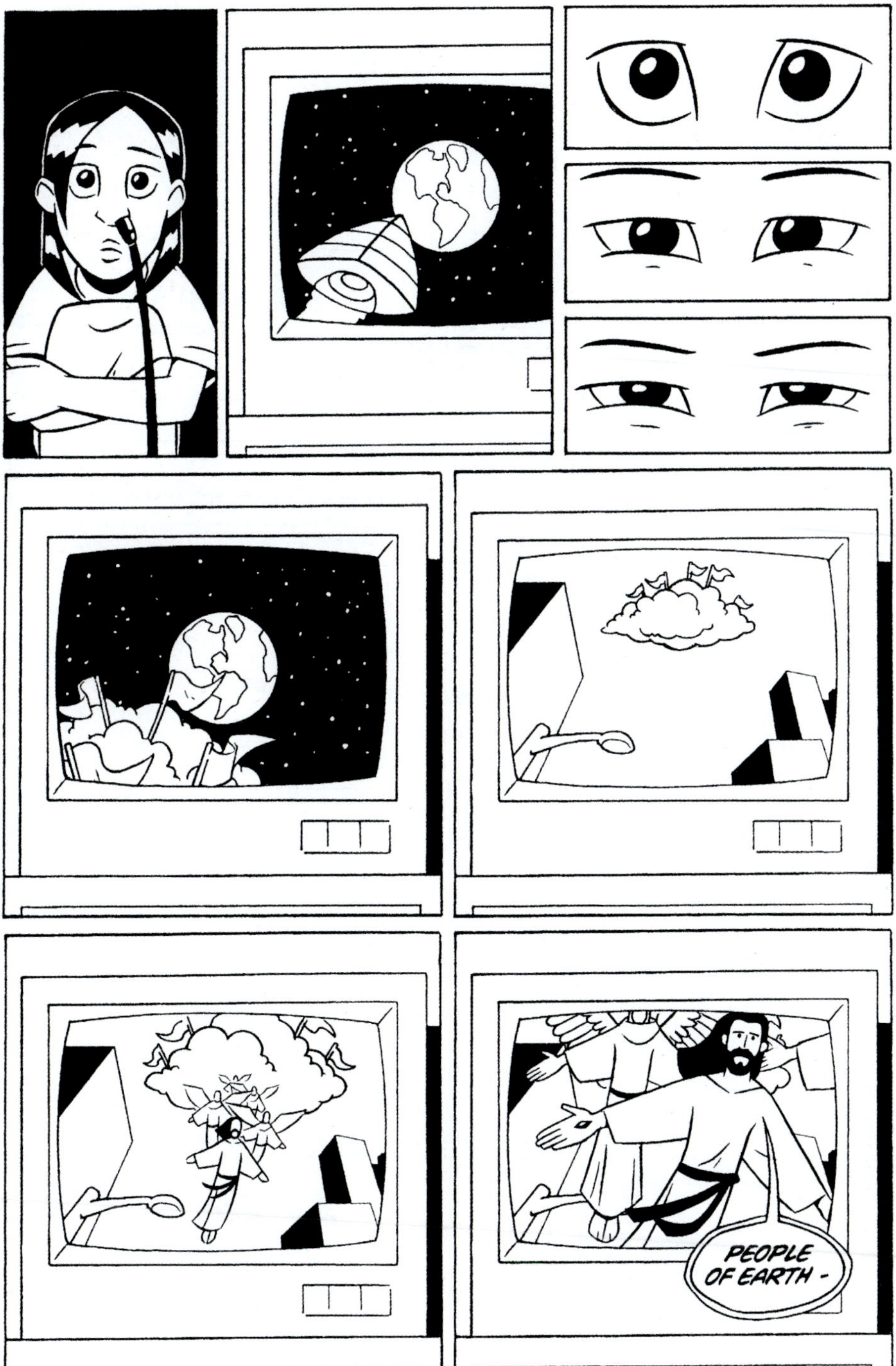
PEOPLE OF EARTH -

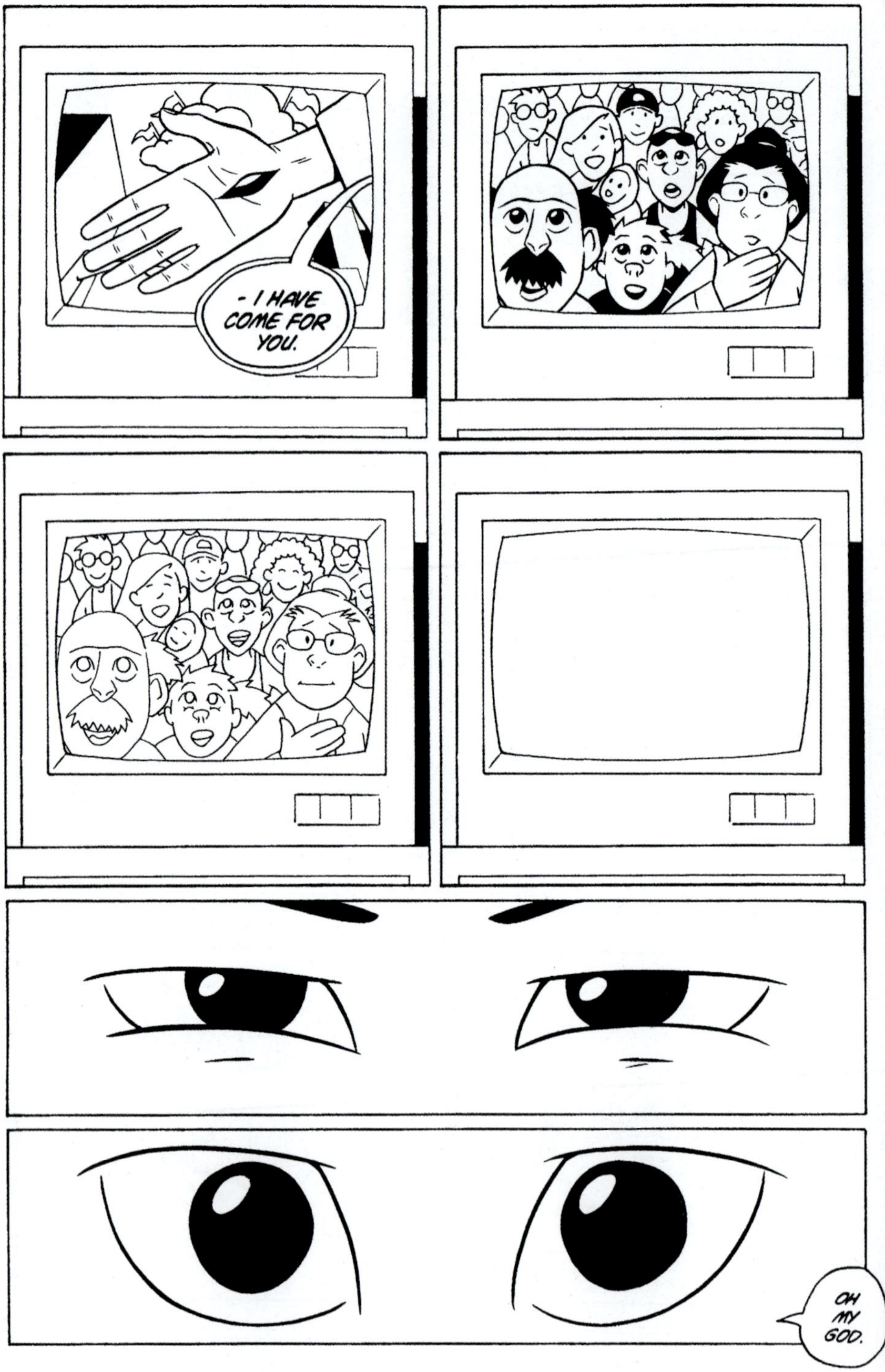
- I HAVE COME FOR YOU.
OH MY GOD.

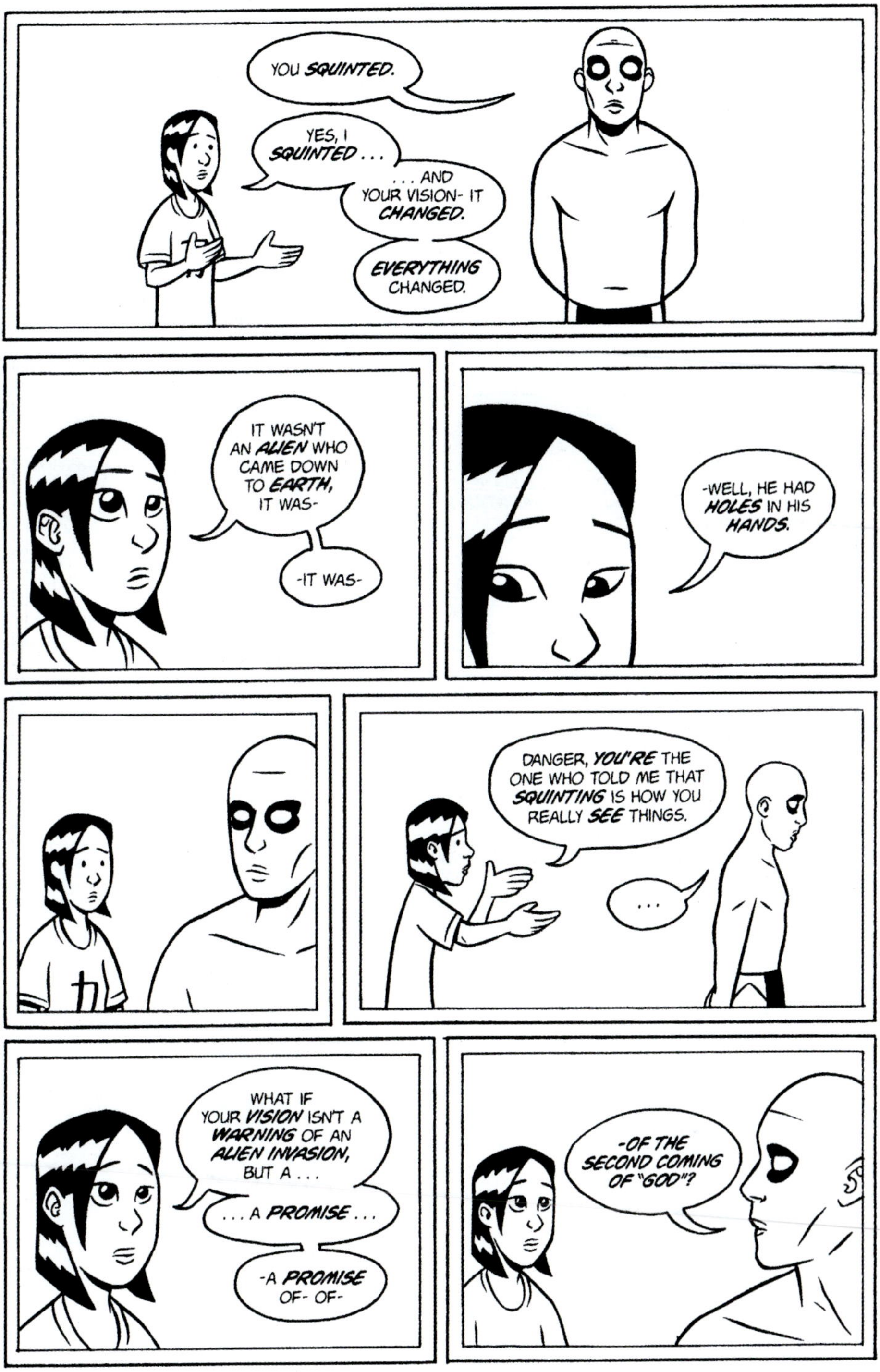
YOU SQUINTED.
YES, I SQUINTED . . .
. . . AND YOUR VISION- IT CHANGED.
EVERYTHING CHANGED.
IT WASN'T AN ALIEN WHO CAME DOWN TO EARTH, IT WAS-
-IT WAS-
-WELL, HE HAD HOLES IN HIS HANDS.
DANGER, YOU'RE THE ONE WHO TOLD ME THAT SQUINTING IS HOW YOU REALLY SEE THINGS.
. . .
WHAT IF YOUR VISION ISN'T A WARNING OF AN ALIEN INVASION, BUT A . . .
. . . A PROMISE . . .
-A PROMISE OF- OF-
-OF THE SECOND COMING OF "GOD"?

DO YOU REALLY BELIEVE "GOD" WILL COME DOWN FROM HEAVEN TO LEAD HIS PEOPLE TO SALVATION?
I . . . I DON'T KNOW.
. . . DO YOU REALLY BELIEVE ALIENS WILL COME DOWN AND ANNIHILATE THE HUMAN RACE?
YES.

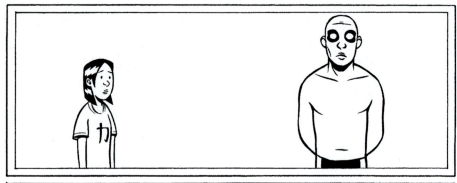

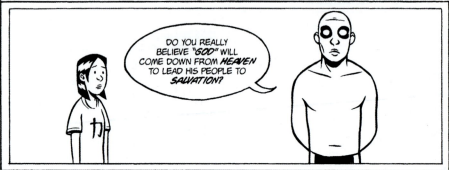

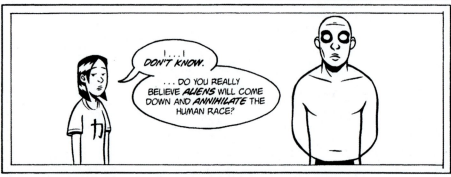

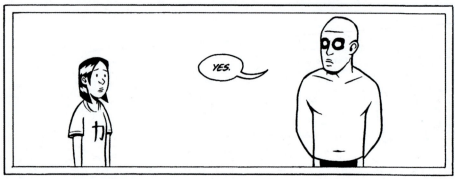

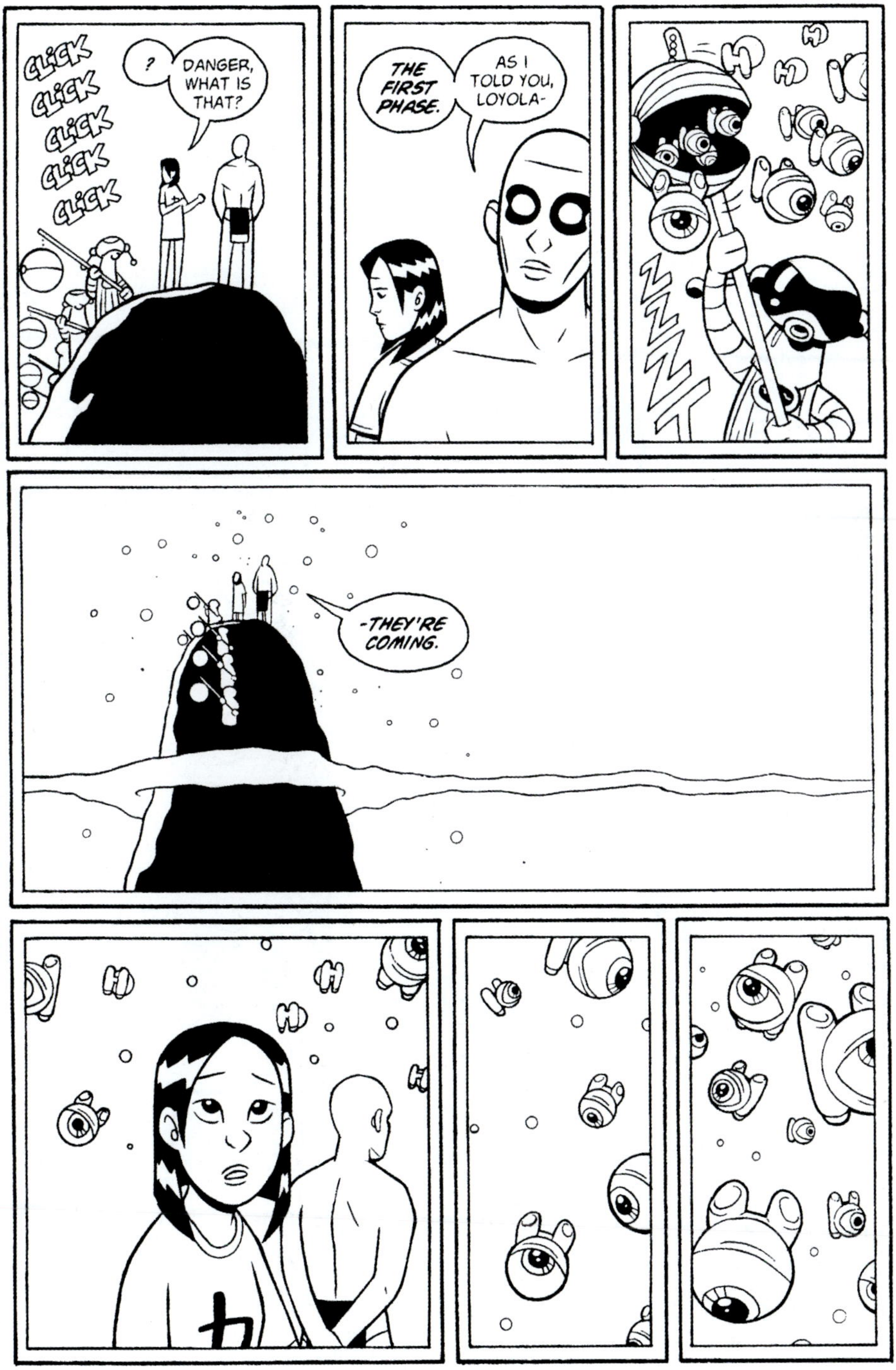
CLICK CLICK CLICK CLICK CLICK
?
DANGER, WHAT IS THAT?
THE FIRST PHASE.
AS I TOLD YOU, LOYOLA-
NNNT
-THEY'RE COMING.

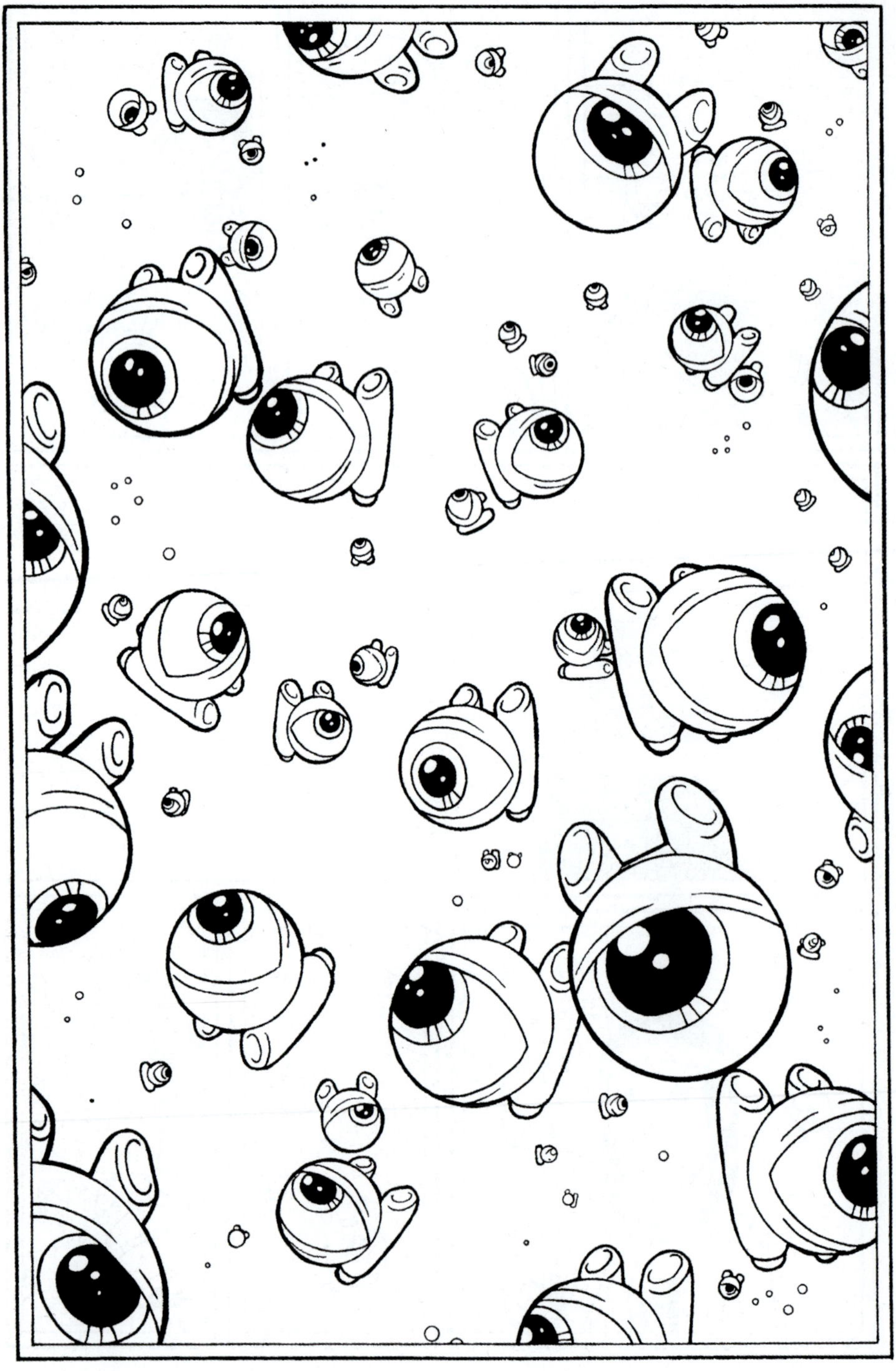

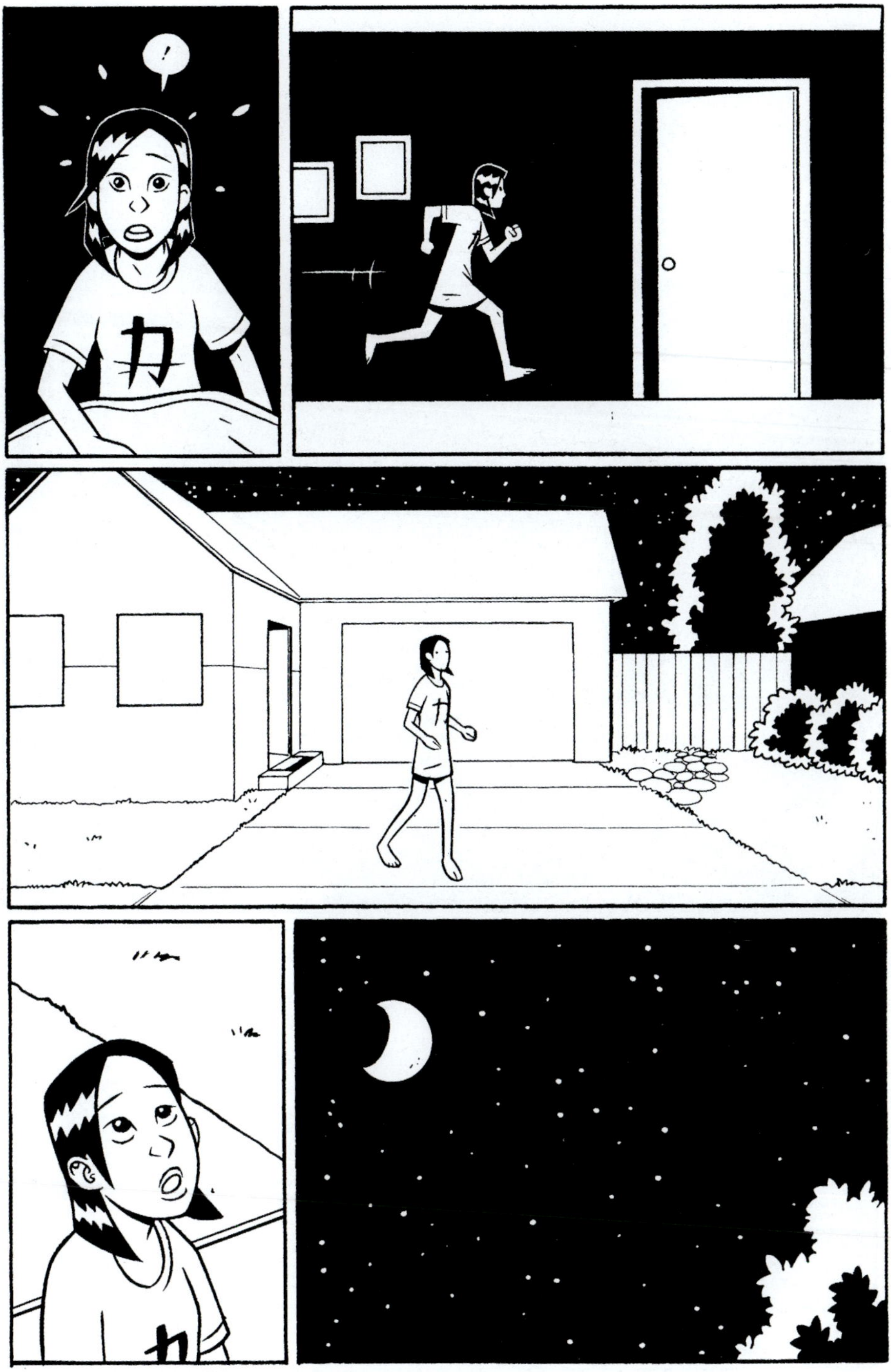
!

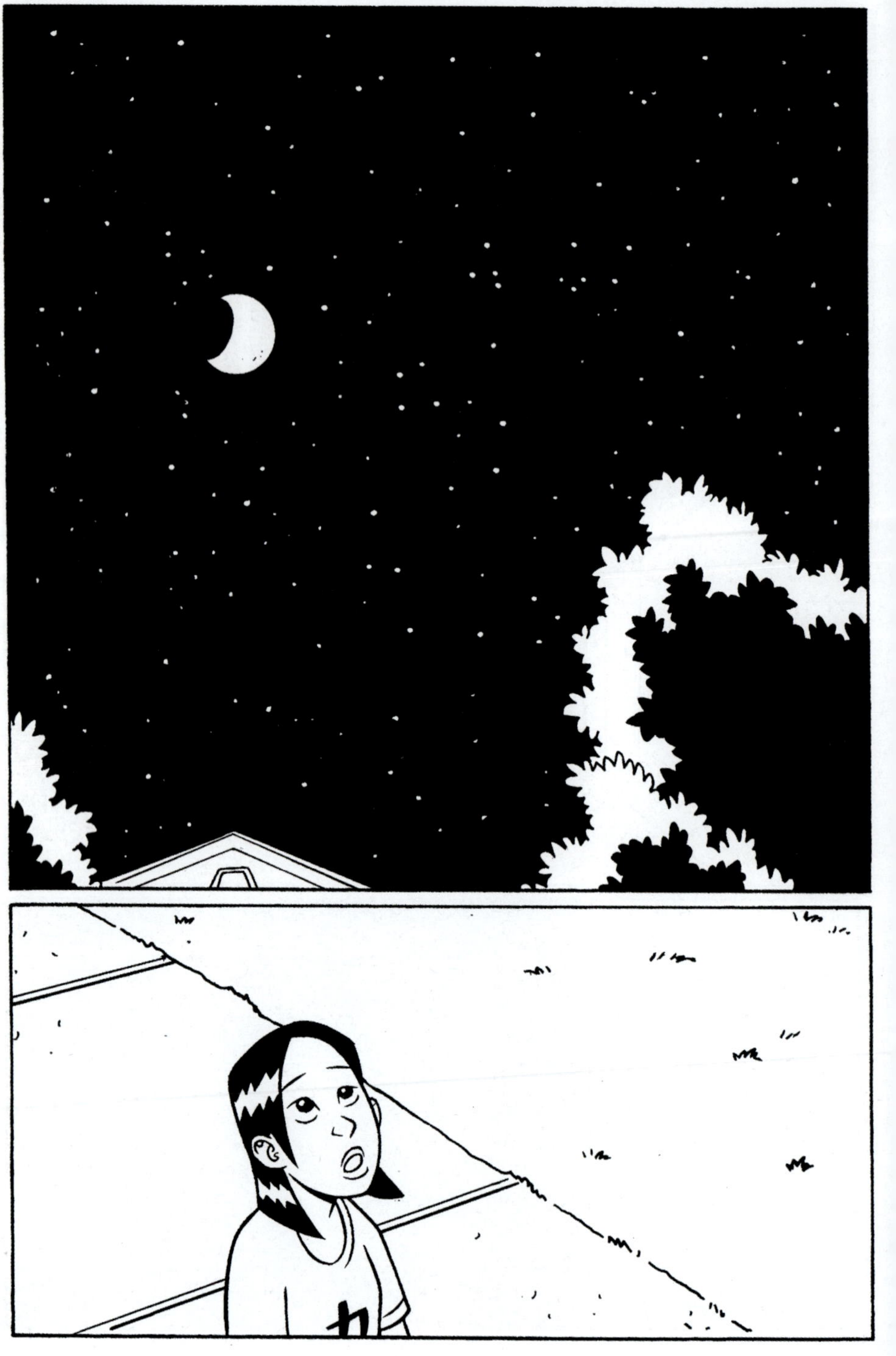

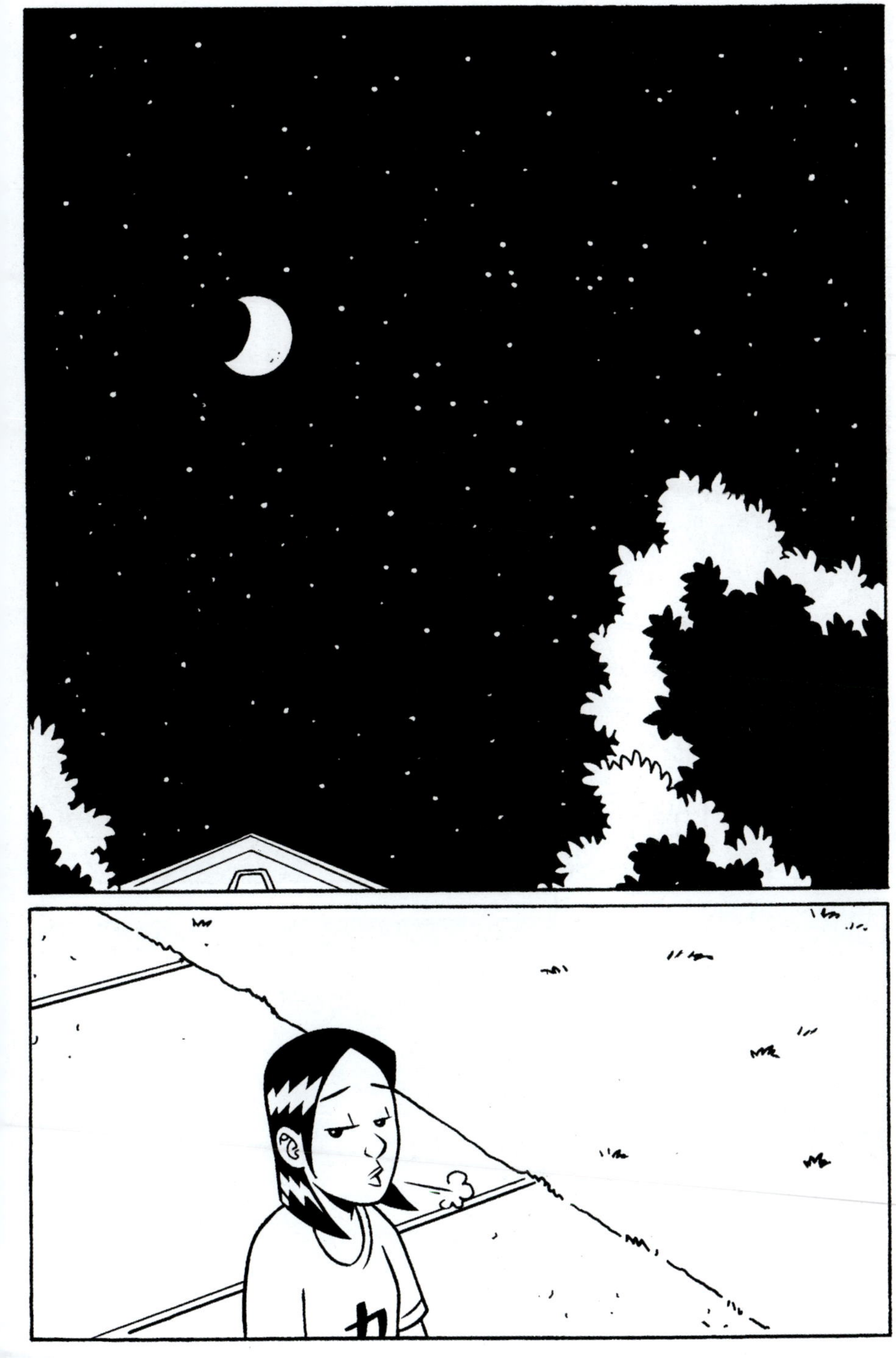

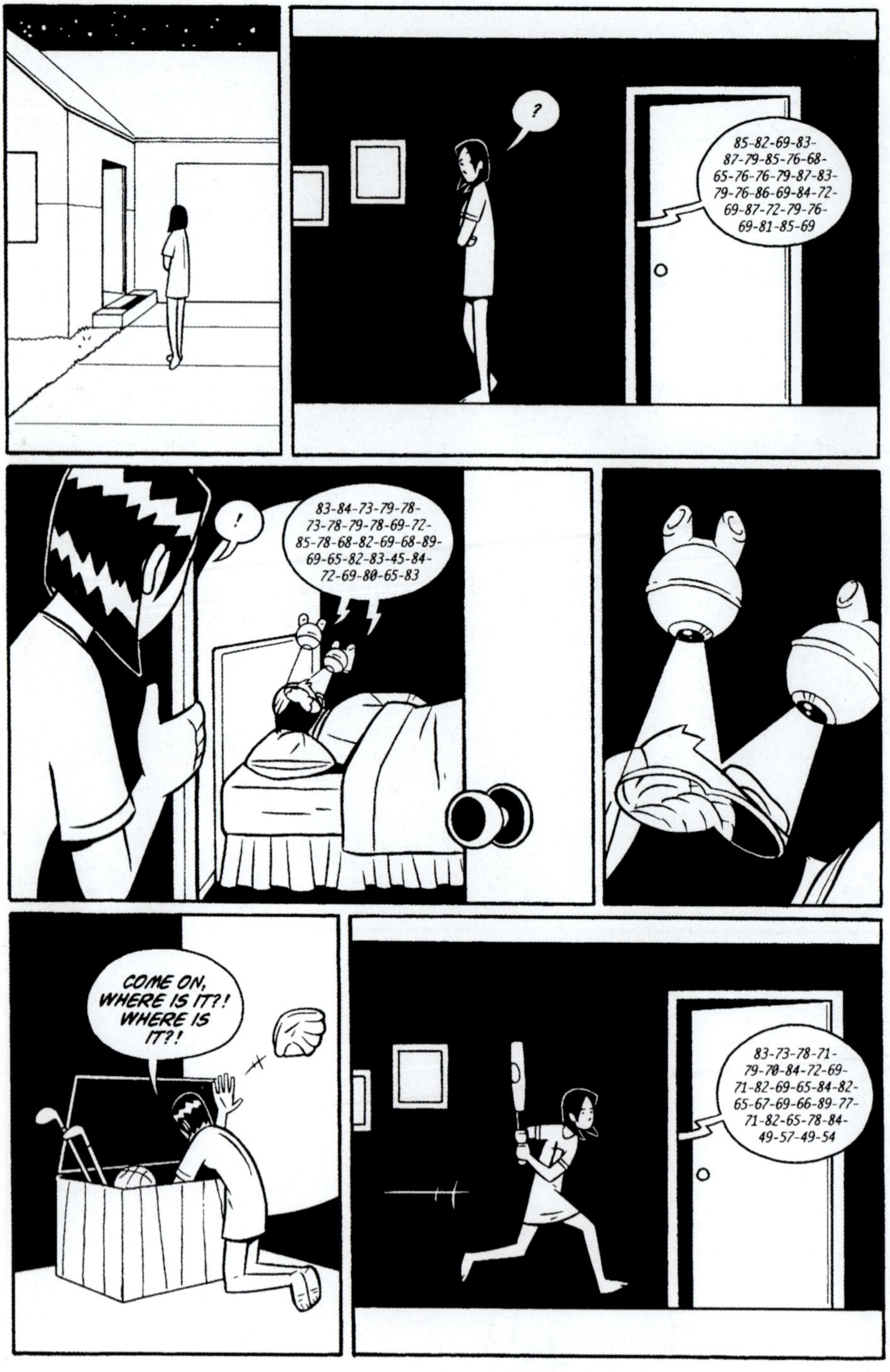
?
85-82-69-83-87-79-85-76-68-65-76-76-79-87-83-79-76-86-69-84-72-69-87-72-79-76-69-81-85-69
!
83-84-73-79-78-73-78-79-78-69-72-85-78-68-82-69-68-89-69-65-82-83-45-84-72-69-80-65-83
COME ON, WHERE IS IT?! WHERE IS IT?!
83-73-78-71-79-70-84-72-69-71-82-69-65-84-82-65-67-69-66-89-77-71-82-65-78-84-49-57-49-54

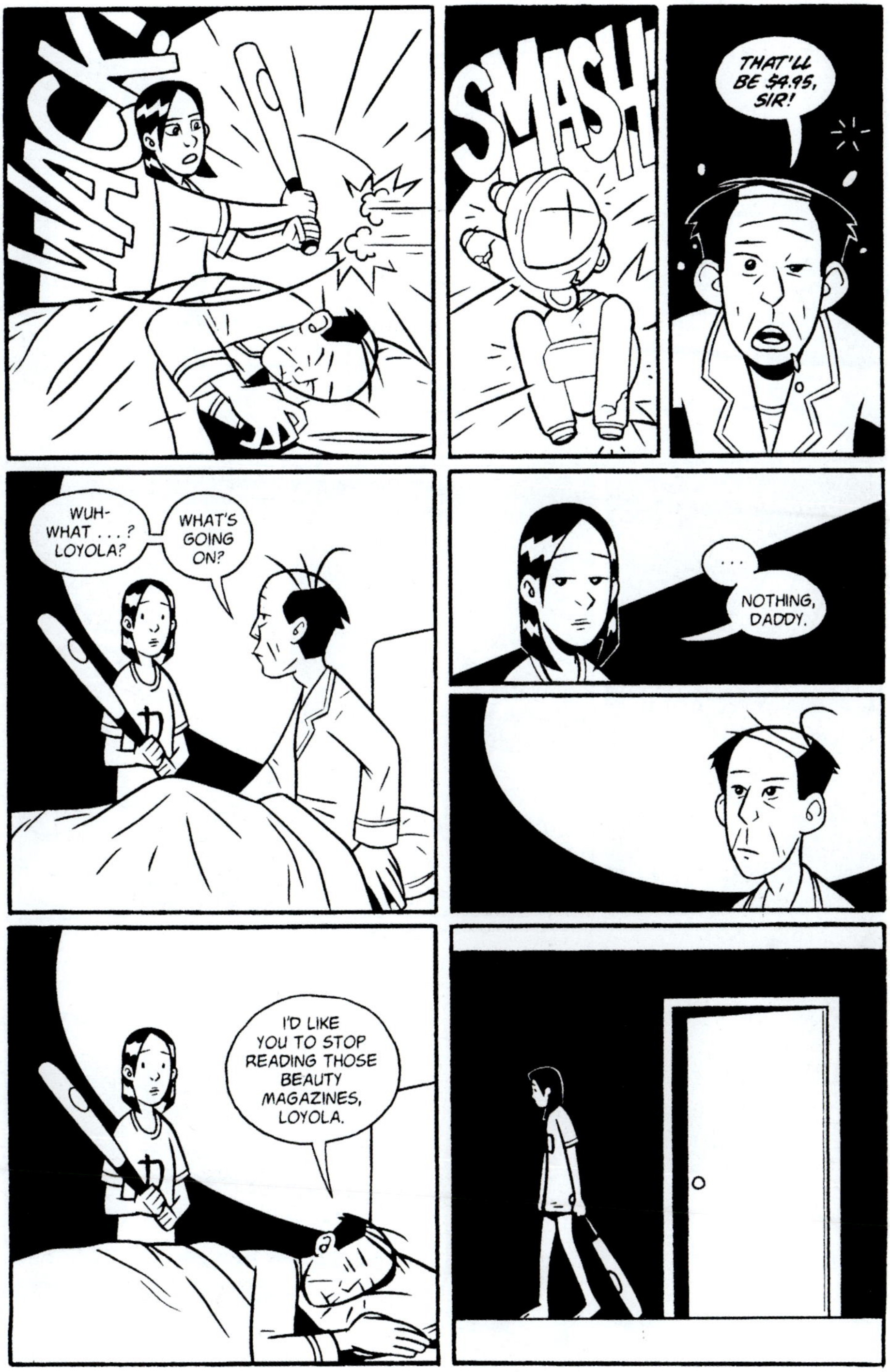
WACK!
SMASH!
THAT'LL BE $4.95, SIR!
WUH- WHAT . . . ? LOYOLA?
WHAT'S GOING ON?
. . .
NOTHING, DADDY.
I'D LIKE YOU TO STOP READING THOSE BEAUTY MAGAZINES, LOYOLA.

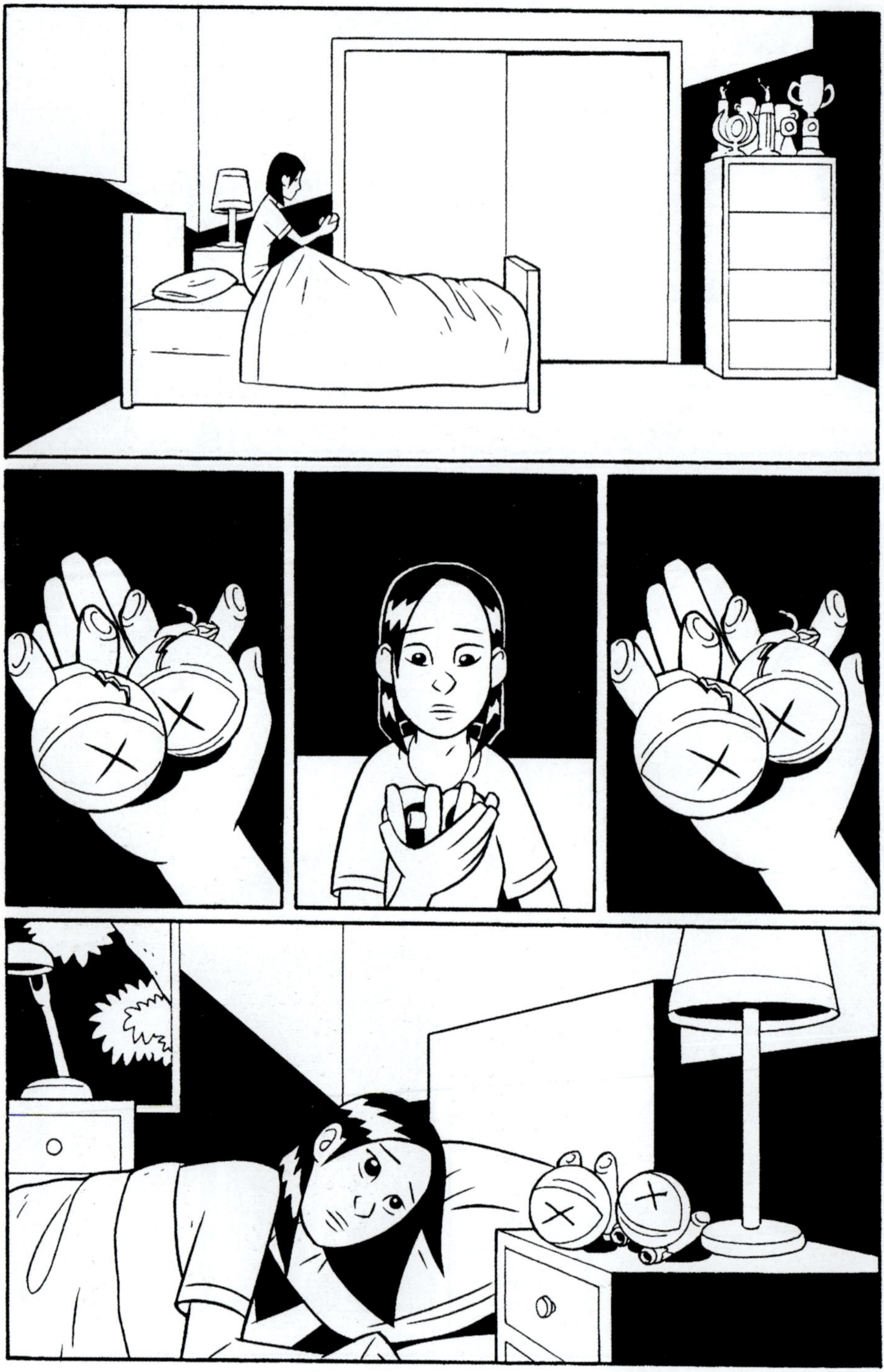

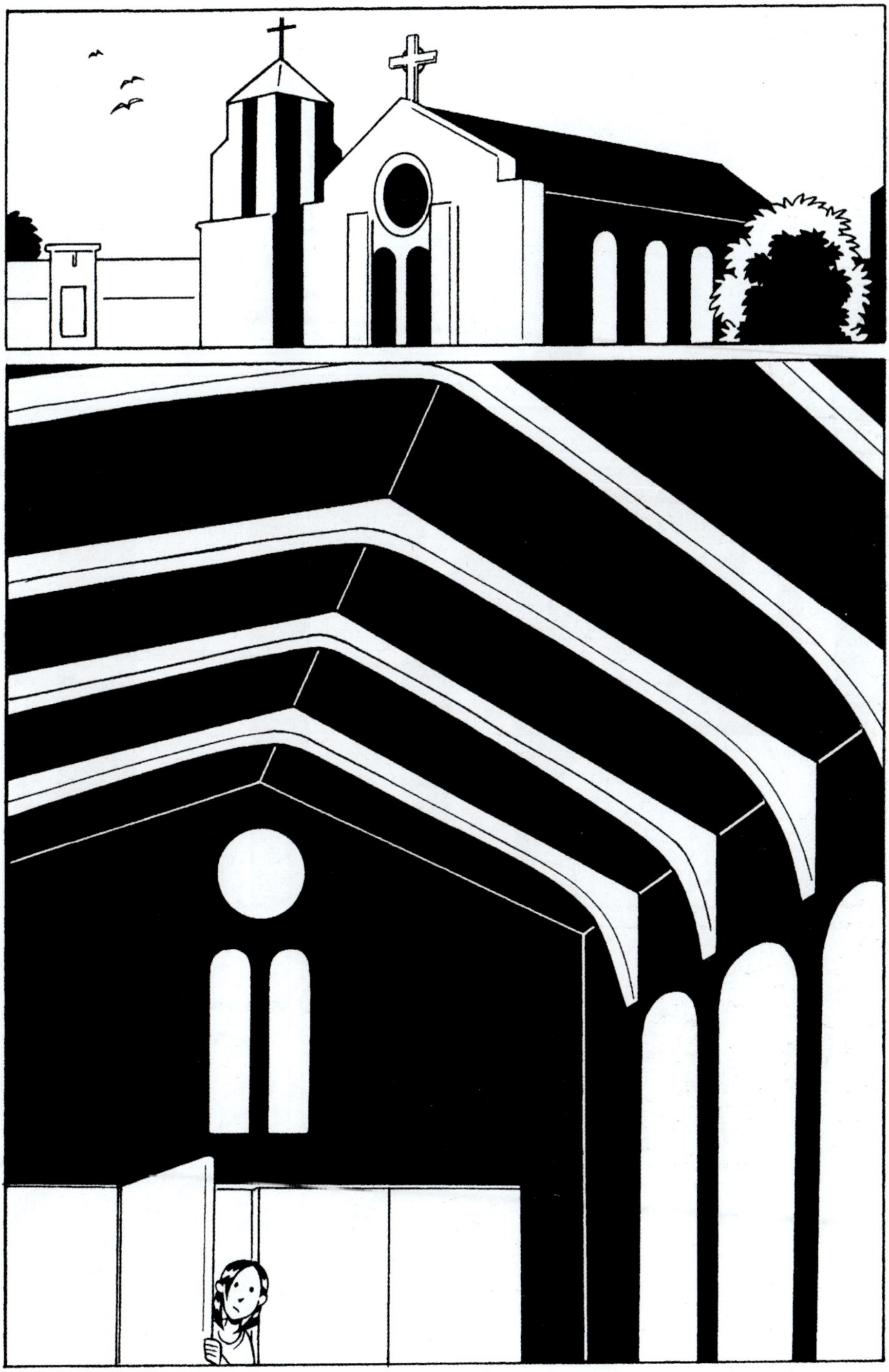

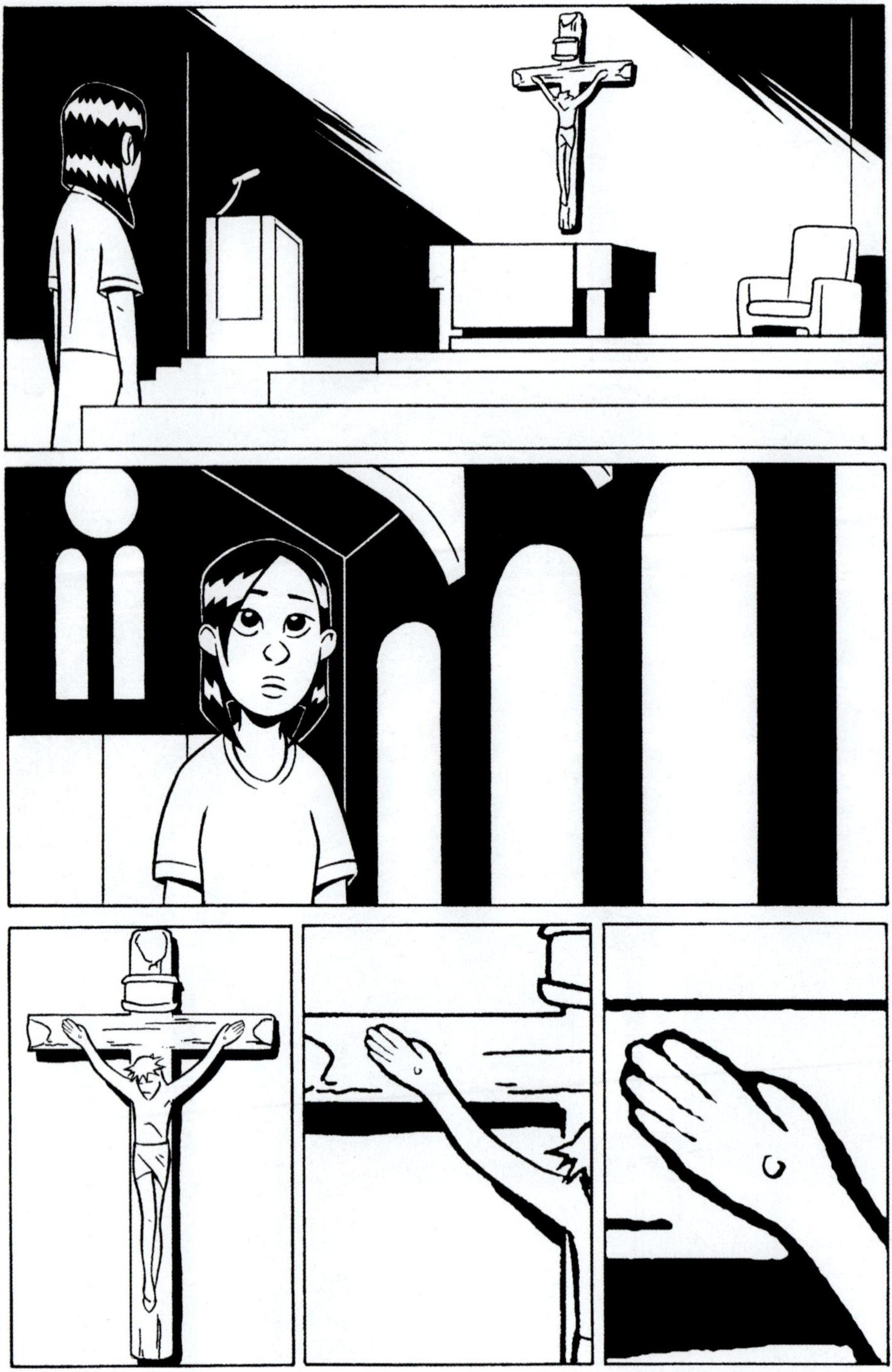

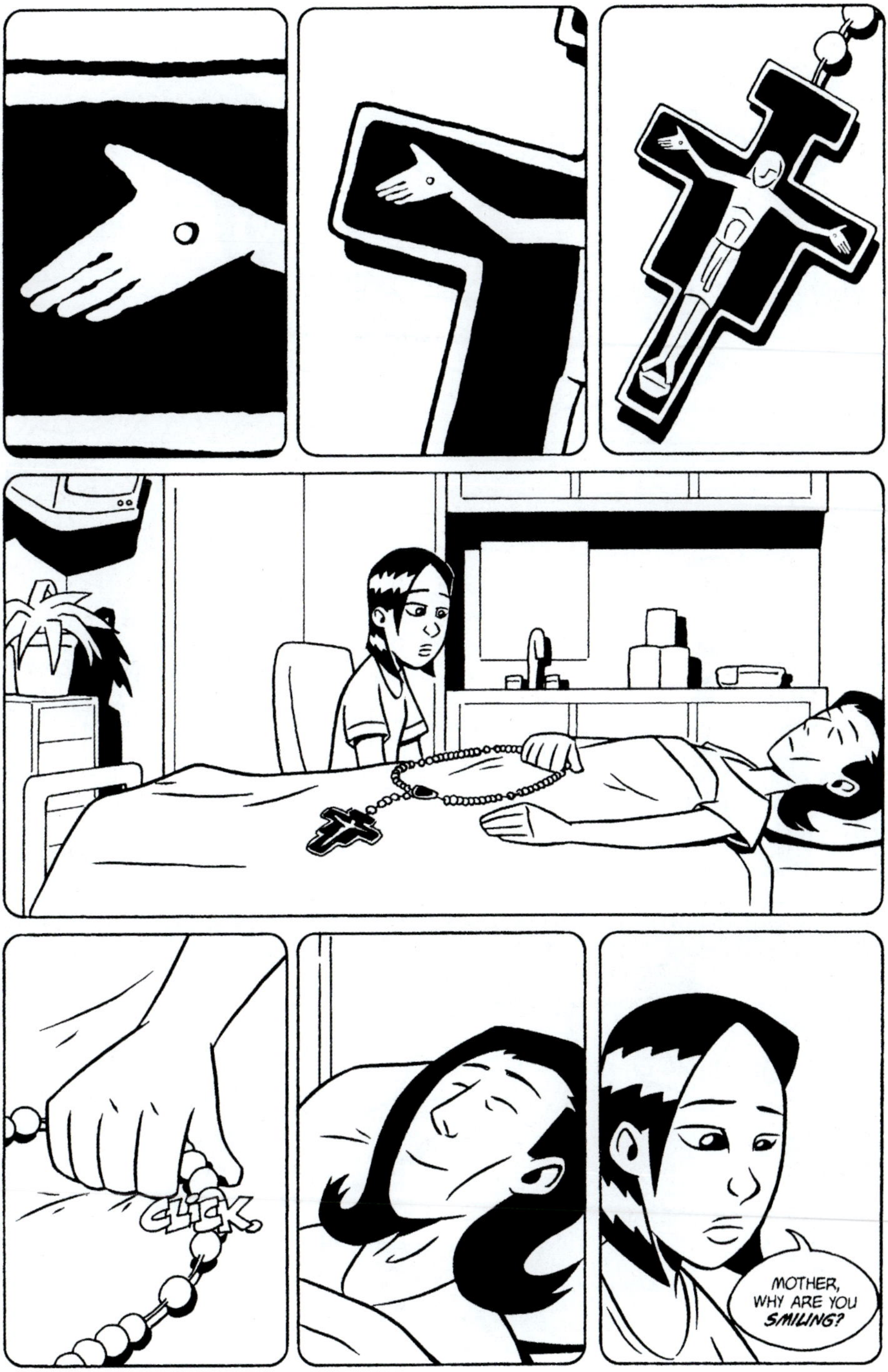
CLICK
MOTHER, WHY ARE YOU SMILING?

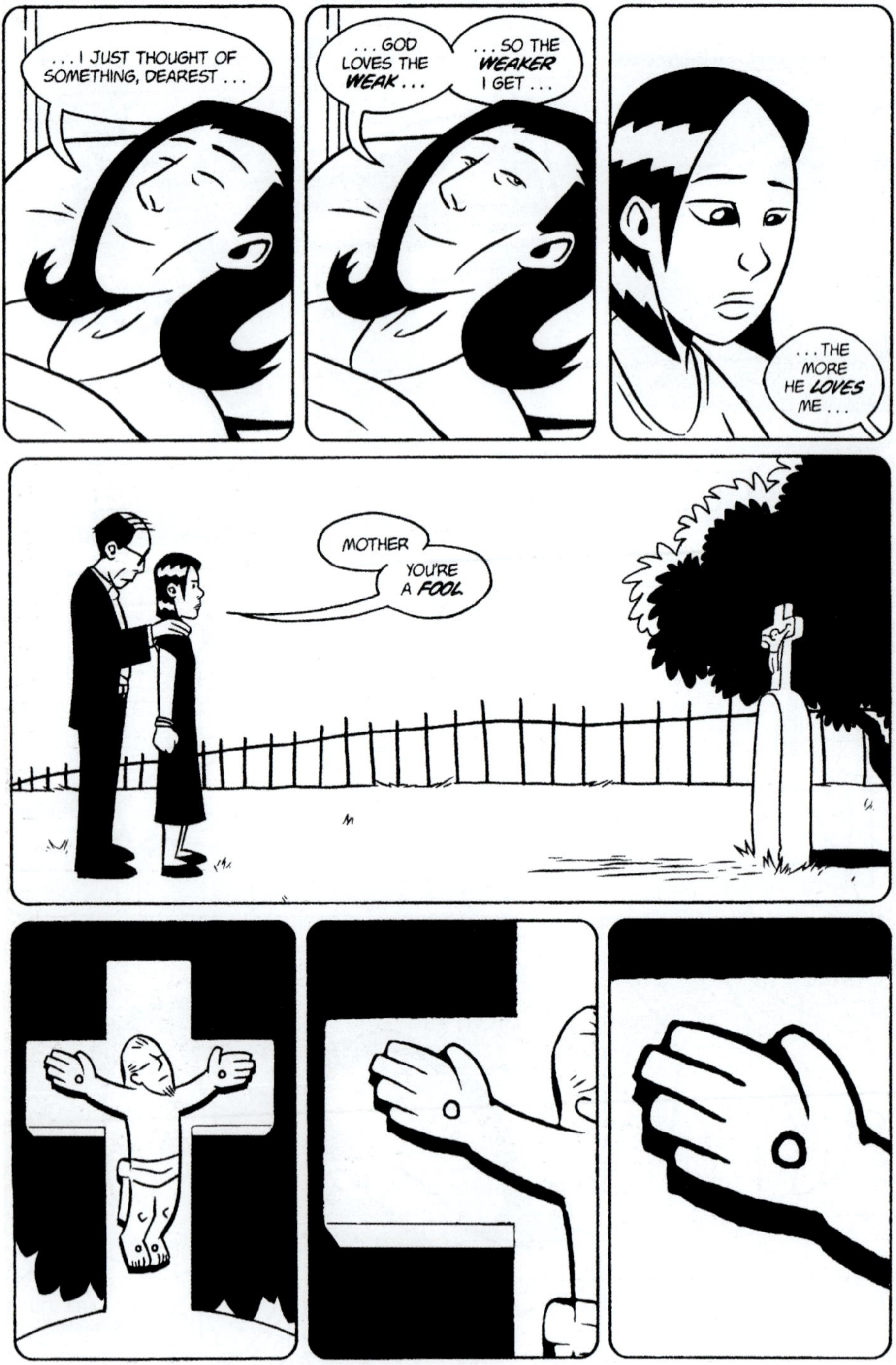
. . . I JUST THOUGHT OF SOMETHING, DEAREST . . .
. . . GOD LOVES THE WEAK . . .
. . . SO THE WEAKER I GET . . .
. . . THE MORE HE LOVES ME . . .
MOTHER
YOU'RE A FOOL

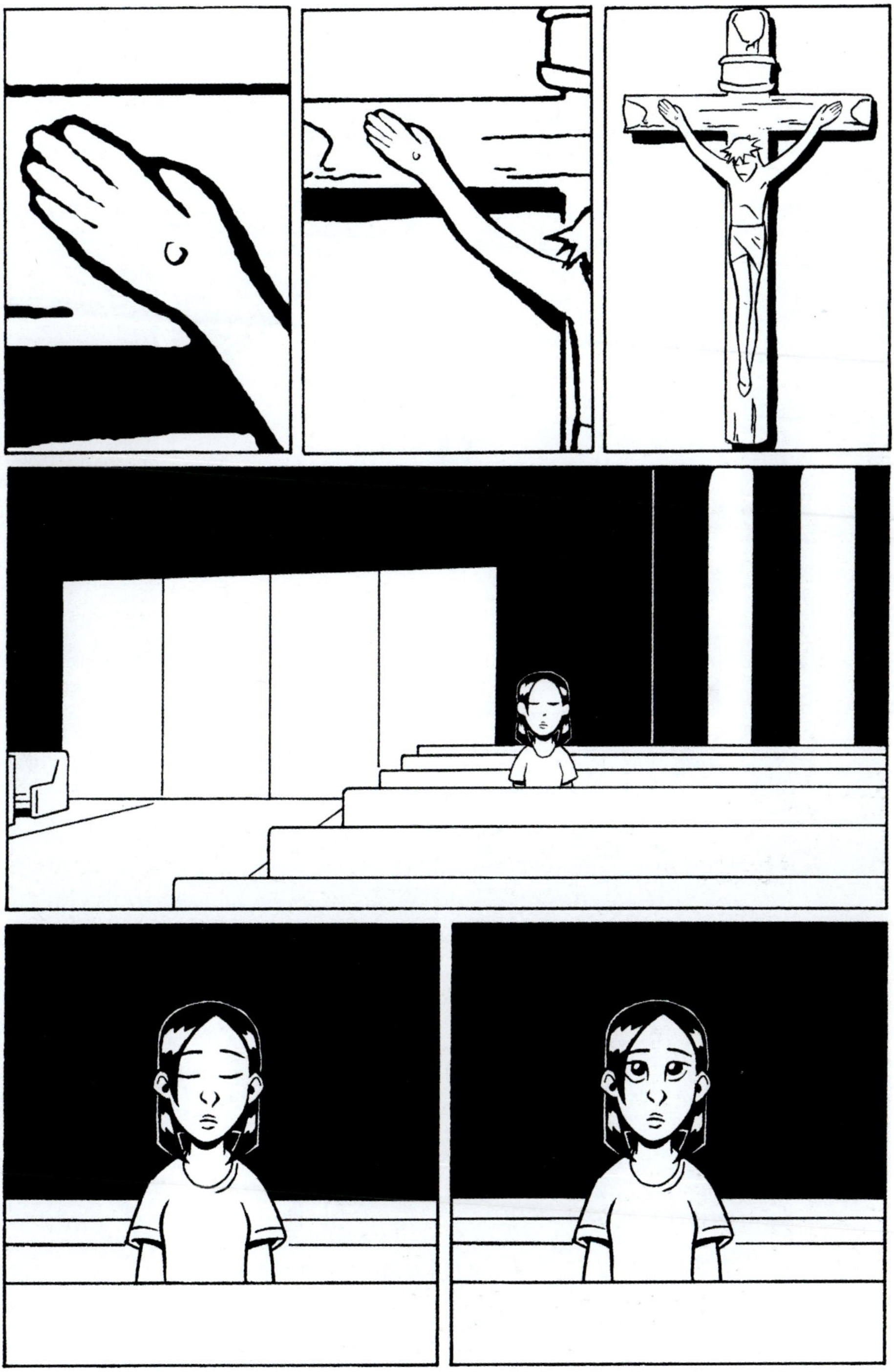

God chose what is foolish in the world to shame the wise, and
God chose what is weak in the world to shame the strong.

1 Corinthians 1:27

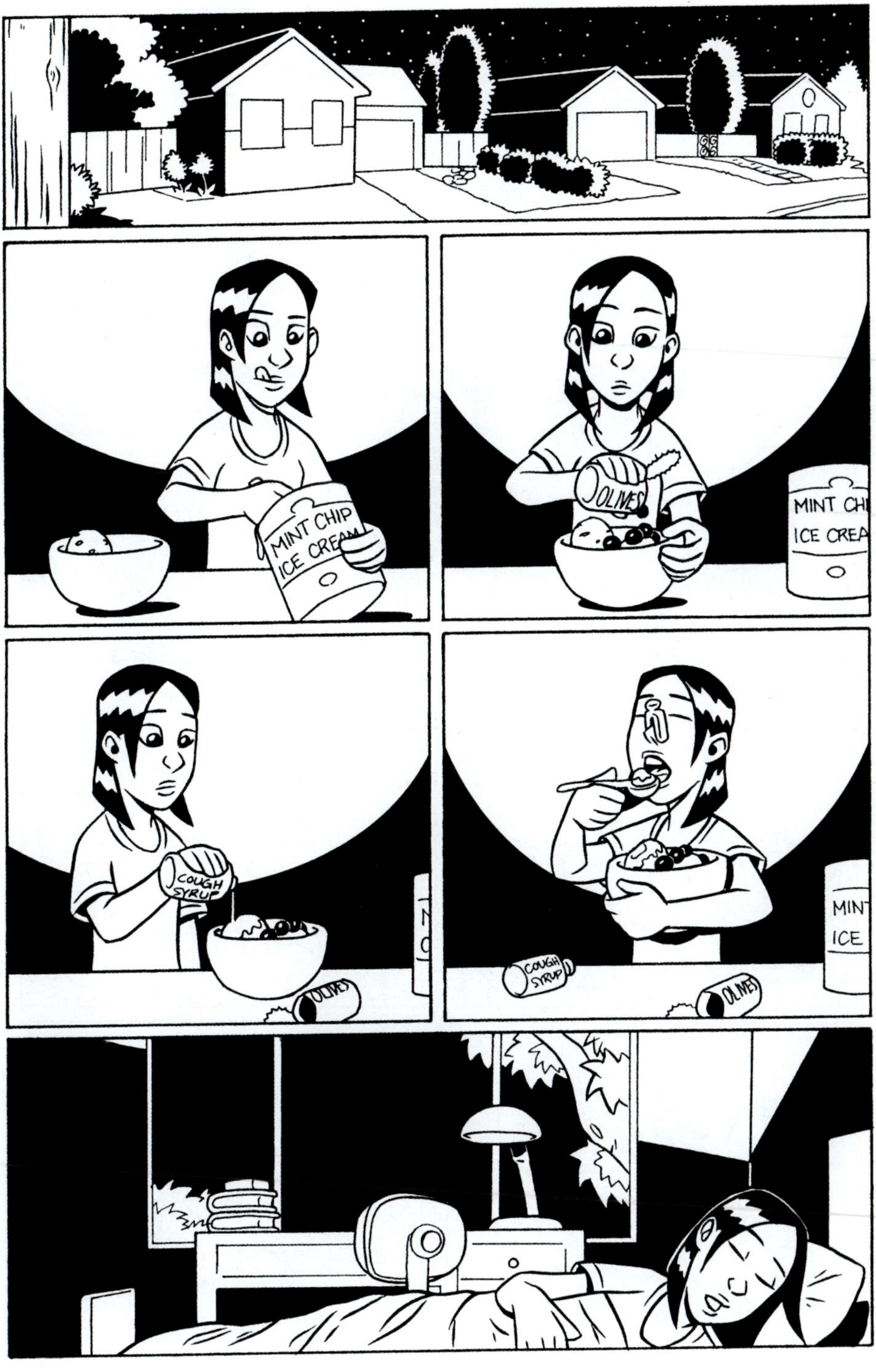

MINT CHIP
ICE CREAM
OLIVES
MINT CH
ICE CREA
COUGH SYRUP
OLIVES
COUGH SYRUP
OLIVES
MINT
ICE

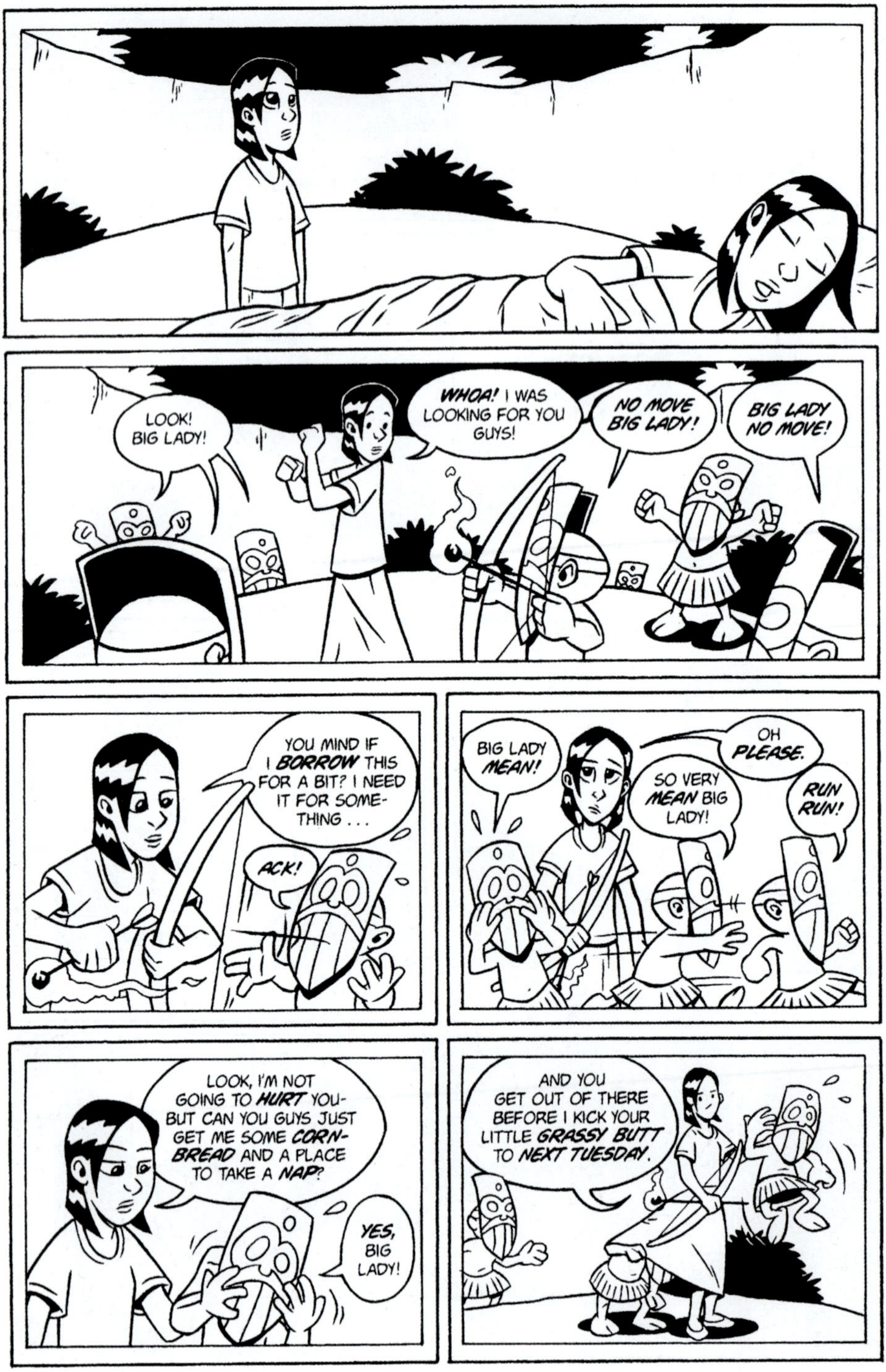
LOOK! BIG LADY!
WHOA! I WAS LOOKING FOR YOU GUYS!
NO MOVE BIG LADY!
BIG LADY NO MOVE!
YOU MIND IF I BORROW THIS FOR A BIT? I NEED IT FOR SOME-THING . . .
ACK!
BIG LADY MEAN!
OH PLEASE.
SO VERY MEAN BIG LADY!
RUN RUN!
LOOK, I'M NOT GOING TO HURT YOU- BUT CAN YOU GUYS JUST GET ME SOME CORN-BREAD AND A PLACE TO TAKE A NAP?
YES, BIG LADY!
AND YOU GET OUT OF THERE BEFORE I KICK YOUR LITTLE GRASSY BUTT TO NEXT TUESDAY.

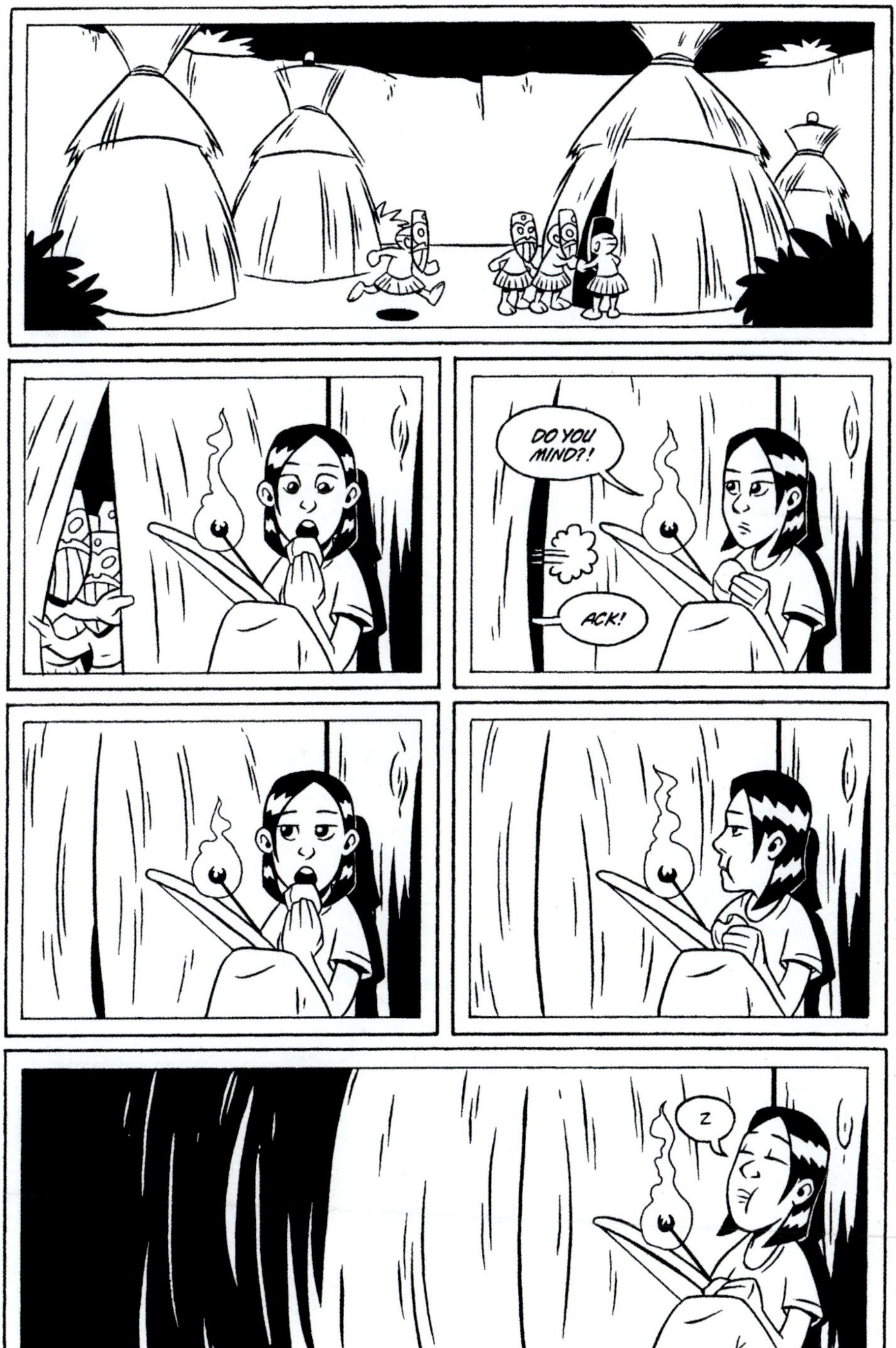

DO YOU MIND?!
ACK!
Z

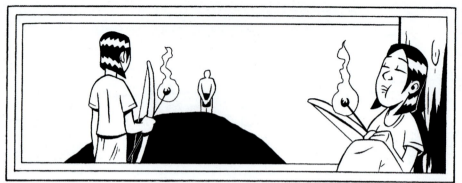

DANGER . . .

LOYOLA! I WAS AFRAID YOU WOULDN'T COME-

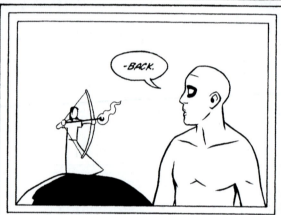

-BACK.

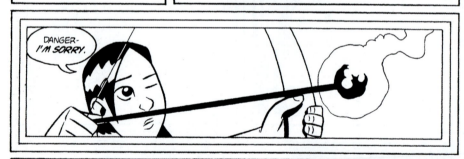

DANGER- I'M SORRY.

WHAT WAS THAT?
DANGER, I'VE THOUGHT ABOUT IT FOR A REALLY LONG TIME . . .
. . . AND I . . . I JUST CAN'T SEE YOUR VISION THE WAY YOU DO.
MAYBE IT'S BECAUSE I DON'T WANT TO.
I HAVE TO LISTEN TO MY HEART . . .

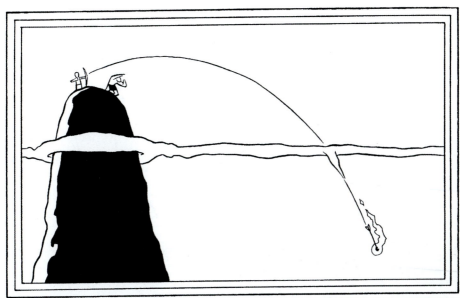

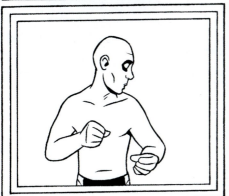

...I'VE BURNT DOWN YOUR TEMPLE.

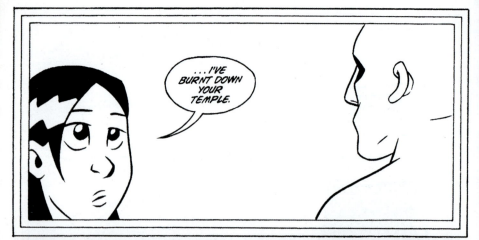

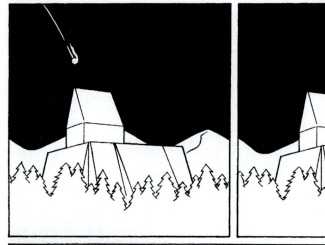

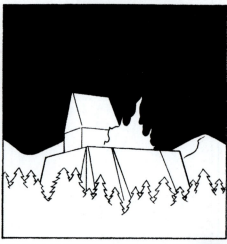

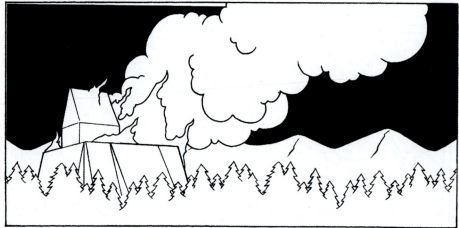

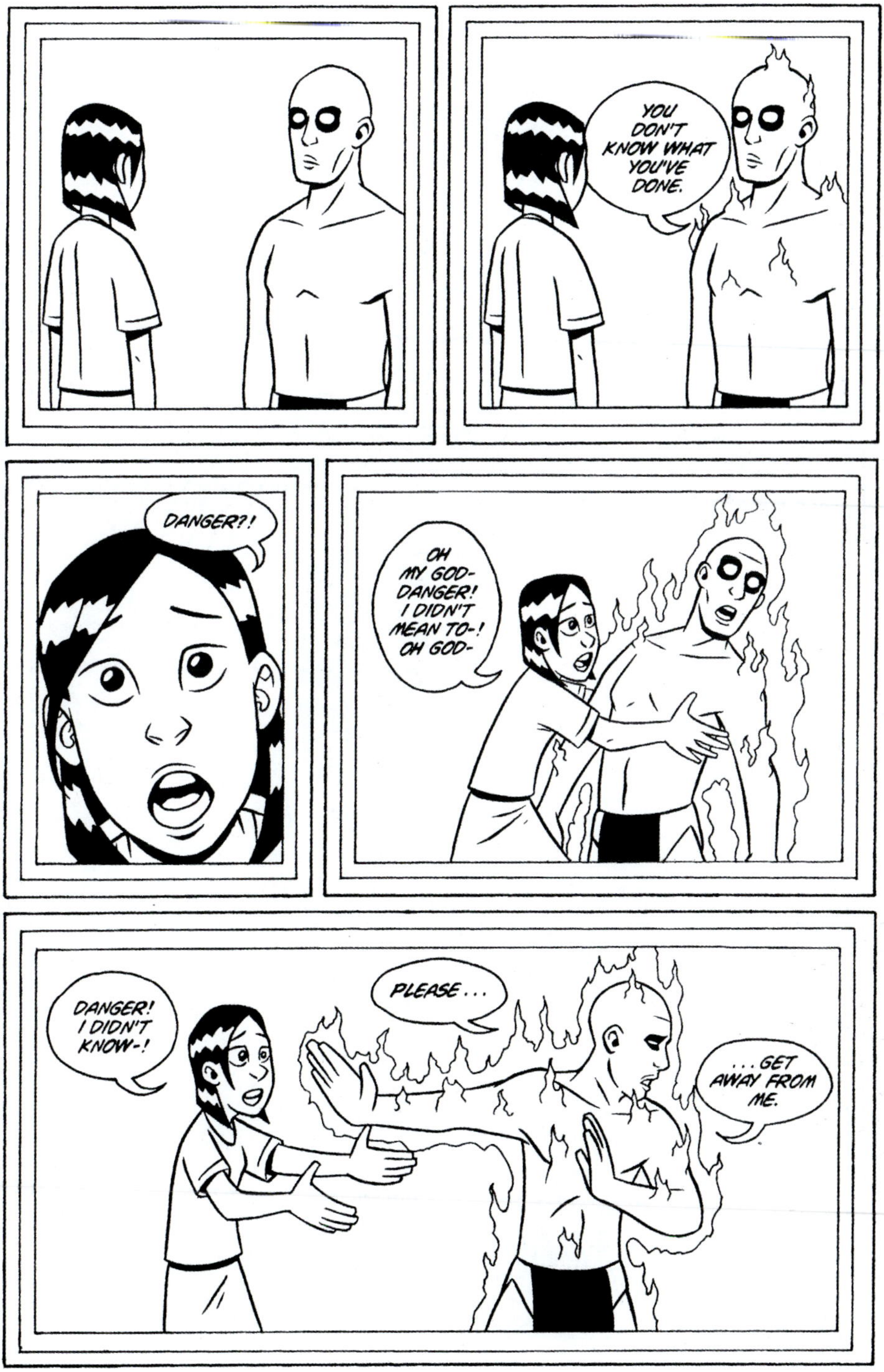
YOU DON'T KNOW WHAT YOU'VE DONE.
DANGER?!
OH MY GOD- DANGER! I DIDN'T MEAN TO-! OH GOD-
DANGER! I DIDN'T KNOW-!
PLEASE...
...GET AWAY FROM ME.

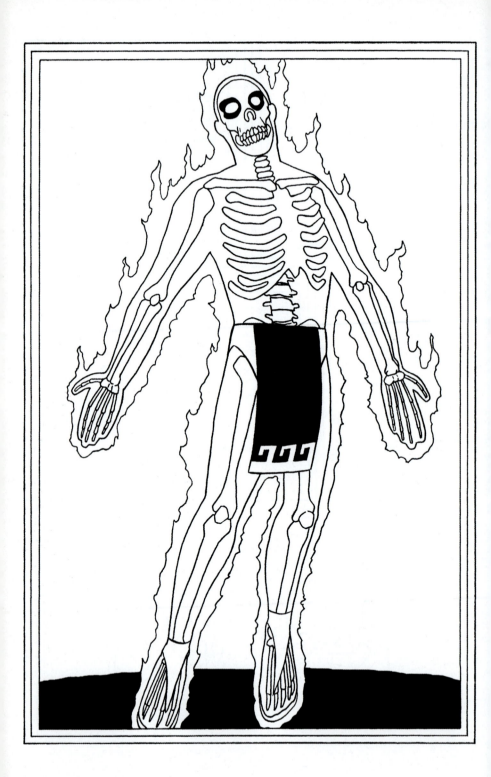

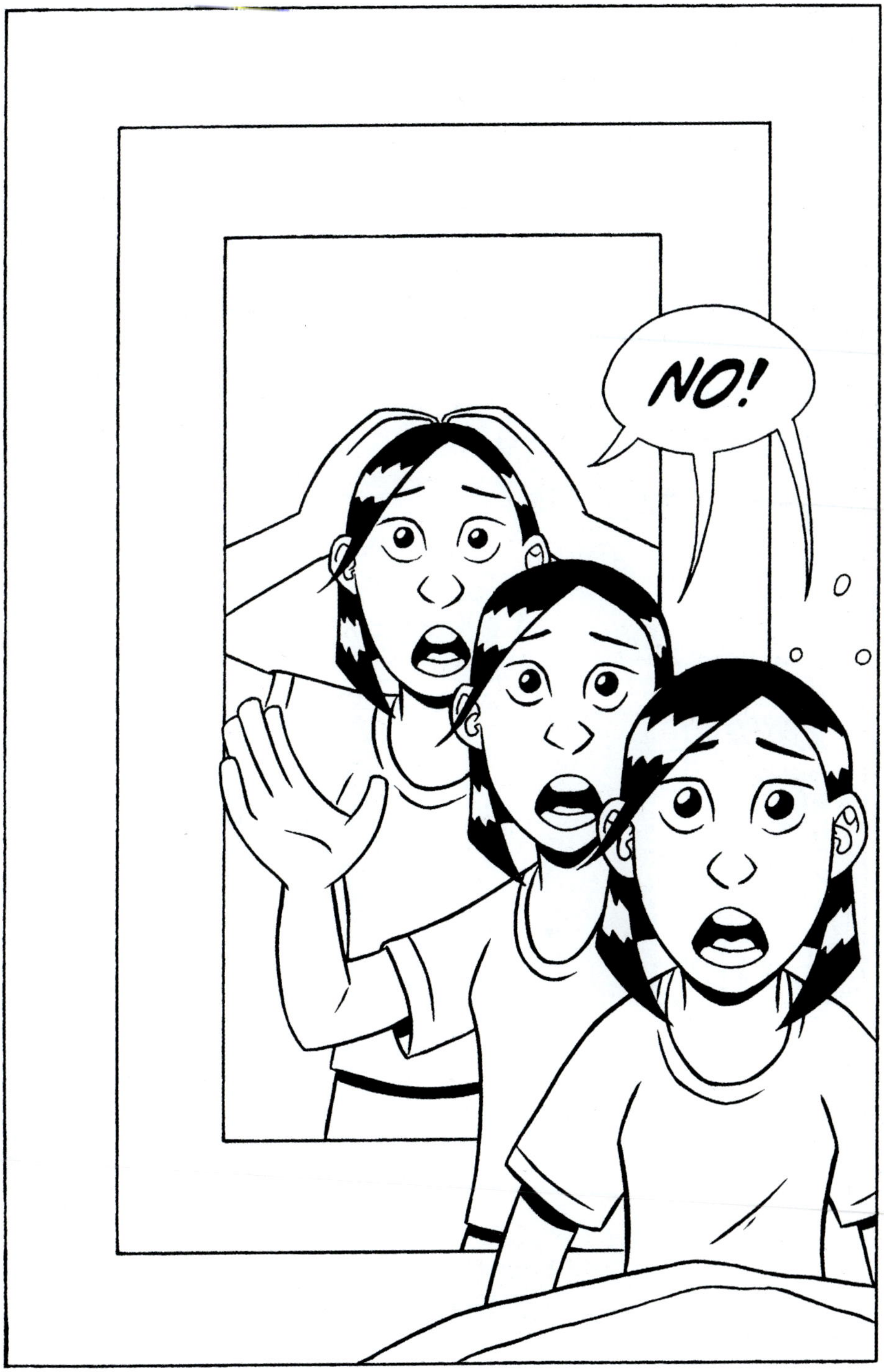
NO!

THAT WAS THE *LAST TIME* I EVER SAW HIM.

I *SEARCHED* FOR HIM FOR *MONTHS* AFTER THAT.

A FEW TIMES, I COULD'VE *SWORN* I CAUGHT A *GLIMPSE* OF HIM . . .

. . . JUST OVER A *HILL* . . .

. . . OR JUST AROUND A *CORNER* . . .

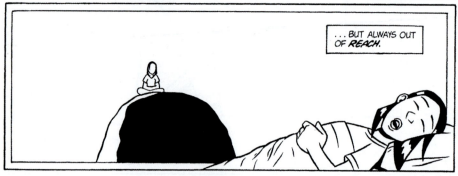

. . . BUT ALWAYS OUT OF *REACH*.

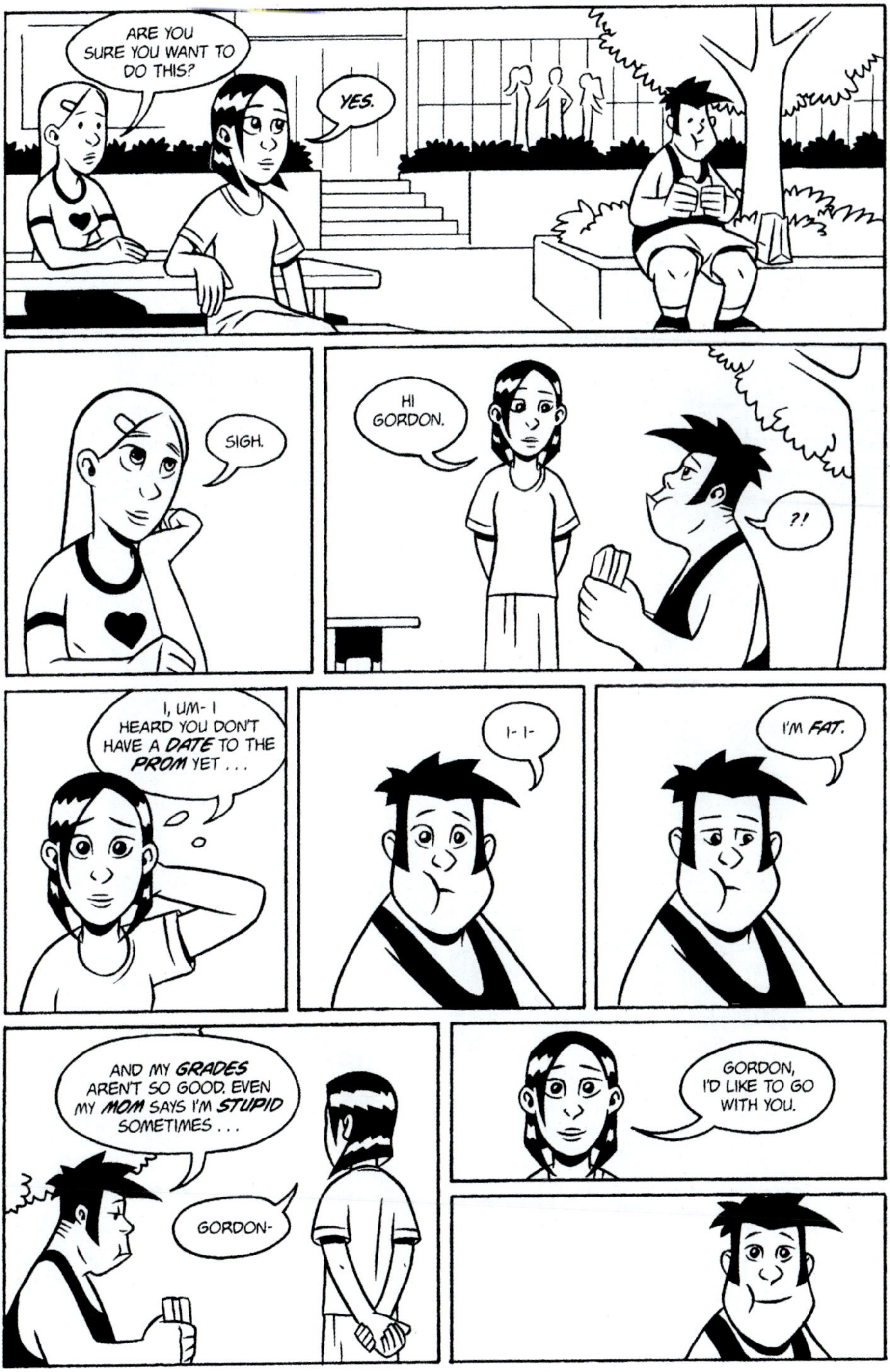
ARE YOU SURE YOU WANT TO DO THIS?
YES.
SIGH.
HI GORDON.
?!
I, UM- I HEARD YOU DON'T HAVE A *DATE* TO THE *PROM* YET . . .
I- I-
I'M *FAT*.
AND MY *GRADES* AREN'T SO GOOD. EVEN MY *MOM* SAYS I'M *STUPID* SOMETIMES . . .
GORDON-
GORDON, I'D LIKE TO GO WITH YOU.

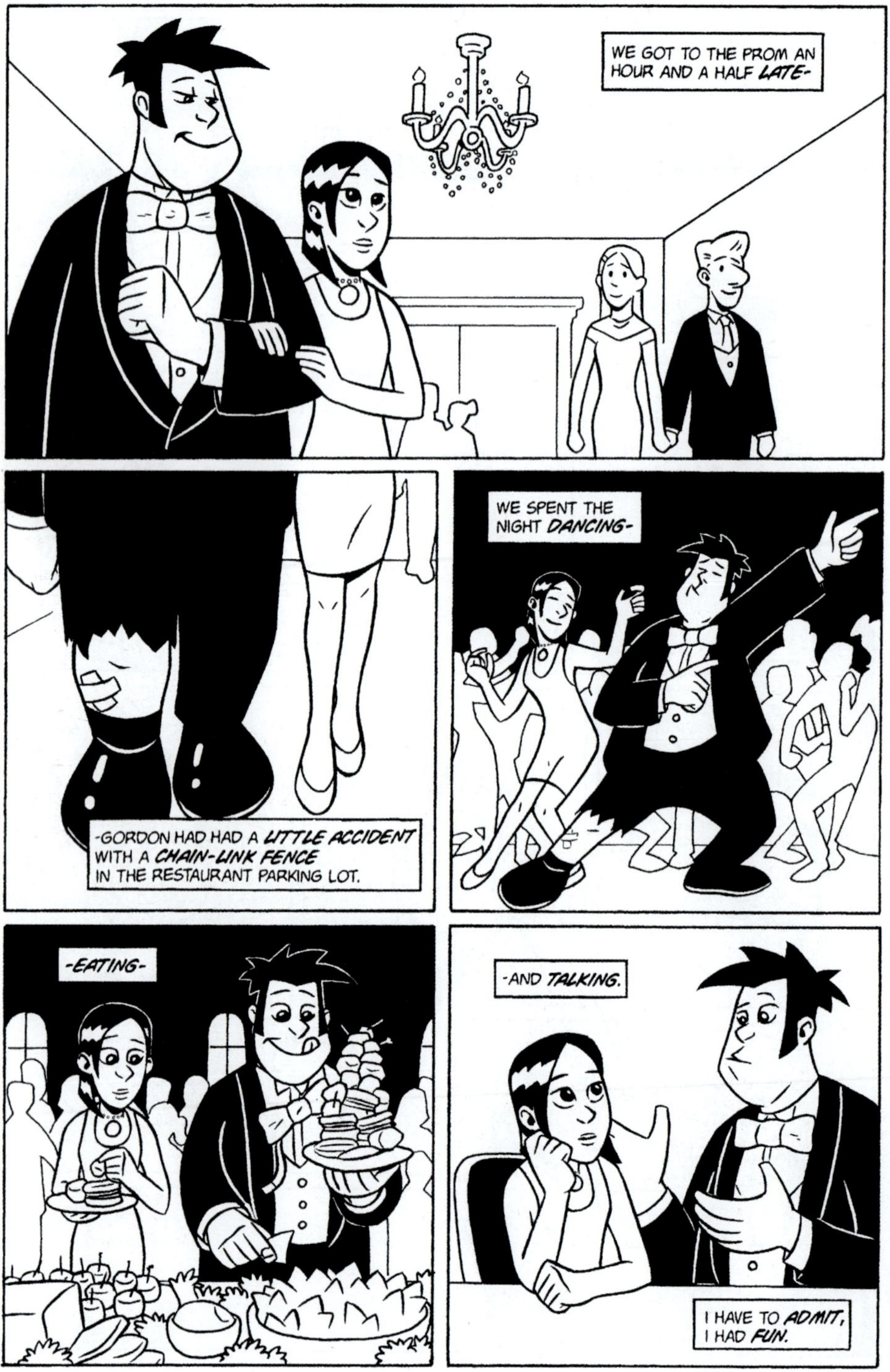
WE GOT TO THE PROM AN HOUR AND A HALF LATE-
-GORDON HAD HAD A LITTLE ACCIDENT WITH A CHAIN-LINK FENCE IN THE RESTAURANT PARKING LOT.
WE SPENT THE NIGHT DANCING-
-EATING-
-AND TALKING.
I HAVE TO ADMIT, I HAD FUN.

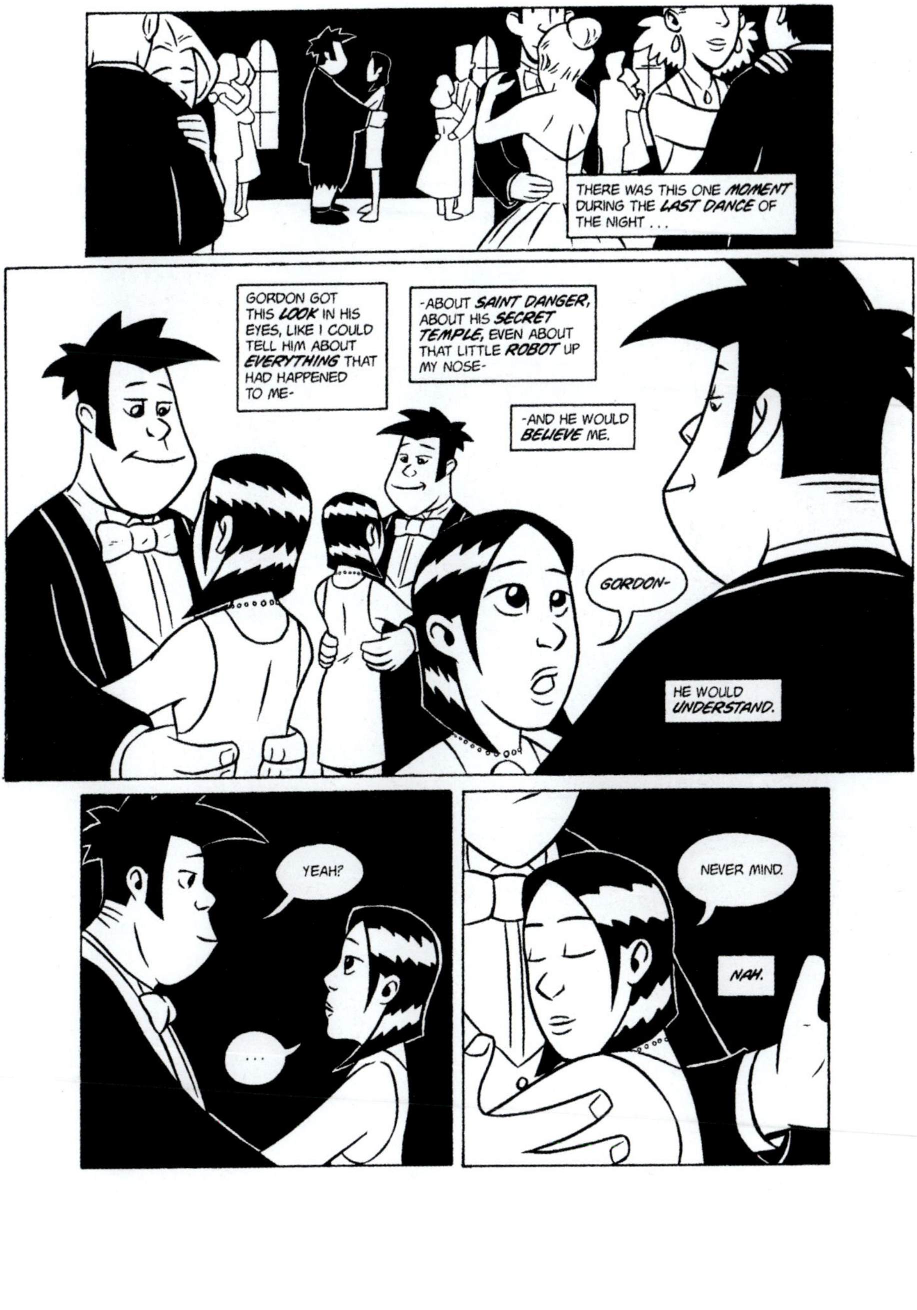
THERE WAS THIS ONE MOMENT DURING THE LAST DANCE OF THE NIGHT . . .
GORDON GOT THIS LOOK IN HIS EYES, LIKE I COULD TELL HIM ABOUT EVERYTHING THAT HAD HAPPENED TO ME-
-ABOUT SAINT DANGER, ABOUT HIS SECRET TEMPLE, EVEN ABOUT THAT LITTLE ROBOT UP MY NOSE-
-AND HE WOULD BELIEVE ME.
GORDON-
HE WOULD UNDERSTAND.
YEAH?
. . .
NEVER MIND.
NAH.

"Dream a Little Dream of Me"
Quiggenberry High School Senior Prom

AFTERWORD
BY GENE LUEN YANG

Lately, I've been contemplating the importance of what I do. Comics, I mean. I've been counting the costs, and frankly, what I've found is that the costs are enormous. Those of you creating your own comics know what I'm talking about.

Even with a sparse (or as some would call it, lazy) style like my own, penciling and inking a single page still take hours. A day's worth of drawing leaves my hand cramped and my neck stiff. I'm not sure how comic book artists who draw more detail than I do (in other words, every other comic book artist) deal with it.

And that's just the drawing part. The writing is even more agonizing, only on a psychological level. Does that dialogue sound right? Would he/she/it really act that way? Does that plot twist make any sense at all? Why would a reader even want to go on to the next page? Thousands of questions tumble through my head like a mob of angry drunks.

Then comes the actual publication and distribution of the comic. My fragile fanboy ego, sheltered for years by reading other people's word balloons and critiquing other people's line work, is suddenly thrust naked before an audience, offering *The Comics Journal* the chance to give it a swift kick in the jewels before it retreats back to obscurity.

But ultimately, it all comes down to the One Real Question. As someone who subscribes to such traditional

Roman Catholic niceties as God and Church and Heaven, I must have that One Real Question answered: Is any of this going to matter in The End? (By "The End" I really do mean the traditional Roman Catholic version of "The End," with all its pomp and circumstance.) Will my comics have any lasting effect on anyone or anything? Will my hand cramps and neck stiffness and psychological torture have been suffered for something meaningful?

When God and I sit down together to review my days on the Great Celestial ViewMaster, will He laugh at the slides of me hunched over my drawing table? Or will He beam with pride? Or will He smile at me politely, the way one does at an acquaintance who's got a bit of spinach stuck between his two front teeth?

Honestly, I don't know.

I stayed up until 5 am last night thinking about it, and I still haven't a clue.

Perhaps I'll figure it out while working on my next comic. I've already got this really great idea....

Gene Yang
October 2000

SKETCHBOOK

The two sketches on the left are my first two sketches of Gordon Yamamoto. Gordon was originally a character in a short story I wrote for a college creative writing class. It was about three fifth graders who try to invent a superhero with a rubber suit and kitchen knives.

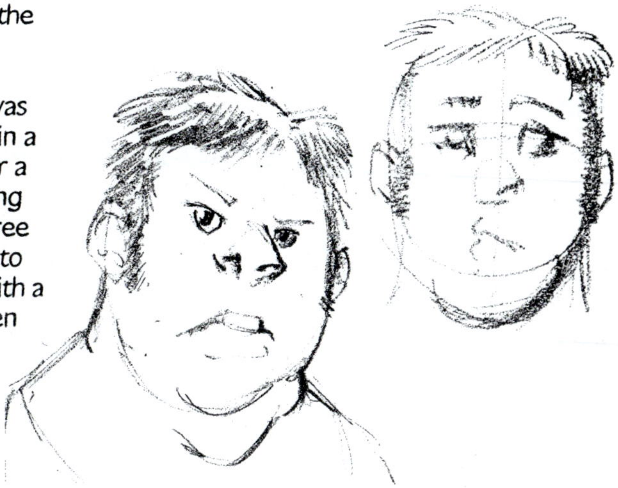

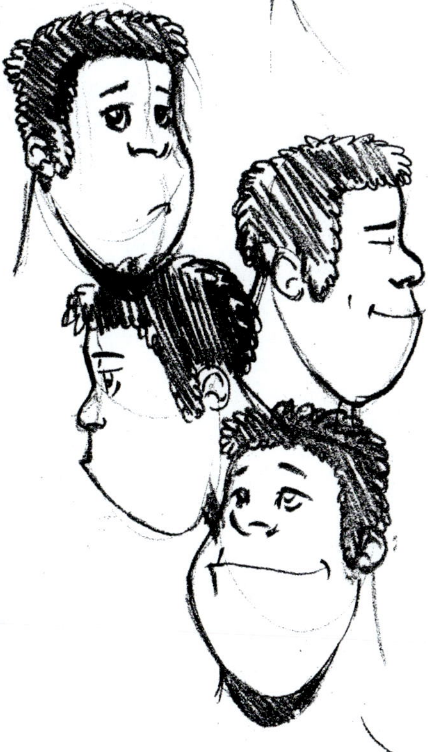

In the sketches to the left, Gordon is sporting his original curly hairstyle. I've never seen a Japanese person with hair like that in real life, so I'm not sure what I was thinking. Below, Gordon's hair gets spiky.

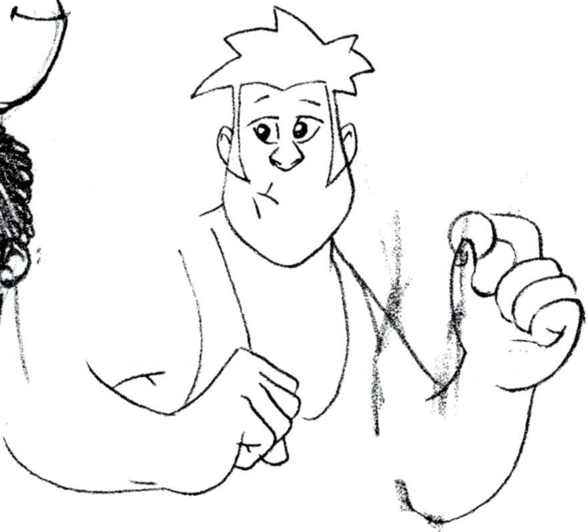

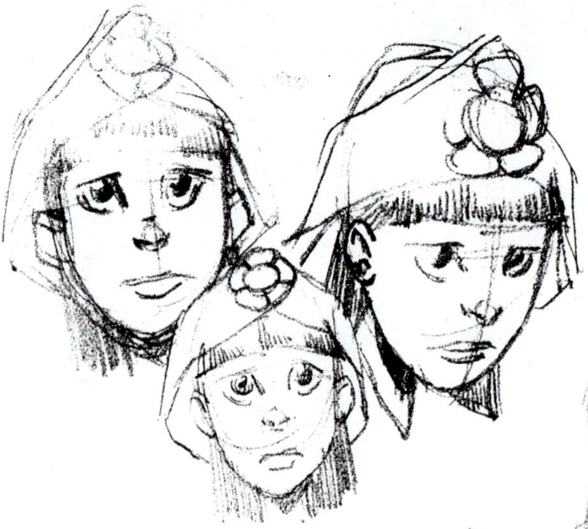

When I first sketched Loyola, I gave her a big, goofy hat with a flower on it. Then one day I realized that I'd given her *a big, goofy hat with a flower on it*. So I took it off.

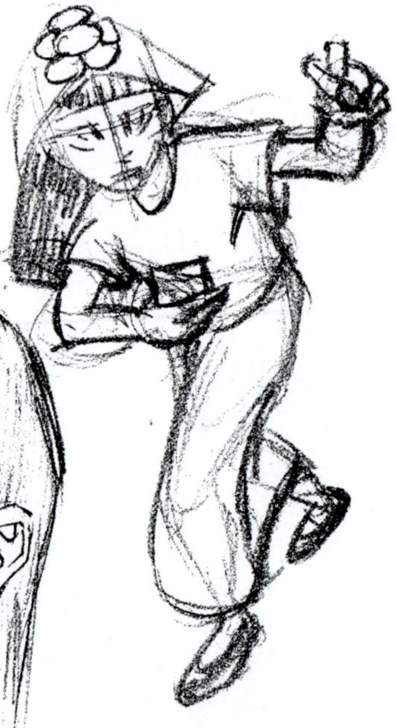

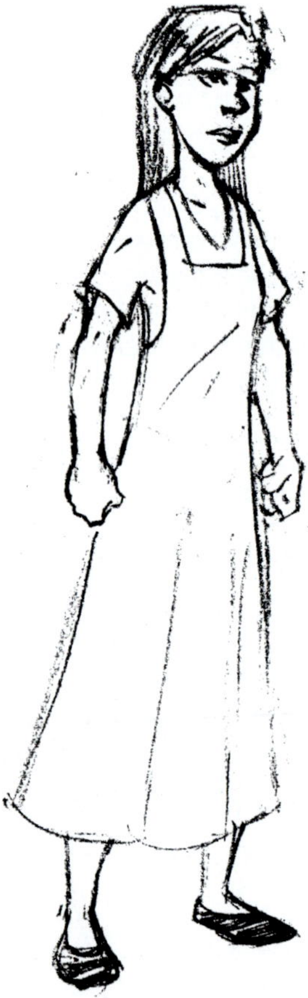

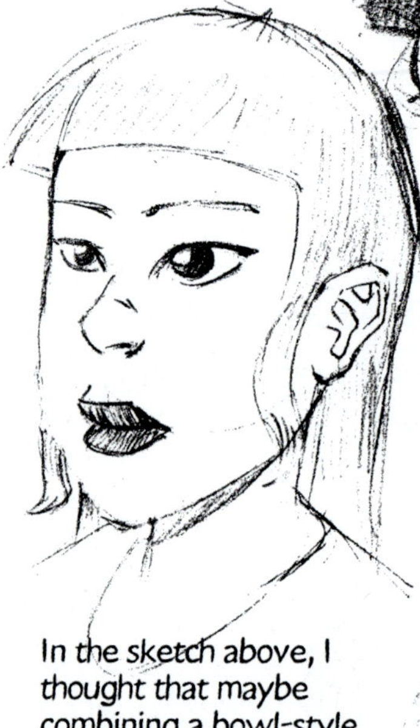

In the sketch above, I thought that maybe combining a bowl-style haircut and voluptuous lips would appeal to the much sought-after nerd/seductress demographic. To the right, I'm getting closer to Loyola's final look.

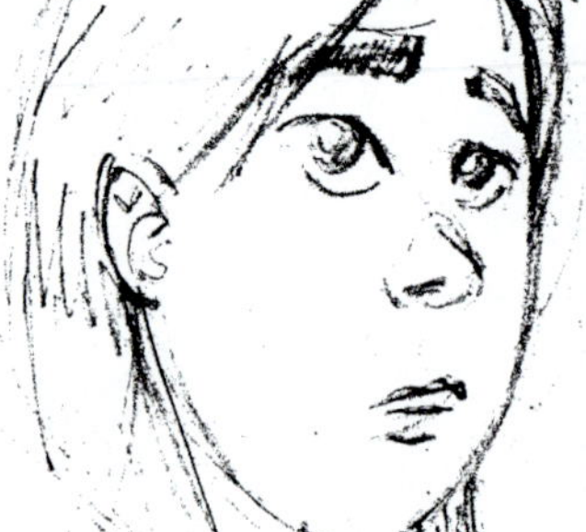

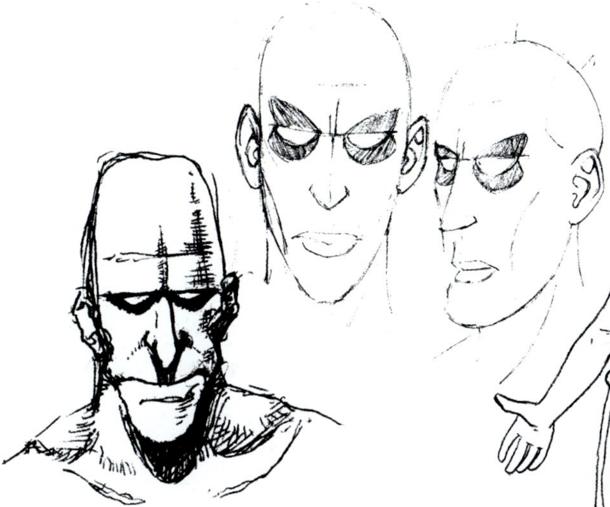

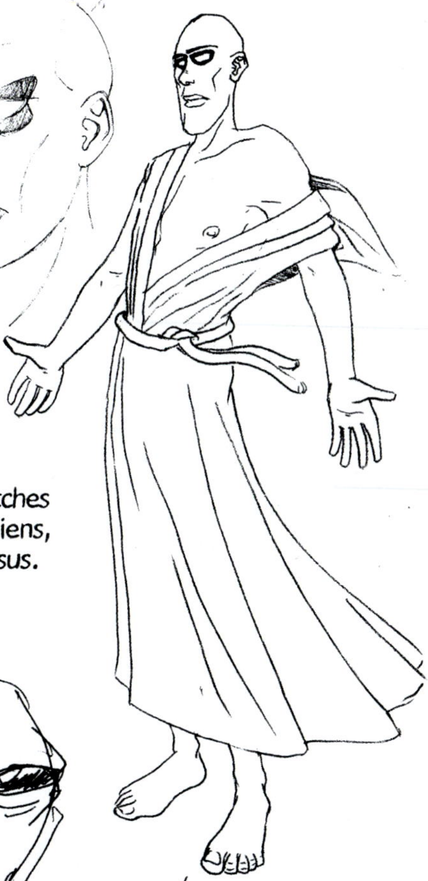

Here are some sketches of Saint Danger, aliens, spaceships, and Jesus.

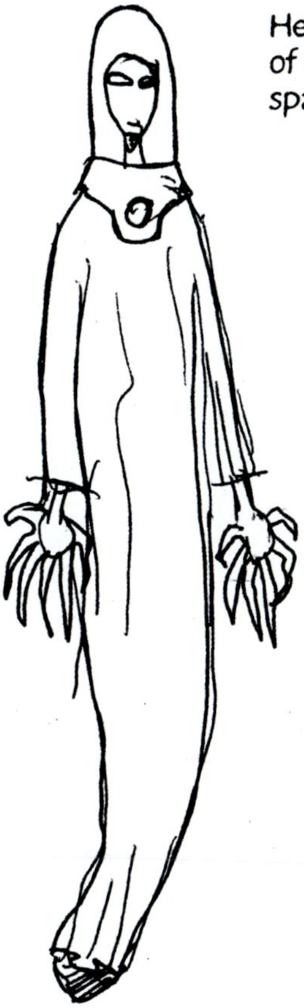

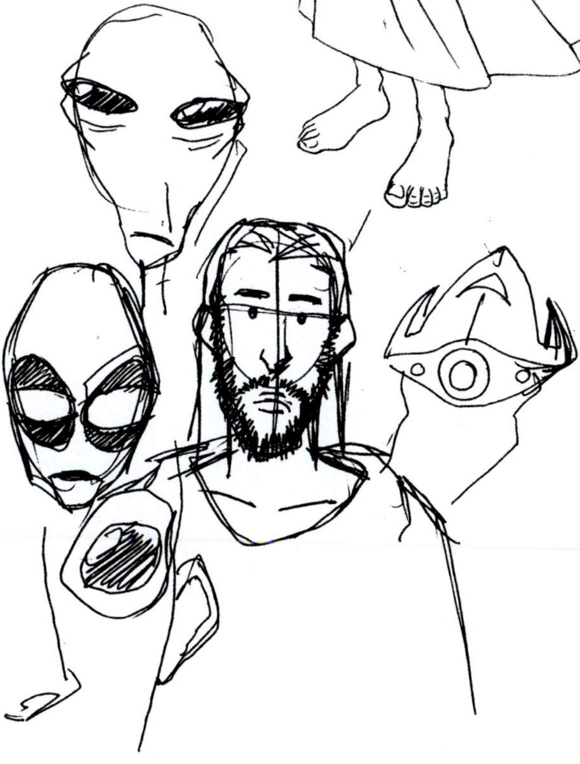

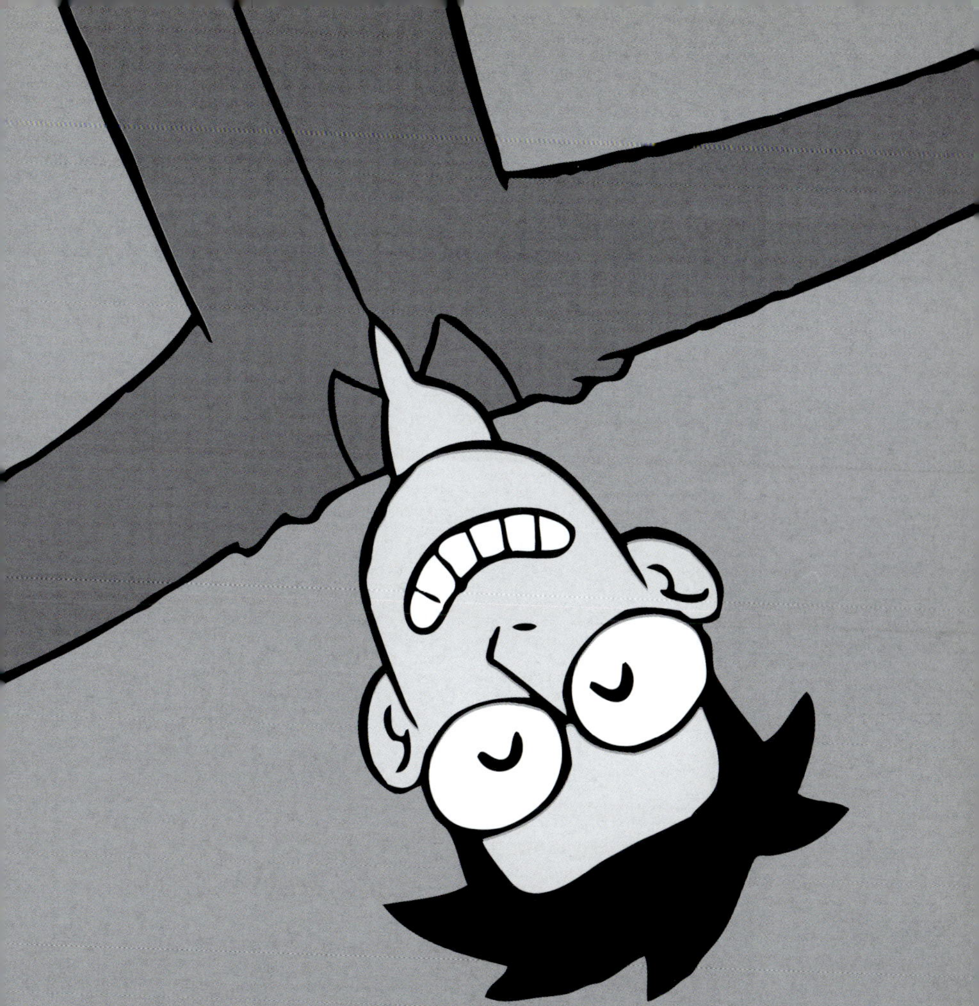

BONUS FEATURE

THE PATH TO PUBLICATION

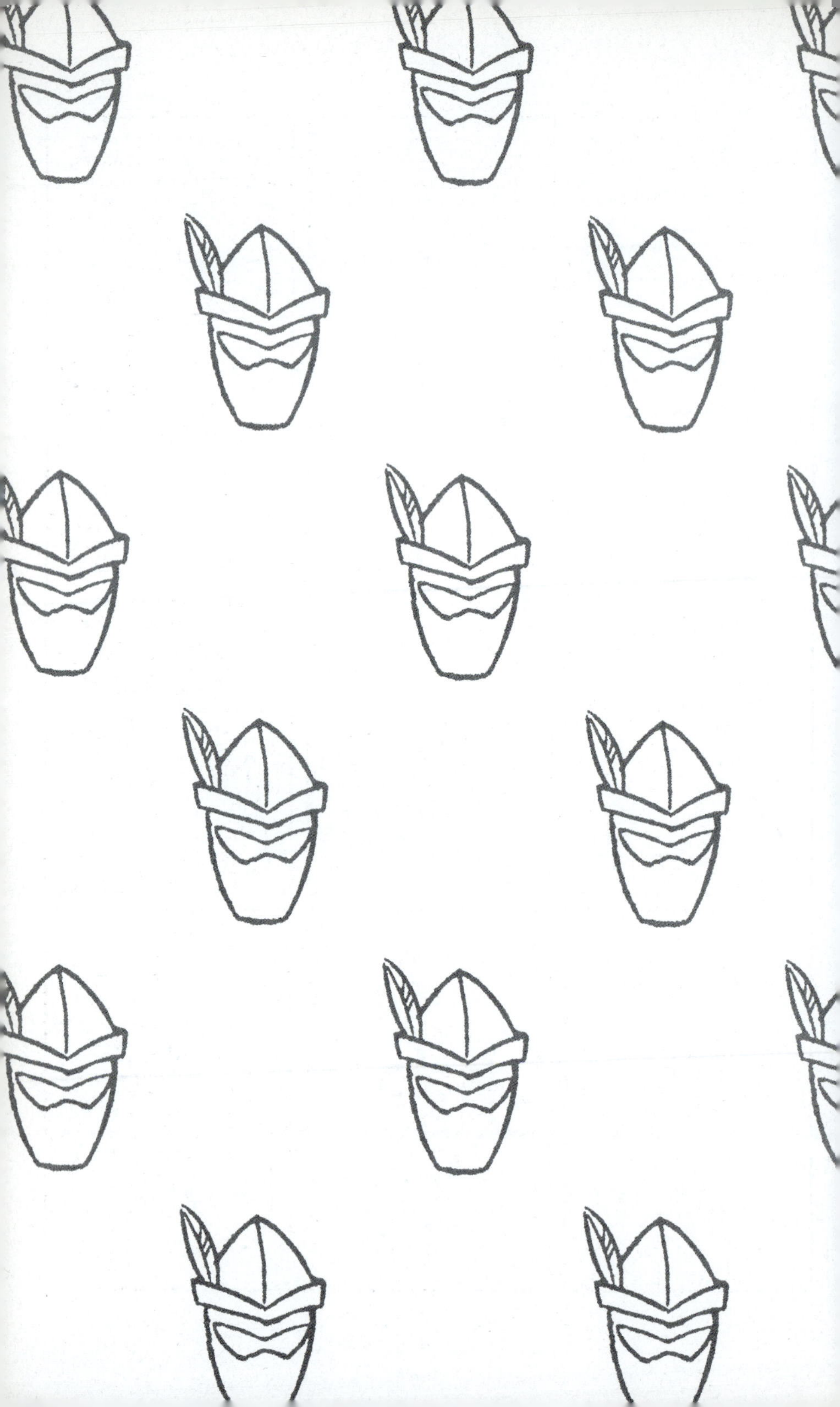

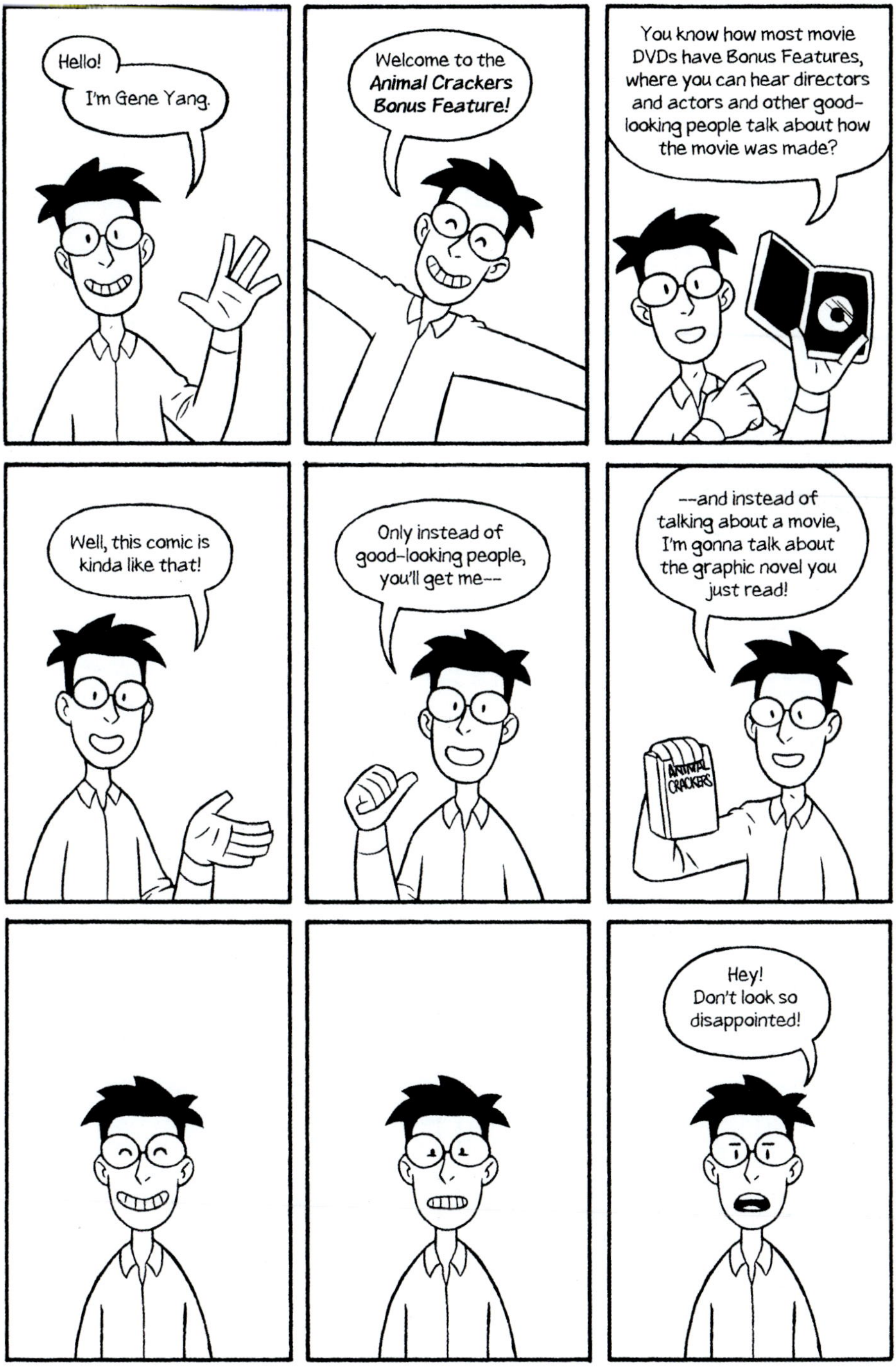
Hello!
I'm Gene Yang.
Welcome to the *Animal Crackers Bonus Feature!*
You know how most movie DVDs have Bonus Features, where you can hear directors and actors and other good-looking people talk about how the movie was made?
Well, this comic is kinda like that!
Only instead of good-looking people, you'll get me--
--and instead of talking about a movie, I'm gonna talk about the graphic novel you just read!
ANIMAL CRACKERS
Hey! Don't look so disappointed!

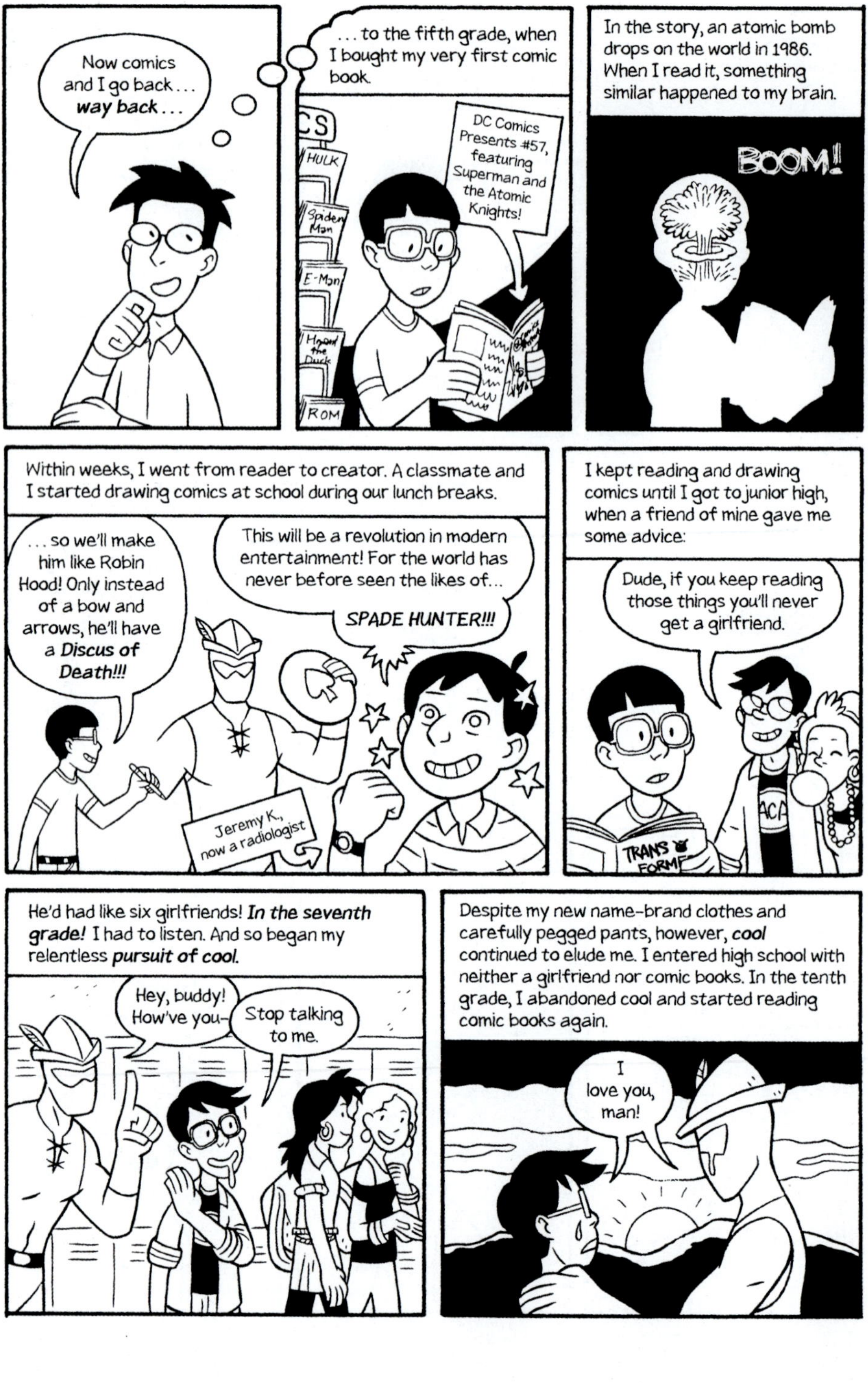
Now comics and I go back... **way back...**
...to the fifth grade, when I bought my very first comic book.
CS
HULK
Spider Man
E-Man
Howard the Duck
ROM
DC Comics Presents #57, featuring Superman and the Atomic Knights!
In the story, an atomic bomb drops on the world in 1986. When I read it, something similar happened to my brain.
BOOM!
Within weeks, I went from reader to creator. A classmate and I started drawing comics at school during our lunch breaks.
...so we'll make him like Robin Hood! Only instead of a bow and arrows, he'll have a **Discus of Death!!!**
This will be a revolution in modern entertainment! For the world has never before seen the likes of...
SPADE HUNTER!!!
Jeremy K., now a radiologist
I kept reading and drawing comics until I got to junior high, when a friend of mine gave me some advice:
Dude, if you keep reading those things you'll never get a girlfriend.
TRANS FORM
He'd had like six girlfriends! ***In the seventh grade!*** I had to listen. And so began my relentless ***pursuit of cool.***
Hey, buddy! How've you-
Stop talking to me.
Despite my new name-brand clothes and carefully pegged pants, however, ***cool*** continued to elude me. I entered high school with neither a girlfriend nor comic books. In the tenth grade, I abandoned cool and started reading comic books again.
I love you, man!

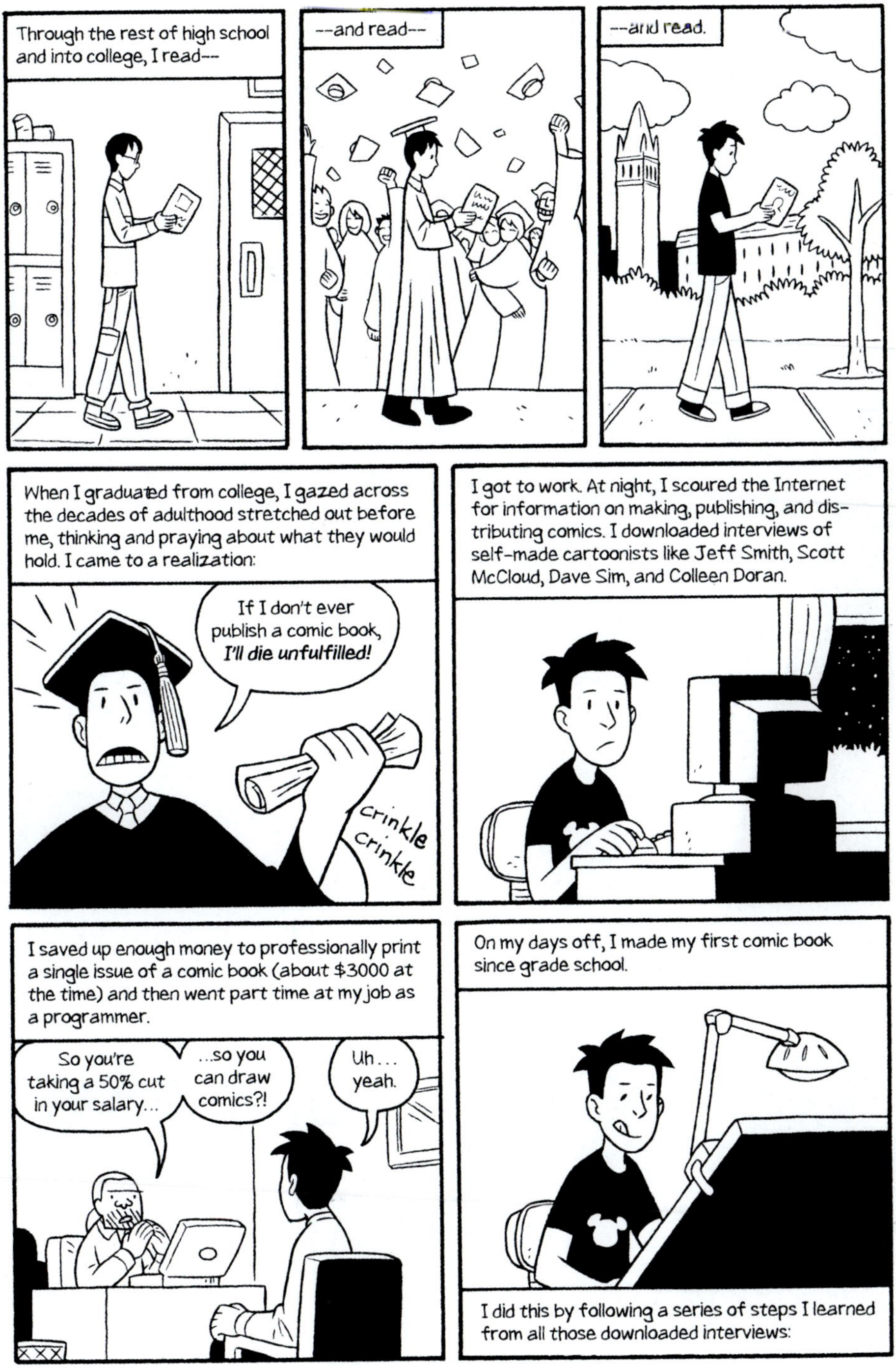
Through the rest of high school and into college, I read--
--and read--
--and read.
When I graduated from college, I gazed across the decades of adulthood stretched out before me, thinking and praying about what they would hold. I came to a realization:
If I don't ever publish a comic book, *I'll die unfulfilled!*
crinkle crinkle
I got to work. At night, I scoured the Internet for information on making, publishing, and distributing comics. I downloaded interviews of self-made cartoonists like Jeff Smith, Scott McCloud, Dave Sim, and Colleen Doran.
I saved up enough money to professionally print a single issue of a comic book (about $3000 at the time) and then went part time at my job as a programmer.
So you're taking a 50% cut in your salary...
...so you can draw comics?!
Uh... yeah.
On my days off, I made my first comic book since grade school.
I did this by following a series of steps I learned from all those downloaded interviews:

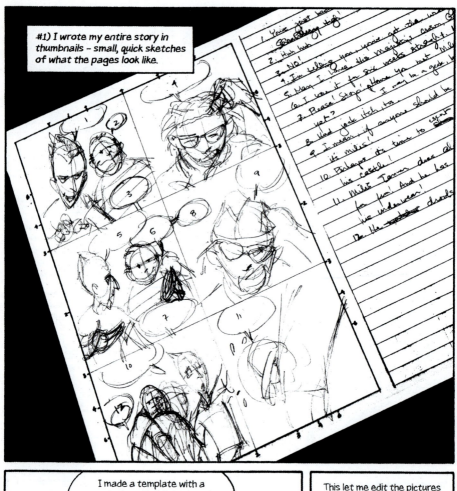

#1) I wrote my entire story in thumbnails – small, quick sketches of what the pages look like.

I made a template with a space to draw the pictures on one side, and a space to write the words on the other.

This let me edit the pictures without affecting the words, and vice versa.

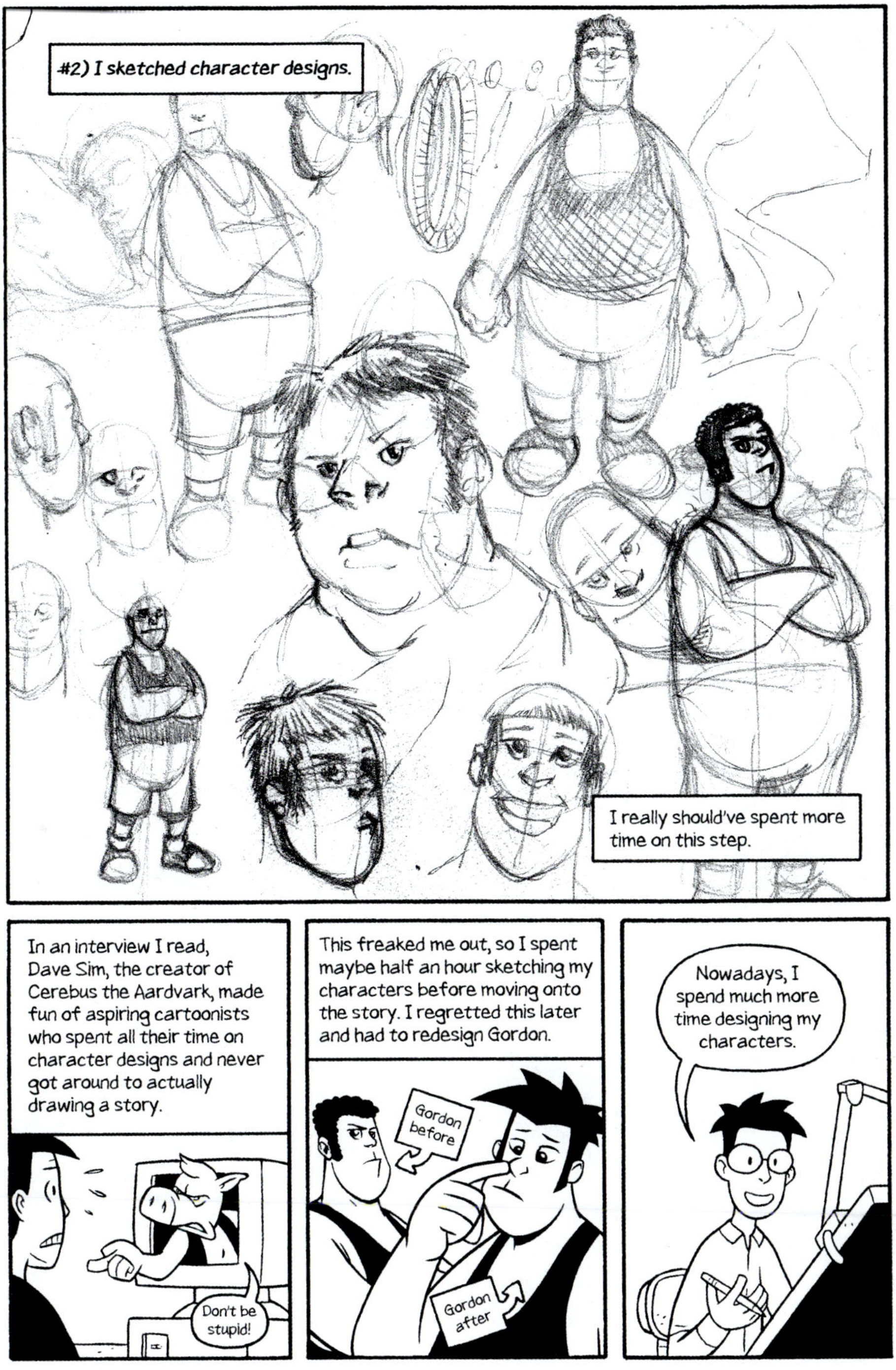
#2) I sketched character designs.
I really should've spent more time on this step.
In an interview I read, Dave Sim, the creator of Cerebus the Aardvark, made fun of aspiring cartoonists who spent all their time on character designs and never got around to actually drawing a story.
Don't be stupid!
This freaked me out, so I spent maybe half an hour sketching my characters before moving onto the story. I regretted this later and had to redesign Gordon.
Gordon before
Gordon after
Nowadays, I spend much more time designing my characters.

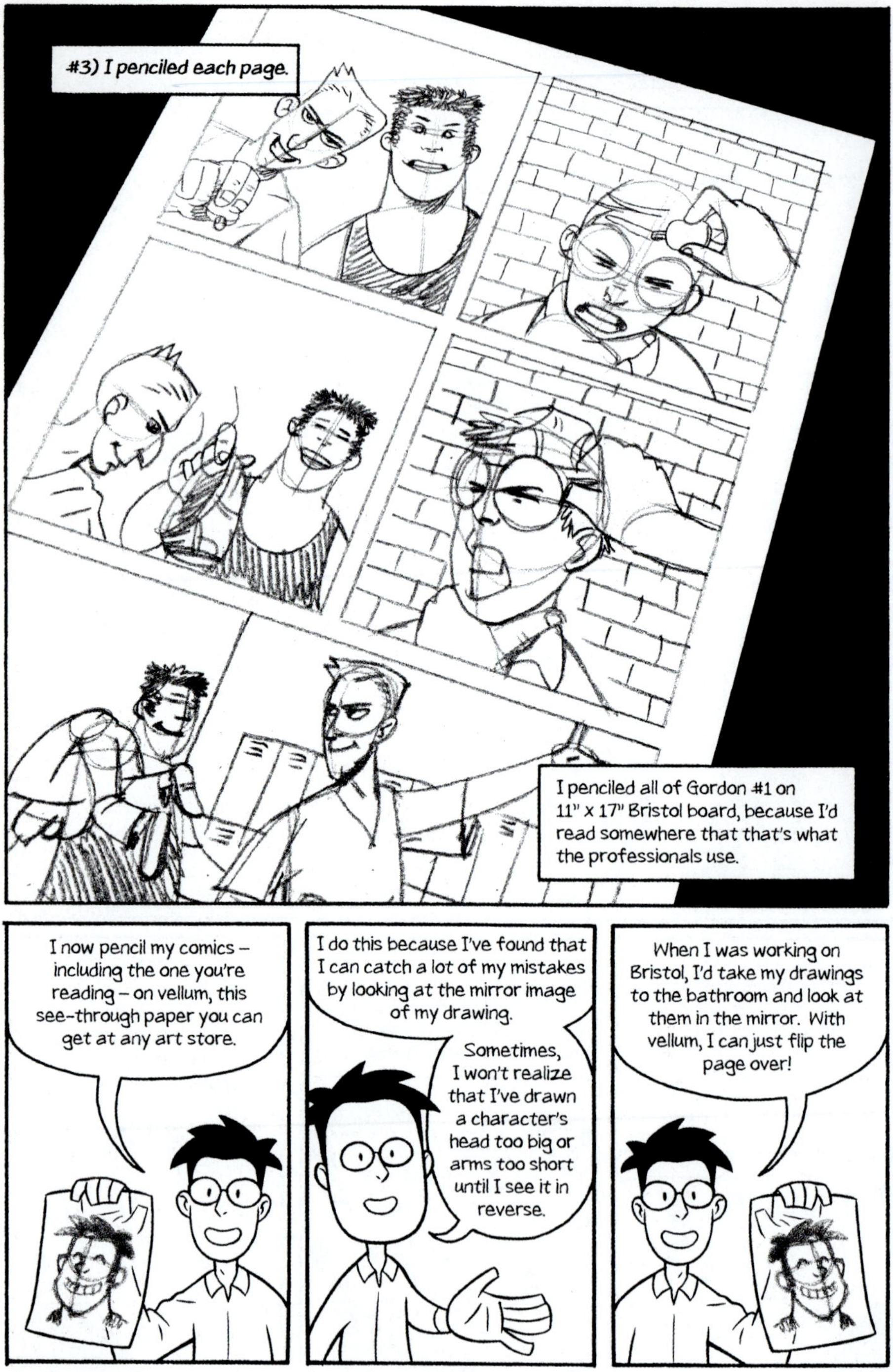
#3) I penciled each page.
I penciled all of Gordon #1 on 11" x 17" Bristol board, because I'd read somewhere that that's what the professionals use.
I now pencil my comics – including the one you're reading – on vellum, this see-through paper you can get at any art store.
I do this because I've found that I can catch a lot of my mistakes by looking at the mirror image of my drawing.
Sometimes, I won't realize that I've drawn a character's head too big or arms too short until I see it in reverse.
When I was working on Bristol, I'd take my drawings to the bathroom and look at them in the mirror. With vellum, I can just flip the page over!

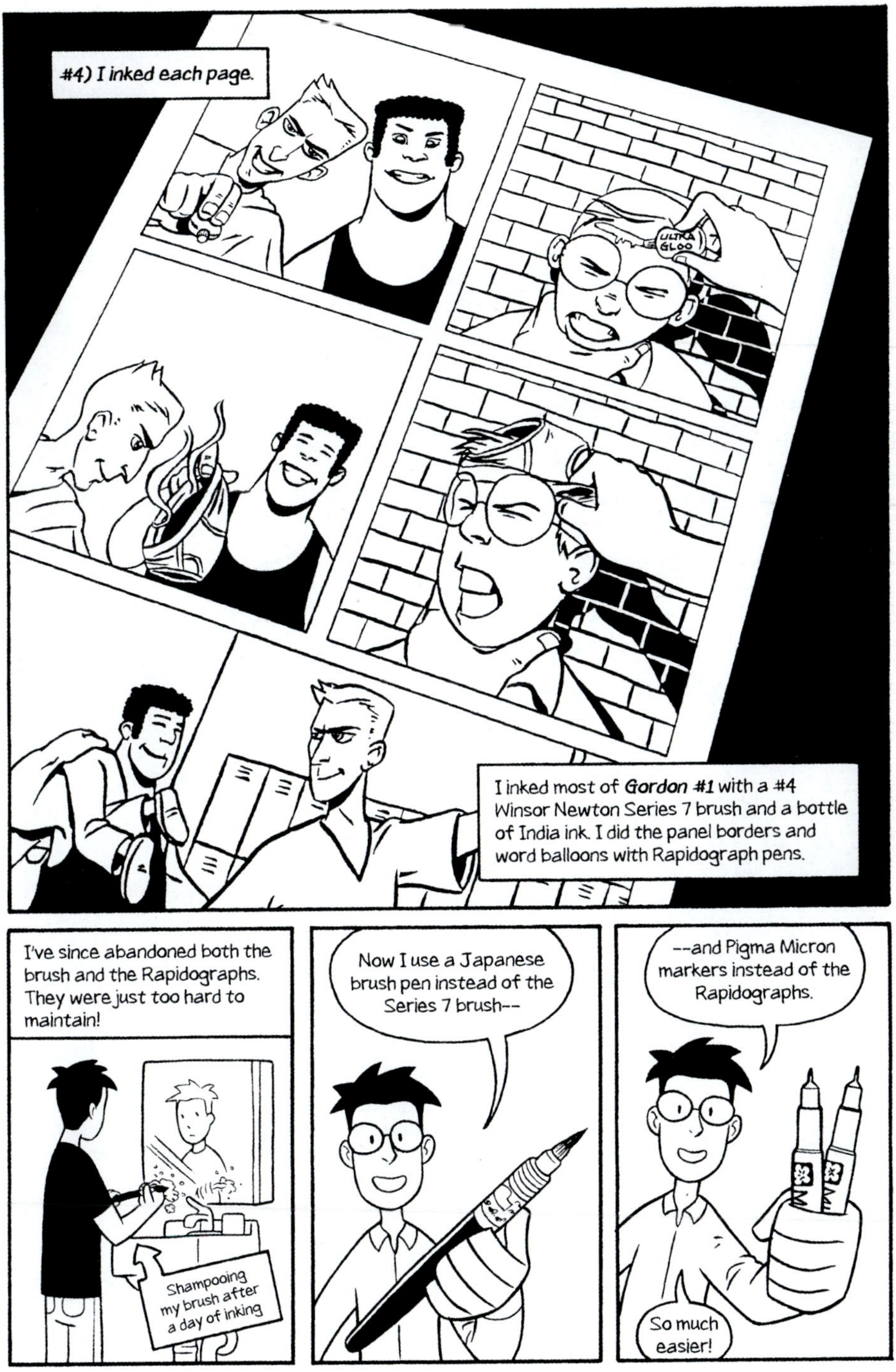
#4) I inked each page.
ULTRA GLOO
I inked most of Gordon #1 with a #4 Winsor Newton Series 7 brush and a bottle of India ink. I did the panel borders and word balloons with Rapidograph pens.
I've since abandoned both the brush and the Rapidographs. They were just too hard to maintain!
Shampooing my brush after a day of inking
Now I use a Japanese brush pen instead of the Series 7 brush--
--and Pigma Micron markers instead of the Rapidographs.
So much easier!

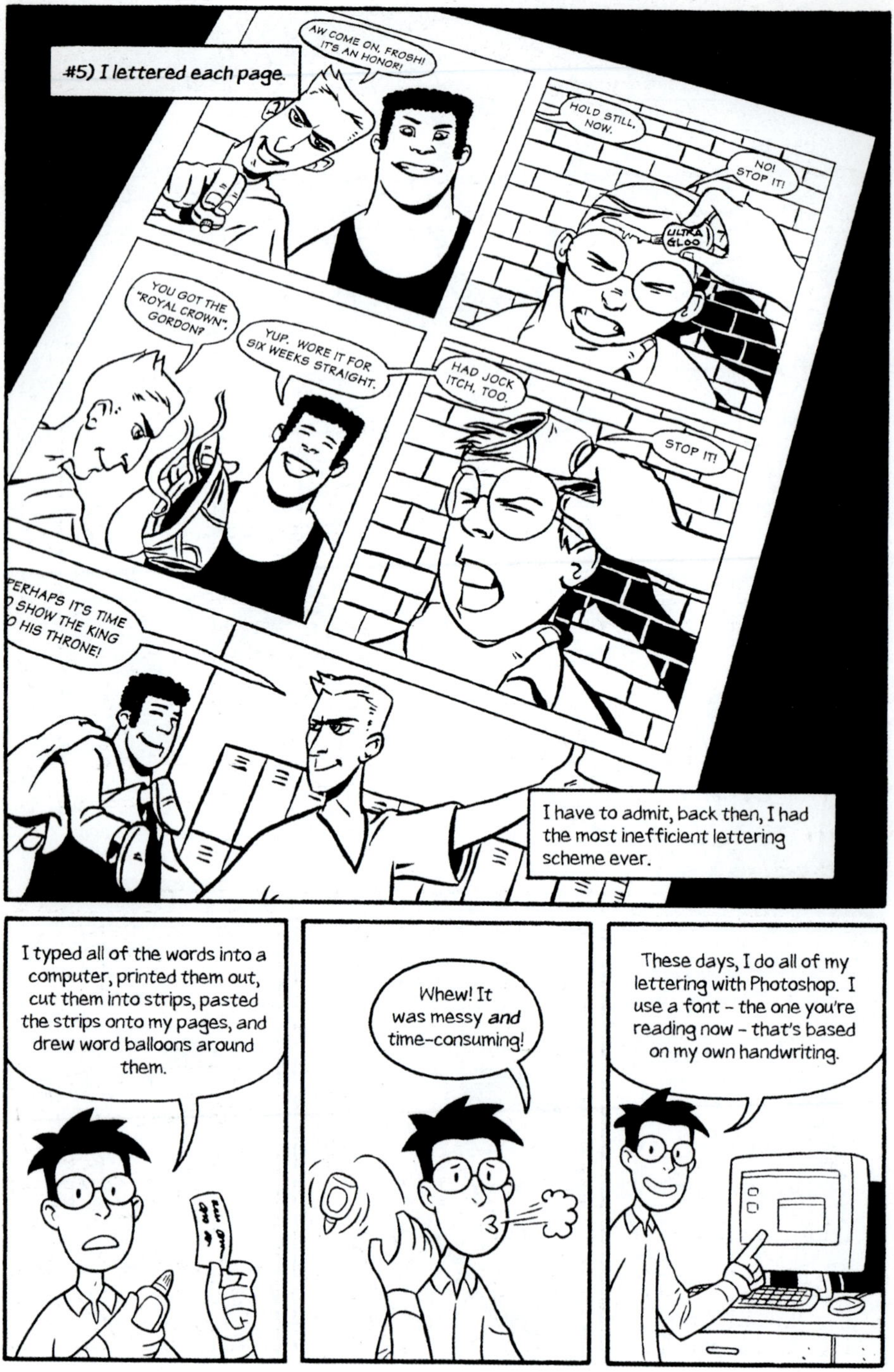

#5) I lettered each page.
AW COME ON, FROSH! IT'S AN HONOR!
HOLD STILL, NOW.
NO! STOP IT!
ULTRA GLOO
YOU GOT THE "ROYAL CROWN", GORDON?
YUP. WORE IT FOR SIX WEEKS STRAIGHT.
HAD JOCK ITCH, TOO.
STOP IT!
PERHAPS IT'S TIME TO SHOW THE KING TO HIS THRONE!
I have to admit, back then, I had the most inefficient lettering scheme ever.
I typed all of the words into a computer, printed them out, cut them into strips, pasted the strips onto my pages, and drew word balloons around them.
Whew! It was messy *and* time-consuming!
These days, I do all of my lettering with Photoshop. I use a font – the one you're reading now – that's based on my own handwriting.

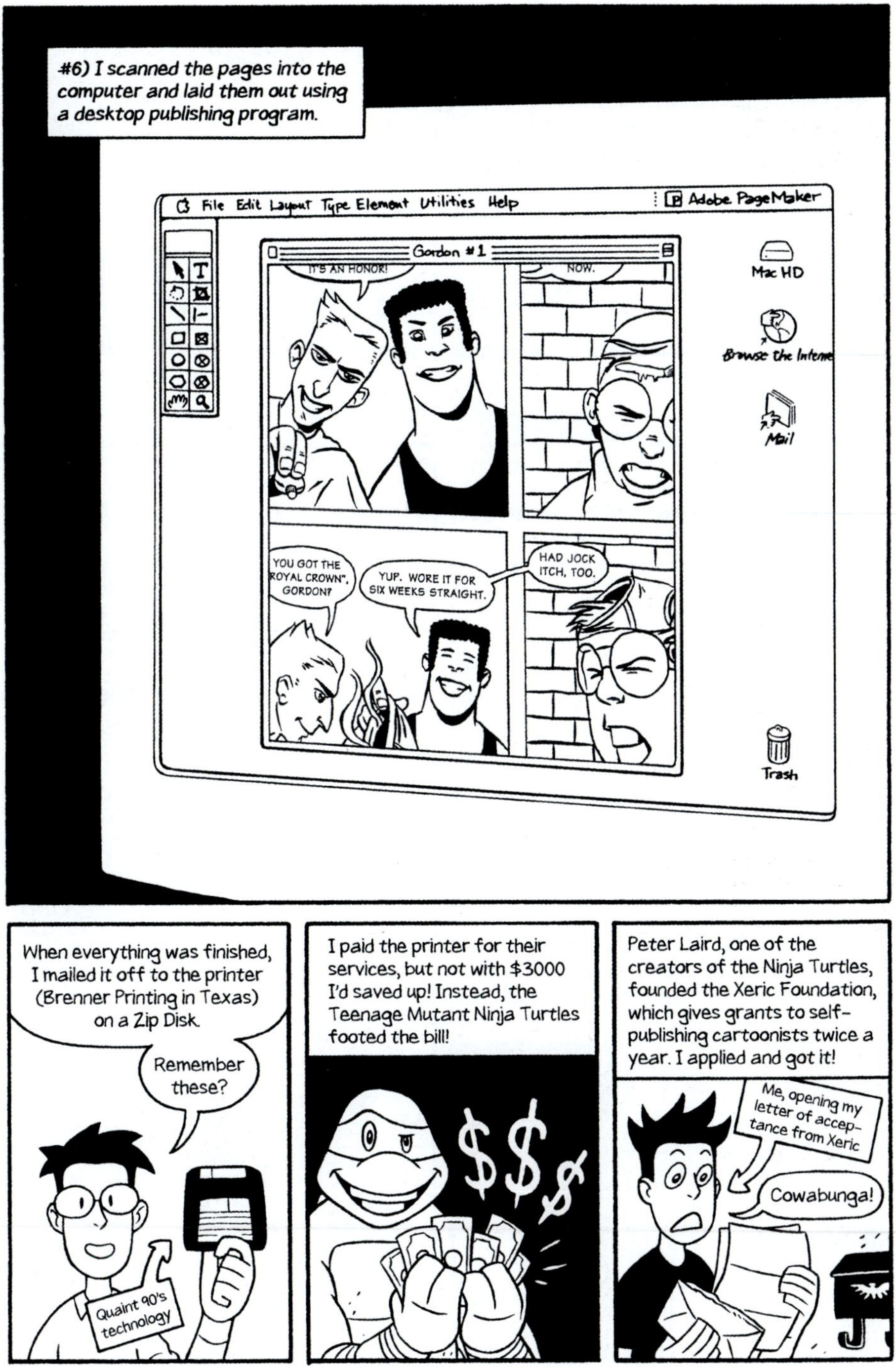
#6) I scanned the pages into the computer and laid them out using a desktop publishing program.
File Edit Layout Type Element Utilities Help
Adobe PageMaker
Gordon #1
IT'S AN HONOR!
NOW.
YOU GOT THE ROYAL CROWN", GORDON?
YUP. WORE IT FOR SIX WEEKS STRAIGHT.
HAD JOCK ITCH, TOO.
Mac HD
Mail
Trash
When everything was finished, I mailed it off to the printer (Brenner Printing in Texas) on a Zip Disk.
Remember these?
Quaint 90's technology
I paid the printer for their services, but not with $3000 I'd saved up! Instead, the Teenage Mutant Ninja Turtles footed the bill!
$$$
Peter Laird, one of the creators of the Ninja Turtles, founded the Xeric Foundation, which gives grants to self-publishing cartoonists twice a year. I applied and got it!
Me, opening my letter of acceptance from Xeric
Cowabunga!

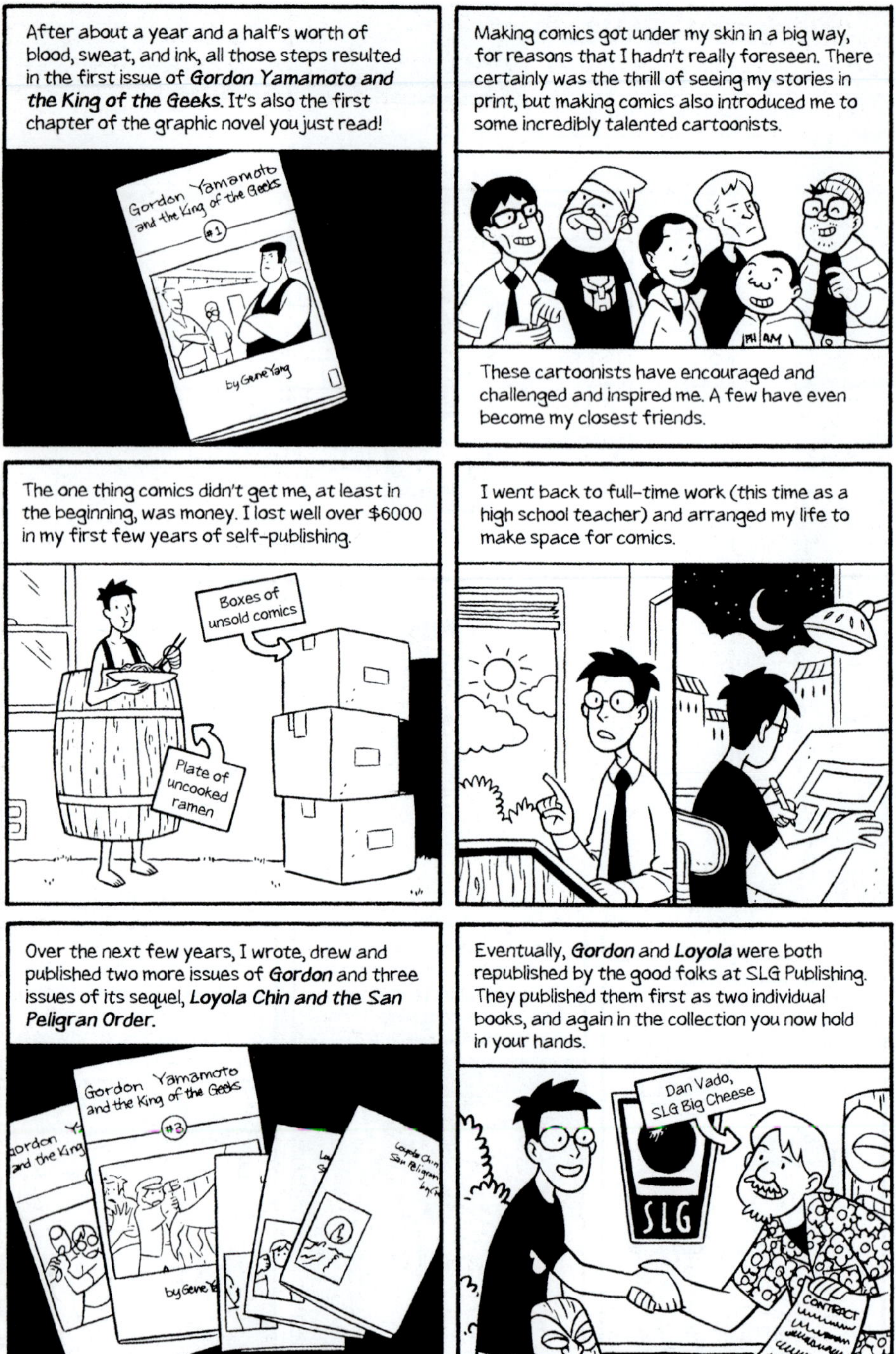
After about a year and a half's worth of blood, sweat, and ink, all those steps resulted in the first issue of Gordon Yamamoto and the King of the Geeks. It's also the first chapter of the graphic novel you just read!
Gordon Yamamoto and the King of the Geeks
#1
by Gene Yang
Making comics got under my skin in a big way, for reasons that I hadn't really foreseen. There certainly was the thrill of seeing my stories in print, but making comics also introduced me to some incredibly talented cartoonists.
These cartoonists have encouraged and challenged and inspired me. A few have even become my closest friends.
The one thing comics didn't get me, at least in the beginning, was money. I lost well over $6000 in my first few years of self-publishing.
Boxes of unsold comics
Plate of uncooked ramen
I went back to full-time work (this time as a high school teacher) and arranged my life to make space for comics.
Over the next few years, I wrote, drew and published two more issues of Gordon and three issues of its sequel, Loyola Chin and the San Peligran Order.
Gordon Yamamoto and the King of the Geeks
#3
Eventually, Gordon and Loyola were both republished by the good folks at SLG Publishing. They published them first as two individual books, and again in the collection you now hold in your hands.
Dan Vado, SLG Big Cheese
SLG
CONTRACT

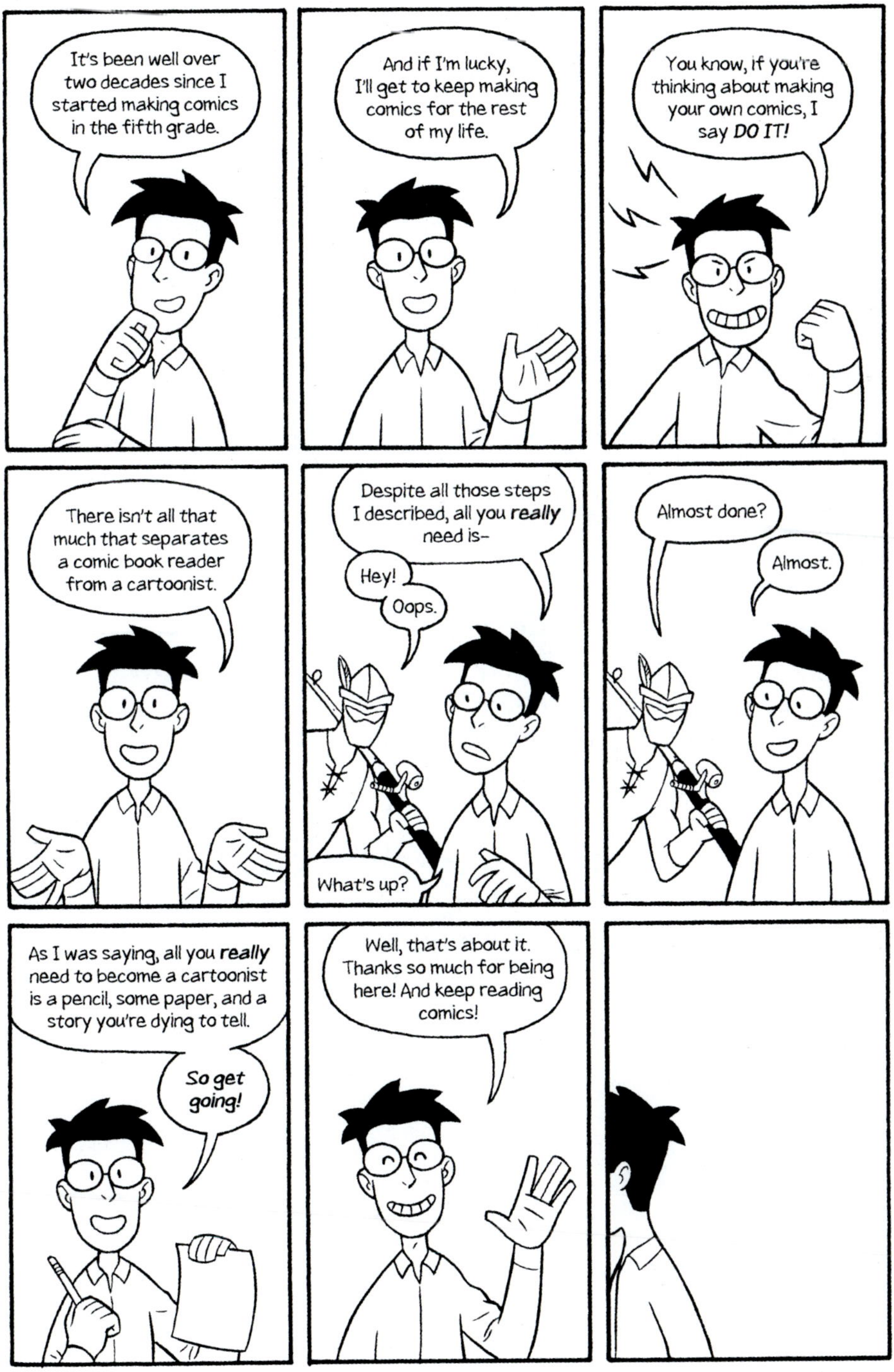
It's been well over two decades since I started making comics in the fifth grade.
And if I'm lucky, I'll get to keep making comics for the rest of my life.
You know, if you're thinking about making your own comics, I say *DO IT!*
There isn't all that much that separates a comic book reader from a cartoonist.
Despite all those steps I described, all you ***really*** need is–
Hey!
Oops.
What's up?
Almost done?
Almost.
As I was saying, all you ***really*** need to become a cartoonist is a pencil, some paper, and a story you're dying to tell.
So get going!
Well, that's about it. Thanks so much for being here! And keep reading comics!